CW01497280

SISTER CLARICE:

VATICAN DEMON HUNTER
Campfire Stories #2

by
D Glenn Casey

www.DGlennCasey.com

The novel *Sister Clarice – Vatican Demon Hunter* is a work of fiction. Names, characters, places and incidents either are the product of the author's imagination or are used fictitiously. Any resemblance to actual persons, living or dead, events, or locales is entirely coincidental.

Copyright © 2024 by D Glenn Casey

Cover design: D Glenn Casey
Cover art: Midjourney

Other works by D Glenn Casey
(All titles available in ebook and paperback)

The Chronicles of Wyndweir
The Tales of Garlan - Prequel
Wicked Rising ~ Book One
The Wrath ~ Book Two
Coming Soon
The War For Wyndweir ~ Book Three

A Cold Shivers Nightmare
Beware The Boogerman
Shattered Prisons
Crossing The Veil
Demon Hunter Academy
Coming Home

Campfire Stories
Darius James: Monster Hunter
Sister Clarice: Vatican Demon Hunter

Other full-length novels
Into The Wishing Well

My writer's blog
www/dglenncasey.com

Sister Clarice ~ Vatican Demon Hunter
Table of Contents

SISTER CLARICE
VATICAN DEMON HUNTER
Campfire Stories #2

Prologue

The mournful wail of the barges on the river was a sound that could keep a person awake at night, or lull them into a deep slumber. The low bass resonance of the horns reverberated through the air and rattled the windows of homes situated close enough to the waterway.

To some, the sound was a comforting lullaby, almost hypnotic. But to others, it was an irritating noise grating on their nerves. Those who couldn't stand it never lasted long in the lowlands near the water's edge, unless they didn't have the means to escape.

Lying in bed, the boy sweated profusely through his t-shirt and pajama bottoms. The sound of the barges moving up and down the Mississippi River was a siren call to him. He imagined himself jumping on a barge and escaping from his life; from the existence he loathed.

Moths and other bugs banged against the screen in his open window, drawn by the dim night light burning in his bedroom. Leaving the window open was the only way to tolerate the sweltering nights, but it was also an invitation for the pests buzzing and fluttering just beyond the thin mesh of wire.

Freddie couldn't stand the thought of those bugs getting in. His eight-year-old mind had no problem conjuring up all kinds of horrible things they would do to him if they got inside the bedroom. Despite his age, he had seen plenty of horror movies. He knew what those bugs were capable of if they ever got to him. He was thankful for the one part of the old house that seemed to work properly, the screen keeping him safe from the night monsters.

In between blasts from the barge horns, the sound of the television in the front room of the house echoed down the hallway. He knew his dad would spend another late night watching infomercials and drinking. It was his usual late-night activity. It wasn't like he had anything else to do.

With his dad not having a job for over a year, it had fallen to his mother to bring in the little money keeping the family afloat. Just one more thing he hated about his life and vowed he would do differently when he got older.

His mom had gone to bed hours ago, probably crying herself to sleep like she always did. No matter how much she pleaded, he wouldn't stop drinking or go out and look for a job. And when he had had enough of her pleading, he became violent. Not every night. Not even every week. It was like a switch was thrown and he would go off with the smallest provocation. When that happened, it was best to be in another room.

Or another state.

But leaving his mama alone to fend for herself was something he would never consider. Even at eight-years-old he knew he needed to be her protector. But what was a scrawny little kid from one of the poorest neighborhoods along the river going to do against the hulking monster he called his dad?

Freddie did the only thing he could think of. He prayed. He prayed his dad would fall asleep and not wake until the alcohol in his bloodstream had faded away, leaving him a little more in control of his anger.

It was just after two in the morning when his eyes opened. He couldn't describe it, but he sure could feel it. Something he had never felt before and instantly he knew he never wanted to feel again. A wave of darkness washed over the house and dropped the temperature so quickly his sweat felt like ice on his skin.

The sound of the television disappeared and he could hear his dad lumbering down the hallway, past his door, to the back bedroom. He could hear something scraping along the walls outside his door, but figured it was his dad running his hand down the wall to keep his balance. What was strange was how with every step he took, the house shook like he weighed a ton.

The bugs clinging to the window screen took flight and disappeared into the night as his dad plodded down the hallway. Freddie stared at the empty mesh and felt a sense of dread. He pulled the covers up and over his body and huddled underneath them, shivering. Something that should not be happening on one of the hottest nights in August in the Mississippi delta.

Freddie heard his mother screaming as his father smashed the bedroom door. Her screams shattered the quiet of the night, mixed with the sound of crashing furniture and breaking glass. He heard his father start beating her.

Jumping out of his bed, he rushed through his door and down the hallway to his parent's bedroom. The door looked like a tank had rammed through it, splitting it in half down the middle. He could hear the violence coming through the shattered door as he ran forward.

Just before he reached the door, he saw an enormous shadow moving on the walls of the room and Freddie could hear his mother crying out for help as the sound of his dad beating her assaulted his ears. He clenched his fists, ready to finally confront his dad and stop the violence.

Running through the doorway, he saw something that would haunt him for the rest of his life. It was something he never would have dreamed possible, except in the horror movies he used to love to watch late at night.

His dad was crouched on the bed over his mother, but he was flickering like an old-time movie. One second he was his dad, the next he was some kind of beast with long claws, black and scaly skin. The demon had two long, curly horns protruding from its head.

When the beast looked up at Freddie, he had some of the reddest eyes the boy could imagine. Redder than the fire engines from town and burning brighter than the fires those fire engines raced to put out. To his horror, he could have sworn a smile crossed the lips of the monster.

"Hey Freddie," the monster growled in a voice straight from Hell. "Stick around. I'll get to you next."

Apparently, old Mrs. Cline next door heard the same thing Freddie was hearing and she called the cops. If something seemed out of place in the neighborhood, old lady Cline knew all about it.

The sound of a siren pierced the night outside and it sounded like it was getting closer. Not wanting to leave his mother to be attacked by this monster, he knew he couldn't do anything about it. The beast was so large his head was bumping against the ceiling, even though it was kneeling on the bed. Its horns scraped deep gouges in the ceiling above the bed, causing plaster dust to rain down on his mother's unconscious form.

When he heard the police car skid to a stop outside, he turned and ran barefoot to the front door and flung it open just as the cops were running up the steps.

"He's hurting my mom!"

One officer took him and pulled him outside and onto the porch.

"Stay here!" yelled the cop as he followed his partner into the house.

The sounds coming from the back bedroom meant it didn't take the police long to locate the continuing attack. In his mind's eye, Freddie could see the cops charge into the bedroom, only to be confronted with the same thing he had seen.

"What in holy fu …!" screamed one officer.

5

The sound of gunfire followed, and though Freddie didn't count, he was sure both officers unloaded every bullet they had on the monster.

Mrs. Cline hobbled up the steps and grabbed Freddie by the wrist and pulled him away from the house.

"C'mon, Freddie. Let's get back," she said as she dragged him down the steps. He tried to pull away from her, but even though she was ancient, she still had quite a grip in her bony fingers.

As they stood in the road near the front of the police cruiser, two more cars skidded to a stop near it and the officers bailed out and charged into the house. Within ten minutes, there were ten cop cars, an ambulance and a couple of plain cop cars jammed into the narrow dirt track serving as the street in front of the house.

The neighborhood came to life with people jostling for position behind the vehicles, trying to get the best view possible. A police presence in this neighborhood was not unusual and it always seemed to be a spectacle when it happened.

Mrs. Cline leaned against the front fender of one car and kept Freddie in front of her, wrapping her arms around him from behind. Though most of the kids of the neighborhood made fun of her, Freddie liked her because she always treated him like a grown up man. Maybe it was because he was the only one in the house acting like a man.

About twenty minutes after the first cops

went into the house, some of them came back out. A large, rotund cop with sergeant stripes on his sleeves followed the first two officers out.

"What in the hell went on in there?" he demanded of the two.

One officer looked like he was in shock from what he had seen. The other just mumbled something, causing the sergeant to yell at him.

"I can't hear you, Tompkins! Did you and Jones really need to pump fifteen rounds into that man?"

Tompkins looked up at him, the terror still clear in his eyes.

"That was no man, sergeant."

"What the fuck are you talking about? I walk into that bedroom and I see this guy laid out across the bed, shot through with more holes than Swiss cheese and you're telling me he's not a man? Well, you got that right! Now he's a dead man!"

"It was a demon," said Jones in a voice no louder than a whisper.

"A what?" yelled the sergeant. "Did I hear you right, Jonesy? A demon?"

"I saw the same thing he saw, sergeant," said Tompkins, "and it was like no man I've ever seen. If I were to describe a demon, it would look just like what we saw."

The sergeant shook his head and said, "You two are on report and on desk duty until after a hearing. Not only will you most likely lose your badges, you may spend some time in prison over this!"

"They're not lying, sir!"

All three of them turned and looked at Freddie.

"And who are you?" bellowed the sergeant.

Mrs. Cline bristled at the sound of his voice and said, "This is Freddie Bishop and this is his home! And I'll thank you for taking a kinder tone with him, young man!"

The sergeant dropped his head and took a deep breath.

"I'm sorry," said the sergeant. "This is going to be a rough night for all of us, especially you, son. What did you see in there?"

"The same thing they said. I heard the monster beating on my mama and when I looked in the door to their bedroom, I saw my dad on top of her. Only ... it wasn't my dad. He kept changing into a monster and was hurting my mom."

The sergeant shook his head and mumbled, "Man, I don't have time for this."

Just then, another gunshot shattered the night.

"Jonesy!" screamed Tompkins.

While no one was paying attention, Officer Jones had walked a few feet away, reloaded his service weapon, stuck the barrel under his chin and pulled the trigger.

As his body fell to the ground, Mrs. Cline spun Freddie around and covered his head, trying to keep him from seeing what had happened. In the background, Freddie could hear some teenager from the neighborhood say, "Cool."

The rest of the night was a blur to Freddie. It was the beginning of him locking himself away in his head and not talking to anyone. No matter how much they tried to get him to say what had happened in the house, he just stared straight ahead.

Within a few days, they turned him over to Child Protective Services and stuck him into an orphanage run by the state. Within a couple of days, a couple of Catholic nuns showed up and spoke with the head of the orphanage and Freddie was transferred into their care.

That was the last time he saw New Orleans.

The sisters had come from an orphanage in the Chicago area and convinced the state of Louisiana that it was in Freddie's best interest to get him as far away as possible from the house he had called home.

In Chicago, where he would remain for ten years, there were very few opportunities for an eight-year-old colored boy to be adopted. Especially when he wouldn't say anything when prospective foster parents came to see the children.

During those ten years, he didn't say more than a few hundred words. He would answer yes or no questions with a nod or shake of his head. The sisters running the orphanage took great care of him and prayed he would come out of his shell. They treated him better than he sometimes believed he deserved.

He finally broke out of his prison of silence on the day he aged out of the orphanage. He gave each nun a hug and thanked them for looking after him. About half the nuns had tears streaming down their faces as he turned and walked out the door and climbed into the car that would take him to the halfway house.

He was told he could only stay at the home for six months. After that, he would need to find a job and prepare to be on his own. It took him less than a week to find a job, a month to move out and another couple of weeks to start night classes at the community college.

His chosen field of study at the college was law enforcement. He knew he wanted to fight the kind of evil he saw on a hot August New Orleans night ten years ago.

He also knew becoming a police officer wouldn't prepare him to fight the kind of monster he saw that night. So, his outside studies took a much darker path. His personal library soon contained books about demons, the occult and the things that would scare the living hell out of the rest of us.

Not to mention the eight-year-old boy he used to be.

Chapter 1 – The Beast

Tonight was especially dark, much quieter than usual. Only the sound of her heels clicking on the sidewalk broke the silence as she made her way home. The *snick snick snick* of her heels seemed to echo off the walls of the surrounding buildings.

Getting off work at midnight each night, Suzanne had grown accustomed to this walk. This part of town was not the worst, but it also wasn't the best.

Clenched in her fist was the small can of mace that she prayed she would never have to use. So far, after seven months of living here, she hadn't deployed the weapon even once. There was no reason to believe tonight would be any different.

Until it was.

Without warning, the calm in her chest evaporated into a cloud of terror, as if something had reached out of Hell and wrapped its cold, evil fingers around her soul.

For the past couple of weeks, her sleep had been nothing more than a late night horror movie, playing the same movie over and over every night. The kind of horror movie that would keep most people awake at night.

A large demon would terrorize her, chasing her through the darkness of a forest, calling her name.

Suzanne, where are you going?

Every night she stumbled and crawled through the woods and every night, the demon

11

almost caught her. She only escaped capture because the alarm would always awaken her from the nightmare.

It always took her a couple of hours to shake off the effects of restless sleep and only after a couple of cups of strong coffee.

Her coworkers had noticed something was wrong, but every time one would ask about it, she would just say she was having a hard time sleeping and it would get better.

Tonight was different, though. She felt the same fear from her nightmares reaching for her soul as she walked home, but she knew it had to be nothing more than her imagination running rampant.

Feeling the grip of malevolence wash over her, she almost stumbled and had to reach out to grab hold of a railing to keep her balance. As she fought to catch her breath, the mace canister fell from her fingers, clattering to the ground in front of her.

"Oh, no!" she stammered as she bent to pick up the small canister, causing the dizziness in her head to amplify.

Just as her fingers reached for the mace, it rolled away and she had to let go of the railing to reach it.

A wave of wooziness washed over her as she fought to catch hold of the small black cylinder. Each time her fingers came in contact with the plastic tube, it moved away, as if something was trying to keep her from getting her fingers on it.

Fighting the feeling of nausea in her gut,

she lunged for the mace canister and wrapped her fingers around it and picked it up.

When she stood up, it felt like she had done so too fast and a wave of dizziness washed over her. Swaying on her feet, she closed her eyes and she took a deep breath. Reaching out to grab hold of the railing again, she found it wasn't there.

Opening her eyes, she saw the railing was ten feet away. Stumbling toward it, she reached out, hoping she would get there before she passed out. When she could grasp the cold metal of the rail, her body swiveled on her heels and she collapsed onto the stairs.

Even though her mind was cloudy, she found herself thankful that she had at least fallen into a sitting position. The last thing she wanted was to be mistaken for a drunk laying on the sidewalk. Especially when she didn't drink or use drugs.

As she bowed her head and took deep breaths, trying to clear the fog clouding her mind, she heard a door open behind her.

"What are you doing here?" she heard a gruff, male voice behind her.

"I'm just..." she started, but couldn't continue. Breathing seemed more important to her.

"Go on! Get out of here! We don't want none of your lot in this neighborhood."

She turned her head and glanced over her shoulder. The man was easily seventy-years-old and looked like he hadn't missed a meal in all those years. Dressed in ragged shorts and a tank-top t-shirt, he had an ample gut that threatened to spill out for all the world to see.

Fighting the feeling of passing out, she said, "I don't feel well. I can't..."

"Probably from all that booze you drank or the drugs you took. Now get out of here before I call the cops."

He didn't give her a chance to answer. Turning back, he slammed his door with a note of finality, completely dismissing her as a fellow human being.

She took another couple of breaths and felt a little better, so she pulled herself up and got steadied on her feet.

I need to get home and get something to eat or get some water. I'm probably just dehydrated.

Just then, she heard the door behind her open again and she decided to just ignore the guy and get moving. She was about a hundred yards from her garden apartment.

"Here sweetie."

She turned at the sound of the woman's voice and saw a woman, obviously about the same age as the man. She was wearing a worn housecoat and had her gray hair bundled underneath a night cap. In her hands, she held an open bottle of water.

"Oh, thank you," said Suzanne softly as she took the bottle. It was ice cold.

"Don't pay no attention to Marvin. He'd step over your dead body before he would ever help you."

Suzanne took a sip of the cold water and

let out a sigh.

Looking at the woman's sparkling eyes, she smiled.

"I don't know what happened," she said. "I just got dizzy and had to sit down."

She looked up at the door and saw the man standing there.

"And I'm not drunk."

"Marvin, get back inside!" said the old lady.

"You get back inside, Esther. You shouldn't be out here like this."

"I'll come in when I'm ready! Now leave her alone!"

Marvin just harrumphed, turned and pushed the door closed. It was easy to see who the boss was in this house.

Esther turned back to Suzanne and just smiled.

"Like I said, pay no attention to him. Do you have much further to go?"

"No," said Suzanne before taking another drink of the Heaven-sent water. "Just a few more buildings."

She pointed down the street.

"Come on, I'll walk with you," said Esther.

"Oh no! Please, I feel much better having gotten this water in me. I think I was just dehydrated. Anyway, I'd be a nervous wreck thinking about you walking back here alone."

"Dearie, I've lived in this neighborhood for the past forty years. I've had nothing bad happen to me here and I don't think it will start tonight."

She reached out and wrapped her arm through Suzanne's arm and started walking with her down the street. The younger woman looked down and saw Esther was just wearing a pair of house slippers and was thankful it wasn't cold out tonight.

As they walked, Esther talked about how she and Marvin moved into their apartment when Ronnie was in the White House. And about how their only son hardly ever visited anymore or even called.

"I'm sorry to hear that," said Suzanne. "I used to call my mama at least once a week when she was still alive."

"She passed?"

"Yes, about a year ago, just a few months after my daddy passed away."

"So, are you all alone in this world now?"

"Oh, no. I have a younger brother, but he lives in California. We talk now and then, but we don't get to see each other much."

"Well, stay in touch with him, dearie. Family is all we have worth anything in this world."

"That is so true," said Suzanne as she patted Esther's hand.

"Well, this is me," she said as she came to a stop outside the small apartment building.

"That's my apartment down there," she said, pointing to the garden apartment just below ground level.

"Are you going to be okay?"

"Yes, I'm feeling much better."

Without realizing she was doing it,

Suzanne leaned over and kissed Esther on the cheek.

"Thank you for looking after me."

Esther just smiled and said, "Wouldn't this world be a much better place if we all looked out for each other?"

"Yes, it would. Now, I'm going to stand right here on the sidewalk and watch as you walk back to your place. I'm not going in until I know you've made it safely back."

Esther looked up at her and smiled.

"What is your name, sweetie?"

"Oh, Suzanne. Suzanne Kelly."

"Well, Suzanne Kelly. You be careful. There seems to be something in the wind tonight and it doesn't feel good."

Suzanne snatched a quick breath, but before she could ask Esther what she meant, the old lady had turned and started back toward her own apartment. Suzanne watched her go, but couldn't shake the feeling the sweet old lady had given her a warning. A warning she did not understand.

A couple of minutes later, Esther reached her own door and turned and waved to her. Suzanne waved back and watched as she climbed her steps and disappeared into her home.

Walking to her own apartment, she stepped down the four steps that led to her garden apartment. It sat about halfway below ground level, with some small windows that looked out to the street in front of the building.

As she fumbled with her keys, trying to

balance the mace and the bottle of water, the light over her head began flickering. Looking up at it, she just shook her head.

Have to ask Charlie to check that light tomorrow.

As she slipped into the apartment, she pushed the door closed and set the contents of her hands on the small kitchen table. Turning back to the door to lock it, she felt the same wave of dizziness wash over her again and it drove her to her knees.

"Oh, God!" she cried out softly. "What is wrong with me?"

As she brought her hands up to her head, she squeezed them together, trying to drive the pain from behind her eyes. She leaned forward until her forehead touched the floor.

Clenching her eyes closed so tightly, she didn't notice the dark figure push the door open and step into her apartment. At least eight feet tall, very broad in the shoulders and curly horns that scraped the ceiling of the apartment. The cracks in its skin glowed orange and red, as if everything under its dark skin was in flames.

It was only when the door clicked closed, Suzanne opened her eyes and looked up through the pain.

And screamed.

Chapter 2 – Our Hero

Gray clouds hung low over the city of Chicago, but there didn't seem to be a threat of rain in the air. That didn't stop Marvin from grabbing the umbrella from the stand inside the door. The sun could have been glaring down on a hot summer's day and he still would have taken an umbrella.

Esther stood on the stoop, waiting for her love to close the door, so she could hold his arm as they walked down the steps to the sidewalk.

As they reached the sidewalk, he went to turn left and go for their usual morning walk. Their walk would take them to the deli, where they would get a couple of small bagels and coffees. They would spend their morning sitting at a table on the sidewalk.

They loved to watch the people going by, making up stories about them. Marvin always made up stories about how bad their lives were. Esther always tried to make her stories bright and cheerful, with these strangers living happy lives.

As he turned to go left, she stopped and gasped.

"What is it, Esther?"

She was looking down the street in the opposite direction.

"Oh no," she whimpered, as she began pulling him in that direction.

As they walked, he could see the police cars and ambulances in the street. Lights were flashing and the emergency vehicles completely blocked the street.

Esther kept trying to go faster, while Marvin tried to slow her down.

When they got closer, they had to cross the street to the opposite sidewalk to get to a place directly across from the small apartment building. There was a small crowd of people gathered and Esther came to a stop. When she looked at the scene across the street, a small cry escaped her lips.

"Man, they said she was completely tore up," said a teenage boy to another standing next to him.

"Like some slasher?" asked the other boy.

"No, like some wild animal got loose in her place."

"Cool," said the second boy.

Esther wanted to rage at the two for showing such disrespect, but held her tongue. She could see the police going in and out of the garden apartment. The one that faced the front of the building.

The one Suzanne had pointed out as her own.

She felt a wave of terror envelop her body as she turned and looked at Marvin.

"Give me your phone," she whispered.

"Esther, don't."

She pressed her lips into a tight line across her face and he knew the best course of action was to surrender the phone without another word. Over forty years of marriage had taught him that.

She took it and dialed a number from memory. He could see tears streaming down her face as she waited for someone to answer.

Her voice cracked when she said, "Sister, I think it's happened again."

~~~~

Less than thirty minutes later, a tiny, rusty white car pulled over to the curb about fifty yards from the building and a small nun got out. She wasn't dressed as one would think of a traditional Catholic nun, black habit with a white wimple around the face. The white wimple was the only thing that looked traditional.

She replaced the black robes of cotton or wool with black leather that hung to the tops of what looked like black motorcycle boots. Engraved in the breast of her top was a blood-red cross, a color that matched the cloak hanging over her shoulders and the veil that draped over her head.

The white wimple under the veil looked out of place, but at the same time, looked like it belonged right where it was.

She couldn't have been over thirty years old, possibly much younger. She had the olive skin of a person from the Mediterranean region, but the shocking blue eyes of someone quite removed from that area.

Though she was small, barely reaching five feet tall, her appearance would make even the toughest biker take a step back if she wanted to

21

get through. As she proceeded from her car to the crowd gathered across the street, the neighborhood toughs moved out of her way, giving her a wide berth.

That always amazed her because she worked really hard at presenting an air of calm and peace as she encountered people.

As she moved toward the crime scene, she saw Esther and Marvin and went straight to them.

"Sister Clarice," cried Esther. "It's so awful. I talked to that sweet young lady just last night. I should have known something was coming."

Sister Clarice reached out and placed a hand on the side of her face.

"Esther, it's not your fault," she said with as much kindness as she could muster.

"That's what I've been trying to tell her," said Marvin gruffly.

The sister stepped back and looked up at Marvin, giving him a bit of a smile.

"Marvin, I see you're still struggling with empathy."

Sister Clarice had the voice of an angel, but it always seemed to cut Marvin right to the core. And being the crotchety old dude that he was, he didn't like it. He just gave her a barely audible harrumph.

Turning back and putting an arm around Esther's waist, she pulled her close and allowed her spirit to wash over the older woman to comfort her.

"So, what do you know about her?"

"I only met her last night," said Esther.

"I've seen her walk by now and then, but last night was the first time we talked. She had such a sweet spirit, but was feeling poorly and I walked her home."

"Do you know her name?"

"Yes, it was Suzanne Kelly."

"Suzanne Kelly? Hmmm?"

"Do you know her?"

"No, I'm sure I don't, but I think I'm going to get to know her quite well."

Then the sister gave Esther a quick hug around the shoulders and then turned to Marvin.

"Marvin, take your sweetheart home. I'm about to go to work."

Marvin just nodded, held out his hand and Esther took it. As they began shuffling away, the sister stared at the group of police officers across the street. The last thing she was expecting this morning was to come to a murder scene that was going to contain what she feared would make her life a nightmare.

I hope he isn't here yet. Well, time to get to work.

Stepping off the sidewalk, she started across the street, weaving her way through the police cars blocking the road. As she reached the other side, she came to the yellow crime scene tape and reached out and lifted it up. Stepping under the tape, she started toward the door, only to have a young, fresh-faced officer step in front of her. He looked her up and down, not sure if she was a nun or a cosplayer.

"Sister, I'm sorry, but you'll have to wait on

23

the other side of the tape."

"Officer Skelling," she said, looking at his name badge, "I am here for a reason and I believe that reason is in that apartment. So, if you don't mind, please step aside."

For some reason, one he couldn't even articulate, he stepped out of her way and watched as she breezed past him. One of the older beat cops laughed quietly and patted him on the shoulder.

"Skelling, that there be Sister Clarice. If she asks you to move out of the way, you best move."

It amazed him to see the other officers and detectives make way for her without being asked and she disappeared down the steps and into the apartment.

As she stepped through the door, she could feel the evil that had breached the apartment. Blood covered the walls of the room, some of it still running slowly down to the floor.

There was a body laying in the middle of the small living room, covered with a white sheet, which was fast turning red from the bloody mess underneath.

There were half a dozen cops in the room and none of them seemed to take notice of the nun as she walked toward the body. Until a police woman reached out and took her arm.

"Sister, I don't think it's a good idea for you to be here."

"No, Mary, this is exactly where I need to be, whether I like it or not."

The officer let go of her arm, knowing who

she was and arguing with her would be pointless.

Sister Clarice stepped near the head of the body and could feel the carpet, wet with blood, squish under her feet. She pulled her habit up a little so she could crouch down without it dragging on the floor.

She heard Officer Danton gasp when she did that. Sister Clarice was wearing her customary black leather boots that rose to just about mid-calf. Fashioned into the sides of the boots were sheathes and the daggers they held. A gold cross on a red background emblazoned the hilt of each dagger.

If it wasn't the daggers that caused the reaction from Officer Danton, it was the gold-plated 9mm pistols in the custom holsters at her ankles. Each had pearlized grips with the same gold cross in a red circle.

Sister Clarice reached out and lifted the white sheet from the face of the young woman and wept silently for her. Suzanne's face, frozen at the time of her death, remained locked in a mask of terror.

That look of terror did not extend to her eyes. Her eyes looked as if they had been burned out of their sockets, leaving just two charred, black holes.

The sister just shook her head, knowing of the horror she must have faced as she died.

Laying her hand on the forehead of the young woman, Sister Clarice gasped as a vision assaulted her mind. A darkness swept over her vision as she saw Suzanne open her eyes and look up.

Standing at the apartment door was a demon. A demon she knew all too well, one that had terrified her in her dreams.

Azrin.

Her vision rocked by the sound of Suzanne screaming, but it was a scream cut short. Azrin had never been one to waste time when he came for someone.

She saw Azrin drive two claws into the eyes of Suzanne and she felt the pain the young woman endured as he ripped her life from her body.

It only brought more tears to her own eyes.

As she shook the vision from her mind, she wiped her hand over the face of the dead woman. She lifted the sheet a little higher and looked at the horrible damage the demon had done to this poor girl. The boys outside had been correct. Azrin had torn Suzanne Kelly to pieces, most likely keeping her alive as long as possible, causing her to suffer greatly before she died.

She leaned down and whispered, "Fly away home, Suzanne. Fly to the loving arms of our Heavenly Father."

When she lifted her hand from the woman's face, the look of terror was gone, replaced with a look of peace.

"Oh Christ, what is she doing here?"

Really Father? Couldn't you have made sure we didn't cross paths today?

Sister Clarice closed her eyes for a second and asked for strength from Heaven. Then she stood up and turned to face the owner of the voice.

"Detective Bishop," she said with a quiet confidence. "How are you today?"

"I believe I made myself perfectly clear last time, you were to stay away from these crime scenes," yelled Bishop.

The sister stepped up in front of him and patted him on the chest. He stood at least three inches over six feet, which put him over a foot taller than her.

"And as I remember, the last time we had this conversation, your chief told you to give me every bit of help I needed."

"Well, he's retired now," said Bishop, "so I don't think he'll be of much use to you this time around."

"Oh, really. I hadn't heard. I guess I'll need to stop down to city hall and introduce myself to the new chief."

Bishop looked like someone had pulled his pin and he was ready to explode. Turning to Officer Danton, he yelled, "Get her out of here! And keep her out!"

"Sister," said Mary, holding her hand out toward the door.

Clarice looked up into Bishop's face and said, "I'll be seeing you, Fredrick. You be careful."

She could feel him bristle at the sound of his given Christian name and if the situation hadn't been so dire, she would have smiled inwardly. She knew he didn't like being called by his first name.

Turning, she followed Danton out of the apartment and up the steps.

"Sister," asked Officer Danton softly, "what did you see? I mean, when you touched her head. I know you saw something."

The sister took a breath, turned to her and reached out, touching her arm.

"Evil, Mary. I saw evil."

She looked down and saw a small puddle just off the sidewalk. Dipping the sole of one boot into the water, then the other, she swished the boots around in the water, turning it red with the blood of Suzanne Kelly. When she looked up, she saw Danton had tears in her eyes.

Stepping back to Danton, the sister took one of her hands and raised it and kissed it.

"Evil that I intend to kill, Mary."

"You're going to kill someone? Sister?"

"Not someone, sweetheart. Something. Something evil and straight out of Hell. I intend to send it back there."

She kissed her hand again and said, "God be with you, Mary."

"You, too, sister."

Sister Clarice turned and trudged back to her car, her heart feeling like it weighed a ton and was on the verge of breaking. When she sat down inside, she reached to turn the key, but stopped. Quickly pulling a tissue from the box between the seats, she buried her face in it and cried for five solid minutes.

After she composed herself, she lifted the lid on the center console and pulled out a phone. Dialing a number, she waited for it to pick up.

"Your eminence, I need to see you immediately."

Chapter 3 – A Friend in Arms

Sister Clarice was on her knees, her head bowed as she fought to contain her emotions. Cardinal Wright stood up from his chair, leaned over his desk and looked down at her. He had an exasperated look on his face. He felt a great discomfort in his soul, seeing her on her knees in front of him.

"And you're sure it was Azrin?"

Sister Clarice nodded her head, but kept it bowed.

"Of that I have no doubt, Your Eminence. I saw her last few seconds of vision."

"Oh, sister, please get up!"

Clarice looked up and then stood up.

"What do I have to do to keep you from dropping to your knees every time you come into this office?"

She bit her lip and shrugged.

"Sit down, please," said the cardinal as he sat back down.

She moved to the chair and gathered the light, black leather of her habit with her hands and sat down.

"I wish you would quit doing that," said the cardinal.

"I do it because of who you are and who your uncle is."

"Sister, I am not my uncle, nor do I wish to be. That he is the Holy Father over this church means nothing between you and me."

Sister Clarice pressed her lips together and he could tell his words were making no impression on her at all. As long as his uncle was the Pope in Rome, she would never relax in his presence.

"Now, tell me exactly what you saw."

"He followed her home last night and attacked her once she was inside. She could feel his presence long before he made himself known to her."

"We haven't suffered Azrin in over three years. Why would he come out of hiding now? What was the young lady's name again?"

"Suzanne Kelly."

"Do we know anything about her?"

"Not yet, Your Eminence. I will look into who she was and find if there is any reason Azrin would target her specifically. I stopped at her place of employment on the way here and talked to some of her coworkers. They said she had been having trouble sleeping for the past couple of weeks. I can only imagine Azrin invaded that sweet woman's dreams."

"I find it hard to believe he would strike her down for no reason other than just to kill her."

"As do I. I've already called the medical examiner. I intend to be at the autopsy this afternoon."

The sister bowed her head and went silent for a moment.

"What's the matter, sister?"

"It's just that ... I don't know ..."

The cardinal looked at her over his steepled fingers.

"You're still unsure of your calling."

She looked up at him and drew a deep breath.

"I think it's time for you to put your doubts about your abilities to rest," said the cardinal. "Very few in the church do the good work you do."

"That's just it, Jon," she said, then winced when she realized what she had done.

"Sister, in this office, I am just Jon. I am not 'Your Eminence', 'Cardinal Wright' or any other name you can think of. Please continue."

"I was just going to say that sometimes it doesn't feel like good work. I battle evil. Some of the worst evil imaginable."

"And you don't consider that to be good work? Because I can assure you, my uncle does. As do I. There is no higher calling you could have than to fight these demons from Hell."

She pressed her lips together and nodded. Then she stood up and said, "I shall take my leave now. The autopsy is scheduled for one hour from now. Traffic can be troublesome at this time of day."

The cardinal nodded and asked, "Is there anything else I can do to help you with this?"

She thought for a moment and then asked, "Do you know the new chief of police?"

Pulling up in front of the police station that housed the medical examiner's office, a parking space was available to her. It never ceased to amaze her that there always seemed to be a parking space for her, even though this was a very busy time of day.

There was even an hour's worth of time left on the parking meter. She placed a couple of quarters in the slot, just in case. If she didn't use the time, she would be happy to help the next person parking there.

As she walked up the steps to the front doors, she reached out for a handle, but the door swung open as a young police officer came out.

"Oh, pardon me, sister," he said as he stepped aside and held the door for her.

"Thank you," she said as she breezed through the door.

As she approached the metal detectors, one officer behind the desk looked up and smiled at her. As she stepped through the detector, he reached under his desk and pressed a button.

Despite being armed to the teeth, she walked through, activating no alarms, lights or sirens. Stepping to the counter, she picked up a pen to sign in as the officer stepped over.

"You here about that young lady that was brought in this morning?"

She looked up and said, "Yes ... the poor soul." She could feel her eyes watering again and the officer held out a box of tissues for her.

"My cousin, Officer Danton, said it was the worst thing she's ever seen."

She nodded and said, "Evil knows no bounds, Kyle."

"No, it doesn't," he said. "They will be in room three."

She dabbed her eyes again and then bid him goodbye and headed for the elevators. As he watched her walk away, he felt the icy fingers of fear run up the middle of his back.

"Godspeed, sister," he whispered.

As she walked down the stark, white hallway, she passed many police officers and medical staff, and none of them paid her much notice. Those that did just nodded and smiled at her.

She came to a door that had the number three on it and pushed it open. Stepping inside, she could see she was the only one there at the moment.

Well, that was only true to a point. In the middle of the room was the exam table and there was a body laying on it, covered in a clean, white cloth. Near the head of the table, on both sides, were the trays that held the tools that were going to be used in the autopsy.

Walking across the room, she stood near the head of the table and reached out, resting her hand on the covered head of Suzanne. Bowing her head, she let her heart sink into prayer for this young lady.

She could feel Suzanne's soul was no longer present, having gone to Heaven already. That was the only comfort she felt as she stood there.

The soft opening of a door broke her from her reverie and she looked over to see the medical examiner across the room, along with a couple of assistants. She smiled and nodded at him, and he returned the smile.

"Sister Clarice, it is good to see you,

though I fear the circumstances will be trying for all of us."

One lady began getting the trays ready for use as the other helped the M.E. put some gloves on. When they finished, he looked at the two of them.

"Ladies, I don't think I'll need anything else from you. You don't need to be present for this."

Both of them breathed sighs of relief and made their way out the door.

"Sister, if you'd like to stand at the foot of the table, I'll try to keep the sight of the body away from you as much as possible."

"Stephen, I've already seen it."

He looked at her with a pained look on his face.

"And that is regrettable. A sweet soul, such as yours, should never see something like this."

She reached out and patted his arm. "I should think no one should see this kind of thing."

As they agreed, the door was flung open and Sister Clarice closed her eyes and bowed her head.

"Oh, for Christ's sake! What the hell are you doing here?"

She turned and said, "Fredrick, please curb your language when you are in my presence. As a matter of fact, you should think of doing it at all times."

"Look, I don't need you to ..."

Bishop's phone began ringing in his pocket.

"I think you should get that," said the sister. "It might be important."

Bishop clenched his teeth and pulled the phone from his pocket. Stabbing at the Answer button, he held the phone to his ear.

"This is Bishop! … Oh, yes sir … Yes, I am here right now … Uhh, yes, she's here, too … But, sir! … And what does that mean, exactly?" His head hung as he sighed and said, "Yes, sir, I understand completely."

Pressing the End Call button, he slipped the phone back in his pocket, trying to calm his breathing. He felt her gentle hand on his arm and opened his eyes and looked at her.

"How do you do that?" he asked.

She just smiled softly and asked, "Can we just agree to get along and work together?"

"Against my better judgment."

"Detective Bishop, I am not your enemy. We are both working toward the same end. To find who did this to this poor young lady and see justice done."

The detective looked into her brown eyes and sighed.

"I'll try, but I'm making no promises."

"I only ask that you try."

Stephen spoke up and asked, "Shall we begin?"

"Yes, doctor," said both of them.

Stepping to each side of the table, they watched as he began his examination. Sister Clarice could feel the rage building within the heart of the detective and prayed silently for his soul to be calmed.

When the autopsy finished an hour later, Sister Clarice had learned nothing she didn't already know.

Azrin had killed this sweet lady, and the only question she had was, why?

As they walked down the steps outside the building, the detective said, "I think you know more than you're letting on."

Sister Clarice came to a stop on the steps and he stopped two steps down and turned to look at her. This put them face-to-face and she looked into his eyes.

Then she reached out with one hand and placed it on the side of his face. Immediately, he felt a memory come crashing into his mind, driving the breath from his lungs. His whole body froze as the images washed through his head. Memories that he had hoped to never see again.

When she took her hand away, she could see the distress in his eyes. Placing both hands on the sides of his face, she pulled his head forward and touched her forehead to his. He felt the memory fade from his mind and soften within seconds. It didn't completely disappear, but it became more manageable to live with.

He looked up at her, his eyes threatening to unload a torrent of tears. He had just seen the same images he saw that night all those years ago.

She said, "It seems we both seek the same beast."

Looking into her eyes, he knew he had

finally found someone that would understand the terrors he'd been suffering most of his life. Fighting with every ounce of power he had, he kept the tears at bay.

"Sister, may I buy you lunch so we can sit and talk?"

"It would be my pleasure," she said as she put her arm through his and they walked down the rest of the steps.

As Sister Clarice sat across from him, she didn't interrupt him while he related what had happened to him as a boy. She could tell it was a struggle for him to even dredge that memory up.

"That night, standing in front of my home, I could tell no one would believe me if I told them what I saw. I decided to just keep quiet and over time, I think I convinced myself I had been mistaken about what I saw."

The sister took a sip of her water and then said, "And now, the things that happened that night are coming back to haunt you."

"Sister, those things have haunted me every night since my parents died. I have not forgotten one detail of that night."

"And what did you feel when you saw what happened to Suzanne Kelly?"

"Like the same evil son of a bitch was … sorry … I shouldn't say things like that around you."

She reached across the table and patted his hand.

"Don't worry about it. I've heard much

worse working with the kids in my neighborhood. You were saying?"

"That the same demon that killed my parents was back in town. Now, sister, tell me I'm crazy and this is just my imagination running away with me."

She looked and their eyes met. She shook her head.

"I wish I could, detective."

"So, this is real."

"More real than the rest of the world knows. Most people go about their daily lives, working, playing, sleeping, without realizing just how thin the veil is that separates their quiet lives from the chaos on the other side."

"Why doesn't the church warn people?"

She leaned forward, resting her elbows on the table and folded her hands under her chin.

"How well did that work out for you? For Officers Tompkins and Jones? What happened to Tompkins, by the way? Did he get over it?"

"In a manner of speaking," sighed the detective. "Within a month of that night, he followed Jones to the other side, eating a bullet."

Sister Clarice bowed her head and wanted to cry for those two police officers, but knew now was not the time.

"Even if I were to go to the town square and cry out that demons are among us, the church would show up with a straight jacket and haul me away."

"Even though they know it to be true?"

"Especially knowing it to be true. The last

thing they would want is for the population to panic. I'm sure you, as a police officer, can understand that."

"You seem to know an awful lot about this, sister. What is your part in this?"

She leaned forward and motioned for him to get closer.

"If I tell you and you breathe a word about it to anyone, I'll have to kill you."

Then she sat back and stared at him. His eyes were as big as the plate his burger came on.

Then she giggled.

"I'm sorry. I always wanted to say *I could tell you, but then I'd have to kill you*. It just doesn't seem to work for me."

Detective Bishop leaned back and let out a belly laugh that made the sister's heart warm, knowing he could still find a reason to laugh.

"Detective, I am one of a handful of nuns and priests that work around the world, battling against the very monsters you've always known to exist. There are four of us here in America."

"Only four?"

"Yes, me here in Chicago, Father Draper in New York and Sisters Helena and Marisol in California."

"Two in California, huh?"

"Right and I can tell you those two sisters are busier than I have ever been."

"Why am I not surprised?" said the detective with a grin. "I guess even the demons like the weather out there."

"Sometimes in the middle of January I wish I was out there, battling demons in the bright, warm sunshine."

"Something tells me I'm going to be glad to have you here."

Then he looked around at some of the other diners and leaned forward and whispered, "If you tell anyone I said that I'll have to kill you."

She stuck out her tongue and gave him a raspberry, bringing another laugh from him.

"So, sister, what do we do?"

The smile fell from her face and the detective could feel a sense of sorrow come over her.

"What?" he asked.

"Detective, you are going to need to work up a story about a sadistic serial killer loose in the city."

"This demon has only killed one person, Suzanne Kelly."

She bit her lips and closed her eyes.

"You don't think she is going to be the only one," he said.

She just shook her head slowly.

"This is going to get a lot worse before it gets better," she said. "I wish I didn't have to tell you that, but it would be irresponsible of me not to."

"At the crime scene, when you were in contact with Ms. Kelly, I heard you mention the name Azrin. Can I take it you've crossed paths with him before?"

She closed her eyes and nodded slowly.

Chapter 4 – A Bright Future

In the dark halls of the ancient church, set high in the hills north of Rome, a young nun is walking briskly to wherever she needed to be. The church was probably older than God, Himself and quite drafty and cold.

The young sister hardly noticed any of that. Her heart was filled with the sunshine that comes from having just taken her vows and entering the life she had dreamed of since she was a little girl.

Maria Saletti had given up that name and would be known for the rest of her life as Sister Clarice. It filled her bright blue eyes with hope for the future. Blue eyes that shocked people when they saw her olive skin.

Being assigned to this church was more than a dream come true. Though it was old and in need of some repairs, the one thing it had in abundance was children. It was one of the largest and oldest orphanages in Italy, dating back to the mid-1600's.

When World War II raged over the land, not one bomb fell within a mile of the church. It had come through many wars unscathed, as did the children that called the Church of Santa Madonna Gabriele home.

As she walked from the library to the main sanctuary, she heard the patter of small feet and when she turned around to search for the source of the sound; she heard a giggle. The hallway was dark, but she knew what she had heard.

Walking back the way she had come, she stopped near a niche and crouched down, looking past the marble stand on which rested the statue of the church's namesake.

"I see you," said the sister with her sweet voice. "Come on out."

After a few seconds, a young girl poked her head out from behind the statue and smiled at her.

"Isabella, why are you hiding back there?"

"Because Father Christof said he was going to force me to eat those horrid vegetables."

"Oh!" gasped Sister Clarice. "The beast! I can't believe he would do that to you."

"You will not make me eat them, will you?"

"Are you kidding? I hate vegetables!" said the sister as she held out her hand and Isabella took it.

"But you know we have a big problem."

"What?" gasped Isabella.

"I heard when Jesus was your age, he hated vegetables, too."

"Really?"

"Yes, I swear it is true. But, his mama, the blessed Maria, told Him if He didn't eat his vegetables, He wouldn't be a very good Son of God."

As they continued walking back toward the dining hall, Isabella squeezed the sister's hand.

"What did Jesus do?"

"Well, He ate his vegetables, but He didn't like it."

As they walked into the dining hall, she saw Father Christof standing near one of the tables with an empty seat and a plate with greens on it. Sister Clarice surmised that must be Isabella's seat.

"But, you know what He did after that?"

"What?" asked Isabella as she was being led to her doom.

Sister Clarice leaned over a table and picked up a bottle and carried it with her.

"He invented something that made vegetables a lot better," she said as she and Isabella sat down.

She held up the bottle so Isabella could see it and she giggled.

The sister leaned over and said, "Everything tastes much better with ketchup on it."

She poured a generous helping of the red liquid over the greens on Isabella's plate and picked up the fork sitting next to it. Then, without a second's hesitation, she popped a Brussels sprout into her mouth and began chewing.

"Mmmm," she said. "Much better."

She held the fork out to Isabella and the girl took it, stabbed a sprout and stuck it in her mouth. Within two minutes, all the sprouts were gone and the plate was empty.

Isabella looked around the empty dining hall with a forlorn look on her face.

"What's the matter, sweetie?"

"They said there was going to be cake for dessert."

The padre leaned over her shoulder and picked up the plate and fork.

"You just sit right there, young lady. I'll see if there is any cake left."

He walked the plate into the kitchen and then returned with a small plate with a large piece of cake, covered with sugar icing. And two forks.

Setting the plate down in front of the two ladies, he turned and walked away, but not before giving Sister Clarice a smile and a wink.

After they finished the cake, Isabella took the plate to the kitchen and gave it to the dishwasher and returned to the sister.

"So," asked Sister Clarice, "what are you supposed to be doing now?"

"I should be in Sister Agatha's classroom. She was going to read to us before we go to bed."

"Well then, let's go. I hear she tells the most excellent stories."

The two of them walked hand-in-hand to the school side of the building and when they got there, Sister Clarice found a chair near the back and pulled Isabella onto her lap. They sat and listened to a truly ancient nun tell the story of the Prodigal Son, making it sound so interesting every child in the room sat in rapt attention.

After story time was over, a few of the older children took charge and led the younger ones back to the dorm rooms. Sister Clarice stood outside the classroom and wished every child a good night.

As she watched the last group walk away, a hand settled down on her shoulder. She turned to see Sister Agatha looking up at her.

"Sister Clarice, I thank the good Lord He has sent you here to help us."

She took the older nun's hand and kissed it, saying, "I go where Heavenly Father requires me. I only hope He will be happy with my work."

Agatha smiled and cupped her face with both hands.

"I'm sure He is already happy with your work, sister. And I see something in you that maybe you don't see yourself."

"What is that?"

"I see a power in you. I can't describe it as I have never seen it before like this. You have the power of Heaven resting on your shoulders."

Sister Clarice looked into the wise, old eyes of the nun and said, "I should hope we all have the power of Heaven looking over us."

"Yes, we do," said Sister Agatha, "but not like you. Be mindful of your strength. It will serve you well."

Clarice nodded and then asked, "May I walk with you to your chambers?"

"Oh no, dearie. I'm going to spend some time in the meditation garden before going to bed. You run along."

She bowed and kissed Agatha's hand again, saying, "Peace be unto you, sister."

"And to you, Sister Clarice."

The older nun turned and walked away, toward the back entrance to the church, which led out to the gardens. Sister Clarice watched her go and couldn't help feeling something tickling at the back of her mind. It was a feeling so foreign to her she had no experience to deal with it.

Shaking off the feeling, she turned and walked back toward the nave and into one of the small chapels off to the side. Her nightly routine would find her on her knees in prayer before going to bed.

Kneeling down in the chapel, she looked up at the crucifix hanging behind the altar. She couldn't understand the feeling that came over her, but it felt like the Jesus hanging on the cross was looking directly at her. It wasn't a feeling of peace and tranquility that settled over her soul. It was a feeling of strength and an admonition to be prepared to fight.

Fight? Fight what?

Chapter 5 – The Hero's Journey Begins

The quiet tranquility of the chapel was a place where she always found peace. Her mind and heart would slow and she felt as if she was floating in the universe.

However, she found this night was not one of those nights. Her mind was racing and she couldn't pin down a reason.

As she struggled to understand the emotions washing over her, a woman's scream shattered the solitude of the night. Then a roar. A roar that sounded like some enormous beast was loose in the church.

As she pushed herself to her feet, she turned to the arch leading out of the chapel and saw the padre running past, followed closely by two monks.

Running into the corridor, she turned to follow the others and it shocked her to see that each of the three men were carrying swords.

Another scream from the woman was cut short and then a roar from the beast again caused the walls of the church to shake.

"Sister!" said the padre as she sprinted past him. "You should not go out there! Mind the children!"

His words fell on deaf ears as she rushed out of the church and into the garden. Why she knew to go straight to the garden, she could not explain. An unseen hand guided her steps.

Charging through the open door leading into the garden, she came face-to-face with the most horrifying sight she could ever imagine. It made her heart stop beating for a second as she struggled to comprehend what she was seeing.

A large demon was standing in the middle of the garden. He was easily eight feet tall and that didn't include the large horns protruding from his head. His eyes burned red as he swung his gaze to the new arrivals in the garden.

What caused the most dread in her soul was the demon's claws seemed to be a foot long and he had Sister Agatha impaled on the claws of one hand. He had driven the claws into her back and out the front of her body. He was holding the old nun's body up, as if he was proudly showing off what he had done.

Before Sister Clarice could understand what was going on, one monk barged past her and went straight at the demon, his sword pointing straight at the demon's chest.

"Brother Michael!" screamed the padre.

In just a second, the monk tried to drive his sword into the demon, but all he got was a backhand from the monster, sending him flying across the garden and slamming into a statue. Sister Clarice heard a gasp of pain and the sound of bones breaking as Michael crumpled to the ground at the feet of John the Baptist.

Sister Agatha dropped a sword she had clutched in her hand and it clattered to the ground, stopping just inches from Clarice's feet.

The sister looked at the demon and could see Sister Agatha was still alive, but wouldn't be much longer. Their eyes met and Sister Clarice felt as if the older nun was looking directly into her soul.

"Fight, sister," gasped Agatha as her body went limp on the talons of the demon.

For reasons only known to God, Sister Clarice bent down and picked up the sword. She felt a surge of power course up her arm and into her chest. Her mind raced back to the words of Sister Agatha, that the power of Heaven rested on her shoulders.

The padre and the other monk pushed past her and approached the demon with a little more caution than Michael had. It was clear they knew to be wary of this demon.

The demon regarded them with disdain as it flung Sister Agatha away like a piece of trash, her body slamming into the same statue as Brother Michael and landing on top of him.

Sister Clarice wanted to go to her, but a small voice in the back of her mind told her to stand and prepare to face the demon. In her heart, she knew it was too late for Sister Agatha and she needed to provide support for the padre and Brother Andrew.

The two men tried to angle themselves to come at the demon from different sides, but the beast was having none of it. Every time they took a step, the demon would back up one step, keeping them in front of itself.

"Azrin," said the padre, "you should have stayed in Hell where you belong."

Azrin? So this monster has a name?

"Hell isn't nearly as much fun as coming

up here and playing with you humans."

Then Azrin turned his gaze to the sister.

"Ahh, so you've brought me a new plaything."

Squinting his eyes at her, he growled, "I shall have a good time with you. I shall test your faith like it has never been before."

She raised the sword in front of her and stared at the beast.

"My faith is strong and it will never waiver in the face of the likes of you."

"Oooo ... a challenge. I do so love a challenge. I shall squash you like a little bug. Little bug. I think that is what I shall call you from this day forward."

Brother Andrew stopped trying to get an angle on Azrin and stepped in between the demon and the nun. His sword glowed in the moonlight as he raised it.

"You shall not harm one hair on her head, demon!"

The demon took a step toward the monk and Father Christof could see it was going to end badly if he didn't do something. He lunged forward and dropped below Azrin's swinging fist. With a mighty slash, he sliced the blade across the back of Azrin's leg, eliciting a howl of pain from the monster.

Azrin swung again, this time connecting with the padre's shoulder and knocking him over a raised flower bed. He rolled and came up on his feet immediately, but it was clear the blow had slowed him down.

Brother Andrew lunged and stabbed at the

demon's chest and almost made contact, but Azrin batted the sword away and raked the monk's back with his claws.

As Andrew went down. Azrin turned his attention to the frightened nun in front of him. She held the sword with two hands, keeping her eyes locked on the demon's eyes. Memories of her childhood flooded in. A time when she and her two brothers would play Three Musketeers with wooden swords.

She remembered how the sword was a little heavy for her small hands, so she would swing it with both hands. She learned quickly and could defend herself against the attacks of her brothers and would even best them once in a while.

Wrapping her fingers around the hilt of Sister Agatha's sword, it all came back to her. The sword felt like it was created for her hands.

She couldn't explain the feeling of power that was coming from the blade, but it buoyed her confidence.

Azrin took a step toward her and she pointed the sword at him.

"Go back to the depths of hell, demon. You are not welcome here."

Azrin stopped and looked at her.

"Welcome here? I certainly hope not. It would not be any fun if I was welcomed here."

He took a swipe at her and she ducked under his fist. She could tell his attack had some power and prayed he would never connect with one of his punches.

As his arm swished over her head, she

stabbed at his belly, causing the demon to roar in pain. As it turned back to her, she remembered how she had to use fancy footwork to keep her brothers at bay. As it lunged at her again, she moved swiftly out of its path and sliced the blade along the demon's side, opening up a gaping wound.

She was aghast as the open wound spit fire and smoke. It was as if the demon was made from the very fires of Hell.

Azrin turned again, its movement would best be described as lumbering, contrary to hers, which would be thought of as graceful. It was six years of ballet lessons paying for themselves.

She caught a quick glance of the padre pushing himself to his feet and picking up his sword and she felt relief that he would come back to the fight and help her. Her relief turned to dismay when she saw him fall to his knee again. He tried to push himself up, but he had taken a severe blow and couldn't stay standing.

Azrin took another step toward her and she found herself backed up against a wall. With nowhere else to go, she prepared to defend this last piece of Earth under her feet.

The demon reached for her and she could feel her skin beginning to singe from the heat of its fingers. She knew if those fingers ever touched her, they would burn her alive.

With one last effort, she swung the sword with all her might and connected with the fingers of the demon, slicing three of its fingers off.

As Azrin reared back and howled in pain, she stepped forward and drove the point of the sword directly into the gut of the demon. When Azrin looked down at her, she twisted the blade and drove it deeper.

"By the power of Heaven, I command you to go back to Hell where you belong!"

Azrin went to grab her, but then his body began to shake and rattle. In a few seconds, the demon's body burst apart in a fiery flash and then disappeared, leaving nothing but a pile of ash in the middle of the garden.

Feeling overwhelmed by what had just happened, the sword fell from her hands and clattered to the ground. She bent double, trying to calm her heart and breathing, thanking God for the strength He had blessed her with.

Suddenly, she remembered she wasn't the only one in the garden and she stood up and looked around. Father Christof was still on one knee, holding onto his sword for support. He was just staring at her.

She saw Brother Andrew was lying on the ground a few feet away and she went to him. As she put a hand on his back, he roused with a groan. He rolled onto his side and looked up at her.

"You're an angel," he croaked.

"No, not yet anyway," she said with a pained smile. "Are you going to be okay?"

He pushed himself up and said, "I think so. Maybe after a week of laying on a beach in Hawaii."

He looked over and saw Sister Agatha

laying on top of Brother Michael.

"Oh no," he groaned.

Sister Clarice stood up and walked over to the fallen nun and monk. Kneeling down, she ran her hand over the sister's forehead. The older nun's eyes fluttered open and she smiled softly at the younger woman.

"You're still alive," gasped Clarice.

"I'm afraid not for much longer, sister."

Father Christof finally got his feet under himself and he made his way to the two sisters.

"Sister Clarice, see if you can hold her up for a moment. I'm going to get Brother Michael out from under her."

"I don't think that's a good idea, padre."

"Sister," said Agatha, "I can't feel anything from my chest down and what I do feel, tells me I am not long for this world. Try to lift me so Brother Michael can be tended to."

Sister Clarice leaned forward and wrapped her arms around the older woman and lifted her up slightly and Father Christof slid the monk out from under her. When the padre rolled him over, it was clear he was already dead.

The padre crossed himself and said a quick last rites.

"Padre," gasped Agatha, "take my effects and give them to Sister Clarice. I believe she shall make a worthy replacement for me."

"What are you talking about?" asked Clarice. "You're going to get better and need no replacement."

"No, sweetheart, I'm not. I am fast coming

to the end of my road."

Then she reached up and cupped Clarice's face with one hand.

"You be strong, young one. Evil walks this Earth and you have been chosen to fight against it. Always walk with God's love in your heart. It will give you strength."

Her hand fell away from the young nun's cheek and her eyes dropped closed for the last time.

"Sister?"

The padre said the last rites and blessed her for her long life of fighting evil. Then he reached under her habit and unbuckled a leather belt and pulled it out from around her body. Clarice saw it was a belt with a scabbard for holding a sword.

"Remove her weapons from her boots, sister," said the padre.

"Weapons?"

Sister Clarice looked under the hem of Agatha's habit and gasped. The older nun was wearing a pair of heavy black boots and there were two daggers in sheathes on the inside of her ankles. There were two semi-automatic pistols in holsters on the outside of her ankles.

"What in the world?" she mumbled as she removed the custom belts from the tops of the boots that held the knives and pistols.

As she was doing this, the padre stood up and walked over and picked up the sword she had dropped. Sliding it into the scabbard, he turned back to them.

Brother Andrew had finally gotten himself

off the ground and stumbled over. He looked like his heart was being ripped out as he looked down at the dead nun and monk.

The padre stepped up to him and put a hand on his shoulder.

"Brother, can you see to these two? I need to make a phone call."

"Yes, padre."

Sister Clarice was holding the two belts with knives and guns, much as a person would hold a dead rat. The padre held out his hand and took them from her, which she was all too happy to give him.

"Sister, would you come to my office in ten minutes? I need to make a phone call and then I need to talk to you."

"Certainly, padre."

He turned and went back inside, only to find most of the children were gathered just inside the door. There were a couple of monks trying to keep them corralled and not letting them see too much.

"Children, get back to your rooms! Now!" stormed the padre.

Sister Clarice heard the outburst and rushed to the door. She saw some children back away from him as if he were a demon. Reaching out, she put a hand on his shoulder and felt his body relax under her touch.

He took a deep breath and said, "I'm sorry. Please return to your rooms and get some sleep. We can talk about this in the morning."

"Go to bed, sweethearts," she said softly and they turned and began heading back to their rooms, shepherded by the other monks.

The padre turned and limped down the hallway and went into his office. She watched him go and could see his once strong shoulders were drooping from the heavy weight of what he had just been through. The weapons dangled from his hands and he walked.

She went to the chapel and dropped to her knees in the pulpit and cried her eyes out for Sister Agatha. She found her hands trembling as she relived the battle she had just been part of.

Never in her life had she been confronted with evil like she had just witnessed. She knew in the back of her mind that evil like that existed in the world, but she had always been protected from it.

Now it seemed to have its eyes fixed squarely on her. She always knew evil would work against her and the church, but she never dreamed it would come at her so directly.

Chapter 6 – A New Calling

After trying to calm herself, she rose and left the chapel and headed for the padre's office. She found him standing at his open door, waiting for her. After she entered, he closed the door and pointed to a chair.

Sitting down, she saw the weapons laying on the desk. She still trembled at the sight of these instruments of death. Until she removed the pistols from Sister Agatha, she had never come that close to holding real guns in her hands.

"First off, let me apologize for my outburst in front of the children. That was completely uncalled for and for that, I beg your forgiveness."

"Padre, after what we just witnessed and went through, I'm surprised I'm not falling to pieces myself."

Her eyes drifted from his to the weapons laying on the desk. The daggers had ivory handles with red crosses inlaid in them. The pistols were gold-plated, with ivory grips and the same red crosses. The sword looked to be a match for the daggers.

"Have you ever heard of the Sisters of the Templar?"

"No, padre, I haven't."

He nodded and said, "About four hundred years ago, there was an off-shoot from the Knights Templar and it was made up entirely of Catholic nuns, such as yourself and Sister Agatha."

"I thought the Knights Templar were no more."

He smiled at her and reached up and pulled the black collar of his tunic down and she saw a red cross in a red circle on his white clerical collar.

"You're Templar Knight?"

"Yes, I am, and Sister Agatha was one of the Sisters of the Templar. It used to be that we, the Knights Templar, would defend the Holy Land. Now, there isn't much call for that. Our calling is now to protect this world from … well … from demons like Azrin."

She swallowed hard when she realized where this conversation was going.

"No," she whispered.

"No? I haven't even asked you anything."

"You're about to ask me to take Sister Agatha's place. I didn't become a nun to become a warrior. I came here to teach the children. I am not a fighter."

"After what I just witnessed in the garden, I can safely say you are very much a fighter. As for teaching the children, you will continue to do that. But you will also protect them. If Azrin had gotten past Sister Agatha, he would have entered the walls of this sanctuary and would have killed every child in the place."

Immediately, her mind went to a scene of horror, where Azrin rampaged through the school and killed everyone, including little Isabella. A shudder ran through her body.

"Scusami, padre."

Sister Clarice jumped at the sound of

another voice and realized it had come from the speakerphone on the desk.

"Yes, Maurice."

"You should notta be scaring her alike that."

"She needs to be scared."

What followed was a short, terse sentence in Italian, causing the padre to bow his head.

"I am sorry. You are correct. It has just been a trying time, this last hour."

"I a understand. It will be trying time for all of us. Seester Agatha was a the best of all of us."

"Yes, sir," said the padre, bowing his head.

"Seester Clahrice, you are a new to order?"

She looked at the padre, not knowing what to do.

"Uh, yes, just six months now."

"Aye, seex months. Eengcredible. Seester Clahrice, we need you accept new calling. Padre Christof knows about."

"Excuse me, but who am I talking to?"

"I'm sorry," said the padre. "Sister Clarice, this is His Holiness, Pope Thomas the Fourth."

The sister felt as if the entire world had just fallen on her head. First, a demon named Azrin, straight from Hell. And now the leader of the entire Catholic Church was changing her calling.

"I feel like I'm going to be sick," she said, trying to keep from hyperventilating.

The padre reached down and picked up the wastebasket next to his desk and handed it across to her. She took it and wrapped her arms around it, holding it like it was the most precious thing in her life.

"I say not scare her," said the pope.

"Actually, I believe you are scaring her more than me."

"I weesh I could laugh at that. Dark times we have now."

"Yes, sir, very dark indeed."

"I see you in two hours. Conveence her."

Then there was a click and the phone went dead.

The padre looked across the desk at a very frightened, very pale nun. As His Holiness said, he wished he could laugh at the sight, but the darkness that was upon them made that impossible.

"What did he mean? He would see you in two hours?" she whispered.

"Actually, he meant he would see us in two hours. Please go pack a light suitcase. We'll be gone for a couple of days."

"Where are we going?" she asked as she clutched the wastebasket even tighter.

"I thought it was clear, sister. We're going to Rome."

That was all it took. Up came those gross Brussels sprouts and ketchup. The sound of her throwing up echoed out of the wastebasket, along with the smell.

After she finished and could open her teary eyes, she saw he was holding a box of tissue out to her.

"You call His Holiness Maurice?" she whimpered as she wiped her mouth.

"He and I have been friends since childhood. I know I shouldn't talk with that level of familiarity to him, but he gets upset if I refer to him as His Holiness. Now, please go pack. His plane will be here to pick us up in less than an hour."

She held up her hand to signal he should stop talking because she felt another round of churning in her stomach. After a few seconds, she could stave off the feeling and set the wastebasket down.

Rising from the chair on two very unstable legs, she crossed herself and then asked, "Would it be possible to just say I'm not going?"

"Nope. But look at it this way. When you are standing in front of him, you can decline the calling if you like."

"What are my chances of getting away with that?"

"How strong is your faith in God?"

"It is absolute, padre."

"And your faith in His Holiness as the leader of this church?"

"Again, absolute."

"Then I'd say your chances of declining the calling are pretty much zero. Unless you intend to renounce your calling and leave the order."

"I would never do that!"

"Then you have your answer, sister. Believe me when I tell you I know exactly how you feel. I was called to the Knights Templar when I was a very young priest and my reaction was pretty much the same as yours."

She stared into his eyes and he could see she was about to tear up again.

"Sister, the church and the Sisters of the Templar need someone like you more than you know."

She nodded, turned and walked out the door. That feeling of having the world dropped on her shoulders remained. It felt like she was now carrying it to her small room.

Chapter 7 – Know Your Enemy

"So, I guess your calling comes from very high up."

Sister Clarice looked across the table at the detective and gave a half smile.

"You could say it comes from the very highest of places. God Himself has chosen me for this work and who was I to refuse?"

"Okay, so what do we know for sure?"

"One thing we know," said the sister, "is we both had dealings with Azrin in the past. I find it hard to believe that is just a coincidence."

"And you think he's back for what reason?"

"To settle some scores. Just to play games with one or both of us."

"Games?"

"When dealing with Azrin, or any other demons from Hell, you should know one thing. To them, terrorizing and killing humans is nothing more than play time for them. Usually they are kept on a fairly short leash, but now and then one of them will decide to break that leash and humans are the ones that suffer for it."

"You said he might have some scores to settle. What scores would a demon have to settle?" asked Bishop. "Seems to me a demon would just be evil one-hundred percent of the time. Do they really hold grudges?"

"I never would have believed it myself, but I have learned since I became a demon hunter, they can hold grudges. They don't like to lose and will keep coming until they either win or they are destroyed."

"You think Azrin is coming after you because of the defeat you handed him in the garden that night?"

Just then, the waitress walked over and asked if there was anything else she could get them.

"Two pieces of your finest apple pie," said the detective. "With ice cream?"

Sister Clarice smiled and said, "Of course."

"Be right back," said the waitress, who then walked back to the kitchen.

"Really? Apple pie?" asked the sister.

"I learned way back when I became a homicide detective that in dealing with the things I see almost daily, I need to take a few moments and enjoy the nicer things in life. Do I need the apple pie? No," he said, patting his belly. "But there are some things that may not be good for the body, but they are good for the soul."

Sister Clarice smiled and said, "I've never heard of pie being good for the soul, but I am quite willing to defer to your judgment."

When they had finished their pie and the detective paid the check, they walked out of the diner and into the parking lot. The detective followed her to her car and held the door for her.

"Thank you, kind sir."

She went to sit in her car when Bishop's phone rang. She was ready to say goodbye, but didn't want to interrupt him, so she waited.

"This is Bishop."

As she stood there quietly, she heard him gasp and then close his eyes. She could see he was hearing something quite disturbing.

"Got it," said the detective. "Text me the address. I'm on my way."

He ended the call and just stood there, gritting his teeth and then starting to shake. He only opened his eyes when he felt a small, gentle hand on his arm.

"What is it?" she asked.

He took a deep breath and then said, "It's happened again and in the same neighborhood as Suzanne."

"Oh, dear Lord," she said, her voice almost breaking.

His phone chirped and he tapped the screen and it showed the address he needed to get to.

"I don't suppose there's anyway I can keep you away from this?"

"I need to go," she said. "And the sooner after the killing I can get to the victim, the more I'll be able to see."

He held the phone up to her and she pulled her phone and typed the address into the map software. She gasped when she saw where the map centered.

"What is it, sister?"

She felt a tear run down her cheek and quickly wiped it away.

"I think that's Marvin and Esther's home."

The detective took her arm and gently

pulled her away from her car and closed the door. She looked up at him.

"I'm not going to let you drive there right now," he said. "You can ride with me."

They hastened to his car and he held the door for her. By the time he had walked around and got in, she had pulled a tissue from her pocket and was holding it to her eyes.

"Are you going to be okay?"

She lowered the tissue and her eyes were red and wet.

"No, Detective Bishop, I am not, but I guess I'll have to be."

He started the car and pulled out of the parking lot, his light and siren blazing. There was not another word spoken between them as they sped across the city.

The sister prayed she was mistaken about the address and what they were going to find. She prayed, but she knew deep in her heart that Azrin had struck again and this time it was a message directed at her.

Chapter 8 – Hits Close To Home

As they turned the corner onto the street, Sister Clarice's heart sank. Just as the day before, the narrow street was completely blocked off with emergency vehicles and the police worked hard to keep people back.

As Bishop brought his car to a stop, he unbuckled his seat belt and went to get out.

Then he stopped.

He looked over at the sister and she was sitting frozen in place, tears streaming down her face as she looked at the scene in front of her.

"I think you really should stay in the car," he said.

Turning her head slowly, she looked at him and took a deep breath.

In a timid, small voice, she said, "Just like you, Detective Bishop, I can't do my job if I sit here in the car."

Then she unbuckled her seat belt and opened the door, but before getting out, she closed her eyes and said a silent prayer, asking for strength.

Climbing out of the car, she walked around to the front and the two of them stood there for a moment, side-by-side, surveying the scene. Neither one was interested in seeing what had happened, but they knew it was inevitable.

They were the only two people standing on that street at the moment that knew what was really going on.

A heavy hand settled softly on her

shoulder and she looked up at Bishop. He looked down and took a deep breath.

"Let's go."

With a small nod, she walked alongside him, one of her hands clutching at his powerful arm. He could feel her trembling as they got closer to the yellow crime scene tape.

As they approached the tape, one officer lifted it and they walked under, though Bishop was getting some strange stares. Bringing the nun to the crime scene was one reason, but seeing her clutching at his arm was another.

As they began climbing the steps Suzanne had taken refuge on just a few brief hours earlier, Sister Clarice doubted her resolve to face whatever was inside the apartment.

As they reached the top step, the door opened and Officer Mary Danton stepped out. When she saw the two, she held up her hand and pulled the door closed behind her.

"What's up, officer?" asked Bishop.

"Sir, they have asked me to stop you from going inside. Both of you."

"Really? It will be hard to investigate this crime scene if I don't get inside to see it."

"I know, sir, and I wish I wasn't the one sent out here to tell you this. They have removed you from the case and, sister, you are not to be allowed inside."

"On who's orders?" asked Bishop.

"Captain Tyrell. He wants you in his office within an hour, sir."

"Who's taking over the investigation?"

When Mary hesitated to say, he crossed his

arms in front of his chest and looked at her. He gave the impression he was expecting an answer.

"Purcell is taking over, sir."

"Purcell? Are you kidding me? He couldn't find his own ass with both hands and a road map!"

Mary winced and closed her eyes as he said this.

"I'll try not to take that personally, Bishop."

The detective spun around to see Detective Thomas Purcell walking up the steps. He had a grim smile on his face, as if he didn't want to be there.

"Sorry, Tom, but finding out they have sidelined me in this way is very unacceptable."

Tom raised his hands as he reached the top step and said, "Hey, I feel you, man. To tell you the truth, I didn't want this. After hearing what happened to Suzanne Kelly, I wanted nothing to do with this case because it sounds like it's going to be related."

Bishop held out his hand and said, "I'm sorry about what I said. It was spur of the moment and I lost my cool. It's just that the sister and I ..."

He glanced at Sister Clarice, and she gave him a quick shake of the head.

"Well, she knows the people that live here and I was just getting started with the investigation."

Tom took his hand and shook it.

"Understood. Now, if you'll excuse me, I need to get in there and see how bad this is."

As Mary opened the door to let him in, Sister Clarice glimpsed blood all over the walls of the apartment.

"Oh, dear God," she cried before Officer Danton could close the door.

"Sir," said Mary, "I truly am sorry. This was your case and I think it should still be your case. But I'm just an ordinary beat cop and my opinion means nothing."

"Don't sell yourself short, Danton. Without you beat cops our jobs would be a hundred times harder. I guess I better head downtown and see the captain."

As he turned, the sister reached out and took hold of his arm.

"I'm going with you."

"Sister Clarice, there may be some harsh words spoken, words that shouldn't fall upon your ears."

"I work with inner-city kids, detective. There isn't a word you can say that I haven't heard before."

"Don't be so sure."

"Besides, I came here with you if you remember. My car is a long way from here."

In a moment of realization, he remembered and didn't want her walking twenty blocks to get back to her car.

"You take care, Mary," said the sister as she turned to follow Bishop down the stairs.

"Sister."

"Yes."

The sister turned back to Mary and she was scribbling something in her small notebook. Then she tore the page out and folded it.

"I could lose my badge for doing this, but," said Mary softly, as she held out her hand.

When Clarice took it, the folded piece of paper slipped into her hand and she stepped closer to the officer and pulled the sleeve of her habit over both their hands. She was able to take the paper with no one seeing.

"Go to her. She needs you more than anyone else right now," said Mary, as she turned to head back inside. She closed the door quickly so the sister wouldn't see the horror inside.

Keeping the paper in her hand and covered with her sleeve, she descended the steps and walked over to the detective's car. He was holding the door open for her.

"Officer Danton say anything?"

The sister jerked a little and she looked up at the detective.

"No, she actually …"

"She what?"

"Let's get going," said Clarice as she sat down in the car.

As the detective walked around the car, she put the piece of paper in one of her inside pockets and then fished her phone out of the other.

As Bishop sat down, she was dialing. Holding the phone to her ear, she waited as Bishop started the car and pulled around and headed out of the neighborhood.

When the phone was answered, she put it

on speaker.

"Jon, we are in serious trouble."

There was a moment of silence before Cardinal Wright spoke.

"If you're calling me Jon, we must be facing end of the world trouble."

Bishop pulled the car over because he wanted to make sure he heard everything.

"I'm sorry, Your Eminence."

"Don't be sorry, sister. Just tell me why I hear more fear in your voice than I ever have before?"

Over the next minute, Bishop stayed silent as she related what just happened.

"This makes little sense," said the Cardinal over the phone. "Detective Bishop is probably the most qualified police officer to investigate this. Wouldn't you agree, detective?"

Bishop's eyes got big as he wondered how the Cardinal knew he was listening.

"Why do you say that?" asked Bishop, finally breaking his silence.

"Because you know what it is we fight, having your previous experience with Azrin."

"You knew about that?" asking Bishop, sounding a little irritated.

"Did we know it was Azrin back then? No. But the sisters at the orphanage knew what had happened to you and though no one else believed you, they did. And so did I."

Bishop bowed his head and closed his eyes, trying to calm his emotions. He felt the sister's hand settle on his arm and he looked at her.

"Did you know?" he asked.

"No, not until I touched your arm this morning and saw your vision."

"Detective," said the Cardinal over the phone, "I'd like to continue this conversation, but right now I need to make a phone call. Continue on your way to the precinct, but might I suggest a rather circuitous route?"

Bishop looked at the sister, wondering what the Cardinal was saying.

"Yes, Your Eminence, we can do that," said the sister.

"Fine. I shall see you there in one hour."

There was a click of finality as the phone went dead.

"What is he asking of us? I was told to be in the captain's office within an hour, and that was about half an hour ago."

She squeezed his arm as she said, "If I know the Cardinal, he is going to make a phone call to someone a little higher than the captain. Don't give up on this being your case just yet, detective."

"So, I've been on the church's radar for over thirty years?"

"Fredrick, your parents were attacked and killed by a demon, which we now know was Azrin. Don't be upset about this. It sounds like they were doing everything they could to protect you. Putting you in a Catholic orphanage could not have been a mistake."

"Protected by a bunch of nuns?"

Then he hung his head when he realized what he had just said.

"I'm sorry. I'm just upset at the thought of

all those years when I thought no one believed me about what I saw."

She squeezed his hand again and smiled when he looked at her.

"I'm sure there was a sister demon hunter at that orphanage who had the duty of watching over you."

He gasped and stared at her.

"Sister Marissa."

"Really? You think so?"

"One day I was sitting in the gardens, back by the bushes, and she was walking across the grounds, heading for the chapel. She dropped some papers and bent over to pick them up and I saw …"

"Saw what?" asked Clarice, as he stopped.

"Something that seemed so out of place with the sister. Even now, I still can't believe it."

The sister gave him a small smile and reached down and pulled a pistol from her ankle holster and held it up.

"Did she carry something like this?"

His eyes went wide as he saw the gun.

"Exactly like that! The gold, the white ivory handles and everything. You're armed?"

"Detective, I'm probably armed better than you."

She reached down to put the gun back in her holster and when she sat back; she saw her phone still sitting in her lap. As she reached into her pocket to put it away, she felt the paper Mary had given her and pulled it out.

As Bishop started the car and began pulling back into the street, the sister opened the paper and read it. Then screamed, causing the detective to slam on the brakes.

"What?"

"Oh my God! Mercy Hospital! Please!"

"What happened?"

She handed him the paper and he read it. Once done, he handed her the paper back. Then pulled his red light from behind his seat and reached out and set it on the roof. Reaching over, he flipped the switch and the siren started blaring and he took off at a very high rate of speed.

The sister sat in the seat and tears were streaming down her face as she looked at the paper in her hands. The quickly scrawled note tore right through her heart.

Esther Morgan is alive
and at Mercy Hospital

Chapter 9 – A Friend In Need

The detective's car slid to a stop just outside of the ambulance lane at Mercy's emergency room. He fumbled with his seat belt, swearing under his breath. He had to hurry because the sister had bailed out of the car almost before it came to a stop.

He left the red light on top of the car and hustled toward the emergency entrance, having already lost sight of the sister's black robes as she disappeared inside.

He burst through the doors just in time to hear her pleading with the nurse behind the window.

"Please, I must see her."

"Sister, she's in surgery right now. There is no way you can go in there."

Sister Clarice turned as she heard the detective walk up behind her. She had tears streaming down her face as she clenched the lapels of his jacket.

"Please, I need to see her."

He put a large arm around her shoulders and guided her toward some chairs.

"Sister, you charging into the operating room will not do Esther any good. I think the best you can do is sit here and talk to God on her behalf."

Sniffing back her tears, she nodded and sat down. Reaching behind her wimple, she undid a clasp and pulled her rosary from around her neck. As she closed her eyes, she bowed her head and began by kissing the crucifix and began praying silently for the life of her friend.

It comforted her as the detective rested a warm hand at the base of her neck. He sat silently as she prayed. He silently prayed for a woman he had never met, if the truth was known.

About thirty minutes later, a young Dr. Collins came through the doors from the emergency room and went straight to the two of them.

Sister Clarice bounced up from her seat.

"How is she, doctor?"

He could see her face was streaked with dried tears and he pulled a handkerchief from his pocket and handed it to her.

"She's going to be fine, sister. Most of the injuries were superficial."

"Can I see her?"

The doctor shook his head and said, "No, not at this time. Though her physical injuries were minor, she's suffered a mental shock and we had to sedate her. She is unconscious and will be for a few hours."

"If I could just see her for a moment and say a quick prayer over her," she said with pleading eyes.

Dr. Collins took a deep breath and let it out slowly.

"I will take you in there. One minute and not one second more. Do you understand me, sister?"

"Yes, doctor. Thank you."

She looked back at Bishop and he said, "Don't forget, we need to get to the precinct and find out what your boss has in store."

"I'll be right out."

She followed the doctor through the doors and back to a room with a sign that said Intensive Care. As they walked into the room, Sister Clarice's heart just about stopped. Even though the doctor had said Esther's injuries were minor, they didn't look like it.

Her face was bruised, like someone had taken a baseball bat to it. She had one arm in a cast from her wrist to shoulder.

"Oh, Esther," she lamented.

Going to the bedside, she reached into another of the seemingly endless pockets in her habit and pulled out a smaller version of her rosary. Kissing the crucifix, she slipped it over Esther's uninjured wrist.

Putting a hand gently on the old woman's forehead, she bowed her head and beseeched God to look after her and heal her.

After what was clearly more than a minute, she heard the doctor clear his throat and she turned to him.

"Please, do not let anyone remove that rosary from her wrist. The evil that attacked her tonight may return and it may be the only thing that protects her."

The doctor cocked his head and asked, "Evil? Attack her here?"

"Doctor, are you a Christian man?"

"Yes, I am."

She reached into her pocket and pulled out another small rosary and handed it to him.

"Yes, doctor. Evil. This will keep you safe."

As he looked at the prayer beads in his hand, she turned and looked one last time at Esther.

"How long will she be out?"

"I should think about ten to twelve hours."

"I shall return to see her then," she said as she headed out of the room.

There was a sound behind her that almost broke her heart. The sound of the rosary being tossed into the waste bin.

When they reached the captain's door, Bishop knocked and heard the captain call them in. Opening the door and stepping inside, it surprised him and the sister to see they weren't the only ones invited to the meeting.

Sister Clarice took a couple of steps and went to kneel.

"Sister Clarice, if you kneel in front of me in this office, I will have to give you a serious reprimand."

She stood back up and clasped her hands in front of her heart.

"I'm sorry, Your Eminence."

The cardinal, dressed in his finest red robes, stepped around behind her and placed his hands on her shoulders and turned her.

"I'd like to introduce you to the Chief of Police, Clark Masters."

A distinguished-looking man with silver hair and blue eyes stood up and held out his hand to her. When she looked at the hand, she hesitated to shake it and the cardinal knew he needed to say something.

"I'm sorry, Chief Masters. The sister is of one of our orders that has vowed to never touch another man until the hands of Jesus touch her in the next life."

"Oh, I am so sorry," said the chief as he pulled his hand away quickly.

"That's okay, Chief Masters," she said softly. "You couldn't have known."

This confused the detective for a second, having touched her hand a few times. But then, he realized, if she touched the chief's hand, she might have seen some of his past life and it might not be something she wanted to see.

"Chief," said the Cardinal, "I don't want to keep you any longer than necessary."

"Yes," said the chief as he walked over and shook Bishop's hand. "Detective Bishop, it is good to meet you."

"Likewise, sir."

"Okay, Captain Tyrell," said the chief, "as you know, I don't really like surprises in this department. I like things to run smoothly and leave my captains to run their precincts as they see fit."

"Yes, sir," said Tyrell.

"About an hour ago, the Holy Father called me from the Vatican to ask why Detective Bishop had been removed from the case he was working on and why Sister Clarice was being forbidden to lend her considerable expertise in this situation."

"Clark …"

The chief just looked at him.

"Chief Masters, Detective Bishop was

proving to be ineffective in this investigation and I felt the need to replace him. And why the sister needs to even be a part of this, I can't even imagine."

The chief twisted his neck a couple of times and the sister was standing close enough to hear a couple of pops from his neck joints, causing her to wince.

"There was a horrific murder last night and then another this afternoon," said the chief. "Do you expect all of your detectives to solve their cases in less than twenty-four hours? Don't get me wrong, I'd love to see it, but it seems unrealistic."

Tyrell sank back into his chair, realizing this would not go his way.

"I have to agree with you, sir."

"Can you assure me that you will reassign the detective to the case and the sister may help in any way she can?"

"Yes, chief."

"Good," said the chief as he clapped his hands. "Now, I'd like to get back to my dinner with my lovely wife."

Looking at the cardinal, he said, "And I hope I never get a call like that again."

"I'm sure," said Cardinal Wright, "we have sorted everything out. And I'm sure His Holiness appreciates your attention to this matter and would probably love to talk to you again after this is taken care of."

The chief shook his hand and then Bishop's.

"Detective, please bring out your A-game

on this one. Something tells me the city is going to need it."

"Absolutely, sir."

"Good evening, gentlemen." He turned and nodded to the sister, "And to you, too, sister. Be careful out there."

She nodded to him, keeping her hands firmly clasped in front of her.

After the chief walked out the door and it was closed, the cardinal looked at the captain and smiled.

"There, that seems to have been handled nicely."

The captain shook his head and picked up his phone and hit a couple of buttons.

"Shirley, can you have Purcell call me? Thanks."

He hung up the phone and looked at the three on the other side of the desk.

"Was it really the pope that called him?"

"Yes, it was," said the cardinal, "after I called His Holiness and apprised him of the situation here."

The captain just looked down and shook his head.

"Captain Tyrell," said the cardinal, "we are not your enemies. We are looking to end the coming reign of terror, just as you are. Detective Bishop and Sister Clarice are our best hope in achieving that goal."

"Reign of terror?"

Cardinal Wright looked at Sister Clarice and nodded.

"Captain Tyrell," she said, "we have had

two murders in just the last few hours and I can feel it in my heart they will not be the last. It is going to get a lot worse."

"How much worse?"

She didn't want to say anything and Bishop saved her from having to speak again.

"Biblically worse, sir."

"Biblically? Are you shi ...," he barked, but then realized the sister was standing there.

Just then, the phone rang and he snatched it from the cradle.

"What! Oh, yes. Purcell, I'm sending Bishop back to the crime scene and you are to turn over everything to him and lend him any support he needs."

After a few seconds, the captain said, "I don't care! You will give Bishop the lead on this and help him in any way he needs! Good!"

Then he slammed the phone back into its cradle.

"He will wait for you at the crime scene," growled the captain.

"Yes, captain."

Bishop turned to the door and opened it, and the cardinal stepped out first.

"What the hell am I supposed to tell the press? And don't give me this biblical crap," asked the captain.

Bishop looked at him and then at the sister.

Sister Clarice stepped closer to the desk.

"Captain Tyrell, you now have a sadistic serial killer working in the city, and the department is doing everything to put a stop to it."

"A serial killer?"

"And you will not be lying," she said.

He sat back and placed a fist in front of his mouth. Taking a deep breath, he let it out slowly.

"That will be all, sister."

She nodded and turned and walked out the door, allowing Bishop to close it.

As they walked toward the front doors to the precinct, Bishop tapped the cardinal on the shoulder.

"Sir, is there any way I can convince you to keep Sister Clarice from going with me back to the crime scene?"

The sister looked at him through narrowed eyes.

"Oh, I'm sorry, Detective Bishop. Allow me to introduce you to our Sister Clarice. She is a single-minded and very ferocious warrior of God. I would never dream of getting in her way when it comes to Azrin, and I would advise you to give her the same consideration."

Cardinal Wright turned and looked at Sister Clarice.

"I'm sure I don't need to tell you to be careful."

"No, Your Eminence."

"I'm sure I also don't need to tell you where you need to start this investigation," he said as he tipped his head toward the detective.

She looked at the detective and said, "No, sir. I was just thinking the same thing. Especially after he told me of something he saw earlier in life."

"Just go slow. I hear she can be cantankerous."

She smiled and asked, "Is that the word you'll use to describe me someday?"

"I hope not, but that will depend on you, I guess."

He turned and said, "Detective, sister, be safe."

He swept out the doors and down the stairs to the waiting car and was gone.

"What did he mean about where to start the investigation?"

She reached out and patted his arm.

"You're going home, detective."

Chapter 10 – So Much Horror

Walking through the door of the apartment, Sister Clarice grabbed Bishop's arm to steady herself. She knew it was going to be bad, but she wasn't prepared for the amount of evil that had been visited on her friends.

There was still a small team of crime scene investigators working throughout the apartment. They were mostly involved with taking pictures and mapping out all the evidence. When they saw the two walk through the door, a couple of them shook their heads and the message was clear.

Get her out of here!

There was a lot of blood on the walls of the living room and a huge swath of it going down the hallway toward the bedroom.

"You could wait outside," said Bishop softly.

"No, detective, I can't."

Detective Purcell came through the archway that led to the kitchen and saw two of them.

"Ah, good, you're here."

Bishop looked at him and said, "You sound like you're not unhappy about turning the case over to me."

"Bishop, after what I've seen this afternoon, I am seriously considering turning in my badge. This is the most horrific murder scene I've ever been to."

Purcell looked at the sister and said, "Sister, I would advise you to wait outside.

This is not something you should be seeing."

"Detective Purcell, I am truly tiring of hearing people tell me I shouldn't be here. I have been to many crime scenes like this one and I can assure you I will see nothing here that I haven't seen before."

Purcell looked at her and licked his lips and clicked his tongue.

"Don't be so sure."

"I assume the body has been removed?" she asked.

"Yes, a couple of hours ago."

"Have you got a timeline of what happened here?" asked Bishop.

"I believe so. Let's start in the kitchen."

Purcell turned and walked back into the kitchen and the two of them followed.

The sister had been wrong. What she saw in the living room was nothing compared to what she saw as they entered the kitchen.

There was blood smeared all over the cabinets, as if someone had taken a person's body and rubbed it across almost every surface in the room.

A couple of the open cabinet doors looked like they had bits of skin and hair hanging on them. As the sister saw this, she could feel her heart breaking.

Oh Marvin, what did he do to you?

The back door leading to the small garden behind the apartment was laying up against the wall. It had been knocked off two of its three hinges and was just barely being held up by the bottom one.

"We're pretty sure this is where the attack started," said Purcell. "Apparently the couple were sitting in here eating lunch when the killer smashed through the door."

Bishop walked over and peered out the door. The patio furniture looked like an enormous animal had stomped on it. The glass table top was shattered and littered the entire patio.

Stepping out of the apartment, he looked up and around. The small patio had an eight-foot fence surrounding it, separating it from the patios on either side.

The thing that intrigued him was the lack of destruction to the fence. How Azrin had come into the backyard without leaving some sort of damage was a mystery.

Sister Clarice stepped into the doorway and he was going to ask what she thought, but stopped when he turned around.

"What in the world?" he muttered.

Purcell was standing behind the sister and he said, "Yeah, I'm still trying to figure that out."

The sister stepped out of the kitchen and into the backyard and turned to see what Bishop was looking at. Her reaction was a little more subdued that the two detectives.

The entire area around the door was charred black, as if someone had hit it with a flamethrower. Even the bricks around the door frame were almost solid black.

"Azrin," she mumbled.

"Who?"

The two of them looked at Purcell, not having anything they could tell him.

"Just a working hunch," said Bishop. "Nothing concrete yet."

Purcell looked at the two of them for a second and they could tell his gears were turning between his ears.

"Okay," said Bishop, "we know the perp came in through the back door. Now we're still hazy about what caused those."

He was pointing up and they looked at the ceiling. They saw two gouges in the plaster that made parallel tracks toward the small table. There were burn marks on each side of the tracks.

"Horns," said the sister before she realized she shouldn't.

Bishop just nodded.

"Horns? Look, it sounds to me like you two know something and I'd sure like to be included in your little club."

The sister looked at Purcell and said, "Detective Purcell, I can tell you what I know about this, but you will never believe me."

"Right about now, I think I'd believe anything."

"Are you a Christian?"

"Yes, I am."

"You believe in the Devil and his workings in this world?"

Purcell stopped and looked at her. The look on his face showed he could see where this conversation was going and he didn't like it.

"Are you going to tell me the devil did this?"

"Not Lucifer, personally, no. But one of his demons did."

"Oh, man," said Purcell, shaking his head. "I knew I shouldn't have asked you. I don't believe in demons or the devil reaching out of Hell and murdering people like this."

"And yet, you just claimed to believe in God, in Jesus Christ."

"I just … I umm …"

She stepped in front of him and put a hand on his folded arms.

"Can you really claim to be a Christian, believing in God, but say you don't believe in the Devil and the things he does?"

Purcell looked into her eyes and then felt a genuine need to avert them. He looked up at Bishop, who was just standing there, watching the scene play out.

"Do you believe this, Bishop?"

Bishop just took a deep breath and let it out slowly.

"Why don't you just show us the rest of what you've found?"

He could tell Purcell was looking at him, trying to figure if he was crazy or not. Knowing what he knew and had seen as a boy, he had no doubts about the things the sister was saying. He just wished she had said nothing to the other detective, knowing it was going to make things a lot harder for them if the surrounding people started wondering if a call to the state mental hospital was in order.

Purcell pulled away from the sister and nodded.

"This way," he said as he walked out of the kitchen.

He turned to the left and started down the hallway toward the bedroom. There was blood smeared on the walls and even some on the ceiling. There was also the black charring on the walls, along with the gouges in the ceiling.

The sister was looking at all of this and feeling more and more desperate with every step. Her heart was breaking as she thought of what Marvin and Esther must have been going through.

Stepping into the bedroom, the sister gasped, clasping her hands over her mouth. She felt an intense evil hanging in the room and almost wanted to check the closet or under the bed to make sure Azrin wasn't still there. Though he was long gone, something still imbued the room with his evil.

There was blood everywhere. On the walls, the ceiling, the bed and the carpet.

"This is just beyond belief," muttered Bishop.

Clarice looked at him with wonder in her eyes.

"I just mean, all the blood we've seen and the fact that Esther is alive and in the hospital, I can't believe that this much blood came from Marvin."

"That's not the most interesting thing about it," said Purcell. "Well, *interesting* might not be the right word, but it's the best I have at the moment."

"What is it, Tom?" asked Bishop.

"Marvin Morgan wasn't dead when that happened."

He was pointing at the wall behind them. When they turned around, Sister Clarice actually cried out in horror. Biting her finger to keep herself under control, she had to work quickly to wipe tears away and not show she was losing it.

The wall had a large splattering of blood and it was clearly in the shape of a person hanging from a cross. There were holes in the walls where the hands would have been and one where the feet would have been spiked together.

Just like Jesus!

"The very few words we got out of Ms. Morgan were that someone had nailed her husband to the wall, like that, while he was still alive. Then the perp broke her arm and forced her to her knees in front of her husband. Then he knocked her unconscious, leaving her on her knees while he made his escape."

Bishop looked at the sister and could see she was struggling to maintain herself.

"Why would he do that?" he asked.

She spoke in a quivering voice about paintings of the Blessed Mother Maria kneeling before Jesus on the cross. "I think Azrin was taking delight in creating that image."

Then she lost it. The tears started flowing as if the dam had broken. She tried to wipe them away, but there was no stopping them.

"I'm sorry ... I'm sorry," she cried as she left the room, almost running to get away from the horror.

"I knew she didn't have it in her," said Purcell. "I warned her to stay outside."

In an instant, Bishop moved in front of him and put a finger in the center of his chest.

"Don't you *EVER* bad mouth the sister in front of me again!"

"C'mon, Bishop! The devil, demons? Give me a break! And what the fuck has gotten into you? It's common knowledge that you hate the sister and would get almost apoplectic if you saw her at a crime scene."

Bishop's finger in the chest became a flat palm as he slammed Purcell up against the wall.

"What the fuck, Bishop?"

Bishop leaned in, getting face-to-face with Purcell, which was interesting because he stood a good five inches taller than the mouthy detective.

"Not ... one ... more ... word ... about the sister," he growled in Purcell's face. "That little lady has seen more evil in her brief life than you can imagine."

"What's going on?"

Bishop didn't even turn his head when he said, "Nothing, Jerry. Just your partner and I coming to an understanding."

He stepped back, taking his hand off Purcell and turned to look at his partner, Jerry Kline. The new arrival had two cups of coffee, having just gone to get them so he could get out of the house.

Bishop walked over and took one cup from him and said, "Thanks."

"Hey, that was mine," stammered Purcell.

Bishop turned and looked at him, causing him to take a step back.

"I'll be expecting your reports and evidence on my desk within a couple of hours. And contrary to what the captain said, I don't believe I'll be needing your assistance on this case."

Turning back, he asked, "Jerry, how are you doing? How's the wife?"

"Oh, she's fine. As for me," he said, motioning to the blood in the room, "not so good. I can't say I'm unhappy the captain has pulled us off this case and given it back to you."

"I feel you, man. I don't want it either, but … well … make sure to have all that stuff on my desk as soon as you can."

"No problem. We'll have it there in an hour or so. By the way, did either of you know there is a nun, on her knees on the sidewalk out front and I think she's losing it. She's crying and praying."

Bishop bit his lip and nodded.

"Take care, Jerry," he said as he pushed past and headed for the front door.

He could hear Jerry say softly, "I told you not to piss him off."

Sister Clarice had fallen to her knees and was crying next to his car. He walked up behind her and stopped.

"Worse than anything you've ever seen before?"

"Fredrick, I just …"

As he waited silently for her to finish, she just gathered herself and stood up. Her face was covered with tears and she reached into her pocket and pulled out a tissue and began drying her face.

"What the chief said earlier, I'm going to say to you," he said. "I need you to bring your A-game on this. This is your area of expertise, not mine. I will do any and everything I can to help you, but in the end, it's going to be you that leads this effort."

She sniffed and looked up at him.

"I don't know what to do, detective."

"Let me ask you something. Other than Sister Agatha or Brother Michael, has Azrin ever struck this close to your heart?"

She thought for a moment and said, "No. Most of his victims I've come across have been like Suzanne Kelly. Someone I didn't know. But detective, I can assure their deaths caused as great a cloud over my heart as if they were long-time friends."

"I'm sure they did, but it seems like this attack has more to do with you than with the Morgans."

"Or, maybe it's aimed at both of us," she said.

"Maybe so. So *WE* need to come up with a plan on how to fight this bastard. Sorry, I shouldn't swear in front of you."

She forced a smile and said, "Don't

apologize. I think I'm about ready to swear, myself."

He smiled and said, "Please don't. It wouldn't sound right coming from your lips and it would break my heart to hear it."

She smiled through the pain and looked at the cup of coffee in his hand.

"You didn't get me one?"

"Oh, this is yours. Purcell was more than happy to give it to you. Besides, I don't drink coffee."

She gave a tiny smile as she took the cup and said, "Detective, I know for a fact that police detectives live on coffee, donuts and fast food."

He laughed as he opened the door to his car for her to get in.

"Not me sister, I live on soda and TV dinners."

"Not alcohol?"

"After my divorce, alcohol became a huge part of my life. But after seeing what it did to my dad, I wised up and started going to AA meetings and haven't missed one since."

"See, he taught you a valuable life lesson without even trying."

After she got in, he closed the door and went around and got in.

"So, we're going home now? It's been a long time since I've been to that house. And you realize we can't go there without a very long drive or an airplane flight. I haven't been there since the night Azrin killed my parents. Not even sure if I can find it nowadays."

The sister took a sip of the hot coffee and then said, "No, detective, not that home."

Chapter 11 – Going Home

Pulling up outside the orphanage, Bishop felt several emotions. When he first became a police officer, he would drop by for a visit at least once a month. Over time, those visits had become less frequent. Sitting here now, he realized it had been almost ten years since his last visit.

He wasn't really sure how he felt about that. One thing he felt was unhappiness, as if he had somehow let the sisters down. The sisters that had looked over him during one of the worst times of his life.

Now, knowing that one of them was specifically tasked with protecting him from a demon from Hell, he felt even worse for not visiting.

What can I possibly say to apologize for not being around more?

He heard the click of Sister Clarice's seat belt, and he knew he couldn't put it off any longer. Climbing out of the car, he stopped to look at the old brick structure that he had called home for eleven years.

It didn't look any different from the last time he saw it. The church had always been good about keeping the place up. He had even helped with some of the maintenance of the buildings when he got old enough to work with the building supers.

"Are you coming?"

He snapped out of his thoughts and looked at the sister.

"Yeah," he mumbled.

When he walked around the car, she reached out and put a hand on his arm.

"If you want to wait in the car, I will understand."

He looked down at her and noticed she had a bit of a weak grin on her face.

He laughed and said, "Yeah, right. If you can take it, I can take it."

She laughed softly and put her arm through his as they walked up the sidewalk leading to the front doors.

As they approached the door, it swung open and was being held by an older nun. She looked truly ancient and looked like she had never heard the word *smile*. She looked at Sister Clarice and clearly didn't approve of how she was clinging to the tall, black man walking alongside her.

As they stepped through the doors, Sister Clarice smiled and said, "We're here to see Sister Marissa."

"All visitors need to stop and see the Mother Superior first," was the curt reply.

"That's fine," said Clarice. "We'll be happy to start with her."

"She may not approve ..." said the doorkeeper as she looked at Sister Clarice's arm through the detective's arm.

Before Sister Clarice could reply, Detective Bishop said, "I can see you have not gained a sense of humor, Sister Beth."

The older sister jerked back and looked closer at the detective.

"Fredrick?"

"Yes, sister. I have returned."

"Oh my," she said. "Let me show you to the Mother Superior's office."

"Thank you, Sister Beth," said Sister Clarice.

Beth spun on her heels and marched down a hallway and stopped at a door and knocked. A short, "Come in," sounded from the other side of the door.

Beth opened the door and said, "Mother Superior, you have visitors."

"Well, please show them in."

Sister Beth stepped aside and ushered the two into the office. As they stepped through the door, Bishop laughed, which caught Sister Clarice off-guard.

"A promotion, I see," said the detective.

The old nun behind the desk smiled and went to stand up. As soon as she did, they could see it would be a struggle for her and the detective told her not to get up and Sister Clarice concurred.

"Oh poppycock," said the Mother Superior.

As she stood up, she grabbed a cane and used it to steady herself and straighten herself up. As she shuffled around the desk, Bishop smiled.

"Sister Clarice, may I introduce you to Sister Marissa, who I guess is the Mother Superior here now."

Sister Marissa looked toward the door and said, "That will be all, Sister Beth."

"Yes, Mother Superior," she said as she

pulled the door closed.

"I see she is still quite protective of you," said Bishop.

"Yes, and she is still a major pain in the butt."

Bishop laughed and said, "Don't be too hard on her. As I remember, she was there for you in all circumstances."

"Yes, Fredrick, but she hovers. She hovers like a helicopter and won't stop it. Now, to what do we owe the pleasure of your visit this day? One that has been too long in coming, I might add."

"I have no words that can convey how sorry I am that I haven't been around in such a long time."

"A long time? It's ten years, five months and twenty-two days."

As Bishop straightened up and looked at her, Sister Clarice giggled.

"I think she has missed you, Fredrick."

Sister Marissa looked at her and smiled.

"He was my favorite charge. Though he talked little, I could see he was destined for greatness. And what can I do for you, sister? I'm sure you are the object of this visit and not Fredrick."

"You are correct, Mother Superior. I am here to talk to a fellow Sister of the Templar."

Sister Marissa straightened up and gripped her cane with more strength.

"So, this is a business visit and not a social call."

"I'm afraid so," said Clarice.

"Is this about those murders in the city?"

"It is."

Immediately, the mood in the room darkened. Sister Marissa turned and began hobbling back around the desk. Sister Clarice let go of the detective and hurried to help her back to her seat. As she helped her sit down, Clarice dropped to her knees at the feet of this truly noble warrior.

The Mother Superior reached forward and cupped the cheek of the younger nun.

"Cardinal Wright has warned me you have a habit of kneeling in front of your leaders."

"Mother Superior, I had very little time to learn about you before we came here and what I know is, you are one of the greatest warriors the Sisters of the Templar ever had."

"And sister," said Marissa as she patted her cheek, "you were there when Sister Agatha was killed and you took up her sword and vanquished that demon back to Hell where he belongs."

"Sadly, it appears Hell is not strong enough to hold Azrin," said Sister Clarice in a very soft voice.

"It will never hold him, sweetheart, as long as he is one of Lucifer's favorites. The Devil will continue to send him to wreak havoc in this world until we can destroy him."

Sister Clarice bowed her head and said, "But how are we supposed to do that? I have bested him in battle and he has come back."

"First, please get off your knees and sit down."

"Yes, Mother Superior," said Clarice as she stood up.

She turned around to see Bishop was pulling a chair around the desk so she could sit directly in front of the older nun.

"Thank you, detective," she said as she took a seat. Bishop turned and pulled the other chair around so he could sit with the two of them.

"He really is a good boy," said Marissa.

Sister Clarice smiled and said, "He is, but I think you're deflecting."

"You're darn right, I'm deflecting. I am not as young as I used to be and I'm not sure I can do battle like I used to."

"I'm not asking you to join me in battle, Sister Marissa. I am here to see if you have any ideas how to defeat Azrin."

"I faced Azrin three times and three times he escaped back to Hell. If there is a way to defeat him once and for all, I certainly don't know what it is."

The detective interrupted Sister Clarice as she was about to speak.

"Hold on just a second," said Bishop. "You faced off against Azrin three times and each time he ran from you, back to Hell? Why would he do that?"

Sister Clarice looked at Bishop and then the look on her face changed as his words sank in. She shifted her eyes back to the Mother Superior.

"He asks a valid question," she said. "What did you do that sent Azrin running back to

Hell like a dog with his tail between his legs?"

Sister Marissa leaned forward and took the young nun's hands and held them.

"I'm sure you know the answer to that question."

"No, sister, I don't think I do."

Sister Marissa leaned forward and looked into the younger nun's eyes. Clarice felt as if Marissa was staring straight into her soul. She became uncomfortable as she felt the fingers of Mother Superior's spirit touch the strings of her heart. She felt as if the Mother Superior was searching her mind, and it felt as if she was looking at her worthiness.

"Sister Clarice, your greatest weapon against the evil that is Azrin is your faith in God and in yourself as a warrior."

"My faith in God is absolute," claimed Clarice.

"But not in yourself."

That statement caused Sister Clarice to stop and rethink.

"His Holiness has chosen you, himself, consecrated you for the work he has called you to, yet you still doubt your worthiness for the task at hand."

A single tear worked its way down the cheek of the young warrior.

"I still remember the night Sister Agatha died. I remember the moment I first laid eyes on Azrin. I can still feel the terror I experienced when I saw true evil. Azrin looked at me and said he was going to have fun with me. Then he killed Brother Michael and tossed Sister

Agatha aside as if she was just a piece of trash to be discarded."

Clarice bowed her head and wept silently.

"When Sister Agatha was dying, she said something to you. What was it?"

"She had dropped her sword and then she looked into my eyes and told me to fight."

"And without hesitation, you picked up the sword and stepped forward to face the demon," said Sister Marissa. "And what did you feel when you picked up the sword?"

"The same thing I feel to this day when I hold the sword. I feel as if the power of God is filling my soul."

"Then I have to ask you one thing, sister. When was the last time you held your sword and allowed the strength of Heaven to come upon you?"

Sister Clarice hesitated to answer because she felt ashamed of what she was going to say.

"It has been a couple of weeks," she whispered.

"A couple of weeks?" exclaimed Sister Marissa. "Why in Heaven's name are you not grasping that sword at every moment?"

Clarice cried and said, "Because I still feel unworthy."

"Sister Clarice! I assume your sword is exactly where it should be."

"Yes, Mother Superior."

"Then I command you to unsheathe it this very instant!"

She hesitated, which brought a stern rebuke from the older nun.

"Now, young lady!"

She stood up and reached behind her head and Bishop heard a snap coming open. Then he almost jumped when she pulled a short sword from under her robes. When he first saw it, his initial thoughts were that the sword looked awfully short.

Then she brought it up in front of her face, the tip of the sword pointing at the ceiling. He almost fell over backward when the blade extended with a heavy *kachunk*, becoming as long as he would have expected.

Sister Clarice grasped the gold hilt and held the sword in front of her face, the gold crossbar hand guard aligned with her chin.

The detective's eyes were as big as saucers when he saw the exact moment the power of Heaven descended on Sister Clarice. Her face took on a glow, as if lit from inside. She let out a slow breath as the sword worked on her.

When she opened her eyes and looked at Bishop, he could see they had lost their unusual blue color and were now a dazzling golden color. Even her hands took on a glow that he was sure wasn't there before.

"What in …," he gasped.

Sister Marissa struggled to stand up and when she did, she reached out and cupped the younger nun's chin with her hand.

"Why on God's green Earth are you not experiencing this every single day?"

"Because …"

She stopped because she knew she had no good explanation for the Mother Superior.

"Sister Clarice, do you feel unworthy at this moment?"

Clarice straightened up and said, "No, Mother Superior."

To the ears of Bishop, it sounded as if there had been two voices that came out of the sister's mouth. One of those voices sounded truly powerful.

Sister Marissa reached out her other hand and cupped both sides of Clarice's face and stared into her eyes.

"I command you to spend at least half an hour every day in meditation, with your sword firmly in your hands."

Sister Clarice opened her mouth, but said nothing.

"Do I make myself clear?" questioned the Mother Superior.

Sister Clarice began to bend her knees as she said, "Yes, Mother Superior."

"And if you kneel in front of me, I will pull my sword and we will go at it. I may look old and frail, but I can assure you I will be all you can handle."

Clarice straightened back up and nodded to the older nun.

"You kneel before no one except for God. Is that understood?"

"Yes, Mother Superior."

"Fredrick!"

Bishop shot out of his chair like they had electrocuted him.

"Yes, Mother Superior!"

"While the two of you are working

together, I expect you to question her every day whether she is following my command. I will expect a phone call from you if she falters. Do you understand?"

"Yes, Mother Superior."

"Good!"

She looked at Clarice again and said, "Put the sword away, sweetheart."

Bishop watched as the sword disappeared back underneath the sister's robes. Then the Mother Superior took Clarice's face with both hands and leaned forward and looked her in the eyes.

"Don't you ever doubt your worthiness again. If you weren't worthy, the power of God wouldn't fall upon your shoulders so easily. The sword of God wouldn't even let you handle it. God knows a warrior when He sees one and you have a power that is uncommon among our ranks."

"Sister Agatha said the same thing the night Azrin killed her."

"And you doubt her?"

"No, Mother Superior."

"Good! Now sit down and tell me what you know so far about the two that Azrin has killed."

For the next hour, Sister Clarice and Bishop related everything they knew about Suzanne Kelly and Marvin Morgan. No matter how hard they tried, the three of them couldn't come up with any connection between the two victims. Other than they lived on the same street, there seemed to be no connection at all.

"And how about you, Fredrick?" asked the Mother Superior.

"What about me?"

"We've concluded there is no connection between Sister Clarice and Suzanne Kelly. We know the sister was quite familiar with the Morgans, having worked with them, or at least Esther, in the past."

"I think," said Bishop, "the connection we're looking for is Sister Clarice."

"Me?" asked the sister.

"Explain, Fredrick," said Sister Marissa.

"My theory is very thin."

"Thin or not, it may be the only theory we have."

"My run-in with Azrin left me an orphan, but that was the extent of my dealings with him. And that was over thirty years ago."

"That is correct," said Sister Marissa, "but as you told us many years ago, Azrin looked right at you and said he would get to you. The police showing up may have impacted his plans for you."

"True, but Sister Clarice had dealings with him just a few short years ago."

"Five to be exact," said Clarice softly.

"And in that encounter, she cut off some of his fingers and stabbed him, almost to the point of killing him. He may not have forgotten that. And these killings may be nothing more than a way to draw you out."

Sister Marissa shook her head, something the detective noticed.

"You don't think so?" asked Bishop.

"No, Fredrick, I don't. Azrin has been silent since his run-in with Sister Clarice five years ago. That doesn't quite square with what we've seen of him in the past. If he felt like he'd been slighted, he wouldn't have waited this long to try to get revenge."

"So, where does that leave us?"

"Not much better off, I'm afraid," said the Mother Superior.

After talking with the Mother Superior for a few more minutes, it was plain there was nothing new to learn. As she walked them to the detective's car, with Sister Beth following behind, she made Bishop promise he would start visiting the children again.

"They so loved your visits, Fredrick."

"Yes, Sister Marissa, I will start visiting again and Sister Clarice can hold me accountable to that."

"And you are to hold her accountable to what I said earlier."

"Yes, sister."

As they drove away, Bishop glanced over at the quiet sister.

"In the words of the Mother Superior, why on God's green Earth would you not be spending time with that sword in your hands every day?"

"You wouldn't understand," she said softly.

"Then help me to understand. I saw what I assume was the power of God come down from Heaven and surround your body. I could see how the power strengthened you. If I could feel that for even one second …"

He let the words drift out and hang in the air.

"Because I was being truthful with the Mother Superior. I feel so unworthy to carry this sword."

"Let me ask you this. Would God let you carry that sword if you were unworthy?"

"No, I suppose He wouldn't."

"Then why in Hell are you questioning His wisdom? Five years you've been carrying that sword and you still feel unworthy? Well, let me clue you in to how I feel on the subject."

He looked over at her and asked, "Are you listening?"

"Yes," she said as she looked down at her hands clasped in her lap.

"I have met no one I would say is more worthy of carrying the sword of God than you. If someone had asked me that a week ago, I would have said get the fu … I would have said get out of here. I hated you. I hated seeing you show up at crime scenes. But now … I don't want to go to any of these crime scenes without you by my side."

He glanced over and could see she was drying her eyes again. He began to wonder how any one woman could have that many tears in her head. He figured it must be one of those requirements to be a nun. An endless supply of tears to shed for the pain and suffering they would see in their lifetimes.

He reached across and squeezed her hands.

"I intend to make sure you do exactly as

Sister Marissa said. I will make sure you spend time with that sword in your hands and I would like to be present every now and then when it happens. I can't explain it, but when you held that sword up and the power of Heaven came down, I could feel it myself and I want to feel it again. Many times."

She patted his hand and they rode on in silence.

Chapter 12 – Opening Old Wounds

Pulling into the parking lot where Sister Clarice's car was, the detective stopped behind her car and shut off the engine. He had been very quiet during the second part of the drive from the orphanage and the sister could tell he was troubled by something.

"What are you thinking, detective?"

Looking across the car, his eyes met hers and she could read the pain.

"I need to go see someone that might not be so happy to see me."

"Your ex-wife?"

He just nodded, knowing the sister had just read his thoughts.

"I think I need to warn her of the evil we face."

"Will she believe you?"

"Highly doubtful, but I need to try and get her to take precautions. I need to know she and my daughter are safe."

"Would you like me to go with you?"

"No, sister. This is something I need to face on my own."

Sister Clarice reached out and placed a hand on his arm.

"Just be honest with her. She may not be ready to believe you, but she will feel your desire to keep her and your daughter safe."

She lifted his hand and kissed it.

"Be blessed and safe, Detective Bishop. I have a feeling I'm going to need you a lot in this task."

"I don't know what I can actually offer you," he said. "You are the demon hunter, called by God. How will I be of any help to you?"

She smiled and said, "Fredrick, you have already been more help than you know."

Then she turned and opened the door and stepped out of the car. Leaning back down, she looked across the car.

"You be careful," she implored him.

Then she closed the door and walked to her car as he started the engine. He sat for a few seconds, making sure she was safely in her car before pulling away.

They went their separate ways, exiting the parking lot. Him, going to see a woman he had done nothing but disappoint and her to see the cardinal and tell him everything she'd learned.

When the door opened, he saw the smile on Angelica's face disappear in a couple of seconds. It had been at least two years since he had stood on her doorstep.

"What do you want?"

He took a deep breath and let it out slowly. One thing she had always been good at was cutting right through his heart with the fewest words possible.

"I need to talk to you. May I come in?"

She looked like she was considering telling him to go to Hell, but then she stepped aside and let him in.

As he walked through to the living room, he tried to remember the speech he had practiced on the way there.

"How are you doing, Angelica?"

He turned to face her and she was looking at him.

"How am I doing? I'm doing fine. Why don't you ask how your daughter is doing?"

Bishop brought his hands together in front of his mouth and just pushed down the ire that was rising in his chest.

"Or do you even remember her name?"

He opened his eyes and stared at her.

"Angel, can we not do this?"

"Angel? You haven't called me that since the first year we were married."

He turned and paced to the other side of the room and tried to think of what he was going to say.

Looking back at her, he said, "Of course, I remember Ashley's name. Something you might not be aware of is she and I talk at least a couple of times a week. She doesn't hate me the way you do. I had lunch with her last week, as a matter of fact."

Angelica's mouth dropped open at this news.

"I seem to remember specifically telling you to stay away from her. To keep your drunken self out of our lives."

"Something I did until she walked into the precinct about six years ago and asked to see me. I was five years sober and haven't had a drink in the last eleven years."

"Well, I guess miracles can happen," she said, the disdain she felt dripping off each word. "I warned her to stay away from you."

"I'm aware of that, but I guess your attempts to poison her feelings toward me didn't work."

"I guess I'm going to need to have another talk with her."

Bishop could feel the anger rising, and it was everything he could do to keep it in check.

"She's twenty-six years old. I think she can make her own decisions."

"Why are you here? It can't be to tell me you've had a better relationship with our daughter than I do."

"She loves you and wishes you would let go of the bitterness in your heart. Something I think God would also ask you to do."

"Don't you bring God into this! You have no right to invoke His name!"

He shook his head and said, "You know what? I can't do this."

He walked past her, heading for the door, feeling like a failure. He came here to try to protect her and he was going to leave without lifting a finger.

"Going to run again? You haven't changed at all," she sneered behind him.

Swinging around, he raised his hands, more in a sign of surrender, but she still took a step back.

"Why do you have to be like this?" he asked.

"I asked you to stop being a cop and my words were just ignored!"

"You knew I was a cop when we met,

Angelica! You knew that and you still married me!"

He took another deep breath and said, "Do you still have that gun I gave you?"

"I do," she said. "It's still locked in the safe, right where I put it after you gave it to me. I haven't touched it since."

"I need you to get it and start carrying it."

He reached into his pocket and pulled out the magazine the sister had given him. He handed it to his ex.

"Switch out the bullets and magazine for this one. You know how to shoot, so just do this for me."

She looked at the full magazine in her hand and then back at him.

"What in the hell is this about, Fredrick?"

He just looked at her and said, "Please do this for me. Oh, and pray for me."

Turning around, he opened the door and walked out, pulling the door closed behind him.

After he sat down in his car, he gripped the steering wheel and stared straight ahead. A couple of minutes later, he realized he was gripping the wheel so tightly his hands were starting to hurt.

Well, I guess that went about as well as I could have hoped for.

Starting the car, he glanced at the house and saw her looking through the curtains. The fear was clear in her eyes.

He pulled away, disappearing down the dark street. He had to fight with every fiber of his being, wanting to go back and grab her and shake some sense into her.

Stepping on the gas, he swung the car up the freeway on-ramp and headed back downtown.

Sister Clarice had to stop herself from kneeling when she walked into the cardinal's office. He looked at her as if he knew she was just about to do it, but the look on his face stopped her.

"What news have you brought me?" he asked.

She sat down and placed her hands in her lap.

"Sister Marissa wasn't really able to give the detective and I anything we could use against Azrin. I think she is just as flummoxed as the rest of us."

"That would be surprising. In all the time I've known that woman, she's never been at a loss for what to do."

"I don't know, Your Eminence. It seems like we are hitting road blocks at every turn. For some reason Lucifer has turned Azrin loose in this world and finding a way to stop him is beyond me."

At the mention of the Devil's name, the cardinal perked up.

"You are under no circumstances allowed to venture into Hell again. I don't want to hear of you going there to have a word with Satan. The last time you did I was pretty sure we would not be getting you back."

"Lucifer wouldn't dream of touching me."

"Sister! You can't keep venturing into the Devil's kingdom and expect to come out unscathed every time!"

"I've only been there once."

"Which was one time too many!"

"I had to bring the padre home."

"Who ended up killing himself not too long after coming back. You should have let Heaven sort that out."

"Yes, Your Eminence."

"Promise me you won't go down there again. I have enough white hairs on my head without worrying about you doing something that stupid again."

"I promise."

She stood up and left. After she closed the door behind her, he just stared at it.

Why do I get the feeling she just lied to me?

Chapter 13 – Toying With The Devil

"Tell me again, why did we come all the way out here."

Bobby Skillings looked over his shoulder at the other five teens that were following him. It was his idea for this little field trip. They were deep inside one of the wilderness areas about an hour west of Chicago.

They had left the car about twenty minutes ago and were hiking along one of the trails that cut through the wilderness area. The further they got from the car, the more the others became agitated.

"I told you, there is an old cabin up ahead and it will be perfect for what I have in mind."

"Which is what, exactly?" asked Carrie Tyler.

"I told you, it's a surprise."

"I'm telling you, if you brought us all the way out here to have your way with us," said Bethany, "we'll bury your body so deep it will never be found."

Bobby laughed.

"I have no doubt the three of you girls could disappear any one of us guys."

"But not all three of us," said Kyle with a silly grin on his face.

"No," said Carrie, "but we'll start with you, Kyle."

The grin vanished from his face as Carrie stared him down. Then she laughed at the look on his face.

"Kyle, you know you are the one us girls

need to worry about the least."

She was right. Of the six of them, Kyle was the shortest and smallest. Even the three girls towered over him, which wasn't hard because two of them played on the girl's basketball team and the other was the captain of the volleyball team.

But the girls liked him because he was the most gentlemanly of all the guys at school.

"We're here," said Bobby.

The group came out of the trees and saw a dilapidated cabin on the other side of a small clearing. To say the cabin had seen better days was an understatement. It looked like one good wind storm could blow it right over.

"We hiked all the way out to this piece of shit?" asked Stan.

He was the exact opposite of Kyle. He was the tallest member of the group, playing starting forward on the basketball team and quarterback on the football team. He was a gifted athlete and he knew it. And acted like it.

Bobby was one of his best friends and also his favorite wide receiver.

That left Kyle as the only non-athlete in the group. But being Carrie's little brother, when she said he was coming along, there was no argument.

"Come on," said Bobby. "I got something fun to do this afternoon."

He started across the clearing and the others fell in behind him. There was a bit of grumbling, mostly from Stan, but the others were genuinely interested to see what Bobby had in mind.

Reaching the front porch, Bobby stomped his feet to clear the mud from his boots, but everyone else wondered *"why bother."* The place would probably look a whole lot better with a good coat of mud. It certainly wasn't going to make it look any worse.

Bobby pushed the door open. It was hanging by a couple of ancient looking hinges and they were the most solid looking things about the cabin.

A couple of creepy crawlies scurried across the floor when the sunlight lit up the place.

"Charming," said Bethany as she looked around.

"Yes," said Carrie. "Is this your idea of a dream home, Bobby?"

"Oh hardee-har-har," he said as he pulled the backpack off his shoulders. He had been the only one carrying a pack, seeing as how he was the only one that knew why they were there.

"Everyone take a seat."

"Where? On the floor?" asked Lydia.

"Hey," said Bobby, "that's why I told you to not wear your good jeans."

He plopped himself down on the floor and the others went ahead and followed his lead. Opening the backpack, he pulled out a Ouija board and placed it in the middle of the circle they had formed.

"Is that what I think it is?" gasped Bethany.

"Yes it is. I found it in a thrift store last week and I thought it would be fun to play with it. They didn't have the little doo-dad you use for pointing, but I thought this crystal my mom had on the shelf in the living room would work just fine."

"It's called a *planchette* and I'm not sure we should be playing with this thing," said Lydia.

"What's the matter, Lydia? You scared?" said Bobby with a laugh.

"Hey! Don't talk to her like that."

Bobby looked at Kyle and just laughed.

"I'm just kidding around."

Kyle might have been the shortest, smallest kid in the group, but he was built like a brick outhouse. His shoulders were strong with muscles because of his penchant for lifting weights and everyone knew not to mess with Kyle Tyler.

Bobby placed the round crystal in the middle of the board and looked around the circle.

"I was watching a video on the internet and these girls, pretending to be witches, used it to try to summon some witch that was burned at the stake.

"Did they succeed?" asked Bethany.

"What do you think, Beth? It's all bullshit. They even had some sort of visitation, but anyone could see it was cheap special effects, worse than anything Hollywood has ever come up with."

Stan said, "Well, I'm game. As you say, it's all bullshit, so let's see if we can get a few laughs out of this thing."

Bobby leaned forward and placed one finger on the crystal and said, "Okay, everyone put your first finger of your right hand on the crystal."

"We're actually each supposed to put a finger of both hands on the planchette," said Lydia.

"You seem to know a lot about this for someone that was ready to bolt just a moment ago," said Bobby.

Bobby was startled when Kyle slapped the floor and just stared at him. Though no words were spoken between them, the message was received.

"It's just I …," she started to say.

"You don't need to explain yourself, Lydia," said Kyle.

She was sitting right next to him and she put a hand on his arm.

"That's okay, Kyle. I was just going to say I used to have this crazy old aunt and she was into this kind of thing. She had a Ouija board and claimed she was able to communicate with the spirits of the dead. Though I never believed it when I sat with her, I always got a strange feeling when she used the board."

"Well, I don't think twelve hands are going to fit around this crystal," said Bobby. "That's why I said one finger each."

He reached forward and put a finger on the crystal and the others followed suit.

"I'll go ahead and start this. I did watch that video and I think I know what needs to be said."

He closed his eyes and began talking softly, asking for any spirits listening to show themselves. He went on for about five minutes without any results.

"Anyone else want to try?" he asked. "Anyone you want to talk to?"

Carrie giggled and said, "Sure, I'll give it a shot, but I think your board is broken."

Bobby laughed and said, "Well, I did find it in a thrift store. If it worked, it probably wouldn't have been there."

Again, they all touched the crystal and Carrie began to say the same things Bobby had just a moment before. She even added her own flair and called for the spirit of Janet Horne to appear and speak with them.

After a couple of minutes she sat back and rubbed her hands together.

"Who's Janet Horne?" asked Lydia.

"She was the last witch killed in England in the year 1727, I believe. I just wanted to get her side of the story."

"Now, that would have been cool," said Stan. "Imagine the history report you could write if you talked to her."

Everyone was sitting back when they heard a scraping sound. Looking down, they saw the crystal was moving across the board.

Carrie reached out and touched the board with a couple of fingertips.

"There's no movement of the ground, like an earthquake or something."

They all just watched the crystal move to the far right side of the board. It stopped over

127

the A. Then it moved to the Z and then to the far right side of the board to the R.

"What's going on?" asked Lydia, with a bit of fear in her voice.

"I think Bobby has messed with the board to make the crystal move by itself," said Kyle.

The two of them stared into each other's eyes and Kyle could tell Bobby had nothing to do with what was happening.

"I think it's spelling a name or something," said Bethany. "First it was A and then Z and then R. It's still moving."

They watched as the crystal settled over the I for a second and then start moving again. When it stopped again, Bobby leaned forward and looked through the clear stone.

"N."

When the stone moved again, it moved to the blank area near the middle of the board.

"$A - Z - R - I - N$," he said. "I've never heard that name before."

He reached out and touched the crystal and said, "Azrin, show yourself to us."

Nothing happened.

At least, nothing happened inside the cabin. Outside the sky began to grow dark, something a couple of the kids didn't fail to notice. Lydia and Stan both looked toward the door, which was still open. The wind had picked up and there were dark, gray clouds moving across the sky.

"Uh, Bobby, I don't think ...," said Stan.

"Azrin, did you not hear me?" commanded Bobby. "Show yo ..."

His voice was cut off when his body flew from the circle and slammed into the back wall of the cabin. The girls screamed when they heard his body snap like a dry twig and drop to the floor.

Kyle jumped up and ran to his friend and could see immediately he was dead.

"What the hell happened?" yelled Stan.

The girls were hugging each other, comforting each other and trying to figure out what had happened.

"I'd like to thank you for inviting me to your little party."

They all turned as one and were terrified as a large, fiery demon stomped up the steps and into the cabin. He was so big his shoulders and horns ripped the sides of the door apart. They could feel the entire cabin shake and it felt as if it was going to cave in.

Kyle reached out and grabbed the three girls and pulled them behind him, placing himself between them and the monster.

"Who ... what are you?" Stan sputtered.

"I'm sorry," said the demon. "I thought you knew. Allow me to introduce myself. I am Azrin, demon of the underworld, minion to my lord, Lucifer. I heard your call and came."

"We didn't call you," cried Bethany.

Azrin smiled, fire showing from his mouth. He looked past them to the crumpled body laying near the wall.

"He did," said Azrin with a laugh.

"Well, we'd ask that you go back to where you came from," said Kyle.

"Now is that nice? I just got here and haven't even begun to have fun."

It was then that Stan decided to show how brave he was and bolted for the door. Thinking freedom was almost within his reach.

Almost.

Just before he reached the door, Azrin lashed out with one hand, the one with all five digits intact and stabbed the boy through the gut and lifted him off the ground.

This brought another round of screaming from the girls when Azrin held the boy up in front of them. Stan was twitching on the claws that impaled him. He wasn't able to scream or even whimper in pain, because the air had been driven from his lungs.

"You die so easily," growled the demon. "It's almost not even worth my time."

Carrie stepped forward and Kyle tried to grab her and pull her back.

"Then don't waste anymore of your time. Leave us and go on your way."

Stan had finally quit quivering and the demon held him up in front of her and then turned his hand over, allowing the boy's body to slide off his claws and drop to the ground at her feet. She looked down into the lifeless eyes of the school's star quarterback.

"Why are you doing this?" she cried. "We didn't do anything to you."

He leaned down and brought a bloody claw up to the soft part of her chin and lifted her eyes to his. She had to raise up on her tiptoes as his claw kept pressing into the soft skin under her jaw.

"I do this because I can," he growled in her face. "I do this to gain the attention of a certain demon hunter."

Carrie was terrified, but at the same time, her eyes showed confusion.

"A few years ago, I did battle with her and she did this to me," he roared as he held up the other hand, showing it to be missing three fingers.

"I know revenge," he said a little softer and with a grin on his face, "it's a little petty, but this injury has cost me more than you can imagine. When she sent me back to Hell, my lord, Lucifer, was not pleased with me at all. For these past years, he tormented me and punished me for allowing it to happen. He claimed I was no good to him in such a state. I was finally able to convince him to let me loose in the world again and I would prove my worth."

Carrie was struggling to keep her weight on the tips of her toes, knowing if she sank downward, his claw would slide up into her head, killing her.

"Please," she pleaded. "We don't know any demon hunters and don't want to die."

"Oh, I know," he said softly, as he caressed her face with his other hand. "It is so hard to face the consequences of your actions. Let me ease your pain."

Without warning, he shoved the claw up through her chin and out the top of her head. Carrie's body went rigid as she tried to scream.

The scream sounded more like a gurgled mess as the claw passed through her tongue as it moved upward through her head.

Azrin shook her body back and forth as she tried to fight her way off his claw.

"Oh, you have a lot of fight in you," he growled into her face as the light began to fade from her eyes.

When her eyes closed for the last time, he sliced across her neck with one of his fingers on his injured hand and separated her body from her head in one clean cut. As the body fell to the ground, blood spurted from the headless neck and spattered across the faces and bodies of the remaining three.

Taking one step forward, Azrin backed the three kids into a corner and hovered over them. He held up Carrie's head, turning it so they could see the scream frozen on her face.

The scream that never came.

"What do you think of my work?" he growled.

Kyle was still standing in front of Lydia and Bethany and he stared down the demon.

"I think you are a sick, sadistic son of a bitch and I hope this demon hunter, who ever she is, finds you and destroys you."

Azrin leaned down and Kyle could feel the heat coming from his mouth.

"You hope she finds me? I am counting on it."

Then he rose up a little and looked at the two girls cowering in the corner.

"Now, who to kill next?"

Kyle reached out and pushed the demon back, but burned his hands on the hot skin of the monster. Azrin looked down at the teenager's hands and the look on his face was that of complete disgust for being touched by a human.

"Leave them alone! You can kill me, but let them go!" yelled Kyle.

Azrin's hand flashed forward and grabbed Kyle by the throat and lifted him off the ground.

"How dare you touch me!" roared the demon. "I am Lucifer's most favored! You are nothing more than a bug to be squashed under his foot!"

"From what you just said," gasped Kyle as he tried to draw breath, "your buddy, Satan, isn't too pleased with you."

Kyle reached into the collar of his sweatshirt and yanked a chain from his neck and slammed the silver crucifix against the face of the demon.

"Die you son of a bitch!" croaked Kyle as Azrin let out a howl of pain.

The fingers clutched around Kyle's throat released and he fell to the ground. Trying to struggle to his feet, he yelled for the girls to run.

Lydia ran for the door as Azrin's attention was diverted by the pain he was feeling as the silver cross burned into his skin. Bethany took a couple of steps toward the door, but then stopped and reached down to help Kyle up, hoping to get him out of the cabin.

"Come on, Kyle!" she cried as she tried to lift him.

Once she got him to his feet, they staggered for the door, but their journey was cut short. Long, blood-covered claws burst through Kyle's chest and he was dragged back.

"Run, Beth," he croaked. "I love you."

Beth took one last look and then turned and fled the cabin. The sun had just barely set, but with the dark cloud that had arrived with Azrin, it was almost as dark as midnight.

As she stumbled through the darkness, she heard the demon's roar and then a scream from the young man that had saved her.

The scream was cut short, silenced forever.

She began running as fast as she could, but had no idea where she was going. She had never been in this forest and there was no sense of direction to safety.

Despite running at her fastest, Lydia repeatedly tripped on tree roots in the dark, resulting in a broken ankle and a fall.

"Help! Somebody help us!" she screamed into the night.

As she laid there, she could feel a tremor in the earth and knew immediately it was the demon walking through the forest. Rolling off the path she had been on, she tried to push herself under a bush.

As she laid there, she could feel her heart beating in her chest and just knew it was going to give her away. She tried to quiet her sobs and put the pain in her ankle out of her mind.

The ground tremors got closer.

Raising her hands to her mouth, she tried to muffle her breathing and even resorted to biting one of her fingers to try to keep silent.

The pounding of the demon's steps got closer.

Silently she started praying, "Please God, get me out of this. I'll do anything you ask if you'll just stop this monster."

She listened and couldn't hear the steps of the demon anymore. Starting to believe he had lost her, she let out a soft, slow breath.

Then she screamed as a burning, black hand reached into the bush from behind her and yanked her out by her blond hair.

"God doesn't make deals like that," growled the demon as he held her up and looked her in the eyes. "You would have been better just asking for his help without promising to be a better person."

"So, He does exist?" she cried.

"Of course he exists. I just told you and your friends I came from Hell and know Lucifer personally. If Lucifer exists, so does God, though he's a bit of a weak god. He can't or won't even protect his creations when they need him most."

Then she gasped, "I will place my trust in Him, no matter how this turns out."

Then she spit in the demon's face. Her spittle could be heard sizzling on the skin of his face.

"That's the spirit!" roared the demon.

Then he stabbed a claw into her chest, just

above her heart. She groaned as the pain hit her, but it was nothing compared to when he sliced her body open, from chest to waist. As her insides tumbled outside, her eyes rolled back into her head and her body hung lifelessly from his hand.

Bethany stumbled through the woods, trying to keep her feet under her. She had heard the scream when Kyle was killed. This tore at her heart because of the last thing he said to her.

I love you.

She knew he had feelings for her and she was just waiting for him to gather the courage and ask her out. She would have fallen all over herself to say *yes*.

Now she would never get to say that one, little word.

Every few minutes, she would come to a stop, trying to figure out where she was and which way she should go.

Then she heard Lydia's scream and she knew the demon had found her. The scream didn't last too long.

This pushed her on even faster. If she was killed by the demon, no one would ever know what really happened out here. She couldn't fail her friends.

Trying to run even faster, she kept her hands in front of her, trying to make sure she didn't run straight into a tree. But that's exactly what happened.

She ran face first into a dark tree and got

knocked to the ground. As she cried in pain, she went to push herself up and keep running.

Then the tree moved.

She screamed as loud as she could when the tree turned around and reached for her.

"Did you really think you were going to get away?"

He reached for her, intending to squeeze the life from her body, but his clawed hand was stayed. He tried again. No matter how hard he tried to grab her, his claws never quite reached her.

Azrin stared into her terrified eyes as he considered this puny female just outside of his grasp.

"You are correct," he said with a fiery grin. "I need to leave one of you alive so you can tell the story."

She could feel the heat from the monster's fingers on her face, but for some reason he never grabbed her.

"I want you to make sure to tell the demon hunter everything that happened here. I want the fear in her breasts to be absolute."

"Let me go," she cried as she felt the skin of her face beginning to redden from the heat.

"I will in a moment. I just need to leave you with a gift, that you will see every day for the rest of your pathetic life. I will haunt your dreams every night and will stalk your thoughts during the day. There will not be a day or moment where I will not occupy your thoughts."

She screamed as he pushed through

whatever had been holding him back and wrapped his claws around her neck. It felt like her skin was going to burst into flames.

After what felt like an eternity, he dropped her to the forest floor. As she rolled onto her back, grasping at her throat and finding it hurt even more if she touched it. The skin felt as if it had been burned away.

"I'll be seeing you in your dreams, Bethany Anderson," said Azrin as he began to fade from view.

Feeling the tears streaming down her face, she laid there and cried over what she had been through and the friends she had lost.

This has to be a dream. A nightmare.

As she rolled her head to one side, she saw light, but didn't understand it. It was coming closer and bobbing up and down. Struggling to keep her eyes open, she watched as two police officers came through the trees, shining flashlights back and forth.

"Over here!" she heard one of them yell.

An older police officer, looking a lot like her grandfather, crouched down next her and held her trembling hand.

"It's okay, sweetheart. We've found you."

The other cop, a much younger one bent down over her and cringed when he saw her neck.

"What in God's name did that to her?"

"My friends," she wheezed. "Find them."

"Are there others out here?" asked the older cop.

She tried to nod, but the burns on her neck

made it difficult. She held up one of her hands and splayed the fingers out.

"There's five more kids out here?"

She nodded and fell into the darkness of unconsciousness.

And the demon had not been lying. He was right there, in her nightmare when she closed her eyes. Grinning that evil grin. With fire behind his lips.

Chapter 14 – Falsely Accused

Sister Clarice was sitting in the library of the church, pouring over anything she could find that would tell her more about Azrin. There was surprisingly little about the demon, considering he had been a terror on Earth since the beginning.

As she was reading, her phone vibrated on the table and she looked at the display before picking it up.

"Have anything, detective?"

"Where are you, sister?"

"I'm in the church doing some research."

"I'll pick you up out front in five minutes."

She could feel the urgency in his voice.

"What's going on?"

There was some hesitation before he said, "It's happened again."

She crossed herself as she felt her body shiver up and down her spine.

"How bad?" she asked softly.

"Worse than anything I've ever heard of. Meet me out front."

He clicked off and she sat for a moment, trying to calm her thoughts and the rage in her chest.

Why is he doing this?

Taking a moment to compose herself, she reached down and checked her ankles for both pistols and daggers were in their places. Leaning back against the chair, she could feel the sword press against her back.

She stood up and gathered the books she

had been reading through and was preparing to put them back when the cardinal rushed through the door.

"Sister Clarice, you need to leave right now!"

"I know. Detective Bishop is picking me up in a few minutes."

She picked up the books and was going to put them back when he reached out and took them from her.

"There is no time for you to do this," he said. "I'll take care of it. Go. And may God go with you."

She could see the terror in his eyes and she just nodded and headed out of the library. Moving quickly through the hallways, she found her way to the front steps outside the church just as Bishop raced to a stop near the sidewalk.

With little time to spare, she closed the door as he swiftly accelerated, lights and siren alerting bystanders. Reaching behind herself, she grabbed her seat belt and struggled to get it around her and fastened.

"Tell me what happened," she said as she tensed up and grabbed the door handle next to her. To say the detective's driving was scaring her would be an understatement.

"Six kids went into the forest a little ways out of town, thinking it would be fun to summon a demon."

"Oh dear God."

"Five of them were killed during the attack, though the local sheriff's department

141

isn't buying the demon story. They are actually thinking the survivor did it and are thinking of charging her."

"Are you kidding me?"

"I know. It sounds ridiculous, but then again, in the minds of the locals the story of a demon killing those kids is just as ridiculous."

"I assume we're going to see this girl."

"You assume correctly. In about twenty minutes the chief is going to make a call to the local sheriff in that town and have the girl turned over to us."

The sister looked at him and could see the look on his face.

"You don't think it will be that easy, do you?"

"The local sheriff is under no obligation to turn her over to us. He may fight this and we'll be left with no way to talk to her."

"Maybe I need to call the cardinal and get him involved again."

"How many times can we go to that well before it dries up?"

"Good point."

The detective raced up the on-ramp to the freeway and nearly sideswiped a truck in the process.

"How far?" asked the sister as she clutched the door handle.

"Not far. Why?"

"I'm just wondering how long our guardian angels can keep up with us before we end up killed in a crash."

"You want me to slow down?"

"No, I want you to go faster if you think you can do it safely," she said with her terrified eyes glued to the road.

The detective swung into the left lane and pressed the gas pedal a little further. The sister closed her eyes and prayed for Heaven to look out for them.

A few minutes later the detective's phone rang and he tossed it into the sister's lap. After fumbling with it for a second, she pressed the Answer button and then the Speaker button.

"Detective Bishop's car."

"Ah, Sister Clarice. Good to have you with us."

She looked at the detective with questioning eyes.

"Yes, chief," said Bishop, "we are lucky to have her. What have you heard?"

"Pretty much what we feared. The sheriff is sticking to his guns on this and I can't say I really blame him. Five kids eviscerated and one survivor is found at the scene."

"Do you think she did it, Chief Masters?" asked Sister Clarice.

"Not for one second, sister. But we know the story about the killer you two are tracking is never going to wash."

"So they will charge this young lady, even if they don't have any evidence to do it?" she asked.

"They will in a heartbeat," said the chief, "which is why I'm calling. How close are you detective?"

"We're about ten minutes from the

hospital."

"Slow down."

"Slow down?"

"Yes, I need you to get there in about fifteen minutes. When you arrive, you will be met by federal agents. Do NOT go into the hospital until they are with you. Understand?"

"Yes, sir. Slowing down right now."

As his foot lifted off the gas slightly, he couldn't miss the sister crossing herself and whispering a silent thank you to Heaven above.

"Once you've secured the young lady and gotten her out of there, take her to a secure location and then let me know."

"Yes, sir."

Without another word, the chief clicked off and the inside of the car was silent except for the dull roar of the engine.

"You're not used to driving fast, are you, sister?"

She looked at him and said, "Detective Bishop, you have seen my car. It can't go fast, even downhill with a tailwind."

A grim smile crossed his face as they approached the off-ramp, which the detective took with a little more control than the last ramp.

He checked his watch and slowed the car even further. She could tell he was having a hard time keeping the speed down. He wanted to get there faster than she did.

As they pulled into the parking lot, he shut off the siren, but left the light on top of his car.

As they pulled around to the Emergency entrance, he saw what was clearly a car of the feds. Black, nondescript and menacing.

Pulling up behind it, the two front doors swung open and two agents got out. One male and one female.

As the detective and sister got out of the car, the agents approached and introduced themselves.

"Hi, I'm Agent Tyler and this is Agent Perry," said the male agent. "And if you make some sort of Supernatural joke we'll turn around and leave right now."

"Supernatural?" asked Bishop.

Sister Clarice leaned over and whispered, "TV show about two brothers hunting and killing demons and monsters."

"Oh," said Bishop, "okay."

Agent Perry reached over and punched Tyler in the arm and then said, "Let's see about getting this young lady out of the hot water she's in."

The sister nodded at her and smiled. The four of them turned and headed for the entrance. As they walked to the admissions desk, they could see a small police presence down one of the hallways.

'Bethany Anderson?" asked Perry to the woman behind the desk.

She just pointed down the hall and said, "115."

"Thank you," said the sister and she followed the others toward the knot of sheriff's deputies standing outside room 115.

Tyler stepped up to the deputies and said, "Gentlemen, we're here to take this dangerous killer off your hands."

"Excuse me?" said a rather rotund man who stepped forward through the group.

"Ah, Sheriff Bostwick, so good to meet you," said Perry.

She held up her badge and ID and Tyler did the same.

"We are here to take control of this situation. We would like you to make a hole and let us into that room."

"I don't know where you think you are, little lady, but we don't take orders from the FBI," said the sheriff.

"Really?" asked Tyler as he tapped a couple of buttons on his phone. Holding the phone to his ear, he said, "Yes, sir. He seems to be reluctant."

Then he held out the phone to the sheriff and said, "It's for you."

The sheriff took the phone and said, "Who is this?"

Then he stiffened and listened. After a few seconds, he said, "Yes, sir. I understand."

Clicking off the call, he handed the phone back to agent and said, "Men, we have been removed from the case. Let's go home."

"This is bullshit," said one of the men in the back and the sister stepped around Bishop and looked at him. When he saw her, he cowered backwards and apologized.

What looked like the entire sheriff's department from this small town turned and walked away from the room.

The sister stepped forward and opened the door and let out a cry of anguish when she saw Bethany laying in the bed. The girl's face was bruised and her neck was bandaged, along with one of her hands.

Bethany opened her eyes when she heard the door open and cried. Sister Clarice swept across the room and picked up the girl's unbandaged hand and held it.

The young girl looked at the others behind her and acted like she wanted to get away from them.

She looked at the sister and pleaded, "Please help me, sister. I didn't do what they say I did."

"Hey, sweetheart, we know that."

"But ...," said Bethany as she looked at the others, clearly recognizing them as police.

Agent Perry moved to the other side of the bed and placed a hand gently on the girl's shoulder.

"We are not here to arrest or accuse you of anything, young lady. We're here to get you out of here and then find out what really happened."

Just then the door opened and a doctor walked in and sized up the group.

"Can I help you?" he asked.

"What are the extent of her injuries?" asked Bishop.

"Are you family?"

Detective Bishop flipped his badge out for the doctor to see.

"I am asking because we need to take her out of here. We need to know if it's safe to move her."

"Though I can't really condone her leaving the hospital, her injuries wouldn't preclude that. She can move if she wants to."

Perry looked down at Bethany and asked, "Do you want to get out of here?"

"Yes, please," whispered Bethany. "I want to go home."

The sister lifted the sheet covering her a little and looked under, then turned to the men.

"Okay, gentlemen, you'll need to wait outside as we help Bethany get dressed."

Without one word, the three men turned and headed out the door. Agent Perry walked to a small cabinet and pulled it open. The only thing she found was a pair of sneakers and a pair of jeans.

"No shirt?" she asked.

"They took it," said Bethany. "It had blood from the others all over it and they were saying it got there when I was killing them."

Then she tensed up and cried, "I didn't kill them. I could never do that to my friends."

"Hey, hey," said the sister. "We know you didn't kill them. That's why we need to get you out of here and someplace safe."

"Yeah," said the agent, "before the townsfolk decide to form a lynch mob."

The sister looked at her and the agent took a deep breath.

"Yeah, I'm sorry. Not funny."

Over the next couple of minutes they helped the girl get her jeans on, leaving her in a hospital gown. The agent found another gown in the cabinet and slipped it over Bethany's shoulders backwards and closing it up.

Then the sister dropped to her knees and slipped her sneakers on and tied them.

"I don't like that, sister," said Bethany.

"What's that?"

"You kneeling in front of me and putting my shoes on."

The sister finished with the shoes and stood up patted her on the shoulder.

"Jesus knelt and washed the feet of his disciples to show them how they were to be of service to others. If my Lord and Savior can do it, so can I. Though I have been told, quite recently in fact, to stop kneeling at the drop of a hat."

"Shall we go?" asked Perry.

They helped her off the bed and found her to be quite in control of her body. As they pulled the door open, the three men jumped up and the doctor brought a wheelchair over for Bethany.

"I don't need that," she said.

"You do to get out of this hospital, young lady," said the doctor.

Bethany wasn't about to argue so she sat down and the sister stepped behind her and started pushing. As the others followed, Bethany looked up and smiled slightly at the nun.

"Still being of service?" she asked softly.

Sister Clarice smiled at her and said, "Always."

When they got outside, they saw there were still six sheriff's deputies and the sheriff standing around. When they came out the doors, Bethany tensed up as she saw them, but relaxed when the sister's hand settled on her shoulder.

The sheriff walked over and said, "You know, I'm thinking of making a call of my own to stop this."

Tyler stepped in front of him and asked, "Really? Someone higher up the chain than the governor?"

"I know a few people."

"Hmm," mused Tyler as he pulled out his phone and tapped a couple of buttons. Then he held it up so the sheriff could see it and asked, "Higher than this?"

The sheriff's face went white and he took a couple of steps back.

"Would you call him?"

"In a heartbeat, though I wouldn't like it. It's a little late in DC and he might not be in a pleasant mood if I wake him up."

"As one of my deputies said earlier, this is bullshit, pardon my language sister."

As Bishop began helping Bethany into the car, Sister Clarice stepped up to the sheriff.

"Sheriff Bostwick, we are on the same team."

"She was claiming a demon killed those kids, sister."

"Haven't you stopped to wonder why a

Catholic nun is in this group?"

He looked at her and she could see the wheels turning between his ears. Then she reached out and touched his hand and the sheriff went rigid. She only held his hand for a few seconds and then she let go.

"We are not your enemies," she said softly.

The sheriff took a second to recover from what he saw and then he turned to his men and said, "Go home or back to the department!"

The six deputies went to their cars and left the hospital parking lot.

He looked back at her and said, "Please tell me you can stop this thing."

"If I can't we're in serious trouble," she said as she took his hand again and eased the vision crashing through his brain.

Bishop walked over and held out his hand and the sheriff shied away.

"Don't worry, sheriff, I can't do the things she can do."

The sheriff took his hand and shook.

"I promise," said Bishop, "we'll keep you in the loop. And if you're a praying man, we could use all the help we can get."

The sheriff just nodded and turned and headed for his car.

As Bishop and the sister got in the car, he asked, "So, what did you show him?"

"I showed him what she saw," she said motioning to the back seat.

"When you touched her hand inside, you saw it. How bad was it?"

"Detective Bishop, you do not want to see it."

He stared into her eyes and then jumped when Agent Tyler knocked on his window. He rolled down the window.

"Where are you taking her?"

"She said she wanted to go home," said Bishop.

"No," came a small voice from the back.

"No?"

"My mom is off in Europe with her new husband. There's no one at home."

Sister Clarice reached into one of her many pockets and pulled out a card and handed it to the agent.

"She'll be right here."

The agent looked at the card and nodded.

"Hallowed ground. I like it."

He turned and headed back to the SUV and they left the parking lot.

"Where to?" asked Bishop.

"Like the agent said, hallowed ground."

"Yes, okay."

As they drove away from the hospital, into the darkness, neither the detective or sister could imagine the horror playing out in the mind of the young lady in the back seat.

Such horror should never be seen by anyone.

Chapter 15 – Safe From Attack

As they pulled into the parking lot behind the church, they found cardinal already waiting for them. The SUV with the agents pulled in and parked next to them.

After they all got out, Cardinal Wright welcomed the agents and then turned to Bethany. Reading the fear on her face was easy for him. He'd seen enough of it in his lifetime of service in the church.

"Ms. Anderson," he said, extending both hands to hold hers, "I apologize for what happened. Rest assured, you'll be safe in this sanctuary."

"Thank you," she said in a meek voice.

"Let's get you inside and settled and then we can make arrangements for you to call your parents and let them know where you are."

"I don't think my mom will care one bit," mumbled the young lady.

Sister Clarice put an arm around her shoulders and gave her a hug. Guiding her through the doors of the church, the sister could feel an immediate relaxation come over Bethany. As if the walls of the church were a barrier to all the terrible things she had experienced over the past day.

"I think she will care more than you think. What about your father?"

"I haven't talked to him in a couple of years. He moved out to the west coast and we have had little contact."

The group followed the cardinal down a

few dark corridors until they came to a dead end with rooms on both sides of the hall, three on each side. He walked to the end and opened the last door on the right and stood back.

When the sister guided Bethany into the room, the young woman gasped.

"This is a lot nicer than I was expecting."

"What were you expecting?" asked the sister. "A dungeon?"

"Kind of."

Bethany stood in the middle of the room and looked at the large, four poster bed, the floor-to-ceiling wardrobe, the antique looking desk and the doorway into the private bathroom.

Sister Clarice wrapped her arms around Bethany's shoulders from behind and whispered in her ear.

"You're not a prisoner here, but it's best to stay in the church for a few days until we know how close Azrin is to you."

Bethany immediately tensed up when she heard the name. The sister gave her shoulders a gentle squeeze and said, "Relax, he can't come into this holy sanctuary, which is why I said you need to stay inside for awhile."

Bethany turned around and looked at her and then at the four others standing just outside the room.

"You don't think he's finished?" she asked, tears already welling up in her eyes.

Sister Clarice reached up and cupped her cheeks between her hands and said, "With you? I believe he is, but with the rest of the world, no. Please promise me you'll stay inside the church."

"I promise. I don't ever want to see that monster again."

Agent Tyler cleared his throat and said, "Agent Perry and I are going to go. We'll be back in the morning to talk to you, Bethany. Please try to get some sleep."

The two agents turned and headed back through the church and Bishop went with them, wanting to thank them for what they did.

The sister turned and looked at the cardinal, who looked like he had no idea what to do with a teenage girl.

"Any word about Esther?" she asked.

"She is going to be released tomorrow morning and we will have someone there to pick her up and bring her here. We'll put her right across the hall. Now, if you ladies will excuse me, I need to make a call to my uncle and see if he can help us."

He turned and walked away, leaving the two ladies alone. The sister turned and looked at Bethany and could still see the fear in her eyes.

"It's okay, sweetheart. He can't get at you in here."

"He can still get into my dreams when I sleep or every time I close my eyes. He promised he would be with me every minute of the rest of my life."

This time the tears began streaming down her cheek. Sister Clarice stepped forward, pulling a tissue from her pocket and dried her face.

Then she cupped her face again and said, "Close your eyes."

When Bethany did that, the sister leaned forward, pulling her face to hers and touched her forehead to Bethany's. Immediately, the girl felt as if walls were being built inside her mind. She could hear Azrin roaring against the barriers being put up.

Before the sister pulled away from Bethany, she said a soft, almost silent prayer.

With each word, Azrin's screams became softer and softer, until they were completely blocked out. Bethany sucked in a deep breath and reached up and put her hands on top of the sister's. She could feel the warmth running through her veins and the power flowing into her head.

After a couple more minutes, the sister pulled back and looked at the young woman. Bethany opened her eyes and could see the sister was drained. Clarice almost fell when her knees began to shake, but Bethany grabbed her and guided her to the edge of the bed and helped her sit down.

"What happened, sister?"

The sister took a deep breath and shook her head slightly.

"Protecting your mind was a very real battle with Azrin and fighting with him is very taxing."

"Then why would you do that, sister?"

"Because he and I have met in battle before

156

and it did not go well for him. I think he's still upset with me. Needless to say, I am much more prepared to face him than you are."

"You're the demon hunter," gasped Bethany.

Sister Clarice looked up at her and just nodded wearily. Bethany sank down to her knees in front of the sister.

"He told me the only reason he was letting me live was so I could tell you what he had done. He seemed to take great pleasure in what he did."

Sister Clarice reached out and took Bethany's hands in hers and held them softly.

"He takes great pleasure in causing pain and suffering among people. Now, it is my job to make sure he never causes that pain to you, ever again."

Bethany jumped slightly as there was a knock on the door and the sister called out for whoever to come in. Detective Bishop opened the door and pretty much filled the doorway.

"I'm going to head back to the precinct. Do you ladies need anything before I go?"

"No, detective," said Clarice. "I'm just going to get her into bed and try to get her to sleep."

The detective looked at her and said, "Sister, you don't look so good."

She smiled at him and said, "I'm just a bit tired. It's been an exhausting day."

"Then you get some rest, too," he said.

Then he looked at Bethany and said, "Young lady, you be strong. The best way you can be of service to your friends is to stay strong and help us destroy this bastard. Oh, sorry sister."

She smiled slightly and said, "Don't apologize to me, Fredrick. You're in His house." Nodding to the crucifix above the bed, he got the message.

He looked at the cross and nodded to it, saying, "Sorry. I'll see you two fine ladies in the morning."

After he pulled the door closed, Bethany looked at the sister and said, "There's something about him. Like he knows what we're going through."

"He does. He had his own run-in with Azrin when he was just a boy and it cost him his mother and father."

Bethany bowed her head and wept even more hearing that. The sister handed her the tissue, which the girl took and started dabbing her eyes.

Then she looked up and asked, "Who's Esther?"

"Another who has recently met Azrin face-to-face and barely lived to tell about it."

Then the sister gave the short versions of what had happened to Marvin and Esther and also Suzanne Kelly.

When the sister mentioned the name of Suzanne, Bethany screamed, "NO!"

Sister Clarice leaned forward and took her face in her hands and asked, "What is it, Bethany? Did you know her?"

All Bethany could do was nod weakly.

"She's my aunt. She was my father's sister."

"Oh dear."

Bethany raised up on her knees and threw her arms around the sister and the nun wrapped her arms around the distraught girl. She could feel her sobbing as her face was pressed into her chest.

She said nothing and just let the girl cry.

Finally, a muffled, crying voice could be heard, "I loved my aunt. She was the sweetest woman I know. She was going to take me to Colorado next week for skiing. I've left messages for her over the past couple of days, but she never returned my calls."

"You don't have the same last name," said the sister.

"Kelly was her married name. Her husband was killed in a crash a couple of years ago."

Bethany pulled back and looked at the sister. Clarice took the tissue and wiped her face dry.

"The crash was never explained," said Bethany. "It was a clear night, no rain and nothing out of the ordinary. He was on his way home when it happened, but, they said there was no reason he should have crashed like that. And they said his truck was completely destroyed, like it had been hit with a bomb or something. There was way more damage than there should have been."

"What was his first name?"

"William. Or Bill, which was what he liked to be called. Bill Kelly. Do you know of him?"

"No, but I will be looking into his death. Tell me Bethany, is there anything about your family, especially your aunt or uncle that you would consider special?"

Beth thought for a moment and shook her head.

"Not that I know of. We're just ordinary people."

"Well, we can talk about this in the morning. You need to get some sleep, young lady. But before I go, we need to do something about this."

She stood up and began removing the bandage from Bethany's neck. When she saw the damage Azrin had done, she clicked her tongue a couple of times.

"This just won't do," she said. "A pretty young lady like you should never be scarred like this."

Then she scared the living daylights out of Bethany by pulling her sword from behind her head. The sword grew in length and then began glowing and spitting lightning bolts.

Sister Clarice ran her other hand over the burned flesh on the girl's neck. Bethany went to pull away, but the sister held her neck firmly.

"Just relax and we'll see if we can get rid of this."

For two solid minutes, Bethany couldn't take her eyes off the blazing sword. Nor could she ignore the feeling of warmth and healing going on under the touch of the sister's hand.

When she finished, Sister Clarice turned Bethany's head one way and then the other, checking out the skin.

"Hmm. Perfect," she said. "That is really going to irritate Azrin when he sees his handiwork has been undone."

Bethany jumped up and ran into the bathroom. Looking into the mirror, she could see no evidence of the wound the demon had left on her neck. As she ran her fingers over the restored, smooth skin, a tear began running down her cheek.

Moving back into the bedroom, she saw Sister Clarice putting the sword away. Stepping up to the nun, she threw her arms around her neck and hugged her, thanking her.

"It's what I do, sweetheart."

"Can I ask you something, sister?"

"Anything, sweetie."

"A couple of times, your sword hit me with those small lightning bolts, but they didn't hurt. As a matter of fact, I felt something so totally unlike anything I've felt before. What is that?"

The sister smiled a little and reached behind her head. When her hand came back out, she was holding her sword, which grew to its full length when she held it up. It started glowing and spitting sparks again.

Bethany took a step back and gasped.

"Don't worry. It's just getting angry that we haven't been able to catch Azrin and end him."

The sister looked at the blade and asked, "Aren't you, my friend?"

The sword sputtered and sparked.

Sister Clarice looked back at Bethany and said, "He gets so testy when he hasn't ended a demon in a long time."

Bethany looked the sword up and down and said, "Looks like he could certainly do the job."

The sister looked at her for a second.

"You say Azrin thought about killing you, but then decided to let you live so you could tell me about the attack. Was there anything strange that happened? Something that surprised you when you think about it now?"

Bethany thought for a second and then said, "Yes, When he reached for me, it was like he couldn't grab me. Like something was keeping his hand away from me. He actually looked confused by it."

"But he was able to grab your neck," said the sister.

"It seemed like it was a struggle for him to do it."

The sister looked at her for a moment and then at the sword. Then she held it out to her.

"Oh no, I couldn't," said Bethany.

"Bethany, it isn't going to hurt you. It would never hurt someone I consider a friend."

The girl looked at it and then reached slowly out to take hold of the hilt.

"Hold it with both hands, sweetheart."

When Bethany's fingers wrapped around the hilt, she gasped. The power of the sword surged through her. Her blond hair began standing out like it was full of electricity and her blue eyes began blazing with power.

She reached forward and begged the sister to take it from her. Sister Clarice took the sword from her and collapsed it and put it back in its place behind her back.

Bethany walked over and sat down on the edge of the bed, gripping the blanket with both hands.

"Well, that was certainly unexpected," said the sister and she sat back down and put an arm around the girl.

Bethany was trying to catch her breath when she gasped, "What was that?"

"Apparently my sword, a sword from God, likes you."

"It likes me? And it did that to me?"

"What did it do to you, Bethany?"

"It ... I think ... I don't really know."

"It sensed a possible warrior for good and tested your heart for purity. I'm pretty sure it saw something it liked."

Bethany jumped up and said, "Does this mean I have to become a nun? I mean, I like you, sister, but I'm not even Catholic."

Sister Clarice reached up and cupped her chin in her hand.

"No, sweetheart, that's not what it means. It just means that you could be a warrior in this fight against evil in this world. God does not care where his warriors come from or what faith they hold. Only that they be good people."

Bethany looked at her and then looked at the crucifix on the wall. She was drawn to the small image of Jesus hanging on the cross.

"He really did die for us, didn't He?"

The sister stepped up behind her and put her hands on her shoulders.

"Yes, sweetie, He did."

"I wish I knew Him better."

Sister Clarice kissed her forehead and whispered in her ear.

"There is still plenty of time for you to get to know Him. And He would love to introduce Himself to you."

She cupped Bethany's cheek and said, "Okay, it's time for you to get some sleep."

She walked over to the wardrobe and opened it, revealing it to be full of clothes on hangers and in the drawers. The sister reached in and pulled out a nightgown and held it out to the girl.

Bethany let it unfold and hang down to the floor. It was long, it was not see-through at all and it looked like something an old woman would wear to bed.

Two centuries ago.

"Not exactly stylish, I see."

The sister laughed softly and said, "Remember, His house," nodding to the crucifix.

Bethany looked at it and said, "Right, right. His house, His rules."

"You will find towels and washcloths in the cabinet in the bathroom and plenty of soaps and shampoos. I am going to get out of here and let you have some privacy."

"Where is your room, sister?"

"Back where this hallway meets the other

one."

"Right where you'd be able to stop any monsters from coming down the hall this way."

"There you go, sweetheart. Anyway, you get some rest."

Without another word, Sister Clarice stepped out of the room and pulled the door closed. As she walked down the hallway, heading for the cardinal's office, she could feel the sword vibrate on her back.

"Yes, I saw that."

Bzzz!

"Hey, she's still just a girl."

Bzzz!

"I don't care what you think. She needs time to grow up and get past this."

Bzzz!

"Ow! You stop that or you're going in the closet and staying there."

Bzzz!

"I forgive you. You know I love you, right?"

Bzzz!

Bethany took her time in the shower, trying to wash the feeling of her friends' blood off her body. No matter how hard she scrubbed, she could still feel the sensation of the blood spattering across her face and body.

When she finally got out of the shower and dried off, she pulled the nightgown over her head and let it fall to the floor. It came to within a couple of inches of the cold tiles under her feet.

Looking at her reflection in the full length mirror, she scrunched up her lips and then sighed at the sight.

And then said, "Sorry, I'm just used to something a little more comfortable to sleep in."

Turning off the light in the bathroom, she walked across the room and checked the door to make sure it was locked. Then she turned off the light and breathed a sigh of relief when she saw there was a small nightlight lower on the wall.

Climbing under the heavy, warm blankets, she laid back and her eyes were drawn to the figure on the wall above the bed. Because the crucifix was directly over her head, she had to crane her neck to see it.

Then she jumped out of bed, pulled the covers out from under the mattress and rearranged the pillows to the other end of the bed. Laying back down, she was now looking directly at the crucifix hanging above her feet.

After a couple of minutes, she tossed the blankets off again and got on her knees in the middle of the bed, facing the figure of Jesus.

I don't know how to do this, but if we could just talk for a few minutes ...

Then she had her very first real talk with Jesus.

Chapter 16 – A New Warrior?

Early the next morning, Bethany peeked her head out of her room and saw the empty corridor stretching back to the rear of the church. Slipping out of the room, she began walking as quietly as she could, trying not to wake anyone that might be sleeping in one of the nearby rooms.

As she snuck around the corner near where Sister Clarice had said her room was located, her entire plan of not being seen came unglued. Sitting in a small chapel off to the side of the intersecting hallway and talking quietly in the pews, were alert eyes.

"Not planning on leaving without saying goodbye, are you?"

She jumped at the sound of the sister's voice and turned to see her and the cardinal looking at her.

"I'm sorry. It's just that I lost my phone yesterday," she said, "and I was hoping to call my dad. Like I told you yesterday, of my two parents, I think he'll be the one to care the most."

"He does care," said the cardinal. "Upon hearing the news of the attack, he frantically called everyone he could in Chicago to find out about your well-being and whereabouts. It took a while, but they put him in touch with Detective Bishop, who told him you were here and safe."

"Cardinal Wright talked to him about an hour ago," said the sister, "and he is on his way here as we speak. He should be here in a few hours."

She patted the seat next to her and said, "Here, come and sit with us."

As Bethany sat down, she slid closer to the sister, who put her arm around her and pulled her close.

"How did you sleep last night?" asked the cardinal.

"I think I slept well, considering what happened yesterday."

Then she looked at the sister and said, "You really did silence him last night. I didn't think of him or hear from him all night."

"It is my intention to silence him forever," said the sister.

"I pray you are successful."

Just then, the two federal agents walked into the chapel and greeted them. Agent Tyler walked over and stood against a wall and Agent Perry sat down in the pew directly in front of the sister and Bethany. She turned herself on the seat so she could look at Bethany.

"Bethany," she said, "this may be the toughest thing you ever do, but we'd like for you to tell us exactly what happened yesterday."

Bethany tensed up as she realized she was going to have to relive the entire story again, but when the sister gave her a gentle squeeze, she relaxed.

Over the next twenty minutes, she related the story as she remembered it. The other four sat and listened, only asking a few questions during the time.

After she finished, the cardinal said, "I think we can safely assume Azrin is interested in this young lady."

"It would appear so," said Agent Tyler.

"What do you mean?"

"We did a little digging into the accident that killed your uncle, The sister believes William Kelly, and correctly, I have to say, was killed by Azrin. We've concluded that Azrin destroyed his truck as he drove down that quiet part of the highway. That is the only way to explain the destruction."

"I still don't understand how that would lead Azrin to be interested in me."

The sister looked at the cardinal and asked, "Do you want to see it with your own eyes?"

The cardinal gave a slight shrugged and the sister stood up and had Bethany stand up. Reaching behind her back, she pulled her sword and it immediately put on its light show.

Holding the sword out to Bethany, the sister looked into her eyes. After hesitating for a second, the girl reached out and took hold of the sword, just as she had the night before. Again, her hair stood on end, her eyes glowed and her face was lit as if from the inside.

"I see what you mean," said the cardinal with no surprise in his voice.

The sister reached out and Bethany thought she was asking for the sword back, but Clarice wrapped her hands around hers and they held the sword together.

Sister Clarice's eyes went from her unusual

blue color to a bright golden color and her olive skin became translucent when the power of the sword acted upon her. Bethany felt as if she was looking at an angel.

What surprised Bethany more than anything was the two agents not reacting to the spectacle in front of them. As if this was something they saw on a daily basis.

After a few seconds, the sister went ahead and took the sword and put it away.

The cardinal stood up and held out his hand to Bethany and she took it.

"I think our Heavenly Father has great plans for you, young lady."

"I don't understand any of this," she said.

"Neither did Sister Clarice when she was called to her work."

Then he looked at the sister and said, "Sometimes I think she still doesn't fully grasp her role as a warrior of God."

The sister gave him a cynical look and thought about sticking her tongue out at him, but realized that might be a little lighthearted for the situation.

The sister guided Bethany back to the pew and sat down beside her, as Agent Perry took her seat again.

"The point is, Bethany, the sword has seen something in you it likes. What it expects of you we don't know. But, as the padre just said, it's clear God has some plans for you."

"But … what if I don't want to be part of those plans?" she asked as she looked up at the crucifix above the small altar. "Sorry."

"Well, you can always turn down the calling just like I tried to do," said the sister. "As you can see, it didn't work out the way I thought it would."

"Bethany," said the padre, "we're not asking you to decide this very moment or even soon. Be open to the idea that God may need your service in the future."

While holding Bethany's hand, Agent Perry disclosed that she and Agent Tyler work in a government department that understands her experience yesterday.

"I just want to say, this world needs more young people like you."

"But, I'm not Catholic."

"God does not care whether you are Catholic, Baptist, Jewish or Buddhist. All He cares about is that you are righteous and pure of heart," said the cardinal. "We believe the sword has already seen those qualities in you."

"He doesn't care if I'm not a member of any organized religion?"

"Let me tell you something, even the sister did not know until a few years after she began her work. There are Sisters of the Templar that are not members of any church. They believe in God, but they don't believe in the Catholic Church."

The sister looked at him with shock in her eyes. "I wasn't told this in the beginning."

"It wasn't necessary to tell you."

Turning back to Bethany, he said, "We just ask you to be open to the idea."

He felt a buzz from his phone and pulled it

171

from his pocket. Standing up, he asked the others to accompany him in welcoming a guest to the church that the sister wanted to greet personally.

"Yes," said the sister.

The five of them headed out of the chapel and to the back door. Just as they walked out the door, an ambulance pulled around the corner of the building and stopped near them.

Sister Clarice stepped out the door and when Bethany went to follow her, the cardinal reached out and put a hand on her shoulder. He pointed down at a strip of tile that marked the edge of the inside of the church and the outside. She knew immediately what he was saying without him actually saying it.

She stepped back away from the line and watched from inside the church.

The back door of the ambulance opened and a nurse, a friar and nun jumped out and they reached in and pulled out a gurney.

Sister Clarice was not to be denied when she rushed to the side of the gurney and took the hand of the woman laying on it. She had tears streaming down her face as she looked down at Esther's bruised face and arm in a cast.

"Oh, Esther," she cried. "I'm so sorry about this."

Esther reached up and cupped her face with her good hand and said, "Stop crying, sister. I lived through it."

"I know, but …,"

"But nothing, young lady."

The nurse said, "Let's get her inside and out of this cold."

"Yes," said Sister Clarice. "Follow me."

She led the way into the back of the church and down the same corridors Bethany had traveled the night before. When they came to the door directly across the hall from Bethany's, the sister opened it and swept in, making sure all was ready for her friend.

"What can I do to help?"

Sister Clarice looked at Bethany and said, "Please pull down the covers on the bed so we can get her into it."

As the friar and other sister went to help Esther off the gurney and over to the bed, she gently pushed them back.

"Oh, stop it, you two. You've been treating me like an old lady all morning."

When she went to take a step, it was clear she was still unstable on her feet and her knees almost buckled. The two sisters jumped to her side and took her arms to steady her and get her in the bed.

"Even a powerful warrior of God needs a little help once in a while," said Sister Clarice.

After they got her in the bed, Bethany pulled the blankets up and laid them over the old woman.

"Thank you, sweetheart," said Esther, as she reached up and patted the young woman on the cheek. "And what is your name?"

"Bethany."

"Oh, such a lovely name. You seem somewhat familiar to me."

A bewildered Bethany didn't know what to say to that.

"Alright," said Sister Clarice, "everyone out."

The others were a bit surprised by this turn of events, but they turned and headed out the door.

"Bethany, you stay."

"Me?"

The sister shut the door and gestured for Bethany to bring a chair to the bed's side while she brought one to the other side.

After the two of them sat down on each side of the bed, Sister Clarice reached out and caressed Esther's fingertips that were poking out of the cast. Reaching up, she softly ran the backs of her fingers over Esther's bruised face. When Esther winced a bit from the touch, the sister pulled her hand back, but the old lady took her hand and pulled it to her lips and kissed it.

"Esther, this is Bethany Anderson. She ...,"

"Are you a warrior, too?" asked Esther. "You seem like a warrior. I think I can see it in you."

"No, I'm not a warrior," said Bethany and then looked at the sister, "but there seems to be some interest in offering me the job."

Esther reached out and took the young woman's hand and said, "Take it. The world needs people like you."

"Bethany," said the sister, "this is Esther Morgan. One of the most insightful people I know. She is also the last person to see your aunt alive."

"What?"

Esther looked at her and asked, "Suzanne Kelly was your aunt?"

"Yes."

"I'm so sorry for your loss, sweetheart. Your aunt was very sweet and I could tell she had purity in her heart. I only met her once and only for a few minutes, but I could see an angel when I looked at her."

Bethany had to wipe some tears away as she said, "She was a wonderful person. I wanted to be so much like her."

Esther squeezed her hand and said, "You can still be just like her, even though she isn't here anymore."

"And," said the sister, "the two of you have met Azrin."

"Oh, sweetheart," said Esther, "No young person should ever have to meet that monster. Did you lose someone close?"

Bethany nodded and the tears flowed unabated.

"Five of my friends," she whispered.

"I'm so sorry."

"I just wanted the two of you to meet each other. I think your separate strengths will be a blessing to each of you."

Just then, there was a tap at the door and when it opened, Detective Bishop stuck his head in and said, "Sister, can I talk to you?"

As she stood up, he looked at Esther, smiled and asked, "How are you feeling, beautiful lady?"

"Like I got whooped by a demon from Hell."

The smile disappeared from his face and she said, "Oh, don't you worry, detective. He better hope I never get my hands on him again."

The detective smiled again and said, "Well, if you get your hands on him, hold him. The sister and I would like to have a little chat with him."

"Can't promise he'll be in one piece," she said without a hint of doubt.

"That's the spirit. I knew I liked you."

He gave her one last smile and pulled the door closed.

Turning around, he looked at the sister and the smile disappeared completely.

"I hate to take you away from this tranquility, but …,"

"It hasn't happened again, has it?"

The detective's head just dropped and the sister crossed herself.

"Three women hiking through the same woods those kids were in yesterday."

"Are you parked out back?"

"Yes."

"I'll be right out," she said as she disappeared into the room again. A few seconds later, he could hear and an anguished *NO!* from behind the closed door. He turned and headed for the car to wait for the sister.

As he was talking on the phone with the captain, the sister came out and sat down in the car. He quickly ended the call as she closed the door. She was just staring straight ahead and had a look of grim determination on her face.

Looking at her, he asked, "What are you thinking, sister?"

"That we are always going to be one step behind this monster."

"This is not the first time I've felt that way."

"What happened?" she asked.

"A case about twelve years ago. We had a serial killer working in the downtown area and we just felt like we were always playing catch up."

"How did you catch him?"

"A little police work, a trap and a lot of dumb luck."

He started the car and drove back out to the street and set course for the same woods they were in the day before.

They drove for about twenty minutes before the sister broke the silence.

"What was the trap?"

"Excuse me?"

"You said you used a trap to capture the serial killer."

"Oh, right. We found a female police officer that seemed to fit the profile of the victims the killer seemed interested in and used her as bait."

"Why do I not like the way you just described her? Bait."

"I suppose for the same reason I didn't like the idea of putting her in that situation. She was the one to overrule me."

As he was talking, the sister could hear

some pain in his voice.

"Did she get through it okay?"

For a moment, he was silent and she feared the answer he might give.

"No, she didn't," he said. "He took the bait, captured her and took her somewhere. He found her tracking device and tossed it in the back of a passing junk truck and we spent an hour tailing the wrong vehicle. By the time we found them, he had been terrorizing her for over an hour."

"Did he kill her?"

"No, but he cut off a couple of her fingers. We rescued her and killed him in a gunfight. Though she could have come back to work, she never did. I've visited her a few times, but she's lost herself in a battle with the bottle."

"Oh, dear."

"Yeah."

After a few moments of silence, the detective said softly, "This job just chews you up and spits you out when it has no use for you anymore."

She reached across and squeezed his arm, but said nothing.

Chapter 17 – It Happened Again

"Good morning, sheriff."

Sheriff Bostwick turned to see who was talking and when he saw the detective and sister walking toward him, he just shook his head and let out a long sigh.

"I don't know what's so good about it, detective."

"You know what, sheriff? You're absolutely correct and I'm sorry for my choice of words."

"Alright," said the sheriff. "You here to take over this investigation, too?"

"No, not that I've been told this time."

"How's the girl, by the way?"

"She's doing okay. We've got her in a safe place and hopefully she gets through this."

"I guess what happened here today let's her off the hook for what happened yesterday."

"It would seem so and I'm glad to hear you say that."

They looked over and could see the sister standing a little ways off, staring over the tops of the trees as the ground sloped away. There were green tree tops as far as the eye could see.

The sheriff stepped closer and asked softly, "Yesterday, she touched me and I saw a monster that seemed to be straight out of some horror movie."

Detective Bishop leaned over, put a hand on his shoulder and said, "About seven feet tall, dark scaly skin like charcoal, horns about a foot and a half long, claws at the end of its fingers and fire in its eyes?"

"She showed it to you, too?"

"She didn't have to. I've seen it with my own eyes."

The sheriff looked up and could see the conviction in the detective's eyes.

"What the hell are we supposed to do against something like that? Is she supposed to be the answer to this problem?"

"She claims to be unsure of what to do, but I believe she is our best chance to defeat this demon."

They looked at her again. She had her back to them, but they could see she had a rosary in her hand and was fingering her way through the beads.

"Well," said the sheriff, "I guess we should get this over with."

They walked over and stopped behind her. A few seconds later, she raised a hand and pointed out at the beautiful forest scene that stretched out before them.

"It is so inappropriate."

"What's that, sister?" asked the detective.

"That a place so beautiful has now become home to the most evil being to walk this Earth."

He reached out and placed a large, black hand on her shoulder and said, "Then let's see what we can do to return beauty to this place."

She reached up and patted his hand and then looked at the sheriff and nodded.

"Right this way," he said as he started down a trail that ran further into the trees.

After a five-minute hike, they came to a

small clearing and they could see there was a small army of CSI investigators working in many places in the field.

As they began walking into the field, one of the female investigators ran over and stopped in front of them. She was wearing a full suit of white plasticized cotton that went from the built-in booties on her feet to the hood over her head. She had a full-face mask with filters near her mouth for breathing.

When they looked down, they could see the legs of the suit were smeared with bright red blood. They knew it was the blood of the victims that was apparently all over the knee-high grass in the meadow.

"Sister, please do not go any further," she said as she pulled the mask off. "You shouldn't even be here and seeing this."

Sister Clarice stepped forward and placed a hand on the side of the tech's face, which caused the woman to emit a sigh and close her eyes.

"I need to be here and to see what this evil has done. And to offer an answer to what you just said. No one should ever witness what happened here today. Show me what you've learned, Shondra."

The woman turned to lead her back to the crime scene, but then stopped and looked at the sister.

"How did you know my name?"

"Your name tag, sweetheart."

Shondra looked down at her name tag and said, "Oh yeah, that."

She turned and walked back to the spot she had been working and there was a body on the ground under a white sheet. At least it was white when they started, but it was soaking up blood and turning an angry red.

As the sister approached, Shondra said, "Your robes are going to get blood on them."

Sister Clarice looked at her and nodded. "It won't be the first time I've had to wash the blood of the innocents out of my habit."

The detective and sheriff stood a few yards away and watched as the sister moved to where she assumed the head was. Lifting the sheet away from the dead woman's face, she saw the same horrified look frozen on her face that she had seen on Suzanne Kelly's.

Setting her hand on the forehead of the woman, she immediately saw the last few moments of her life. The attack had been brutal and quick.

Azrin rose from the ground, terrifying the women as he confronted them. He had killed two of them almost instantly while this third victim was toyed with.

Almost as if Azrin knew the sister would look and he wanted to put on a show for her. And what a horror show it was.

Never had the sister seen such depravity from the demon. It was almost as if the demon had learned all kinds of new ways to torture a human and was trying them all out at once.

After she felt she'd seen enough, the sister opened her eyes and felt a tear drip off her face and fall onto the face of the dead woman. She brushed it away and covered the woman's eyes for a second. When she pulled her hand away, the look of terror was gone from her face.

She gently placed the sheet back over the woman's face and stood up. Turning and looking, she pointed to a spot about ten yards away. There was an overgrown depression in the earth.

"He came up from there."

As she began walking, Shondra stepped next to Bishop and whispered, "How does she know these things?"

"If you want to really have your mind blown, look at your name tag again."

Then he walked away as she looked down and read the name tag.

Crime Scene Investigator
Ms. Collins

The detective called over his shoulder, "Never try to lie to the sister. It's impossible."

As she looked at the name tag and wondered, a single gunshot shattered the calm of the meadow. Then two more.

Sister Clarice whirled around and looked toward where the shots were coming from. She saw the sheriff and the detective running toward the far edge of the meadow and took off after them.

They found a terrified deputy, drawing down on the darkness of the forest beyond the sunlight of the meadow.

"What the hell, Smithers?" shouted the

sheriff.

"There's something here, sheriff!"

"What's here?"

"I … I … know it was here."

The sister ran up and moved slowly to the deputy's side, not wanting to startle him. She reached out and placed her hand over the trembling hand that held the smoking gun.

When the vision hit her, it was fast and caused her heart to skip a beat.

Jumping back, she reached behind her head and pulled her sword. It immediately extended itself and burst into flames. Small lightning bolts spit off the blade as she began turning back and forth, her eyes searching for something in the darkness.

The detective moved up beside her, his gun in his hand and pointing toward the forest.

"What is it, sister?"

For a moment she didn't answer, but he could hear her heavy breathing. Then she spoke in a voice barely above a whisper.

"He's still here."

"Detective, sister!" yelled the sheriff. "I think my deputy just has an overactive imagination! Please lower your weapons."

The sheriff walked over and positioned himself in front of Deputy Smithers and commanded him to holster his gun, but the deputy's eyes were still wide with terror.

Just as the sheriff was about to issue the command again, a branch from the nearest tree lashed out and knocked the sheriff twenty yards through the air.

Bishop and Smithers both opened up on the tree, firing every bullet they had. The tree turned and they saw it wasn't a tree at all. It was a demon from Hell and it had the most evil grin on its face they had ever seen.

Azrin stabbed at the deputy, but could only impale his shoulder. Bishop reached over and grabbed the man by the back of his collar and pulled him off the demon's claw and dragged him away.

The sister charged forward, placing herself in front of the demon, swishing her blade back and forth in its face.

"We meet again, little bug," growled Azrin.

"And you will wish we didn't," snarled the sister in a voice that surprised even the detective.

Azrin charged at the two of them and the detective fired every round in the new magazine he had loaded. He fired so fast it sounded like a machine gun. His bullets had no effect on the demon.

She jumped forward, placing herself between him and the monster. She reached into a pocket and pulled out a gold-colored magazine and tossed it over her shoulder.

"Try these!"

He snatched the magazine out of the air and rammed it into his 9mm pistol. While he did that, the sister and the demon came together on the field of battle.

It became clear to Bishop that Azrin was quite leery of the sword she was brandishing. He would take a swipe at her, but when she went to counter his moves, he pulled back, like he was afraid to even touch the thing.

Bishop raised his weapon, took careful aim at what he deemed to be the head of the demon because he was still in the shape of a tree. Squeezing the trigger, he almost lost his grip when the gun erupted with the loudest shot he'd ever heard from his gun.

The gun almost kicked itself out of his hand and he was a pretty big guy. While he was struggling to control the gun, he almost missed the reaction Azrin had to the bullet.

The demon snapped back as the bullet tore a hole through his head and howled in pain. Before he could recover from the wound he'd taken from the bullet, Sister Clarice attacked and slammed her sword straight into the belly of the monster.

For a brief few seconds, fire and smoke erupted from the place where the sword sliced into the demon's body. Azrin swung again and this time, he connected and slammed the sister to the ground, causing her to release the hilt of the sword.

Azrin tried to grab the sword and wrench it from his body, but every time he touched it he screeched in pain. Finally, he just grabbed it and yanked it out of his belly, but everyone could hear the sword fighting back and burning him even more.

It was amazing to hear the sword burning the hand of a demon that was already made up of charred skin on the outside and fire on the inside. He raised the sword and flung it as hard as he could at the sister, who had just finished rolling on the ground from his crushing hit. If she didn't move, the sword would have sliced right through her.

Little did Azrin know her sword would do everything it could to avoid hurting her.

She saw the sword coming and rolled. When she came back up to her feet, her hand lashed out and grabbed the hilt of the sword as it flew past. In the split second she was regaining her feet, she filled her left hand with a pistol that was strapped to her ankle.

Without a second's hesitation, she fired five rounds with her left hand, straight into the body of the demon, who was now back in his usual form. Each round tore a hole through him, causing him to yowl in pain.

The detective fired more rounds, each one causing significant damage.

"Die, you son of a bitch!" yelled Bishop as he stepped close to the sister.

He said, "Sorry, sister," as he fired one more round.

"This keeps up much longer, Fredrick, I may join you in using curse words," she said as she raised her left foot and slammed the pistol back into its holster.

With her hand free now, she could go back to a two-hand hold on the sword and she started advancing on the demon.

Azrin was showing signs of being injured by the bullets, but she knew well enough what happens when an animal is wounded. It becomes meaner and more aggressive.

As she stepped forward, she heard the detective fire two more times and could even hear the bullets zip past her head.

Oh, I hope he's as good a shot as he seems to think he is.

She got within a few feet of Azrin and he swung his arm at her with such force that if he connected, she would cease to be among the living. The sister countered by ducking under the swinging fist, but raised the sword up to where her head had been.

Even though she couldn't see it because her head was down, she felt the blade slice through and was rewarded with the sight of Azrin's injured hand landing on the ground next to her.

Coming back up, she saw he was backing away from her and heard another couple of shots from the detective fly past her head. She made a mental note to not make any side-to-side movements of her head while he was behind her, firing that gun.

Then Azrin did something completely unexpected. Something the sister hoped she wouldn't see.

He ran.

He ran back into the meadow heading for the depression the sister had pointed out earlier. One thing the sister was quick to notice was the CSI team were standing near the bodies they had been investigating. They were completely transfixed by the sight of what was happening at the side of the clearing and none of them had thought to get the hell out of there.

When the sister saw his path would take him right past Shondra, she screamed, "Run!"

Shondra realized the danger coming her way and turned to run, but wasn't nearly quick enough and Azrin scooped her up as he loped toward the depression.

Turning around, he looked at the detective and sister, who were racing to catch him and he held the screaming tech up in front of him. The detective couldn't shoot without possibly killing her. For an instant, he thought about those victims he'd already seen and wondered if it wouldn't be better to kill the woman than let the demon get away with her.

It was enough of a quandary to cause the detective to hold his fire.

"We will meet again, little bug," howled Azrin as he continued to hold the terrified tech in his one good hand. "Now, me and my new toy shall be off!"

Jumping into the middle of the depression, the two of them disappeared through the grass and into the ground.

Sister Clarice and Bishop skidded to a stop at the edge of the depression, with the detective sweeping his gun back and forth.

"Where the hell did they go?"

A couple of other techs ran over, thinking they would see the demon and their friend in the swale's bottom, but cried out when they saw nothing.

The detective looked at the sister and could see a grave look on her face. She slid her sword back into the scabbard on her back.

The sheriff was able to hobble over and when he saw the empty hollow, he raged.

"Where are they? Where did they go, sister?"

Bending down, she pulled both gold pistols from her ankles and checked them for ammunition. Patting herself down, she was satisfied she had enough magazines to hold off a small army.

"What are you doing, sister?" asked the sheriff with a genuine look of concern.

She looked up at him, her eyes still glowing gold from her contact with the sword and the heat of the battle.

"I'm going to get Shondra back."

"Oh no," said Bishop as he reached out and grabbed her arm. "Not until you tell me where you're going."

She looked down at his hand on her arm and then back up at him. The fire in her eyes told him to get his hands off her. When he let go, she gave him a nod.

"You're a good man, Fredrick. Never forget that."

Then, without another word, she turned and jumped off the edge of the depression and the ground swallowed her right in front of everyone's eyes.

Two women around the hole screamed. Maybe it was a couple of the men. It sounded like someone who had just watched a person leap to their death.

"Son of a bitch!" yelled the detective as he

popped the magazine out of his pistol and checked it for those magic bullets of hers. He had five left.

He shook his head as he slammed the mag back in the gun and growled, "Oh, I hate her even more now."

Then he jumped.

The last thing he heard was the sheriff yelling, "You stupid son of ..."

Chapter 18 – Into Evil's Domain

How long did he fall? He had no clue. It felt like hours and the longer he fell, the hotter it seemed to get.

Well, if I'm falling into Hell I guess I'm heading in the right direction!

As he looked up, he could see the light of whatever hole he jumped into getting smaller and smaller. Within seconds, the light disappeared and the darkness was absolute.

Looking down, there was nothing. No light whatsoever. He was expecting to at least see the fires of Hell burning below him, but he didn't even see that.

He wondered how long it would take to reach the center of the Earth as he fell.

Let's see, the Earth is about 25,000 miles around, half that is 12,500 miles. Flatten that out and subtract … shit, I don't know. Stay in school kids, just in case you decide to visit Hell and want to know how far down it is.

The further he fell, the more he wondered if he should get some sleep on the way down. He thought about bouncing off the sides of whatever this hole was. In the dark, he didn't even know if he was two inches from the edges or two miles. All he could think of was a rock sticking out and dashing his brains out when he slammed into it.

Why the hell did I jump after her?

He was looking down, trying to see if there was any light below, something that would give him an idea he was approaching anything.

Then he screamed like a little girl when something grabbed him around the shoulders from behind. Whatever had just attacked him latched onto his back and was just about to choke the life out of him.

A voice growled in his ear, "What are you doing down here?"

I know that voice.

He yelled over the sound of the hot wind rushing past his ears, "Following you, you crazy woman!"

The arms released him and he could feel her moving around him in mid-air until she was directly in front of him. Her eyes were still glowing and he wasn't sure if it was just her natural state when going into battle or if she was really pissed at him.

Maybe it's a little of both.

"This is the last place I would have wanted you to go, Fredrick," she yelled above the noise of the wind rushing past their ears.

He wrapped an arm around her and pulled her closer. She raised one of her pistols and it was glowing softly, providing a very soft light between them.

"We're working this case together, remember?" he said as he stared into her eyes.

"If you kiss me, I'm going to shoot you right here."

"I wouldn't dream of it, sister. I just don't want to lose you again."

She gave him a tiny smile and looked down.

Finally, there was a bit of a red glow

appearing below. As they got closer, the red became more of an orange and then there was a mix of red, orange and yellow.

"The fires of Hell?" he asked.

She just looked up at him and nodded.

"Tell me something, sister. Are we going to get smashed to bits when we hit bottom?"

She just gave him a bit of a shrug.

"You jumped and you don't know what's going to happen when we get to the bottom?"

"I figured if Azrin can make the jump and survive, I can, too. Besides, this isn't the first time I've visited Hell."

"Been here before, have you?"

"Yes, and believe me when I tell you, it's everything you've been taught it is."

She wiggled herself around so she had her back up against him and he could see she still had the two pistols in her hands. She looked like she was ready to unleash, well, Hell on whoever she met at the bottom of this descent.

"You wouldn't have another one of those magazines with those demon killing bullets in it, would you? I only have five more rounds."

She switched one pistol to her other hand, holding both in one hand and reached into whatever magic pocket she had in her robes and handed him two mags.

"Use them carefully," she yelled.

"Good grief, sister. How many pockets do you have in there?"

"Are you seriously asking a lady about her undergarments now?"

"Um … uhh … no, I really don't want to

know."

She giggled softly, though he could just barely hear it over the wind.

She shifted one gun back to her open hand and, like a boss, flipped the safeties off with a flick of each thumb.

As he reached for his pocket, he noticed his arm was against her breasts.

That is the last damn thing I need to be thinking about right now!

To distract himself, he looked down and noticed specific features, predicting a difficult landing. Or a boiling one. Or both.

She yelled over her shoulder and said, "Remove your arm from around me! If you feel the need to touch my body, put a hand on my shoulder!"

"I wasn't thinking anything," he yelled as he put his hand on her shoulder and grabbed a fistful of sacred nun garment.

"Remember when you told Shondra to never lie to me because it was impossible?"

"You know, I actually came down here to tell you I really hate you right now!"

"That's okay, I still love you … like a brother!"

"Oh, shit!" he yelled just as they hit the ground of the underworld.

They hit on a sloping piece of ground and slid a good hundred yards before coming to a stop.

As he laid on the hot ground, trying to catch his breath, he heard the voice of the sister. It sounded strangely muted. Raising his head, he looked around and seemed to be missing one nun.

"Uh, Fredrick, can I get a little help?"

He scrambled to his hands and knees and low-crawled toward the sound of her voice. Looking over the edge, he saw she had slid a little further than he did and was now hanging onto a bit of rock.

A few hundred feet over the aforementioned bubbling, burning lake of fire.

Reaching down, he grabbed her wrist and hauled her up. When he set her down on solid ground, she wrapped her arms around him and whispered her thanks.

"Kinda glad I came now, aren't you?"

She looked up and said, "Fredrick, I am happy to have you backing me up wherever I go. I just wish you hadn't come here."

"Sister, I'll follow you into Hell to stop Azrin, if that's what it takes."

"Well, that's where we are."

He looked around at the dismal landscape that seemed to stretch out as far as he could see. It was a world of fire and smoke. He could feel the sweat running down his back as he shed his suit coat.

Looking at the coat, he realized the slide on the ground hadn't done it any favors. The entire backside was shredded. Looking down, he could see his pants weren't in any better condition, but being with the sister, it didn't seem prudent to shed what was left of them.

Removing his badge, he threw his jacket over the cliff and watched it fall into the fiery lake. It caught fire before it even touched the surface of the lake.

"Guess Hell is pretty much like what we're told it is," he muttered.

"Oh no. It's going to be much worse."

"Please tell me you're joking," he said as he looked over his shoulder at her.

"I wish I could, detective. "

Looking down from the edge, his eyes focused on the lava lake below. It took a few seconds, but he was able to discern the shapes of people in the fire below, screaming and begging for death. But the fire didn't consume them, meaning their torment would go on forever.

The sister stepped beside him and looked down. He could see tears on her face as she witnessed the suffering of the people below. He knew she was feeling every bit of pain those people were.

Climbing back up the slope, he came to a stop in front of her and asked, "So, what comes next?"

"Well, first we get you outfitted properly."

Reaching into her robes, she pulled out another rosary and had him lean down and she slipped it over his head. She took the crucifix in one of her hands and kissed and blessed it.

Looking up, she said, "Please promise me you'll never take this off."

"Are you kidding? Down here, I will hang on to it with my teeth if I have to."

He didn't fail to notice her habit was in much better condition than his suit, though it was still torn and had gaping holes. He figured it was because God liked her more than him.

"Okay," she said. "We need to climb back up to the level ground above us."

Looking up the hill, he saw it disappear into the darkness.

"Just how far up do we have to go?"

"I couldn't even tell you," she said with a sigh.

Turning and facing up the hill, he offered her his arm. She reached down and placed one pistol back in its holster. Then she gladly took his arm and they started the long climb back up the hill.

"So, Fredrick, what do you think of Hell so far?"

For some reason, he found it easy to laugh, even though he was walking through the literal Hell of the Bible.

"Well, if it weren't for the residents down here, I think it would be a great place to have a retirement home. I mean, I'd never have to shovel snow."

She laughed and said, "I don't think that saying, when]Hell freezes over', is ever in danger of happening."

They didn't say too much after that. Even though they knew they were just trying to keep the mood light, their mission seemed to demand a different tone.

The detective kept his head on a swivel, looking for anything that might be a danger to them. The sister didn't look to either side, but just kept her eyes focused on the trail in front of them.

"We haven't seen anyone other than those in the lake of fire."

She looked up at him and asked, "What do you mean?"

"I mean, we've been in Hell for what seems like hours and we haven't seen a single soul other than them."

"Hell is a vast place, Fredrick. We could walk for days and never see another person."

"Can you do me a favor, sister?"

"Sure, what can I do for you?"

"Stop calling me Fredrick."

"That's the name your mother and father gave you out of the love of their hearts."

"I know and I don't wish to belittle that, but please, just call me Fred or Bishop. Fredrick sounds a little too much like my mama when she was about to whoop my behind for doing something wrong."

"Okay. I won't call you Bishop because I'd like to think we've reached a first-name basis. But Fred? I don't know. That just sounds a little too … I don't know … unfriendly. How about Freddie?"

He laughed a little at that and said, "That will be fine, but be warned, that's what my ex-wife used to call me when we first met and then got married. Of course, that's better than what she used to call me toward the end of our marriage."

"It sounds like it didn't end nicely."

"That's an understatement," he said with a sound of wistfulness in his voice.

She squeezed his arm as they continued to climb in silence. The only sound they could hear was the sound of their footsteps and the occasional slide backwards a few inches.

Reaching the top of the climb, after what seemed like hours, they stood on a small plateau. Bishop looked around and saw nothing but smoke and fire as far as his eyes could see.

"I don't mind telling you, sister, I am scared out of my mind."

"That's understandable, but let me give you a bit of advice before we go any further. Your belief in God and His power will protect you, even down here. Lucifer and his demons will do whatever it takes to cause you to falter, knowing if they can get you to deny God or curse Him, they will have you."

He nodded as he continued to look around, expecting to see Lucifer himself, walking across the landscape toward them.

"Now comes the really scary part," said the sister.

"And what's that?"

"I need you, in the loudest voice you can muster, to announce our arrival. I need you to call Azrin."

"You're kidding? They don't already know we're here?"

"Lucifer does, but he considers us to be a minor nuisance and won't waste his time. Of course, that's because he doesn't realize a demon hunter has come into his kingdom."

"It's actually shocking to know he doesn't

worry about people coming in and out of his domain like this."

"I think he's just bored and doesn't care too much anymore."

"I would think with all the people that get sent here, he has plenty to do."

"How many people do you think are down here?"

"Oh, I don't know, but I would guess a lot."

"Not as many as you think. Most people are good in their hearts. They might not have lived their best lives before being judged, but God doesn't send his children to Hell just because they weren't absolutely perfect. Obviously, most don't reach the highest levels of the kingdom of Heaven, but most don't get sent here either."

"Only the truly evil, huh?"

"Yes. Now, stop stalling," she said. "Call Azrin to us. Make it sound like a demand."

"Oh boy," he said as he stepped closer to the edge of the cliff.

Call a demon from Hell for a face-to-face chat and make it sound like a demand. Yeah, right.

He stared out over the lake of fire and then took a deep breath. The smoke and heat filled his lungs and it surprised him he hadn't noticed it before.

"Azrin, demon from Hell! I demand you show yourself! And bring the girl with you!"

A few seconds passed and there was no response. As he went to repeat his demand, the sister reached out and took hold of his arm.

"Once is enough," she said. "You don't want to sound desperate. He heard you."

"So, you've been here before. How did that go?"

"Only once," she said, as she kept her eyes moving all around. "His Holiness said I needed to come back and get my hands dirty doing the work I was called to do from time-to-time, despite my vow not to return."

"You mean the Pope."

"Yes, Freddie, I mean the Pope. Every few months, he calls me to ask me how I'm doing."

"Well, at least he takes an interest in your well-being."

"Usually it's just to give me another assignment. He sent me here to retrieve a priest that had been snatched from his church.

"I'm assuming that turned out well."

"Well yes, and no. I returned with Father Cameron, but this experience had so affected his mind he couldn't put it behind himself once he was back in the world."

"So, he lives with the nightmare just like you and I?"

"Not anymore. He took his own life a few months afterwards."

She reached up and turned his face to hers and said, "Promise me, if you ever have urges to end yourself, you will come talk to me or the cardinal. I don't want you to harm yourself."

Looking into her eyes, he could see the complete concern she had for him.

"I promise."

Checking his pistol to make sure it was

ready to fire if needed, Bishop wondered what was taking Azrin so long to show up.

"He doesn't seem to be in a hurry to come and meet with us."

"Would you be? A man and woman just walked straight into Hell and demanded to speak with him. He's probably cowering behind Lucifer's skirt."

"Fair point," said Bishop.

As the two of them kept their eyes moving, the sound of thunder rocked the top of the hill, just about knocking them to their knees.

"You flatter yourself, little bug."

The two of them turned and saw Azrin a few yards away. One thing they didn't see was Shondra.

Bishop raised his pistol and fired without a second thought. The bullet slammed into Azrin's forehead, causing the demon to rock backwards and howl in pain.

"Do I have your attention now?" growled Bishop.

As the demon regained his footing, he looked at the detective and took one step forward. Then fell to his knees when Bishop fired again, this time striking the demon in one of his kneecaps.

"I told you to bring the girl."

The sister was trying as hard as she could not to smile.

"I don't take or …"

Bang!

Another shot and another bullet right between the demon's eyes. Again Azrin was rocked backwards by the impact, screeching he was going to kill them both.

"Oh, I'm sorry," said Bishop. "What were you saying?"

"Freddie, please watch your ammo."

"I still have two in the gun and a couple more mags. How many bullets will it take to kill this piece of filth, anyway?"

"Probably more than we have."

"That's a pity," he said as he fired the last two rounds in his gun into each shoulder of the demon. Then, in a lightning fast move, he ejected the mag and slammed a new one into the pistol.

"I'm rather enjoying shooting him, knowing I won't have to fill out a report on this. I'm not sure what I'd put in the report."

She patted him on the arm and said, "Allow me."

She put her pistol back in its holster and pulled her sword. It immediately burst into flames and sent one lightning bolt straight into the right eye of the demon.

"His bullets may not kill you, but I'm sure you remember this blade," she said as she waved it back and forth in front of his face. "How's your hand, by the way?"

Azrin cursed her and swore he was going to end the two of them.

Sister Clarice proved to be in no mood for his antics and jabbed the blade straight into one of the bullet holes Bishop had put in the demon's shoulders.

Azrin screeched in agony and tried to pull

away from the sword, but she stepped forward and embedded it deeper into his shoulder.

"My friend told you to bring the girl. Where is she?"

When the demon hesitated, she yanked the blade from his shoulder and spun around him like a ballerina. In the blink of an eye, she stabbed the blade back through his shoulder from behind.

She leaned over and whispered in his ear, "I won't ask you again."

Wrenching the sword back and forth caused the blade to spew lightning bolts into the demon's body, bringing another howl of pain from the demon's mouth.

"Would you stop it? His screeching is giving me a headache."

The sister felt a shiver of terror course through her body at the sound of the voice.

Bishop jerked around and pointed his gun at a new arrival. Two new arrivals, actually.

One, a man with dark red skin, standing about eight feet tall, dressed in black robes and two large, leathery wings protruding from his back. He had one of his clawed hands resting on the back of the second person's neck.

Shondra.

Her body was shaking like the leaves of a tree in an earthquake. Bishop could see her eyes filled with more terror than any one person should ever have to suffer. When he looked at her, he could see his own daughter.

"Lucifer," gasped Clarice. "Lower your weapon, Freddie. It won't do anything to him."

Lucifer looked at the detective and sneered, causing Bishop to lower his gun slowly.

"All we want is the girl," stammered Bishop.

The devil cocked his head and said, "All you want? Just exactly where do you think you are, Fredrick?"

Bishop bristled at the sound of his name coming off the lips of the king of Hell.

"I am in Hell," he said. "The kingdom of Satan and I seek the return of that young woman, who doesn't belong here."

Lucifer smiled again and said, "I could simply squeeze my fingers and pop her head right off her body, and there would be nothing you could do about it."

Another screech of pain rolled across the plateau, and the two of them turned to see Sister Clarice had pulled the sword from Azrin's shoulder and then slammed it through the back of his neck. The fiery blade protruded straight out of his throat.

The sister wiggled the blade back and forth, making sure Azrin knew it was there.

"You could kill her," said the sister, "that is true. But God doesn't take too kindly to you killing innocents, brought into your kingdom without just cause."

To emphasize her point, she wiggled the blade again, coming very close to relieving Azrin of his head.

"Please, master!" screamed Azrin. "Give her what she wants!"

"Silence, you worthless piece of dung!"

roared the devil.

Lucifer leaned over, his nose pressing up against the back of Shondra's ear. His pointed tongue snaked out of his mouth and ran around the top of her ear.

"You sure you wouldn't rather stay here with me?" he whispered. "I can save you an entire lifetime of pain and suffering. I can make you my queen. All you need to do is ask."

His words were smooth as honey as he licked the side of her cheek, bringing a shudder of revulsion from the young woman. She took a breath as she shivered under the touch of his hand.

"Jesus is my savior," she hissed. "You will never be."

Shondra's confession of faith in God caused Lucifer to groan in agony and pulled his hand away from her neck. Bishop could see the power of Heaven had protected her as Lucifer flexed his fingers in pain.

Holding out his hand to her, Shondra stepped away from the devil and walked toward the detective. When she reached him, he wrapped an arm around her and pulled her close.

"We're getting you out of here," he whispered in her ear.

"Send us back," commanded Sister Clarice.

"I take no orders from you!" yelled Lucifer, and he clenched and stretched his fingers to make sure they still worked. "You found your way down here. Find your own way out!"

The sister applied a little more pressure to

the sword, bringing more screams from Azrin.

"Would you like me to call one of your brothers down here? I'm sure Michael, or even Gabriel, would love to pay you a visit."

Lucifer was at a crossroads. He knew he had just met one of the most pure demon hunters the church had and he could do nothing against her.

He also knew if one of the Sisters of the Templar was in enough trouble and called for help from the archangels, they just might come to her rescue. Maybe not, but he wasn't willing to take the chance.

Lucifer moved a little closer to the center of the plateau, which backed the detective and Shondra up toward the sister and her captive demon. As they got closer, the demon reached out feebly toward them.

"Azrin! You will not touch them or harm them in any way!" thundered Satan.

The sister pulled her sword from the demon's throat and Azrin fell to the side, groaning in pain.

Clarice walked around his writhing body on the ground, not paying him any mind. As she stepped around him, she dragged the tip of her blade across his shoulder and the sword had its own bit of fun, sending lightning bolts through the demon's body, eliciting even more screams.

Stepping in front of Bishop and Shondra, she placed herself directly in front of Lucifer. She kept her blade in her hand, but knew if Lucifer decided to attack her, it would be nearly useless. Not completely useless, but it was a demon killing blade, not an archangel killing blade.

Lucifer was not a favored son of God anymore, but he was still an archangel.

Then, in a show of complete defiance, she turned her back on Lucifer and reached out and cupped the young woman's cheek.

"Be strong, sweetheart. We're going home."

She could feel Lucifer's hot breath on her neck and could see the terror in both Shondra's and Bishop's eyes.

Turning back, she looked up into the face of Lucifer and said, "You know I can't lie and say this has been fun. I will tell my superiors that when the time came, you did the right thing."

"Oh, spare me your platitudes," growled the devil. "One day, maybe soon, I shall have all three of you and then I will make your eternities more horrific than you might imagine."

"Hmm," said the sister, "don't count on it."

It became a staring match between the sister and the King of Hell. She could tell he was trying to come up with some way to keep all three of them right there in Hell.

In the end, he blinked first.

In an instant, the three of them felt lightheaded and fell over. As they hit the ground, all three of them had the thought go through their minds that they hadn't landed on the hot, burning sands of that plateau. They could feel cool blades of grass against their faces.

"Over here!"

The voice jolted the detective and he opened his eyes and then shut them again immediately. The beautiful, bright sun was shining directly into his eyes.

He could hear footsteps pounding on the ground as people were rushing to them. He held his arm up to shield his eyes from the sun and tried to raise himself up. He found he couldn't quite make it up and then realized it was because he still had a terrified young lady clinging to him.

"Hey, beautiful lady. We're home."

Shondra opened her eyes and looked around and then sat up. Bishop climbed to his feet just as the sheriff and the others ran up to them.

Or near them. They were still in the swale's bottom and the others were staring down at them from the rim.

The sister was getting to her feet and Bishop reached down to help Shondra up. When the CSI tech was standing and looked around at her friends and coworkers, she wrapped her arms around the detective, buried her face into his chest and began bawling her eyes out.

Sister Clarice went to climb out of the swale and a large hand reached down to help her. As he pulled her to the top, she looked up and smiled.

"I told you, sheriff. I was going to get her back."

"Yes, you did," he said with a look on his face that he was seeing a genuine superhero.

Especially when she took the flaming sword in her hand, raised it and kissed it, telling it what a good job it had done. Then the flames turned pink, as if it were blushing and then extinguished itself. She quickly put it in the scabbard on her back.

She heard some grunting as Bishop was trying to climb the sides of the depression with a woman clinging to him. As they got closer to the top, two other ladies reached out and took her off his hands.

A little later, as Shondra was sitting in the back of an ambulance, the sister walked over and climbed and sat next to the paramedic.

"Can you give us a moment, Jerry?"

"Sure, I ca ... How?"

Shondra reached over and patted his arm.

"Keeping secrets from the sister is impossible."

Jerry looked at her and then patted her on the shoulder.

"It's good to have you back, Shondra."

Then he climbed out, giving the two ladies some privacy.

"How are you feeling?" asked the sister.

"I feel good. No broken bones or ..."

"That's not what I mean," said the sister. "How are you feeling?"

Shondra looked at her and could feel the tears beginning to well up in her eyes again. Clarice reached over and pulled a tissue from a

211

box and then switched seats and sat next to her. She dried her eyes, putting an arm around her.

"I was so scared," said Shondra. "At first, I thought it had to be a dream. But before too long, I knew it was real. Azrin presented me to Lucifer as if I was to be his new pet. I could hear screams of pain and saw people being tortured with fire and lava."

She started crying again and the sister wrapped both arms around her shoulders and held her tight.

"It was so horrible seeing what those people were going through," Shondra cried. "I don't know if I'll ever be able to get that vision out of my head."

Sister Clarice reached out and took her hand and gave it a gentle squeeze.

"No, you probably won't ever forget what you saw and heard. And like I told the detective, if you ever have thoughts of ending your life, please come find me. I am always willing to talk."

Shondra mumbled, "If I were to kill myself, would I end up back there?"

"That's a possibility."

She sat up and looked at the sister.

"Then I intend to live to be a gray old lady."

The sister smiled and squeezed her hand and said, "That's what I want to hear. And you can always come down to the church and talk to me about anything."

Then Sister Clarice stood up and said, "I'll

let Jerry know you're ready to go to the hospital."

"Oh, no," said Shondra, jumping to her feet. "Hospitals are where people go to die. I'm ready to live. Besides, I still have a crime scene to investigate."

The sister smiled and the two of them climbed down out of the ambulance and Shondra headed directly back to work.

As Sister Clarice watched her go, she knew she was going to be alright.

"The sheriff said we were only gone for a couple of minutes."

Turning around, she saw Bishop walking toward her.

"Time moves a little faster in Hell. But remember, Freddie, eternity is a really long time."

Bishop nodded, knowing he never wanted to spend eternity in the realm he just left.

"I'm so sorry, master. I can go back up and end them. Just give me the command."

Lucifer looked down at the sniveling demon, fighting every urge to destroy him with the snap of a finger.

"I told you, you were not to touch them or harm them. Was I not clear?"

The rage in Lucifer's voice was impossible to miss. Azrin cowered away from him. This caused Lucifer to become even more enraged.

"Stand up when I speak to you!" roared the devil.

Azrin slowly climbed to his feet, keeping

his eyes down, not wanting to look at Satan.

"You were to antagonize the warrior, bringing her to the point of denouncing my Father. Then I would have her. You were not supposed to cause her to come down here!"

Azrin flinched backwards again at the sound of the rage in his master's voice, and Lucifer reached out and grabbed him by the throat. Pulling the demon forward, they were now nose-to-nose, and Azrin was trembling.

"You are not to harm the warrior or the detective! Is that clear?"

"Yes, master," croaked Azrin through his closed throat.

Lucifer released his hold on the demon and shoved him backwards. Azrin was just barely able to maintain his footing.

Then Lucifer reached out toward the demon who gasped and raised his handless arm. A new hand was growing where the sister had deprived him of his other.

"However, you are free to do whatever you wish to all those around them."

Azrin bowed his head and said, "Yes, master. Your commands are why I live."

Satan's eyes narrowed as he looked at this pathetic excuse for a demon.

"You would do well to remember that. Now get out of my sight!"

"Yes, master," said Azrin as he bowed low and then faded out of sight.

Lucifer stepped to the edge of the precipice and looked out over the fiery landscape of his kingdom. His eyes narrowed as he reveled in the sounds of the tormented souls below.

He growled, "Yes, little Maria Saletti. I shall have you, and when I do, the very foundations of Heaven will rock and fall."

He took a deep breath and a grim smile formed on his evil lips.

"Soon."

Chapter 19 – The Beast Attacks

"Can I ask you something?"

The sister looked at the detective as they headed back to the city.

"You can ask me anything, detective."

"If you called out to Heaven, would the archangels come to your rescue?"

"That would be something, wouldn't it? To see Michael come strolling in with his flaming sword, ready to do battle."

Bishop smiled and nodded.

"The answer to your question is probably not. From what they have led me to believe, the archangels, or any angels, have been forbidden to go to Hell and save anyone, no matter whether that person belongs there."

"Forbidden? Why?"

"Picture this. The archangels would love nothing more than to breach the gates of Hell and destroy Lucifer and his kingdom. The problem is, that would be the start of Armageddon. But our Heavenly Father keeps his angels on a pretty short leash to keep that from happening."

"But Armageddon is a forgone conclusion, isn't it?"

"It is, but only God gets to decide when."

"I certainly hope He waits until I am long gone from this world before He lets it begin. I don't think I want to be around for it."

"Won't do you any good."

"I get the feeling I won't like the answer, but … why?"

She smiled and said, "Because, when the last battle begins, it will empty the streets of Heaven of all the angels to do battle with the armies of Hell."

"So even after I'm dead, I still won't find any peace."

"Not for about a thousand years. But look at it this way. You'll be fighting alongside Michael and Gabriel and all the other angels. Fighting to destroy Hell and all its evil, which will lead to the eternity of the true Heaven. Do you think that would be something worth fighting for? For your daughter?"

"Are you really going to go there?" asked Bishop. "That's some dirty pool, right there."

The sister smiled slightly and said, "I'm not the angel you might think I am."

"I think you probably are. I think you're an avenging angel, ready to fight and destroy anything that causes pain and suffering here on Earth."

She laughed and said, "Please don't tell the cardinal that."

They drove on in silence for a few minutes before Bishop said softly, "I will fight for the rest of eternity to make Heaven a better place for my daughter. And I will fight at your side forever, if needs be."

He never took his eyes off the road, and it appeared he was talking more to himself than anyone else.

She reached across and patted his arm, but said nothing at first.

Then she said, "Let's get back to the

217

church. I'd like to check on Esther and also talk a little more with Bethany."

"Yes, ma'am. Let's do that."

As they walked through the backdoor of the church, Bethany came running toward them. She had been looking out the window in her room and saw them pull up.

She skidded to a stop when she saw the sister and looked her up and down.

"What in the world happened to you?"

Sister Clarice looked down and remembered her habit was in a bad way, having slid halfway down a mountainside in Hell.

She reached out and took Bethany's hand and pulled her close. Wrapping an arm around the young woman's waist, she asked, "How are you feeling?"

Someone interrupted Bethany before she could say anything.

"Yes, what happened to you?"

They turned to see the cardinal walking down the hallway. He looked at Detective Bishop and could see he was in the same state as the sister.

"Looks like both of you had an interesting afternoon."

The detective said, "An afternoon I'd prefer not to repeat soon."

"The church is going to go bankrupt keeping you in habits, sister," the padre said with a smile.

Bishop reached into his back pocket and

pulled out his wallet and extracted a $100 bill and handed it to her.

"What's this for?" asked the sister.

"For getting us out of there alive."

She smiled as she pushed his hand back.

"The church will not go bankrupt, detective. He's just kidding."

The detective looked at the cardinal, who had a smile on his face.

"If you are so inclined, there is a donation box right over there," said the cardinal, pointing at a wooden box on the wall.

Bishop walked over and dropped the bill into the box and returned to the group.

"She was amazing, sir. We wouldn't have made it out alive if it wasn't for her."

"I keep trying to tell her how indispensable she is, but she doesn't want to believe me."

"Well, we just have to keep telling her."

"Would you two stop?" said Sister Clarice. "I'm going to go get cleaned up."

As she turned and began walking away, Bethany stayed right beside her with her arm wrapped around the sister.

"It was bad, wasn't it?" asked the cardinal after they were out of earshot.

The detective turned and looked at him.

"Padre, I have never been more scared in my life. And I've gone up against some of the most evil people in this city."

The cardinal nodded knowingly and turned.

"Walk with me, detective."

As they began walking down the dark

corridor, the cardinal asked him what happened that afternoon. As they came to a small chapel off the main sanctuary, he invited Bishop to sit down in the pews.

The detective looked up at the tiny figure of Jesus on a cross hanging over the small altar. He felt like even Jesus wanted to hear how things went.

"I'm not sure she would want me to say this, but I could tell she was terrified when Lucifer showed up. But, being a true warrior of God, she sucked it up and stood toe-to-toe with the devil and demanded he return the woman we went there to save."

Cardinal Wright closed his eyes and said a silent prayer. When he opened his eyes, he looked at the detective and just shook his head.

"There are few people alive that have been in Lucifer's presence, maybe less than a dozen, which I guess now includes you. And that little lady has done it twice now. It terrifies me to my core every time she goes out to face the evil of Hell. I am afraid she might not come back."

The cardinal looked at the crucifix on the wall and crossed himself.

"You're in love with her," said Bishop.

The cardinal jerked his head around when he heard that. He took a deep breath and calmed himself before he spoke.

"Yes, detective, I love her. But not in the way you think."

The detective realized he might have overstepped with his question and thought if the cardinal wanted to rip into him, he'd deserve it.

"I love her for reasons you probably don't see. Seeing her enveloped in God's power as she drops to her knees in my office makes me uncomfortable. This is the same thing my uncle, the Pope, saw when he met her for the very first time. She is an angel walking among us. And I'd appreciate it if you didn't tell her I told you this."

"I understand, sir," said Bishop. "Do you really see it? I mean, with your eyes, like an aura or something?"

"Something like that, yes. His Holiness said when he first laid eyes on her, the light within her was so bright he almost couldn't look at her. I'm guessing you don't see it because most do not."

"No, I don't see it, but I feel it," said Bishop.

"Really?"

Bishop looked up at the crucifix and took a deep breath. He remembered back to the first time he saw her at a crime scene. She had walked right in and though officers had tried to stop her; she passed by them with little difficulty.

"I felt something the first time I walked up behind her and asked what she was doing there. I was upset she was possibly contaminating a crime scene, but more than that, I felt bad a nun was witnessing what was in front of her. She turned around and looked up at me and I felt like ... I don't know ... I can't really explain it."

"Like you were in the presence of absolute goodness?"

"Yes, but it was more than that," said the detective. "I wanted her out of there immediately. Not because I didn't want her to be there, experiencing the horror of the dead body, but because I felt so unworthy to be in her presence. Does that make any sense?"

"More than you know, detective. Nuns raised you during the second half of your childhood. Though I'm sure some of them could remind you of Army drill sergeants when you did something wrong, I'm sure you could also feel the love they had for you."

"Yes, I came to learn at a young age, the nuns can be some of the nicest and wisest people on Earth. And please don't tell her I said any of that."

Bethany sat on the sister's bed and looked at the damaged habit the sister had taken off and laid on the bed.

The sister had left the door to her closet open slightly, and Bethany could see the sword and the holsters that held the two pistols. Sitting on the floor near the closet were the two boots with the ivory handles of the daggers sticking up.

As she looked at the sister's effects, she could feel an urge to hold the sword again, to feel its power. It was almost as if the sword was calling out to her.

When she held the sword for the first time, a feeling of terror ran through her body. But after she held it the second time, with Sister Clarice's hands over hers, she knew it was the power of Heaven speaking to her.

Why would God want anyone as insignificant as me to be one of his warriors?

She could hear the shower running in the small adjoining bathroom.

She had so many questions, but the sister had put her off until after she could wash up.

So she sat patiently.

Finally, she heard the shower shut off and heard the sister drying off. A couple of minutes later, she came out of the bathroom with a towel wrapped around herself. She was running a hairbrush through her short auburn hair.

Bethany just stared at her.

"What?"

The young woman snapped out of her thoughts and looked at her.

"I don't know. It's just that seeing you like this ..."

She hesitated to saying anything else.

"It's hard for you to imagine me as a nun? Seeing me not wearing my habit?"

"Well, yes, but it's more than that. You seem like an ordinary woman and yet you are a demon hunter."

The sister smiled as she pulled some fresh underwear from a small dresser to the closet. When she pulled the towel off and laid it on the bed, Bethany turned red and averted her eyes.

"I am just an ordinary woman, Bethany. An

ordinary woman that has been called to do extraordinary work. And believe me when I say it was the last thing on my mind when I took the vows."

Bethany could glance her way only after she covered herself appropriately. As she pulled a black t-shirt from the dresser and slipped it over her head, the young woman couldn't help but giggle.

"You find my choice of attire funny?" asked the sister.

I never thought you would be a Led Zepplin fan."

'Isn't one of their more famous songs called *Stairway To Heaven*? Besides, when I was your age, I had such a huge crush on Robert Plant."

"Really?" gasped Bethany. "You surprise me more and more with each passing moment."

Reaching into the closet, the sister pulled out the harness with the sword. Pulling the sword from the scabbard, she handed it to Bethany, which the young lady was reluctant to touch. Sister Clarice just shook it at her and she reached out slowly and took it from her.

Immediately, Bethany felt the power of Heaven descend upon her shoulders again and it caused her to gasp and struggle for breath. Sister Clarice wasn't watching because she had turned her back and swung the harness around her shoulders and fastened the buckle in front.

She had a small smile on her lips because she knew what the sword was doing. She

224

hoped Bethany would get used to the feeling and would decide to be a fighter for God.

Reaching into the closet, the sister selected a clean habit from the hangers and stepping into it, pulling it up to her shoulders. The scabbard poked out slightly over her left shoulder, ready to receive the powerful sword.

Zipping the habit up in front, the black leather closed, bringing the scarlet red cross together over her chest. She immediately felt a power settle down over her, protecting her from the evil in the world.

When she turned around, she couldn't keep the smile off her face.

"You did that on purpose," said Bethany breathlessly as she laid the sword on the bed.

"Moi?"

Bethany was just barely getting her breathing back under control as the sister sat on the bed and pulled some socks on. Then she pulled her boots in front of herself.

Bethany watched as the sister pushed her feet into the boots and couldn't help but stare at the white handles of the daggers sticking up from the outsides of the boot tops.

When the sister saw what she was staring at, she said, "Tools of the trade, I'm afraid."

She stood up and pulled a fresh wimple from the dresser and pulled it on. Bethany watched as she pushed her dark hair underneath the white fabric, concealing it from the eyes of the outside world.

"That's a shame."

"What's that, sweetheart?"

"Your hair looks like it would be really beautiful if you let it grow out."

"When I first took my vows, I had beautiful hair down to the middle of my back."

"What happened?"

"Sitting in my little room in the back of that church, I combed my hair, taking pride in how beautiful it was. It was then I realized how that wasn't something I should take pride in. I took a pair of shears and cut it all off."

"That's kind of sad," said Bethany.

"Not really. Do you have any idea how hot it can get under this wimple with hair that long? The next morning, I gave the hair to a nurse at the city's children's hospital for Locks of Love."

"I take it back. Your hair is the most beautiful hair I've ever seen."

The sister smiled at her as she put her veil on. She was looking in a mirror and tried to get it just right.

Bethany jumped up and stepped behind her.

"Let me help with that."

Sister Clarice turned around and Bethany reached up and reset the veil, getting it straightened out and fastening a couple of clips underneath to keep it in place. She stepped back and looked Sister Clarice up and down.

"Perfect."

"Well, not yet, but someday," said the sister with a smile. "How is Esther feeling?"

"I think she's feeling what she lost," said Bethany. "She was crying earlier and then fell asleep as I was sitting with her. I just let her sleep. That was about three hours ago."

"Okay, we'll let her sleep a couple more hours before looking in on her."

Bethany walked back and sat down on the edge of the sister's bed, sitting a little further away from the sword than before. But then she tensed up when the sister reached into the closet and pulled the two ankle holsters out, filled with the gold-plated 9mm pistols.

Sister Clarice walked over and put one foot up on a bench at the end of the bed and wrapped the holsters around each boot.

She looked at Bethany and asked her to hand her the sword.

"No!"

"No?"

"I've held that sword enough for one day, thank you very much."

The sister giggled and walked over, picked up the sword and slipped it behind her veil and into its scabbard.

Then she leaned over, cupped Bethany's chin with her hand and looked into her eyes.

"The sword likes you."

"I'm not sure I like it."

"I felt the same way when I came in contact with it for the first time."

Then she took Bethany's hand and pulled her up.

"I'm going to tell you the same thing the sword's previous owner told me. Sister Agatha said she could see courage in me, even though I couldn't see it in myself. Then later she told me to fight."

When Bethany looked into the sister's eyes, she could see a bit of sadness.

"Sister Agatha was the owner of the sword before?"

"Yes, she was."

"What happened to her? Did she retire from demon hunting?"

"No," said the sister softly. "Azrin killed her."

The sister took a moment to gather herself before continuing.

"Back then, I didn't understand what she meant about seeing courage in me. Now when I look at you, it's as if I'm seeing you through her eyes."

Sister Clarice patted her on the shoulder and said, "I'm hungry. How about you?"

Bethany gave her a smile and the two of them walked arm-in-arm to the small dining room where one of the monks laid out a simple meal.

While dining, the sister eased the young woman's apprehension about becoming a warrior and fighting demons for the church. Sister Clarice only asked her to keep an open mind about it.

About twenty minutes later Bishop came rushing through the door and straight to them. The look on his face wasn't one she welcomed.

"Trouble?" she asked.

"In more ways than one. First, your father is here," he said looking at Bethany. "And it appears we didn't scare Arzin as much as we'd have liked. I got a call about another attack."

Bethany jumped up and ran from the hall, looking for her dad.

"Why is her father being here a problem?" asked the sister as they headed toward the door.

"You'll see as we get closer to the back door."

As they approached the back door, heading for the detective's car, she could hear some raised voices. Bethany's father was obviously throwing a fit and demanding his daughter leave with him. Bethany and the cardinal were trying to tell him to calm down.

He was having none of it.

Sister Clarice split off from Bishop and headed toward the office.

"Sister, we don't have time," said the detective.

She held up her hand to signal for just a few seconds. Stepping through the door, the sound of the man's voice lowered considerably. Apparently, the sight of a nun walking in calmed him down immediately.

Bishop heard her say, "Your Eminence, I leave this in your capable hands. Bethany, you know better than anyone what you face outside these walls. The choice is entirely yours what you do."

Without another word, she reappeared from the office and joined the detective in heading out to his car.

As he pulled out of the parking lot, he asked, "You think she'll stay put?"

"Bethany? I don't think wild horses could drag her out of here."

They drove on in silence for a few seconds before she asked, "What do we know about what we're heading into?"

"Not much. Some neighbors called about what sounded like a monster tearing a house apart and the captain immediately called me and told me to take you. I guess he's beginning to warm up to you."

She reached over and squeezed his arm and said, "He's not the only one."

He harrumphed and said, "The jury is still out on me."

Not another word was spoken for the rest of the drive.

As they pulled onto the quiet street, a familiar sight confronted them. Police cars blocked the entire street and there were a couple of ambulances, too.

As they climbed out of the car, they heard a roar coming from the house in question. That brought the sister to a stop.

"It's still going on and you're all out here?" she demanded of one of the officers.

"We can't get in, sister. The door is blocked so tight we can't budge it. We have a SWAT team on the way to breach the door."

The sister started across the street and the officer grabbed her arm. When she gave him the look of a nun with a ruler, Bishop reached out and eased his hand off her arm.

"Officer Jennings, God's SWAT team has arri ..."

Sister Clarice looked up at him and he was looking at the house. Jennings let go of her arm and she reached over and touched the detective's arm.

"What is it?"

"That car. I think I've seen it before."

Jennings spoke up and said, "This is Mary Danton's house."

Before anyone could blink, the sister set off at a dead run, straight for the steps leading to the door.

Detective Bishop took off after her, muttering, "Here we go again."

Before she reached the steps, the sister had her sword in her hands and it was spitting fire and lightning. When she reached the top step, she swung the blade and sliced the door from top to bottom. Bishop barreled past her and crashed through the door, sending its pieces scattering into the living room of Mary's house.

As he stumbled over the wreckage of the door and fell, a swinging demon's claws barely missed taking off his head. Rolling to his right, he rapidly fired three shots from his pistol, thankful he still had demon killing bullets loaded in it.

Arzin felt every bullet and roared in pain as each one hit its mark.

As the bullets knocked the demon back a couple of steps, Sister Clarice jumped over the pieces of the shattered door and swung her sword, its blade glancing off the demon's forearm. As a charred slice of demon arm fell to the ground, Arzin screeched in pain again.

"Another small piece," yelled the sister. "I shall take you apart one piece at a time if needs be."

Just as Bishop popped up and fired two more shots at Arzin, Jennings came stumbling through the door and face-to-face with the demon.

"Holy shit!" he screamed just before Arzin slammed him across the room and head-first into the wall. The sound of him hitting the wall reminded the sister of Brother Michael's body breaking on the statue of St. John.

Hearing that sound, her rage was ignited and she advanced on the demon, swinging her blade so fast, Arzin kept backing up. He was almost brought down when Bishop fired two more shots into the demon's knees and then had to reload.

The sound of more police officers running up the sidewalk got Arzin's attention and he waved his new hand at the door. Broken pieces flew at the shattered opening and sealed off the doorway. The pounding and yelling on the other side of the door was deafening.

As Bishop was reloading, he looked through the doorway to the kitchen and saw Mary laying face-down on the floor. Clambering through the door, he knelt next to the police officer and checked for a pulse. Finding a good, strong heartbeat, he turned his attention back to the battle.

The sister was still advancing on the demon and Bishop put two more bullets through the chest of the monster. Arzin stumbled back and fell against the wall, shaking the entire house when he hit.

Sister Clarice could see this was the chance she needed to bring an end to the demon's reign of terror and she went to drive her sword through its heart. When the tip of her blade pierced the black skin of the demon, he blinked out of sight, causing her to drive the sword into the wall.

A scream of frustration escaped her lips and she ordered him to return and face them. Straightening up, she turned circles in the center of the living room, her sword at the ready, expecting to see Arzin reappear at any moment.

The demon remained absent from the room.

Hearing a groan behind her, she turned around to see Officer Jennings trying to push himself up. Moving to his side, she reached down and helped him to his feet.

"Let's get you out of here, Brent," she said as she helped him toward the door.

As they reached the door, she stabbed at it with her blade and it fell to the ground in pieces. There was a crowd of dumbfounded officers just looking at her and Jennings. She turned him over to a couple of other officers and refocused her attention on the room.

Arzin was still nowhere to be seen, but that didn't lessen her feeling that he was closer than she liked.

Walking to the door of the kitchen, she saw Bishop trying to see if he could wake Mary up.

She steadfastly refused to open her eyes. Though she was still alive, Arzin had dealt her a serious blow and looked like she might be in a coma.

"I can't wake her," said Bishop, his eyes on the verge of tearing up.

"Is she breathing?"

"Yes."

"Is her heartbeat strong?"

"Yes."

"Then she's still alive. Don't go to pieces on me, Freddie."

Bishop stood up just as a couple of paramedics stormed into the room. He looked like he wanted to say something pithy to the nun, but realized she was right. He had seen many terrible things in his life and Mary was not on that list.

"Let's get out of here and let these fine gentlemen have the room," she said, motioning him out.

As he followed her toward the front door, she asked, "You really like her, don't you?"

Bishop came to a stop and she turned and looked up at him. She had a bit of a smirk on her lips.

"Officer Danton? No!"

"Don't lie to me, Freddie. It never works."

"Okay, maybe just a little."

"Hey, I don't judge. Besides, she is a nice lady and one of the very few you know that will understand your chosen profession better than most."

Bishop was about to agree with her when

the color drained from his black face. Grabbing for his gun, he tried to bring it up as fast as he could, but it wasn't fast enough.

Sister Clarice tried to turn, but felt a searing pain in the middle of her back, knocking the breath from her lungs.

Bishop's hand came up and he fired two shots straight into the face of Arzin, knocking him backward.

As the sister slumped to the ground, Bishop tried to grab her and fired two more shots.

Arzin laughed and disappeared in a flash.

As he wrapped an arm around the sister, Bishop felt the sickening crunch of charred skin in his hand.

"I don't feel so good, Freddie."

Looking down into her glassy eyes, he could see she was fading into unconsciousness quickly.

He could feel the sword in her scabbard turn as cold as ice and he could tell it was doing whatever it could to ease her pain.

"I need paramedics here now!" he screamed.

As she went to the ground, he went with her and ended up sitting and cradling her in his arms. He was about to yell for help again when he saw a couple of paramedics rushing toward the door.

"Hang on, sister. Help is coming."

When the paramedics turned her over to see the damage, Bishop felt his heart stop. Arzin had driven his open hand into her back, leaving a large, charred imprint of his demon hand. His hand had burned right through the leather of the sister's habit, leaving a wound so deep the detective could see bone.

As the paramedics worked on her, she weakly said, "Freddie, take my weapons and deliver them to the cardinal. He'll keep them safe."

"I'll only do that if you promise not to go."

"I'm afraid that may be out of my hands."

"Don't you say that!"

"Please, Freddie, do this for me."

Then she stopped talking.

"Sister? Sister!"

"She's still breathing," said one paramedic. "Just unconscious. We need to move her now."

"Just a minute," said Bishop as he began removing the belt holding the scabbard. Then he removed the ankle holsters and dagger sheathes from her boots.

When he had her entire armory in his hands, they lifted her onto a stretcher and began pushing it over the debris and out of the house.

As he stood there, watching them go, the other paramedics asked him quietly to move so they could wheel Mary out of the same door. As he moved aside, he looked down at the police officer on the stretcher. Reaching out, he ran a hand over her cheek.

"Be strong, Mary. It's not your time."

Standing in the middle of the street and watching the two ambulances roll away from the scene, Bishop felt the weight of the entire world on his shoulders.

It took him a good five minutes before he could make his way to his car. He put the sister's weapons in the backseat before sitting down in the driver's seat. It was another five minutes before he started the car and pulled away from the scene.

When he walked in the church's back door, the cardinal walked out of his office. The color drained from the old man's face in an instant when he saw the detective carrying the sister's effects.

"Detective, where's Sister Clarice?"

Bishop took a little longer than he should have answering and the cardinal assumed the worst.

"Oh, dear God," said the cardinal as he looked like he was going to fall to the floor.

"No, no, padre. She's still alive, but it doesn't look good."

The padre walked a few steps and sank down on a pew, gripping the sides of it so tight his knuckles turned white.

"What happened?"

Bishop could barely hear the man speak. His voice was on the verge of breaking into tears.

"Azrin happened," said Bishop. "He came out of nowhere and before she could react, he attacked her."

He set the weapons down on the bench next to the cardinal and sat down on the other side.

"I wasn't fast enough," said Bishop as he

buried his face in his hands.

Neither man spoke for a minute. Bishop was feeling more pain in his soul than he knew what to do with.

A shudder went through his body when he felt a hand settle down on his shoulder.

"Do not blame yourself for what happened."

"If I had been just a little faster, I could have fired and slowed him down. She would have had time to react and defend herself."

"Detective Bishop, do you think she is blaming you for what happened?"

"I wouldn't be shocked if she turns out to blame me."

"She is not the kind of person who blames others, so I would be very surprised if she blamed you. That isn't in her nature."

Silence again for a moment.

"We always knew this could be a possibility," said the cardinal.

Bishop exploded up from the bench and turned to the cardinal.

"Then why let such a sweet, kind soul do this kind of work?" he raged.

"Please calm yourself, detective."

"Calm myself? She should never have been pushed into this kind of life!"

During the few seconds after his outburst, the sound of feet hobbling down one of the corridors could be heard, along with the rattling of metal. Bishop turned just in time to see Esther maneuver her walker around the corner.

"What happened?"

The cardinal jumped up and went to her.

"Sister, you should still be in bed. Let me help you back there."

"Don't patronize me, cardinal. What is the fuss all …"

She stopped when she saw the weapons laying on the bench.

"Where is Sister Clarice?" she asked, unable to take her eyes off the sword and pistols.

When Bishop's head dropped, she did the same the cardinal had done and assumed the absolute worst. And her knees failed her. It was a miracle the two men could catch her before she hit the floor.

The cardinal scooped her up in his arms and said, "Back to bed with you, Esther."

As he began walking down the hall, he said over his shoulder, "Please bring the sister's things, detective."

Bishop turned around and walked back to the bench and picked up the weapons. As he did, he looked into the gold hilt of the sword and thought it looked a little less bright than usual. Holding the belt up, he stared at the sword.

"You know I'd do anything to help her right now."

He knew he shouldn't, but he ran the fingertips of his free hand up and down the gold metal. He felt a slight shock, but didn't feel the need to stop touching the blade. In his mind, he heard the blade speaking to him.

I know you would and it may come down to that.

Chapter 20 – Leaving The Sanctuary

Bishop walked into Esther's room just as the padre was laying her down and pulling the covers back over her. Esther opened her eyes and the first thing she looked at were the weapons in the detective's hands.

"What happened to her?"

He gritted his teeth, not wanting to answer her, but finally decided it would do no good to keep it from her.

"Arzin attacked her," he said as he felt the anger rise again in his chest. "She's been hurt."

"Is she going to be okay?"

"I don't know, Esther, I don't know."

He hung his head and said, "It doesn't look good."

"No!"

He and the padre spun around to see Bethany standing in the doorway. It broke Bishop's heart to see the look of pure grief settle on the young woman's face. Even he had seen how close to the sister she had become.

Bethany clung to the frame of the door and the padre walked over and put an arm around her shoulders and led her to the chair beside Esther's bed. As Bethany sank into the chair, Esther reached out and took one of her hands.

"Be strong, child. It's not her time."

Bethany looked at her and a myriad of

241

questions floated across her face.

The padre walked over and took the weapons from Bishop and laid them on the bed in front of Bethany.

"I want you to look after these," he said to the bewildered girl.

"She's not dead!"

Esther squeezed her hand and said, "He knows that, dear. He just wants you to look after these items because …"

She looked at the padre and asked, "Why do you want her to look after them? Surely they would be safer in your office."

The cardinal looked at her and then at the girl.

"Show her, Bethany."

"I don't want to," cried Bethany.

She looked up at him and cried, "If I take hold of the sword, it will be as if I am accepting her death."

"Please show her," said the cardinal. "You and Esther have more in common than you know."

The tears were running fully down her face as she reached for the hilt of the sword. Wrapping her fingers around the gold handle, she pulled it from the scabbard. As she held the sword up, it filled the air with electricity.

Bethany's brown hair stood straight out as small lightning bolts snapped from the blade to her hair and hands. Her brown eyes glowed and became a bright golden color.

Esther's mouth opened slightly as she watched the spectacle. A couple of lightning bolts flashed out and touched the old woman's hand.

It didn't escape Bishop's notice that Esther didn't flinch when the charges touched her hand. It was almost as if her breathing became stronger and a mask of determination settled over her face.

After a few more seconds, Esther picked up the scabbard and held it toward Bethany, who slid the blade back into the holder and released the hilt. Her hair slowly fell back to her shoulders. The glow in her eyes faded, though if a person were to look closely, there were now little gold specks mixed in with the brown of her eyes.

She finally let out the breath she had been holding since the episode started.

"Cardinal Wright, may I have a few moments alone with this extraordinary young woman?"

"As you wish, sister," he said as he turned and ushered Bishop out of the room and pulled the door closed.

"Let's go to my office," said the padre. "I could use a cup of coffee."

"Do you have any soda?"

"Oh that's right, you don't drink coffee."

As they entered the office, the padre motioned to a chair as he walked over to the coffee machine and poured a mug. Then he opened the small refrigerator and pulled out a cola.

"Why do I feel there is more to Esther than meets the eye?"

"You're a great detective," said the cardinal without turning around, "with a sense for when things are awry."

Turning around, he walked over and handed the soda to Bishop and set the mug down on the small table next to the chairs. Then retrieved a small basket of sugars and creamers and set them down next to the mug of coffee.

Taking a seat in the chair next to Bishop's, he stirred some sugar into his coffee and then sat back and blew on it to cool it down a little.

"Right now, I'm sure Esther is telling Bethany that before she met and fell in love with Marvin, she was a Sister of the Templar."

"She used to be a Catholic nun?"

"Oh no. Remember, I said earlier that not all the Sisters of the Templar were nuns or even Catholic."

"Yes, I believe you even surprised Sister Clarice with that one."

"Yes, I guess no one ever got around to

telling her that. Esther is Jewish, as was Marvin, obviously. Esther saved Marvin one night from a demon and he was smitten with her from the moment he laid eyes on her. And to say she was quite taken with him would be an understatement."

"How did she work her life as a demon hunter around being married and having a family?"

"Oh, she didn't. She left the order behind to devote herself to her new life."

"And the church let her leave the Sisters of the Templar to be with him?"

"Detective, the church would never stand in the way of true love and there was never a love more true than between those two."

"I guess that's why she didn't act surprised when the sword was stinging her with those lightning bolts."

"They weren't stinging her. They were getting reacquainted. At one time, she carried all those weapons. They passed to Sister Agatha and then to Sister Clarice and I'm pretty sure she doesn't even know of Esther's past involvement."

After they sat and talked for a few more minutes, there was a light knock on the door. The cardinal called for them to enter and they turned to see Bethany come into the office. She was carrying the belt with the scabbard and sword, but they noticed she didn't have the holsters with pistols or the daggers.

Bishop got to his feet and gave her a hug.

"How are you doing, young lady?"

"I'm doing okay," she said.

As she broke away from the detective, she saw the cardinal was looking at the sword in her hand.

"Esther says I should keep this with me. I don't want to carry the guns, but she was insistent that I carry some sort of weapon."

"She's a smart lady," said the padre. "You would do well to listen to her."

"So, she was a demon hunter, too?"

The padre nodded and said, "A fiercer warrior you will not find."

"Other than Sister Clarice," said Bethany, with a hitch in her voice.

The padre took a breath and then said, "Forgive me. You are correct."

"How is Esther doing?" asked Bishop as he pulled a chair over for her to sit in.

"She's putting on a brave face, but I'm sure it's all an act. She can't even mention Sister Clarice's name without breaking down."

The two men nodded, knowing just how the old woman was feeling.

"The reason I came to your office," said Bethany, "is because I'm going to see Sister Clarice."

"Not a good idea."

She looked at the padre and he could see the fire in her eyes. Even the little bits of gold now in her eyes glowed and he was sure it wasn't because she was happy. It also didn't escape his notice the hilt of the sword began to glow.

"Cardinal Wright, I am not a Catholic, nor am I part of the Sisters of the Templar. I didn't come here to ask if I could go see her. I came here to tell you I was going."

"Sister, you are unprotected outside the walls of this sanctuary. Azrin might choose your excursion as an opportunity to come after you."

She stood firm and looked at him.

"I certainly hope so. I'd like to have a little talk with him."

"While your bravery is quite admirable, I can't sanction it."

Bishop stood up and put a hand on her shoulder and said, "I'll take you."

"Detective!"

"Padre, I'd like to have a chat with our friend from Hell, myself. Now, can I ask, do you have anymore of those demon killing bullets? I'm running low."

The padre took a deep breath and let it out slowly. Looking up at the two of them, he saw a united front and his chances of swaying them were very low. Pushing himself up, he walked to the door.

"Come with me, you two fools. And those bullets do not kill demons, only slow them down."

Leading them down the dark hallway, they found themselves outside Sister Clarice's chambers. The padre pushed the door open and motioned them through.

Walking over to the wardrobe, he pulled the doors open and pushed aside the sister's habits hanging on hangers. There was a compartment behind the clothing, with a lighted number keypad. After entering a code, the door popped open and he stepped back.

"Take what you need."

Bishop stepped forward and let out a soft whistle. The compartment was filled with about a dozen boxes of bullets, each labeled as containing one hundred rounds each.

He ignored the boxes, though. His eyes were drawn to the dozens of filled magazines stacked neatly next to the boxes. The sister obviously liked to have plenty of ammunition at the ready.

Reaching in, he pulled out six magazines and checked them to make sure they would fit his service weapon. They were a perfect match.

After loading a fresh magazine into his pistol, he slipped it back into his shoulder holster under his jacket. He turned around and could see the look on the padre's face said this was a terrible idea.

The padre looked at Bethany and said as he stepped back to the wardrobe, "Let's get you ready, too, sister."

"I wish you would stop calling me that. I am unworthy of being called that when compared to Sister Clarice."

He swung around and looked at her.

"Bethany, one thing you will find that will protect you as you venture outside these walls is your faith in God. I know it might be a little weak right now, but rest assured, He has great faith in you. Catholic or not, you will always be worthy of the title, Sister."

She looked at him and he could see the tears forming in her eyes. As she bit her lips, her hair stood out again and she held up the sword she had been holding. It was glowing, with her fingers firmly wrapped around the hilt.

"I wish it would stop doing that," she said, almost in a whisper.

The padre smiled and said, "No, you don't. It's just showing it likes you and will do everything in its power to protect you."

Turning back to the wardrobe, he reached inside and pulled out a black leather jacket. Holding it up, he compared it to her body.

"Looks like it will be a perfect fit."

Bethany's mouth was hanging open. Her eyes were fixed on the jacket and the emblems it bore.

"I can't wear that," she stammered.

"You can and you will. I'm not asking you to wear it, I'm telling you."

Looking into her fierce eyes, he could tell there was no fight in them. Just uncertainty.

"Bethany, you can't go walking around carrying that sword like that," he said. "This will help conceal it."

He laid the jacket on the sister's bed and held out his hand for the belt she held in her hands. When she handed it to him, he turned her around and held the straps out and she slipped her arms through them.

Turning her back around, he fastened the two straps in front, one above her breast and the other just below. Then, picking up the jacket, he helped her put it on and then told her to zip it up. When she did, the red cross embossed on the front came together seamlessly.

Bishop, who was standing behind her, said, "That is one righteous looking jacket."

He was looking at the red cross on the back, which took up most of the surface. When she turned and looked at him, he saw the cross on the front.

"Looks like you're protected front and back," he said with a smile.

"Detective," said the padre, "it is your job to watch her back."

Bishop nodded and said, "Understood."

"Now, young lady. You can probably feel the scabbard is angled slightly across your back. The hilt is just over your left shoulder. Reach back with your right hand and pull it out."

Bethany reached back and felt the sword move slightly to meet her hand.

"That's weird," she said as she pulled the blade out. "It moved."

"It will do whatever it needs to get into your hand easier. Now, put it back."

When she did, the tip of the sword found the opening to the scabbard easily. After sliding it down, she fluffed her hair over it and it was invisible to anyone not looking for it.

Standing back, the two men looked at her.

"I'd say she looks quite like a warrior," said Bishop.

"Looks can deceive, detective."

"You're supposed to be building her up, padre."

"NO! What I should do is lock her into her room and forbid her from leaving this church! I feel it is a grave mistake letting her leave the safety of this sanctuary."

"I'm sorry, padre," she said in a soft voice. "I just need to see her."

"I know," he said with a sigh, "and I apologize for raising my voice. It's just that you fought with your father this afternoon, telling him you would not leave these walls until you knew it was safe. And now, you're walking out the doors freely."

"Let's go, Bethany," said Bishop. "I want to get you there and back here as soon as possible."

Before they could leave, the padre reached into the bottom of the wardrobe and pulled out a small bag. Taking one of the sister's habits off the hanger, he rolled it reverently and slipped it into the bag. He also opened a drawer and pulled out one of the sister's customary black t-shirts and smiled at the Iron Butterfly logo on the front.

"In-A-Gadda-Da-Vida," he said with a smile on his lips.

After placing the t-shirt in the bag, he zipped it up and handed it to Bishop.

"From what you told me, the habit she was wearing is destroyed. She'll need these."

"She really is going to bankrupt the church, isn't she?" asked Bishop with a grin.

The cardinal gave a half-hearted smile at the comment as Bishop followed Bethany out of the room and down the hallway.

Before the two of them walked out the back door to the detective's car, the padre stopped them and gave each one a blessing. Then he stood just inside the door and watched them climb into Bishop's car and drive away.

I hope I didn't just make the most monumental mistake of all time.

Chapter 21 – A Hero In Need

Walking into the hospital, Bethany suddenly felt like this was a mistake. Not that she was feeling danger lurking around the corner. She was pretty sure she didn't have the same abilities to sense something bad like Sister Clarice.

Her hesitancy centered around her fear of seeing the sister in the kind of condition she heard the detective describe. The last thing she wanted to see was her new friend laying in a bed, barely clinging to life. She wasn't sure she was going to be able to handle this.

Bishop pulled his badge as he approached the front desk and asked where the sister was. After checking, the nurse on duty said she had just been taken from surgery to the ICU, but was sure there would be no visitors allowed at this point.

The detective gave her a look that probably could have melted steel and the nurse just pointed down one corridor. As they were leaving, Bethany looked at the young nurse and mouthed an apology.

Stopping at the desk for the ICU, the detective explained they were there to see the sister and wouldn't take no for an answer. At first, the nurse put up a small fight, but when Bishop asked to see Dr. Collins, the nurse jerked back.

"Dr. Collins is dead, detective."

"What?"

"He died yesterday morning on his way to work. They still haven't told us how it happened, but we've heard rumors his car went off the road near his home. It makes little sense, though."

"How so?" asked Bishop.

"The road was flat and straight. There was no rain or anything like that. And his car was found over one hundred yards off the road in the trees. One paramedic that worked the scene said there was no way he could have driven the car into those trees."

Bishop looked at Bethany.

"Azrin," she whispered.

He turned back to the nurse and said, "We need to see her now! I don't care what rules are broken or who we have to walk over."

The young nurse swallowed and nodded, leading them around the counter and back into the unit.

Bethany almost cried out when she saw the sister laying face-down on a burn bed to keep her back off the surface. She could see a small puddle of water on the floor directly under the sister's face and realized it was tears.

The sister moaned, but they were sure it must have been unconscious. Surely the sister was sedated to help ease her suffering.

There was a sheet suspended over the sister's body by a few inches and when the detective looked under it, he felt his knees just about buckle. Though he had already seen the wound, its severity was almost more than he could take.

Bethany saw it and let out a small cry.

"It's not as bad as it looks."

The tiny, soft voice shocked both of them as they realized the sister was awake and knew they were there.

Bethany dropped to her knees at the head of the bed and looked up into the blue eyes of the sister. Sister Clarice gave her a pained smile.

"Hi, sweetheart." Then, looking at the jacket the young woman was wearing, she said, "That coat looks good on you."

Bethany smiled and reached up with a tissue and wiped the tears from the sister's face.

"I'll do anything necessary to give it back to you."

The sister smiled and then said, "Detective, have you stopped looking at my bum, yet?"

The nurse let out a small laugh as the detective's face turned seven different shades of red.

"Your bum is covered, young lady."

"Oh, is it? I can't really feel anything down there right now."

"Are you paralyzed?" gasped Bethany.

"No, sweetie. I'm just so full of pain killers I can't feel much of anything right now."

Bishop bent down and looked up into her eyes.

"Hi, beautiful lady."

"Stop flirting with me," wheezed the sister.

"Never," he said with a grin.

"I think it's time to get me out of here."

"I don't think that's such a good idea," said Bishop.

The nurse spoke up and said, "I have to agree with the detective. You won't be leaving this room for quite a while."

The sister shook her head as much as she was able.

"Oh, ye of little faith."

Looking at Bethany, she said, "I feel as if that jacket isn't the only thing of mine you've brought. If I know the cardinal, he never would have let you out of the church without some kind of weapon and I can sense which one it is."

Bethany nodded and reached behind her shoulder and pulled the sword from the scabbard. The nurse's eyes went wide as it extended itself and began glowing and spitting lightning.

In a raspy voice, the sister said, "Lay it on my back along the wound."

Bethany stood up and reached the sword under the sheet as the nurse moved around to see what she was doing. When the sword was laid flat on her back, it began spitting more sparks and lightning and the sister's body jerked and convulsed.

"We need to take that off her," demanded the nurse.

"Please," gasped the sister. "Leave it."

Bishop reached out and guided the nurse back, telling her it was going to be okay. At least, he hoped it would be okay. For all he knew, it was going to kill her.

For the next several minutes, the sword sparked and hissed, sending electricity through the woman's body, bringing a few cries of anguish from her.

An older doctor came rushing into the room, demanding to know what was going on. He pulled out his phone and was going to call security, but Bishop reached out and took the phone out of his hand.

"Watch and learn, doctor," he said.

"Oh my God," said the nurse, who was standing in a place where she could see under the sheet.

Bethany was just holding the sister's hand and didn't look, but Bishop and the doctor did.

What they saw just about floored them.

Where the sword was sparking and sending lightning into her body, the skin was growing back and closing the wound. Within seconds, the bones the detective had seen earlier were no longer visible.

Tears dripped from the sister's face and it was clear this was not a painless process. She was in severe agony, but what they were seeing helped them to stay their hands and let it run its course.

Bethany kept drying the sister's face and a couple of times, cupped her face with her hands and kissed her on the top of her head.

"Hang in there, sister," she said. "I think it's almost over."

Sister Clarice reached forward with one hand and clutched at one of Bethany's and held on. The younger woman wrapped her other hand around the sister's and held it tight. She could feel the pain in the sister's body with every tight squeeze of the sister's fingers.

After about ten more minutes, the activity from the sword lessened. The sparks and lightning were dying down and it almost completely healed the damage to her back. The sister could finally breathe a little easier and loosened her grip on Bethany's hands, though the younger woman wouldn't let go.

Finally, the sword went dark and silent.

"Oh, I hope I never have to go through that again," gasped the sister.

Bethany released her hand and stood up. Looking under the sheet, she could see the covering over the sister's bottom had shifted. She reached under and covered her back up.

"Stop looking at her bum, detective," said Bethany.

"Well, it was rather nice," he said with a small grin.

"Oh, would you two stop it," said the sister as she tried to push herself up.

Bethany and the detective helped her into a sitting position on the bed and then she realized she was also uncovered in the front. Quickly grabbing the sheet from the bed, Bethany covered her up and then looked at the doctor and Bishop.

"Could you two please give us a little privacy?"

"I still need to examine her," stammered the doctor. "I'm still not sure what I just saw."

With a still weak voice, the sister said, "You just witnessed a miracle, doctor. Now, I need to dress and get back to the safety of the church."

The doctor looked at her and she could still see doubt on his face.

"Listen, doctor. I understand your reluctance to allow this, but if you still feel the need to check on me, please stop by the church.

You can do it there. While I stay here, I not only bring danger to myself but also to everyone here."

"Let's step out for a few minutes, doc," said Bishop as he handed the bag he still carried to Bethany.

After the men left, the nurse went to a small closet and pulled out the sister's boots and clothing. Holding up the damaged habit, she let out a soft whistle.

Sister Clarice looked at it and moaned.

"That was one of my favorite habits. Azrin better not show his face for quite some time."

Without warning, Bethany grabbed the sister by the sides of her face and kissed her right on the lips. When she pulled back, still holding the sister's face, the shock was quite clear in the nun's eyes.

"Don't you ever let something like that happen to you again," implored the younger woman. "I love you and never want to see you in that kind of pain again."

Sister Clarice reached up and cupped the side of Bethany's face.

"Yes, mother," said Clarice, though she had to fight the urge to pull Bethany's hands away. As they were on the sides of her face, she was catching glimpses of the younger woman's life. Some of those glimpses were not things she wanted to see. Her mother, though not evil, was one of the most uncaring women she'd ever experienced.

For the next few minutes, the two women helped her get dressed. Even though the sword had done what it could to heal her, she was still weak and couldn't move without some stiffness.

"I guess it will take some time to get back to full strength," she said as she struggled to pull the zipper up on the front of her habit. Being a somewhat form-fitting piece of clothing, it was fairly tight. Bethany reached out and pushed the sister's hand away and zipped it up for her.

"I might need some help for a few days."

Their faces weren't more than a few inches apart when Bethany said, "Whatever you need, no matter the time of day, I'll be there for you."

"I like your eyes," said the nun with a smile.

"Yeah. That thing did it," said Bethany, motioning to the sword still laying on the burn bed. "It's actually affected the way I see things."

"One thing you'll learn about that sword is it has a sense of humor."

Bethany looked at the sword and said sarcastically, "Haha."

The sword just glowed a little before fading back to normal.

After they helped the sister get her boots on, Bethany realized the padre hadn't sent a new veil or wimple.

"That's okay," said the sister. "I think I can manage a few minutes with the wind in my hair."

Bethany smiled as she began taking off the jacket she was wearing.

"What are you doing?" asked the sister.

"I was going to give you the belt with the sword holder."

"First off, it's called a scabbard. And second, keep it on and put the sword back where it belongs. I'm in no condition to wield it. It will be better in your hands for the time being."

Bethany zipped the coat back up while the sister picked up the sword. Holding it up, she thanked it for healing her. It answered by sending a spark straight into the tip of her nose, bringing a squeal of surprise.

"What was that?" asked Bethany.

"It's still mad at me for letting myself get surprised and attacked like that."

Bethany took the sword from her and looked at it. Then she smiled as she slipped it behind her right shoulder and back into the scabbard.

"I don't know about the sword being better in my hands," she said. "I have no training with anything like it."

"That can change," said the sister. "All you need to do is ask."

The nurse finished rolling the damaged habit and other items and stuffed them into the bag and zipped it up.

"All finished," she said as she picked up the bag, intending to give it back to the detective.

The sister reached up and caressed the nurse's face.

"Thank you for taking such good care of me. In the state I was in, I wasn't aware of who you were, but I could feel your spirit watching over me."

A tear ran down the cheek of the nurse as she said, "I have a little sister who is a postulate right now. When I saw you come in, I could only see her face and it terrifies me she may face the things you do."

Sister Clarice reached up and touched the nurse's cheek.

"Very few of us ever face the evil I do. She will most likely go through her entire life facing nothing more evil than an obstinate teenager."

The nurse laughed softly and then threw her arms around the sister's shoulders and hugged her.

"Thank you, sister. Please be safe out

there."

After they parted, Sister Clarice said to Bethany, "I think it's time to get back to the church. As quickly as possible."

When Bethany walked over and pulled the door open, Bishop was standing there. When he saw the sister walking through the door, his smile could not have been any bigger.

"You look ready to do battle again."

She smiled and said, "Not for quite some time, I'm afraid."

"No matter. It's good to see you on your feet again."

He turned and offered his arm and she gladly took it. After she had signed out of the hospital, they quickly got her in the car and headed back to the church. The sister sat in the front seat with him, as Bethany sat in the back seat.

During the drive, Bishop told her about what happened to Dr. Collins and she let out a small cry.

"Can you inquire about it? I suspect it was Azrin, but I shouldn't jump to conclusions."

"Will do."

As they walked into the back door of the church, the cardinal met them, who unabashedly grabbed her in a bear hug. He only let go when she groaned in a bit of pain.

"Don't you ever get hurt like that again!"

he commanded her.

She smiled at Bethany and said, "That point has already been made."

Bethany took her by the hand and said, "Let's get you to bed."

As she was being led away, she looked over her shoulder and said, "I have a mother hen now."

"And you listen to her!" said Bishop.

As they disappeared around the corner, the cardinal looked at Bishop.

"What's that look for, detective?"

Bishop just shook his head.

"Until about an hour ago, I was sure we were going to lose her. But then I saw something I still can't wrap my head around."

As Bethany helped Sister Clarice get undressed and into bed, she found it easier to do things for the sister. Things like undoing the laces on her boots and pulling them off. Things like getting her out of the habit and helping her into one of her granny nightgowns.

After getting her into bed, she went to the bathroom and got her a glass of water and set it on the nightstand next to the bed.

"Bethany, there is something I need to say to you and I don't want you to misunderstand."

The younger woman sat down on the edge of the bed and took her hand.

"What is it?"

Sister Clarice just looked at her for a few seconds before speaking.

"When you kissed me in the hospital, that was unexpected. I would ask that you never do that again."

Bethany looked down, not wanting to meet the nun's eyes.

"I'm really sorry about that," she said softly. "When the detective returned to the church with your weapons and told us what had happened, I was certain I was going to lose you. But after the sword healed you and I knew I had you back, I guess I couldn't take it anymore."

She looked up at the sister and said, "I love you, Sister Clarice and I don't ever want to feel that way again."

The nun squeezed her hand and said, "You have to know that I will never love you like that. I will love you like a sister and fellow future warrior. But my heart belongs to God. It always has and it always will."

Bethany closed her eyes and nodded. Then she lifted the sister's hand to her lips and kissed it.

"I will make a better effort at controlling myself," she said.

The sister smiled and said, "Thank you."

Bethany could see the sister's eyes were

getting heavy and she stood up.

"Get some sleep, sister. I'll check on you in the morning."

"Good night, sweetheart," said the sister as she settled back into the pillows and closed her eyes.

As Bethany stepped into the dark hallway and pulled the door closed behind her, she felt a tear run down her cheek. As she wiped it away, she felt another sensation she wasn't sure she would ever be able to get away from.

The feeling of the sister's lips pressed against hers at the hospital.

How could I have been so stupid? She'll never trust me again.

She felt a vibration on her back and remembered the sword still placed there.

Walking to her room, she closed the door and pulled the sword from its scabbard. It started glowing and sent a surge of power through her arms and into her chest.

A vision opened in her mind, showing her the love the sister had for all the people she came in contact with. It was a love that was absolute and without condition.

However, the love the sister felt for Bethany went much deeper than that. Though she had no siblings, she felt as if their bond was even stronger than if they were actually sisters. A bond that showed Bethany the sister would lay down her life to protect her if needs be.

Something she hoped the sister would never find the need to do.

Chapter 22 – I Want To Play

Small sounds in the dark house didn't seem too out of place for her as she walked down the hallway toward her bedroom. It didn't cross her mind that she was alone in the home, alone ever since she and her husband had parted ways.

Angelica still harbored a small amount of animosity in her heart toward Freddie. Not that she didn't love him. She still did. It was his refusal to leave the force and find another job that wouldn't put him in the firing line every time he walked out the door to go to work.

It was just too much for her. Sitting at home every night, seeing the news stories about police shootings and more on the television caused her mind to conjure up every bad thing that could possibly happen to him.

Turning off all the lights in the house, she moved to the bedroom she used to share with Freddie. Almost every single night, she would stop at the doorway and look at the king-size bed and wish she didn't have to crawl into it alone.

Taking a deep breath, she refused to let herself cry about this. He had made his decision and she would not go back on hers.

Pulling back the covers, she took off her clothes and sat down on the edge of the bed.

The cool of the evening prickled at the skin of her naked body, but for some reason she felt hot.

She reached over and picked up her phone and considered calling Ashley and finding out how she was doing, but looking at the time, she decided it was a bit late. She made a promise to call in the morning.

Setting the phone back on the nightstand, her hand bumped against the 9mm pistol and she pulled back from it. The magazine of bullets laid next to it, but not in it. The gun was completely empty and unloaded.

A shiver ran through her body as she looked at the gun. Freddie had taken her to the shooting range a few times and they found out she was a natural with a 9mm pistol.

That was fifteen years ago and she hadn't touched the gun since then. It got locked into a gun box and stuck deep in the back of the hall closet. That's where it stayed until a couple of days ago.

She trembled as she remembered the look on Freddie's face and the quaver in his voice. Something was scaring him and if it scared him, she was terrified. She had falsely believed nothing could ever scare her ex-husband.

Reaching over, she picked up the gun and the magazine. Checking the weapon, she looked at the magazine. She looked at the top bullet and could see it was different somehow, but didn't know enough about bullets to know what it was.

Slamming the magazine into the grip, she felt it click into place. Her hands trembled when she racked a round into the chamber. Checking the safety one last time, she slid the gun under the pillow that used to cradle Freddie's head.

She turned off the light and laid down, facing his side of the bed, wishing she could see his head laying on the pillow next to hers. Before she met and married him, she had not been in the habit of sleeping naked, but after they went to bed together that first time, she never wore nightclothes again.

Hundreds of times she had fought the urge to pick up the phone and ask him to come back and share their bed again. And hundreds of times she had beat back that urge, not allowing herself to show a moment of weakness.

A tear fell from the tip of her nose to her pillow and she wiped it away. She desperately wanted to feel his hands on her body again.

Stop it, Angel. He's gone and that's that.

Then she gasped and then cried even harder. She had used his pet name for her. Something she had never done since the day she forced him out the door.

Call him tomorrow and see if there's still a

chance for us.

As she cried silently into her pillow, she closed her eyes and drifted off to sleep.

Like she'd done many nights before.

Isn't it amazing how a dream will seem so lifelike? Especially if the dream is a nightmare. The sound of some horrible monster lumbering down the hallway outside your door would be enough to cause many a heart to freeze over with terror.

Angelica's eyes opened and for a moment, she couldn't piece together what was going on. It took a second or two to realize she had been having a bad dream. Something about some beast loose in her house.

Looking at the soft moonlight coming in the window around the edges of the curtains, she realized it had just been a dream and nothing to worry about.

Until she heard the scratching at the bedroom door. Staring at the door, she almost had to will her heart to beat again. When she heard a low growl, she feared some wild dog had gotten inside her house.

That was until she heard her name.

"Angelica. I want to play."

The voice was low and guttural. The sound felt like it rattled the entire house.

Reaching for the nightstand, she felt

around the gun. Not finding it there, she remembered and drove her hand under the pillow and clasped her fingers around the cold steel.

In one smooth movement, she pulled the gun out and flipped the safety off. Pointing the weapon at the door, she felt her hand trembling and brought up the other hand to steady herself.

The scratching at the door was accompanied this time with a couple of knocks.

"I am armed and willing to shoot!" she yelled at the door.

"Oh really? This should be fun."

She couldn't ignore the feeling of cold terror forming in her chest, like a block of ice building around her heart.

"I mean it!"

The voice just laughed and then the door exploded inward, shattering into hundreds of pieces. The force of the explosion almost caused her to lose her grip on the gun, but she held fast.

What she saw next drained all the will from her resolve and her hands shook so wildly she couldn't even begin to take a proper aim.

An eight-foot tall monster stepped through the door, it's horns leaving smoldering marks across the ceiling. Its eyes blazed with fire and when it smiled at her, she could see the flames inside its head.

"Hello Angelica. I need to send a message to Detective Bishop and I'm afraid you won't survive it."

In the blink of an eye, her hands came up and she fired. One … two … three rounds in rapid succession. Each round hitting the monster in the center of the chest and knocking it backward. The beast groaned each time a bullet found its mark.

"That hurt," said the beast as it leaned back against the wall. "I was going to kill you quickly, but now, you're going to feel every second of your death."

Pushing itself away from the wall, it started moving toward the bed and she opened fire again. The bullets kept pushing the beast back, but it didn't take it down.

She raised her aim and put a round right between the fiery eyes of the beast, knocking it backward and against the wall again.

Click … click … click.

She gasped when she realized she had emptied the magazine and the beast was still on its feet. Jumping out of the bed, she made a run for the door, her bare feet crunching over the debris of the broken door.

She almost made it.

Almost.

A demon hand missing a couple of claws snapped out and grabbed her by the throat, lifting her off the ground. As the monster rose back to its full height, she saw its horns drive up through the ceiling, scorching anything they came in contact with.

"What are you?" she gasped through her closed off throat.

He brought her face up to his and she could feel the heat from off him.

"I'm sorry. I should have introduced myself. My name is Azrin and Freddie has become a thorn in my side, so you are going to be my message to him."

She struggled to push herself away from him, but the heat of his hand was burning her neck and every time she grabbed at his wrist, her hands got burned.

The holes where the bullets had struck closed up in front of her eyes.

Outside, she could hear some noises as neighbors were coming out of their houses to see what the commotion was about. She tried to scream, but Azrin was squeezing her throat too tightly.

A siren could be heard in the distance.

"I guess it's time for me to get on with this," growled Azrin.

He took two steps toward the bed and slammed Angelica down on her back, his hand still clenched around her neck.

"Just so you know," he said with a grin, "this isn't personal. Well, not toward you. This is all for Freddie."

He slapped his other hand down over her mouth and pressed her head into the mattress. Then, with his other hand, he drove one of his claws into the base of her throat, bringing a muffled scream from her.

"I hope this hurts," he said with a grin as he began sliding his claw down her body, slicing open her torso from neck to crotch.

She screamed, but he kept his hand over her mouth, stifling the sound.

Using his cutting hand, he pulled the skin of her upper body to one side and then the other. She continued to struggle, but she was getting weaker as the life was fleeing from her body.

He slammed his hand on top of her exposed rib cage and spread it away from her heart, The sound of sizzling meat could be heard and it smelled like burning steak.

She tried to scream one last time, but didn't have the strength. Azrin leaned down and stared into her fading eyes.

"Good night, Angelica. Too bad you won't get to find out if you and Freddie could have made another go of it."

Just as the last bit of life was leaving her

body, he growled, "I will give your regards to Ashley."

Her eyes opened wide when she realized what he had said, but he pushed down so hard her heart burst and she died instantly, carrying with her the thought this monster was going to go after her baby.

A couple of police cars screeched to a stop outside as Azrin stood up and admired his handiwork. He reached up and used his bloody claws to scratch a message in the wall over the headboard.

To Freddie, with love. Azrin

Smiling one last time, he faded out of view just as the police crashed through the front door of the house. As three officers moved into the bedroom, two of them turned back and threw up in the hallway.

Freddie was sitting at the sister's bedside, with Bethany sitting on the other side. He was holding her hand and confessing to her that if she had been killed, he didn't know what he was going to do.

"You'd keep fighting the fight, Freddie," she said. "Remember, you know the truth."

He jumped slightly when his phone rang in his pocket. Pulling it out, he answered, putting it on speaker.

"Detective Bishop," he answered.

"Fred?"

"Captain? What's up?"

"You need to go home."

"Actually, I'm off duty and I don't have to …"

"No, detective. I mean, you need to go to Angelica's house."

Freddie rose slowly to his feet.

"Angelica's house? What's happened?"

"Fred, just go."

The click on the phone signaled the captain had nothing more to say.

When his eyes shifted from the phone to the sister, he could see absolute pain in her eyes.

"Freddie," she said with tears forming in her eyes. She reached out and took one of his hands and squeezed it.

"I have to go," he said, barely able to contain the tremor in his voice.

"Take Bethany with you."

"What? No!"

She squeezed his hand again and implored, "Please, take her."

Bishop looked across the bed and the sixteen-year-old's eyes were wide, but full of pain. She stood up and walked over to the closet and pulled out the scabbard belt and put it on. Then she swung the jacket around her shoulders and zipped it up.

Looking back, it surprised her to see Bishop was no longer in the room.

"Go after him," said the sister. "He is going to need you tonight."

She gave a quick nod and rushed out the door. Bishop was just reaching the end of the corridor and turning toward the back doors of the church.

She heard him slam through the doors before she got to the corner and the cardinal stepped out of his office to see what was going on. Bethany ran past him and out the door just in time to see the detective slam his car door shut and already had the car backing out of the parking space.

"Bethany! Wait!" yelled the cardinal.

"Talk to the sister," she yelled back as she jumped in front of the detective's car, bringing him to a stop.

"Open the door, Detective Bishop!"

He eased his foot off the brake and the car crept forward a couple of inches, but she didn't budge.

"Open the door," she said through clenched jaws.

He shook his head slowly, but stopped when the cardinal stepped in front of the car, urging the young woman toward the passenger door. He took a couple of deep breaths and then hit the door unlock button.

She pulled the door open and slid into the seat beside him. Then she nodded to the cardinal, who stepped out of the way, allowing Bishop to proceed out of the parking lot.

He felt a surge go through his body when she reached over and put a hand on his arm. It was the exact same feeling he'd get when the sister did the same thing.

He glanced over at her and saw a faint glow around her face.

It has to be the damn street lights shining on her face.

Chapter 23 – Touch Not God's Weapons

Over the next five days, Sister Clarice didn't know what to do. She wandered around the church as if in a daze. The cardinal tried to get her to stay in bed and relax, but she wouldn't stay down.

Detective Bishop hadn't returned to the church since the night he left and found out Azrin had gone after his ex-wife.

What they found in the house was more horrific than anything the detective could have imagined. Even though the body had been removed before he got there, the bloody mess in the middle of the bed was more than he could handle.

When Bethany stepped into the bedroom, she felt a wave of revulsion go through her body and almost cursed the sister for sending her. Though five of her friends had been killed by Azrin, their deaths paled compared to this.

The detective silently stared at the bed while she pondered how to support him. Being just sixteen-years-old, she had no clue what to do. It didn't take much urging for the police officers to get her to leave the bedroom and wait in the living room.

When Bishop finally came out of the bedroom, he didn't even look at her or say anything to her. He just walked out the front door. Before she knew what had happened, he was gone, not even giving her a ride back to the church.

He just left.

She ended up calling an Uber to return to the church and admitted being the most terrified she had ever been. She was sure Azrin was going to attack her during the ride back.

She hardly left the sister's side, trying to get her to open up about what she was feeling. She felt inadequate, trying to bolster the emotions of the older nun.

It all came to a head one afternoon when Bethany was walking the sister around the corridors of the church to get her some exercise. She still wore the scabbard, but not the jacket while they were inside.

Sister Clarice was getting her strength back slowly, but Bethany could feel a melancholy in her spirit.

As they were walking past the back door it flew open and Sister Marissa stormed in, looking like she was ready for battle. She may have been old and walking with a cane, but Bethany could see she was not someone to trifle with.

She was followed by two other nuns, who looked to have even less of a sense of humor than her, if that was even possible.

"Sister Clarice! We need to have a talk!"

"Mother Superior, what are you doing here?"

Bethany stiffened her hold on the arm of the sister. Having heard of the aging nun, it surprised her to meet her face-to-face and feeling the anger in her voice.

"I've been hearing some disturbing rumors about you and what's going on here," said the older nun.

She looked Bethany up and down, seeing the sword hanging from the young woman's back and she bristled with even more anger.

"What is this child doing with your sword?"

Bethany straightened up and said, "Hey! I am her friend and here to help!"

Sister Marissa stepped up in front of her and looked her right in the eyes. Her face almost sneered in derision. Almost, but not quite.

"I don't care who you think you are, young lady, that is a weapon of the most high God and you are not to be handling it!"

"I know exactly what it is and as long as Sister Clarice wants me to carry it, I shall do that!"

The other two nuns took up positions on each side of Bethany, looking as if they were intending to relieve her of the sword on the Mother Superior's command. One even reached for the sword and received a nasty shock from the hilt, bringing a yelp of pain and surprise.

"Please, Mother Superior," pleaded Sister Clarice. "Calm down and leave Bethany alone."

The door to the cardinal's office flew open and he stepped out, causing the five women to become silent. Walking across the empty space, he stopped next to Bethany.

"Mother Superior, had I known you were planning a visit, I would have asked the brothers to fix us a lunch."

He looked at the sister that had tried to grab the sword, who was trying to rub some feeling back into her hand and gave her a wry smile.

"I would advise against trying to take that blade against the will of the person wielding it."

She bowed her head in apology and said, "Yes, Your Eminence."

Sister Marissa straightened up and said, "I demand she turn that weapon over to us freely and without hesitation. If Sister Clarice feels unworthy of carrying it, we shall find someone who is."

Bethany stepped forward, placing herself within a foot of the senior nun and looked her right in the eyes.

"Do not suggest Sister Clarice is unworthy

of carrying this sword or in any other way," she said through gritted teeth.

"Ladies!" stormed the padre as he reached forward and put a hand on Bethany's shoulder. "Let's calm down right now!"

Bethany stepped back and glanced over to see tears on the cheeks of Sister Clarice. She wrapped an arm around the sister's shoulders and hugged her closer. Even though the sister was older, Bethany stood about three inches taller than her and at that moment, she looked more like the protector.

"It's going to be okay, sister," she said softly.

"It will not be *okay*," yelled Sister Marissa. "This church is under attack by the very forces of Hell and if Sister Clarice is not up to the challenge, we need to find someone that is!"

Something in the back of Bethany's mind snapped and her hand flew to the hilt of the sword and in the blink of an eye, it was in her hand.

It caught Sister Marissa and her attendants off-guard and they looked as if ready to attack. Seeing the sword in the hands of this girl was too much for them to handle.

The padre tried to calm Bethany by reaching out, but she raised the sword and a blinding flash sent him and the others reeling backwards. The Mother Superior fell to her knees and the other two crowded next to her, holding her up.

The only one that didn't retreat from her was Sister Clarice. She firmly stepped forward and placed a hand on the girl's shoulder.

In a voice that sounded like it came straight from Heaven, Bethany said, "This is the Sword of God, carried at one time by the Guardian of the Garden."

The walls of the church rocked as she spoke. Bethany's face glowed, her hair turned white, and her eyes blazed, causing the three visiting nuns to cower backwards.

"No one in this world shall choose who wields the Sword of God. That choice resides with He, who is Most High."

The blade crackled and blazed as she held it up and none except for Sister Clarice dared look at it. For a solid minute, she held the sword aloft.

After that short time, her countenance dimmed and the back foyer of the church darkened. As things returned to normal, Bethany blinked and gasped for air. Her arm fell to her side, the blade drooping from her fingers.

Sister Clarice leaned up and whispered in her ear, "Put the sword away, sweetie."

As she slipped the blade back into the scabbard, the padre reached out and helped

Sister Marissa to her feet. The other two nuns moved to her sides and then dropped to their knees. The padre held both the older sister's hands and gave them a gentle squeeze.

Bethany looked down and saw the Mother Superior's cane laying on the floor and she stepped forward and picked it up. As she handed the cane to the older woman, the Mother Superior looked into her eyes, which were still gleaming.

Then the older woman dropped to her knees right between the other two.

"Please forgive me, child," she cried.

Bethany stepped backward, looking at the three kneeling nuns. Her face was one of consternation.

"I wish they wouldn't do that," she said. "Please get off your knees."

As the padre helped them back to their feet, he smiled at Sister Clarice and said, "Now you know how I feel."

She gave him a small grin. Then stuck out her tongue, bringing a small laugh from him.

"Ladies," he said, "let's step into the chapel around the corner and talk about this."

He offered his arm to the Mother Superior and they all went into the small chapel and sat in the pews. Bethany took her usual position next to Sister Clarice, both of them holding hands.

The two attendant nuns took seats in the back pew, never taking their eyes off Bethany. Their faces still filled with the wonder of what they had witnessed.

For the next hour, they talked about the challenges the church faced from the threat of Azrin, about the attack on the detective's wife and where Bethany fit into this. Mother Superior kept glancing over at her, nodding her approval with each detail that came out.

When all things were discussed, the Mother Superior stood up, leaning on her cane and said, "I'd like to visit with an old friend before we leave."

The padre offered his arm and said, "Allow me to show you the way."

After they left, Bethany helped Sister Clarice to her feet and the other two came forward and hugged her, wishing her a speedy recovery from her injuries.

About twenty minutes later, the padre and the Mother Superior reappeared and they all headed for the back door. As they approached the door, Sister Clarice knelt before the Mother Superior and held her hand.

"Mother Superior, I thank you for coming and may I ask a favor?"

"Of course, but only if you stand up."

"Sorry," said the sister and she stood up.

"What is it, Sister Clarice?"

"As you can see, I am still injured and not able to do the things I would like. One of those things is training Bethany in using the sword and how to defend herself."

The Mother Superior nodded and snapped her fingers.

"Sister Nina!"

One of the attendant nuns stepped forward and bowed.

"I need you to stay here for a time and assist Sister Clarice in training young Bethany. I shall send some of your belongings for your stay."

Sister Nina nodded and said, "Yes, Mother Superior."

Then the older nun stepped forward and kissed Sister Clarice on both cheeks.

"Stop dropping to your knees, child. It is unbecoming of a warrior of God."

"Yes, Mother Superior."

With that, the two nuns walked out the door and the padre accompanied them to their car.

After getting Sister Nina situated in a room, Bethany walked Sister Clarice back to hers. After helping her get undressed and into bed, she sat on the edge of the bed and held the sister's hand.

"Can I ask you something, sister?"

"Anything, Bethany?"

Bethany took a deep breath and then asked, "What happened after I pulled out the sword?"

"You don't remember?"

"I remember nothing from the time I grabbed the sword until you told me to put it away."

Sister Clarice smiled and squeezed her hand.

"Let's just say the Mother Superior will never again question your right to hold the sword. And you should never question your worthiness again."

After they sat for a moment in silence, Sister Clarice said, "You should go get some sleep. If I know anything, it's that Sister Nina is going to put you through hell training you."

Bethany sighed and said, "I hope I'm up to this."

"Just remember, you are one of God's chosen and you have the strength of Heaven to help you."

Bethany squeezed her hand again and got up and walked to the door. Looking back as she turned off the light, she nodded to the sister and slipped out of the room.

As she walked along the dark corridor, she had just one thought.

I hope I can count on You to watch over me.

Without thinking, she found herself turning around and walking back the way she came. Before she knew it, she was on her knees in the chapel, looking up at the small crucifix and the figure of Jesus on it.

Chapter 24 – Training Begins

Sister Clarice was not kidding when she said Sister Nina would put Bethany through hell with her training. The new sister was older than Sister Clarice and knew a thing or two about fighting.

Being a black belt in three different martial arts disciplines would attest to that. She was wearing a baby blue martial arts outfit, but the dark color of the belt terrified Bethany.

Bethany wore a simple pair of sweatpants and a t-shirt Sister Clarice had loaned to her. She was still trying to figure out what it was about the Doobie Brothers that put the shirt in the sister's wardrobe.

By the end of the first morning of training, Bethany had plenty of bruises to show for her efforts. She was in agony, wondering if Sister Nina had some sort of grudge against her. The only thing that kept her going was the gentle encouragement from Sister Clarice, who sat in a chair just on the edge of the training mats.

Every time Bethany looked over at her, she remembered the scars on her back and how she got them.

She also remembered the sight of Angelica's bed, where her mutilated body had been splayed in a pool of blood. The look on the detective's face was enough to break her heart.

The thought of her own aunt Suzanne being killed by this demon was enough to get her fired up. She was ready to take any punishment if it meant she would be prepared for some future battle.

After a quick break for lunch, Sister Nina was teaching her blocks, trying to get her to defend herself, when she connected with a full-force kick to the sternum. Bethany went down like she had chopped her down with an ax, clutching her ribs and gasping for breath.

"Sister Nina!"

She turned to the sound of the voice and dropped her gaze.

"Yes, Your Eminence?"

"We've actually become quite attached to Bethany. Could you please try not to kill her?"

The sister bowed and said, "Yes, padre, but …"

The padre looked at her with one raised eyebrow.

"It's just that Azrin will not be gentle with her when they meet."

The padre looked at her and then shrugged.

"You are the teacher. I leave this in the capable hands of the two of you," he said, giving a nod to Sister Clarice.

Turning around, he headed to the doors of

the small gymnasium. As he pushed his way out the door, he stopped and held the door open. Stepping aside, Esther pushed her walker through the door and hobbled her way across the floor.

Sister Nina reached down and helped Bethany off the mat. When the younger woman had regained her feet, the nun did something that caught Bethany off-guard.

Nina leaned in and cupped her cheek, exactly the way Sister Clarice would.

"I hope you know I love you like a sister."

Bethany was rubbing her ribs and still wheezing a little when she breathed.

"Do you usually beat the crap out of your sisters?"

"Only when I'm training them to face demons from Hell."

Sister Clarice jumped off her chair and gave it to Esther, who sat down and folded her hands on her lap. The sister walked over and grabbed another chair and sat down beside the older, retired demon hunter.

"Have I missed much?"

"Oh, no," said Sister Clarice. "Sister Nina was just giving Bethany a few lessons in pain management."

"Ooo, I never did like those kinds of lessons."

Bethany looked at the two and asked, "Are

you two enjoying yourselves?"

Esther smiled and said, "Oh yes, quite."

Sister Clarice got up and walked onto the mat, asking for a moment of privacy from the other sister. Sister Nina turned, walked to the edge of the mats and knelt down with her back to the two.

"I'm sure you're wondering what you've gotten yourself into," she whispered in Bethany's ear.

Bethany looked at her and nodded.

"If you were to ask for His help sincerely, I know He will give it to you, even though your faith in God is not strong."

"My faith is not as strong as yours."

"It doesn't need to be. The little faith you have will be enough. You just have to ask."

Their eyes met and a glow flickered between them. Bethany nodded and turned around. She walked to the opposite edge of the mat and dropped to her own knees and closed her eyes.

I need a little help here. I'm getting my butt kicked by one of your nuns and it doesn't feel good. Please ... help.

At first, she felt nothing. It appeared Heaven was ignoring her. As she rose to her feet preparing for another beating, she felt a warmth wash over her body. It almost caused her to gasp as it filled her chest. The pain from the previous kick lessened and she could breathe easier.

Turning around, she saw Sister Nina was standing and waiting quietly for her. When the sister looked into her eyes, she involuntarily took a step back.

Then she smiled and said, "It's about time, Sister Bethany."

"Please don't call me that."

Sister Nina had a smirk on her face when she said, "Make me."

Bethany looked at the two women on the sidelines. Sister Clarice was biting her lip to keep from laughing. Esther's eyes just danced.

Nina's attack came fast and furiously. Much faster than any other that day. Bethany immediately stepped back into a defensive stance and her hands came up. Feeling as if something else was guiding her hands, she blocked every punch and kick the sister threw at her.

For the next hour, Sister Nina attacked in every way she could think of and only a handful of punches got through, but none caused any serious pain.

And not a single kick landed.

The afternoon's training ended when Bethany threw a punch and caught the sister precisely at the bottom of the rib cage. The gymnasium echoed with the sound of the breath being knocked out of the sister's lungs.

As Sister Nina dropped to her knees to catch her breath, Bethany dropped next to her, apologizing profusely. Because she couldn't speak at the moment, Nina reached up and placed a couple of fingers over Bethany's lips.

When she could finally squeak out a few words, she said, "Stop apologizing. It is unbecoming of a warrior."

As she went to stand up, Bethany jumped up and helped her to her feet. The sister was still trying to draw a full breath.

"I believe we've trained enough for one day," she said as she rubbed her ribs. "Tomorrow morning we shall review today's lessons, but in the afternoon, we'll start weapons training."

Then she turned and began walking slowly to the doors.

"I really am sorry for hitting you," Bethany called after her.

This caused Sister Nina to turn around and walk right back into Bethany's personal space.

"I told you to stop apologizing. Are you going to apologize to Azrin every time you deal him a blow?"

"No, but I don't like Azrin."

Nina smiled and said, "Please stop saying you're sorry. You have nothing to be sorry for. And, true to my word, I will stop calling you

Sister Bethany, though it will pain me to do so."

"I'm only sixteen."

"Joan of Arc was only seventeen when she led the French armies against the British."

"Yes, and she was only nineteen when they burned her at the stake."

Sister Nina giggled and said, "Touché."

The sister patted her on the cheek and headed out the door. Bethany turned and looked at the two ladies still sitting there.

"Well, I hope the two of you enjoyed yourselves."

"Very much so," said Esther. "I especially liked the moment I saw the power of Heaven fall upon your shoulders."

"You saw that?"

"Would have been hard to miss," said Sister Clarice. "It even scared Sister Nina."

"I didn't mean to."

Sister Clarice stood up and helped Esther to her feet and pushed the walker in front of her. Then she turned and smiled at Bethany.

"Believe me when I say she does not hold any ill feelings toward you. As a matter of fact, I'm sure she is smiling inwardly at your progress this afternoon. Now, let's stop by the kitchen and get you an ice pack for your ribs."

The three women left the gym with Esther in between the two of them. She was nattering at them about not needing them to watch her every step. They both smiled at each other, knowing they were privileged to just be walking alongside one of the older demon hunters.

As they entered the kitchen, the ancient cook, who was not a priest or monk, smiled big at the sight of the three. His smile was especially wide for Esther. Then his smile faded when he remembered why she was there.

"I'm so sorry, Sister Esther, for your loss."

She looked up at him and her eyes twinkled slightly.

"Even if I have to do it myself, I will make sure Marvin is avenged."

"That's why I always liked you, sister."

Then turning to Bethany, he asked, "And who is the lovely young lady"?

Sister Clarice said, "This is Bethany, who is also suffering from the loss of those close to her at the hands of a demon."

"My sincere condolences," he said as he took her hand and kissed it. "Azrin?"

Bethany just nodded.

Sister Clarice said, "She is training and considering taking up the sword."

He looked back at her and she could see his eyes growing wet.

"Why does he do that?" asked the cook.

"Do what?" asked Bethany. "Kill people?"

"Not just kill people, sweetheart. He seems to target those that are destined to become the very warriors that will battle against him. Like he is drawing them out. And to go after one so young?"

She looked at the sister and could see her face agreeing with him.

When the sister mentioned an ice pack he smiled and went into the walk-in freezer. He came back out with a bundle made of a soft pouch and two wide straps.

"What is that?" asked Bethany.

"This, young lady," said the cook, "is the kind of ice pack needed by those that are training to be demon hunters. I remember Sister Clarice needing one almost every day when she was training here."

He handed the ice pack to the sister and went back to his cooking.

Bethany looked at her and asked, "You trained here?"

"Raise your arms, sweetie," she said as she placed the ice pack under her t-shirt and against her lower rib cage. "Yes, I did. A few years ago."

Bethany gasped when the cold hit her tummy just under her breasts and then winced in pain when the sister stretched the straps around her and fastened them.

When the sister pulled her t-shirt back

down, Bethany looked at her.

"You must have been really young when you trained here."

"Only about four years older than you are right now."

She looked at Esther, who had been standing quietly by, her hands gripping the walker. When their eyes met, the older woman just nodded.

"You too?"

"I was just eighteen when I joined the Sisters of the Templar. Fought as one of them for over ten years, until the day I met Marvin. Back then, I didn't think anything would draw me out of the sisterhood except for death. Then that rascal smiled at me and I was done for."

They thanked the cook for the ice pack and he said to come back tomorrow because he had plenty of ice packs ready to go. Bethany blew a raspberry at him and he just laughed.

As they were walking down the darkened corridor, Bethany said, "So, Marvin got you to do something even Azrin couldn't."

Esther came to a stop and when they looked at her, she had her eyes closed and a tear was falling down her cheek.

"Oh, Esther," cried Bethany as she pulled a tissue from her pocket. "I didn't mean anything bad by that."

Esther reached up and patted her cheek.

"I know, sweetheart. It's just that ... Marvin is dead because of who I was. If I had ignored his advances and not fallen in love with him, he'd still be alive today."

Sister Clarice reached out and ran a hand across Esther's shoulders.

"Marvin is not dead because of who you were. He is dead because of who Azrin is. Marvin loved you more than life itself. As cantankerous as he could be sometimes, he placed himself between Azrin and the woman he loved."

Esther broke down, her shoulders bobbing up and down with her sobs. She confessed this was the first time she had truly cried about his death.

Bethany handed her the tissue and the three of them stood in the darkened hallway, letting Esther regain control of her emotions.

When they continued on, they walked her to her room and helped her into bed and sat with her for about an hour. She told them what a dashing young man Marvin had been in his uniform of the Israeli army.

After ten years of being a demon hunter, they assigned her to work in the area around Jerusalem.

One night she felt the pull of a demon on her spirit and she walked the darkened streets of the holy city. It didn't take her long to find the demon, who was battling with a small group of soldiers. The soldiers were having no luck because their weapons were useless against it.

When she went racing past them, straight at the demon, a couple of them tried to grab her, but she was too fast.

Then they watched in horror as this woman went toe-to-toe with the demon, but horror turned to amazement when she killed it by removing its head. As the demon head bounced down the gentle slope, it ended up at the feet of one soldier. He looked up at her and his face was frozen in wonder.

When their eyes met, she felt as if a lightning bolt had struck her in the heart.

"I'm still a little peeved at you for not telling me who you were," said Sister Clarice.

Esther patted her hand and said, "The Holy Father admonished me to never reveal my past when he separated me from the sisterhood."

"Even Marvin said nothing!"

"Yes, dearie. That's why he was always so gruff and grouchy. He was afraid someone would come along and convince me to go back to the fight. You were always a reminder to him of where I had come from. I could never convince him that the only fight I wanted to wage for the rest of my life was for the love in his heart."

Then Esther squeezed her hand and asked, "You never wondered why I always called you when I suspected the work of a demon?"

"No, it never occurred to me. I guess it should have."

They sat with her for about an hour, listening as she regaled them with the battles she had fought before she turned her sword over to Sister Agatha.

The two younger women could see she was tiring so they left her to fall asleep.

As Sister Clarice stopped and looked at Bethany at the door to her room, her eyes filled with sadness.

"Bethany, I truly wish you weren't being called to this work. It scares me more than you know, to see you beginning to train to fight demons."

"I still haven't decided."

"You can lie to yourself, sweetie, but you can't lie to me. It's as plain as the nose on your face. You will answer the call because you've seen the damage and sadness demons like Azrin can do. To your aunt, to your friends."

"To you," said Bethany, "and to Esther."

"Leave me out of your decision."

"I will not!" said the younger woman, raising her voice.

Sister Clarice took her by the arm and

guided her into her room and closed the door. Turning around, she could see defiance in Bethany's eyes.

"I just meant do not make your decision based on what happened to me."

Bethany stepped forward until she was standing nose-to-nose with the nun.

"You listen to me, sister, and listen good. I may only be sixteen and lack your knowledge about demons and evil, but when Bishop came back with your weapons I thought Azrin had killed you. It felt like someone had ripped my heart right out of my body. I don't ever want to feel like that again."

The sister reached up and held both sides of Bethany's face and looked her right in the eyes.

"That's what I'm trying to tell you, sweetheart. If you go down this path of becoming a demon hunter, it will fill your life with moments like that. Do you have any idea how many times I've felt the same way you did? Every time I arrive at the scene of an attack, I can feel it. It gets no easier."

A tear trickled from Bethany's eye and began running down her cheek. She reached up and placed her hands over the sister's. After a second, she went to lean in and the sister pulled away.

"And if you kiss me again, I shall have to

hurt you."

Bethany gasped and stepped back, breaking their contact.

"I'm so sorry," she said as she wiped the tear away.

A pained smile crept across the sister's face as she leaned forward and tapped her cheek. Bethany giggled as she leaned in and kissed her on the cheek.

"I promised my lips to my Lord and Savior."

Bethany turned and looked at the crucifix on the wall and said, "I'm sorry for kissing her in the hospital. It won't happen again."

Sister Clarice wrapped her arms around her waist from behind and hugged her close. Being a bit shorter than the younger woman, she just rested her cheek against her back. She smiled when Bethany placed her hands on top of hers and held them.

"Get some sleep, sweetie. I'm sure Sister Nina is going to put you through some tough drills tomorrow and maybe a little payback for that last hit you got on her."

Bethany laughed and said, "I didn't mean to hurt her."

"I know and she knows that, too."

The sister gave her a gentle squeeze and then turned and walked out the door.

Chapter 25 – The Hunt

The next couple of days were spent with Bethany being tortured at the hands of Sister Nina. Sister Clarice and Esther would sit on the sidelines, cringing each time one would deal a breath-taking blow to the other. There were a few times one combatant would be laying on the mats, gasping for breath and clutching their ribs.

A few times the cardinal would be standing near the door of the gym and watching. Each time one of the ladies ended up on the floor, he would just shake his head and walk out.

By the fourth day, each of the women had the measure of the other and there were few blows that connected. Bethany was feeling much more at ease stepping onto the mats and facing off against the sister.

That afternoon, as the four ladies were sitting at the dining room table, Cardinal Wright walked in with a man only Sister Clarice had seen before. He had a very sour look on his face.

"Captain Tyrell? How are you doing?"

asked the sister.

"Not very good, I'm afraid," said the captain. "Have you been in touch with Detective Bishop recently?"

"No, sir. I haven't talked to him since the night his ex-wife was killed. What's happened?"

"Nothing's happened. That's the problem. We haven't heard from him since that night either. No one knows where he is. No one has heard from him. It's like he's dropped completely off the map."

Turning around, she looked at Bethany.

"Did he say anything to you that night that might tell us where he is?"

"No, sister. As soon as he saw what had happened in that bedroom, he never said another word."

"Nothing at all?"

"No. I could see he was devastated, so I kept my distance. I didn't even realize I needed to find another way back here until after he'd disappeared. That was about half an hour after we got there."

Sister Clarice looked at the cardinal and he could see nothing but fear in her eyes.

He said, "I'll start making some phone calls."

Then he reached out and placed a hand on the captain's shoulder.

"Captain, I'm sure we can find the missing detective. Have your people keep looking and we will put the resources of the church into action."

The captain nodded and the two of them turned and headed out of the dining room. The captain walked with a droop to his shoulders that signaled he felt whipped,

"We need to find him, sister."

Clarice turned to see tears in Bethany's eyes. The other two ladies just sat and waited for her to say anything that would cause them to spring into action.

"Sister Nina. Can I assume you will work with Esther here in the church, assisting the cardinal as he tries to locate the detective?"

"Of course. What are you going to do?"

"I think it's time for me to get back in the game. Bethany and I will hit the streets and try to locate the detective."

"Are you sure you're ready? I'd be happy to go with Bethany and help her."

"Sister Nina, ready or not, I need to get back out there."

"I just think you might …"

Nina stopped when she saw the look on Sister Clarice's face and realized the best thing to do was stop talking.

Esther stood up and took hold of her walker. As she shuffled around the table, she stopped in front of the sister and reached out and took hold of her chin.

"You listen to me, young lady. We can't afford to have anything happen to you. You be careful out there."

"Yes, mother," said the sister as she leaned over and kissed the older woman on the cheek.

Esther looked at Bethany and said, "And you watch over her."

"Okay, but who's going to watch over me?"

Esther smiled and reached up and patted her on the cheek.

"Sweetie, you are much stronger than you know. Azrin should run in fright if he ever sees you coming."

Bethany couldn't help herself and she threw her arms around the older woman's shoulders and hugged her tight.

She and Sister Clarice hurried to their rooms and changed clothes. As Bethany stood up after tying her boots, her eyes were drawn to the sword and scabbard in her closet. She reached in, pulled them out and held them up.

"Should I take you to the sister? Or should I keep you with me?"

As she watched, the gold in the hilt of the sword began to glow and she could feel the power of the blade reaching out to her. Wrapping her fingers around the grip, she slid the sword out and dropped the belt on the bed.

It only took a couple of seconds for the power of the sword to descend on her and light her body up. There was a rush of wind that swirled around her, whipping her hair around. A glow came from the blade and she held it pointed straight up. It was so bright she had to close her eyes to withstand it.

A voice boomed in her ears and she clenched her jaws tight and tried to hear what it was saying. It was so loud and distorted she couldn't understand the words, but she knew exactly where they were coming from. And it caused her to grit her teeth even harder, trying to push the pain from her head.

Then she jerked a little when she felt two hands wrap around hers on the hilt of the sword.

Opening her eyes, she was looking into the glowing eyes of the sister. Suddenly she felt the pain lessen and the voice softened, allowing her to understand the words.

YOU ARE A WARRIOR OF HEAVEN!
I WILL NEVER ABANDON YOU.

After a couple of minutes, the sword began to release its hold on the two of them and Bethany found herself breathing a little easier. She closed her eyes and tried to relax.

"It never gets easier, Bethany."

She opened her eyes and could see the sister was smiling at her. She almost had to close her eyes again because the sister was glowing brightly.

"I don't want it to get easier," she said with a trembling voice. "All of my life I've felt like a frightened kitten. I don't feel that way when I hold this sword. I'm just not sure I'm worthy to be holding it."

Sister Clarice reached out and placed her hand on the side of Bethany's face.

"You are not meant to feel afraid. You have courage and strength I could only wish for. And if you weren't worthy of holding this sword, it would never allow you to touch it."

The two women stood for a moment, staring into each others glowing eyes, feeling their souls bonding.

"Let's go find the detective," said Sister Clarice as she took the sword and slid it into the scabbard and then helped sling it across Bethany's back.

The two of them left the room and headed to the back door. They were met by the cardinal, who was just saying goodbye to Captain Tyrell. As they approached the men, the captain looked at the two of them.

"You're taking her out of the church?"

"She has to leave sometime, captain," said the sister. "And her safety will be my number one priority, followed closely with finding the detective."

Despite not being a God-fearing man, the captain prayed for their safety outside the church.

After the cardinal blessed them, they headed out the door and to the sister's car. As the two of them got themselves situated in their seats, Bethany looked the car over.

"I guess the church isn't going to go broke buying you a nicer car, either," said the younger woman.

Sister Clarice smiled and said, "Cardinal Wright keeps telling me the church would be happy to provide me with a nicer car. I keep telling him to use that money for the families and children of the church. This one gets me around just fine."

The sister turned the key and the small engine under the hood turned over once and fired right up.

"Aren't you worried that it will let you down someday?"

"Not at all. One of the brothers in the church volunteers to maintain it and he does a wonderful job. It has never failed me yet."

After fastening their seatbelts, Sister Clarice pointed the car to the exit of the parking lot and drove out onto the streets. Bethany watched her and wanted to ask where they were going, but stopped herself.

Sister Clarice looked very alert as the driver, but at the same time, looked like she was allowing someone or something else to guide her.

After about twenty minutes, Bethany couldn't take it anymore.

"Where are we going?"

The sister snapped out of whatever trance she was in and looked over at her.

"Oh. I don't know exactly, but I think we're heading out to Northwestern University."

"Well, yes, this is the way out there. But why?"

"If I'm not mistaken, the detective's daughter is a student there. I did a little research and found she is living in the dorms. I guess that's as good a place to start as any."

"Okay. Just be warned. The dorms out there are co-ed and you may see things you might not approve of."

"Warning noted," said the sister with a slight smile.

As they drove onto the campus, Bethany looked out the windows, watching the students walking from one class to another, bundled against the chill of the afternoon.

It was a bright early winter day and the snows hadn't come yet, but they were expected any time now. The students didn't seem to mind the cold as they walked together, laughing and joking around.

I wonder if they would be smiling if they knew about the evil that walks this planet?

"Don't think like that."

She turned and looked at the sister.

"You knew what I was thinking?"

"Yes I do and it is my job to make sure as few of these young ones as possible learn of that evil."

"Our job."

"Bethany, do not make your decision yet. I know I'm going to feel bad if you decide to do this because of my coaxing."

"Sister, it won't be because of you, though you are playing a small part in it. It's because I know of the evil that is Azrin and I want to put an end to him just as much as you do."

Sister Clarice gave a grim smile as she reached over and squeezed Bethany's hand. They rode on in silence for a couple more minutes.

Before they knew it, they turned into a parking lot for a set of dorm towers. Finding an open parking space right near the first building, they got out of the car and stepped onto the sidewalk.

"Which one, sister?"

The sister looked back and forth across the five towers and then pointed at one.

"This one," she said as she started walking toward it.

As they headed toward the building, those walking on the sidewalk gave them a wide berth. The sister, with her long, black leather habit, emblazoned with red crosses or the young woman with the black leather jacket with the same red crosses.

As they stepped through the doors, into the lobby of the dorm, there was a small counter with a young lady sitting behind it. She held her breath as the two approached her.

"We're here to see Ashley Bishop," said the sister.

The young woman was just staring at the two of them, apparently not hearing what the sister said.

"Young lady."

"Oh," said the woman, snapping out of her daze, "I'm sorry. Who did you need to see again.?"

"Ashley Bishop."

The woman typed a couple of things in the computer and said, "She is in room 816. But I don't think she's there. It says here she has classes for the next twenty minutes."

"We can wait," said the sister. "Thank you."

"She's not in trouble, is she?"

Sister Clarice smiled and said, "Sweetheart,

we are not the police."

"No, of course not."

The sister turned and walked across the small lobby and took a seat on one of the sofas and Bethany sat down beside her.

"This just looks so ... normal," said Bethany.

"What do you mean?"

"It's just that, this is where I was planning to go to college in a couple of years. I guess I've built it up to be some sort of cathedral of education when it's just another school."

"It's where your journey to adulthood begins," said the sister, touching Bethany's knee. "It will be one more step in you learning who you are and what you will become."

Then Sister Clarice leaned over and laid her head on Bethany's shoulder. Her breathing softened as she tried to relax.

"You're still hurting, aren't you?" asked the younger woman, as she took one of the nun's hands in hers.

"Azrin certainly did a grievous injury to me."

"Maybe we shouldn't have brought you out here."

"There was no one else."

"Sister Nina could have come with me."

"Sister Nina is not a warrior. She is a trainer and a fighter to be sure, but she is not a warrior."

They sat for a moment and the sister said, "I'll be okay. Don't worry about me."

"I think I made it perfectly clear the other day, I will always worry about you, sister."

"Yes, mother."

They both giggled at that.

A few minutes later, a young, black woman came through the doors, huffing and puffing under the loaded heavy book pack on her shoulders.

"I swear to God, Tina! It's colder than a witch's tit out there!"

The woman behind the counter just shook her head and pointed past her. She turned to see Bethany helping Sister Clarice up from the sofa and her eyes went wide. As the two of them walked toward her, she looked like she didn't know whether to stand or run.

As they got closer, she said, "I'm so sorry, sister. I shouldn't have spoken like that."

"That's okay. You're right. It is colder than a witch's tit out there."

"Sister Clarice!" gasped Bethany.

The sister just squeezed her arm.

"You're Sister Clarice?"

"You know of me?"

"I talked to my father a couple of weeks ago and he told me a little about you."

"I hope he said good things about me."

Ashley giggled and said, "Said he didn't know whether to hate you or love you."

Sister Clarice gave her a small smile and then asked, "Can we go up to your room and talk privately?"

A look of concern crossed Ashley's face as she asked, "What's wrong? Something's happened to my dad, hasn't it?"

Bethany spoke and said, "Please, Ashley. We need to take this somewhere private."

Ashley looked at her and then nodded.

"This way," she said as she turned and led them to the elevators.

As they rode up, they could see she was trembling.

"I wish you two would tell me something."

Bethany reached out, patted her arm and said, "In private."

As they exited the elevator and turned left, they walked down the darkened hallway and came upon a sight that made Bethany blush. And decide not to move into the co-ed dorms.

A young man, probably from the football team was walking toward them, having come from the showers. He was wearing nothing but a pair of tight briefs that left nothing to the imagination. His towel was thrown over his shoulder.

Bethany felt the sister's hand tense on her arm and looked over to see she had her eyes closed. She had obviously seen more than she wanted to.

As she guided the sister down the hallway, following behind Ashley, she gave a death stare to the man and was pleased to see the color drain from his face. He immediately grabbed the towel and wrapped it around himself and almost ran to the other end of the hallway to his room.

"It's okay, sister. He's gone."

The sister cracked one eye open and then opened her eyes.

"You did warn me," she said.

"Yes, I did."

They came to a room at the other end of the hallway and Ashley opened the door and ushered them in. They were surprised to find another young woman sitting at one of the desks doing some homework.

"Hey, Ash. Glad you're her …:

She stopped when the two black clad women stepped into the room.

Sister Clarice quickly reached into one of her many pockets and pulled out a couple of dollar bills.

"Kerry, could you go downstairs and get yourself a soda and take a break? We need to speak with Ashley alone for a few minutes."

Kerry got up and said, "Sure. You don't need to pay me to leave, sister."

"I'm not paying you, sweetheart. I'm buying you a drink because you work too hard."

She took the young woman's hand and pressed the bills into it.

"Give us about ten minutes."

"Okay," she said as she looked at Ashley, who gave her a quick nod.

After she left and the door was closed, Ashley broke her silence.

"Okay, what is going on? Is this about my dad?"

Bethany walked over to the window and looked out. They had a view of the Chicago skyline in the distance and she was sure it was spectacular at night.

She could feel Ashley looking at her back, at the red cross. She worried that the hilt of the sword might be showing, but she knew the sword would never reveal itself like that.

"Ashley," asked the sister, "do you know where your father is?"

Ashley looked at her as the reason for this visit seemed to come into focus.

"No. He never even showed up at the funeral for my mom a couple of days ago. Has something happened to him?"

"That's what we're trying to find out. No one has heard from him since the day your mother passed."

"You mean the day someone killed her."

The tone of her voice had gone from friendly to coarse and angry in the blink of an eye.

Sister Clarice bit her lip and then said, "Yes, the day someone killed her."

"How could somebody do that to her? I couldn't even look at her face during the funeral because they had the coffin sealed."

Bethany, who was still standing at the window, said softly, "You didn't want to see it."

Ashley whirled around and looked at the younger woman from behind.

"What do you mean, I didn't want to? She was my mother. I wanted to see her face!"

Bethany turned around and there were tears welling up in her eyes.

"I meant, your mother's face was destroyed by the monster that killed her. You did not want to see that."

Sister Clarice said, "Please remember your mother as she was, Ashley."

"She was a cold, conniving bitch," said Ashley, looking directly at the sister. "She did nothing for the past ten years than tear my father down and poison me against him. He did not deserve that!"

She turned around and tried to catch her breath. There was a picture of her and her dad pinned on the bulletin board. They were sitting at a small table in what appeared to be an ice cream shop and the smiles on their faces were as bright as the sun.

Bethany and the sister just stared at her back, not knowing what to say.

She spoke in a softer voice but remained angry. "I wanted to spit in her face when she was in the coffin, but I couldn't."

"Ashley."

Bethany could hear the pain in Sister Clarice's voice.

Ashley turned and looked at her.

"I'm sorry, sister, but she was a vindictive, mean person who robbed me of years with my dad. Simply because she hated the job that he did. A job she knew he was doing before they got married."

The sister's eyes closed and both women could tell she was holding back tears. She took a couple of steps back and sat down on one of the beds, trying to ease her breathing and calm herself.

Bethany dropped down to her knees in front of her and placed a hand on her knee.

The sister opened her watery eyes and said, "This isn't going at all like I thought it would."

Bethany jumped up and faced the woman.

"Now I understand how you would be back at school just days after your mother was

324

murdered, acting like nothing happened."

"Oh, what do you know? How old are you? 15?"

"My age is of no importance."

"Maybe someday you'll find out what it's like to have a mother like that."

"I already do!"

Bethany felt the sister take her hand and squeeze it, asking her to stop.

"No, sister!"

Turning back to Ashley she continued, "A couple of weeks ago five of my friends and I were attacked and they were killed. My mother, who I know was told of this, couldn't be bothered to even call me from her European vacation with her new husband, to find out if I was okay! The only one that cared was my dad, who flew across the country to be at my side. So don't tell me I don't understand!"

Bethany looked down and saw the sister had her face buried in her hands and was crying. She reached down and put a hand on her shoulder, just as the door opened and Kerry came back in.

"Oh, you're still ... sister? What's the matter?"

Kerry sat down next to the distraught nun and put a hand on her shoulder. Bethany walked back over to the window and looked out. Her voice came out soft and without fire.

"Ashley, I have been angry with my mother. More than you can imagine, but I have never felt the way you do toward yours."

Ashley took a couple of steps and sank down on her bed across from the sister and Kerry.

"I'm so sorry," she said. "I never meant to take my hostility out on either of you. And for the record, I never would have done that to my mom. I think I'm just angry that I never got to make things right with her."

Sister Clarice stood up and then dropped to her knees in front of Ashley.

"Sister," said Bethany.

"Hush."

"Yes, ma'am."

Reaching up, she cupped Ashley's face between her hands and the young woman gasped. The images flooded her mind and took her breath away. Within seconds, tears flowed down her face like a faucet had been turned on.

After a minute, the sister broke the contact and reached into her pocket and pulled out a fresh tissue, which she used to dry Ashley's face.

The young woman opened her eyes and looked at the nun.

"Is she really in Heaven?"

"There was no reason to send her to Hell, Ashley. She was just a little misguided, that's all."

"She said she loves me," cried Ashley.

"She never stopped loving you."

Ashley leaned forward and threw her arms around the sister's neck and they held each other while she cried.

"I don't know what's going on," said Kerry, "but this is some serious Hallmark Channel stuff."

After a moment, the two ladies parted and the sister stood up.

"Ashley, we need to find your father. We're afraid something bad has happened to him or is going to happen."

She looked up at the sister and said, "I don't know. He hasn't answered my calls."

"I know where he is."

All three women turned and looked at Kerry.

"You know where he is?" asked Bethany.

"Yeah, I was going to tell you. He's downstairs. He's talking all crazy and shit ... I mean, stuff. I think he's drunk."

Three ladies trying to squeeze through one doorway will never work, but they tried it anyway. Running to the elevator, they stopped and pushed the buttons, demanding the elevator get there faster.

A young man, dressed in blue jeans, sweatshirt and sneakers was standing a little ways off, not wanting to get any closer. The sister gave him the side eye.

"You look much better with your clothes on, young man. You should be a little more respectful of the young ladies on this floor."

"Yes, sister," was all he could squeak out.

When the elevator door opened and the ladies were getting in, she looked at him and asked, "You coming?"

"Uh, no, sister. I'll wait."

Bethany stepped out of the elevator and took him by the hand and led him in.

It was the longest elevator ride of his life.

Chapter 26 – Horror Branches Out

Sister Nina and Esther spent a couple of hours working with the cardinal, trying to locate the detective. All their calls were proving fruitless and Esther began to show signs of weariness.

Cardinal Wright told her she needed to get some rest and told the sister it was time for her to take a break, too. Sister Nina helped Esther back to her room and got her tucked into bed and said a quick blessing over her and left the room.

Despite feeling tired, she prioritized finding the detective over taking a nap and planned to ignore the cardinal on her way back to the office.

As she was passing by the back doors she could hear the sounds of kids playing behind the church. Stepping to the back door, she pushed it open and looked out.

Despite the chill, a group of boys played basketball on the court at the far end of the parking lot. There were a handful of girls sitting on the brick wall at the edge of the property watching the boys.

The sister decided she could use a quick break and stepped out of the church and walked across the open lot. The girls saw her coming and they smiled and waved at her. She walked right up and hopped onto the brick wall, sitting next to then.

"How are you young ladies doing today?"

"Good," said a couple of them.

"Are you new here, sister?" asked one of them.

"Just here to help out for a short time. I'm usually at the orphanage over on Stewart."

"Oh," said one of the girls. "You're one of those."

Sister Nina kind of smirked and asked, "What are *one of those*?"

"You're one of those angels that works with the kids that don't have any parents."

"Well, I'm not sure about angel, but thank you."

"So, you're here helping out," said a pretty blonde.

"Yes, I am. Just as long as Sister Clarice needs some help."

"That's right," said another girl. "How is she? I heard she got hurt really bad."

The sister nodded and said, "That's true, but she is coming along nicely. She will be back at full strength in no time."

She looked to the court, watching the boys play. A couple were trash talking each other and she smiled as she listened to them.

"Hey, guys!" said one girl, "You have the sister sitting right here. Could you watch your mouths?"

The boys mumbled an apology and Sister Nina laughed and said, "That's okay. They have said nothing too terrible."

"Still, they should watch what they say," said the girl.

"Boys! You can't live with them and you can't shoot them," said one of the other girls.

The first one turned and looked at her in surprise.

"Marcie!"

Sister Nina laughed even harder and said, "No, Marcie, you certainly can't."

She looked at the blonde and asked, "And what is your name?"

"I'm Taylor."

"Well, Taylor and Marcie, I'm Sister Nina."

Then looking at the third girl to her left, a petite Asian girl, she asked, "And what is your name, young lady."

The girl mumbled something. The sister leaned over and said, "I'm sorry, I didn't get that."

"I'm Betsy."

"Betsy. That's a lovely name. You should be proud of it."

Taylor leaned over and said, "She's a bit quiet. She's not Catholic so she feels uncomfortable being here."

"Taylor!" whined Betsy.

Sister Nina reached over and patted Betsy's hand and said, "It's okay, Betsy. We are happy to have you here, no matter what your beliefs are."

Betsy smiled slightly and said, "Thanks."

Sister Nina watched the boys for a few more minutes and then stood up.

"Well, ladies. I need to get back to work. You have a lovely day."

"You, too, sister," said the three of them as she started back across the parking lot.

She reached the other side of the basketball court and then felt like the breath was getting sucked out of her. She stopped and turned slowly, her eyes darting back and forth.

Taylor was watching her and called out, "Sister Nina, are you okay?"

The boys stopped playing and looked at her. Taylor stood up and started walking toward her and the sister held up her hand.

"Stop right there!"

"Sister, what's wrong?"

The sister could feel a tear falling down her cheek and she wiped it away. The feeling of intense pressure got stronger and she could only think of two words to describe what she was feeling.

Impending doom.

Before she could take another breath, there was a loud crash that almost knocked her down. The power of the blast forced her to close her eyes against the sound. As she struggled to stay on her feet, she could hear the kids screaming.

As she regained her footing and opened her eyes, a large demon was standing right in the middle of the basketball court. The kids were frozen in terror at the sight of the monster.

"RUN!" she screamed at them.

Not needing any more encouragement than that, the boys and two of the girls scattered, disappearing around the buildings.

All except for one.

Betsy had fallen when the demon appeared and was backed up against the wall. Her terror was so complete she couldn't even force herself to get up and run. The demon just looked at her like she was a piece of meat and he was going to devour her.

Sister Nina ran as fast as she could, back across the basketball court and jumped in front of the demon, placing herself between the girl and the monster.

"You will not touch her, demon!"

She pulled her rosary from her pocket and held up the cross.

"By the power of God I command you to return to Hell from whence you came!"

"Aww, another little bug to play with," said

Azrin with a cruel smile on his face.

The sound of Betsy's terror-filled screams kept her rooted in place. Sister Nina waved the cross in front of the demon's face and commanded, "Begone!"

Azrin's right hand lashed out and grabbed hers, embedding the cross into his palm. The sister screamed in pain as the demon's burning hand closed over hers.

Out the corner of her eye, she could see Cardinal Wright sprinting across the parking lot, carrying a sword. He was yelling at her to get away.

She could feel the heat from the demon radiating up her arm, toward her body. The pain was so intense she couldn't even scream in pain. She couldn't even draw a breath.

Lord, please help me!

Before the cardinal could cover even half the distance, her body burst into flames. She screamed in agony as the cardinal raced up behind the demon and stabbed him in the back of the thigh.

Azrin released his hold on the burning nun and stumbled to his knees. The padre rounded on him and brought his blade around in a mighty, sweeping arc.

Before it could connect, Azrin winked out of sight, leaving the echoing of his laughter ringing in the padre's ears.

The cardinal raged in frustration as he looked around, hoping the demon would reappear.

"Come back here and face me!"

The screams of the girl behind him forced him to turn and look. She was fixated on the burning body of Sister Nina, who was almost burned to ash by then. She couldn't stop screaming.

The padre reached down and took her by the arm and pulled her to her feet.

"Stop it, young lady!" he yelled as he shook her.

"Padre, be careful with her!"

He turned and could see Esther standing at the back door of the church in her nightgown, leaning on her walker. Her face had a look of concern. Realizing what he was doing he softened his grip on the girl's arm.

"I'm sorry," he said as he guided her away from the scene.

"See that woman over there? Can you please go and help her back to bed? She shouldn't be up."

Betsy looked up at him.

"You'll be safe inside the church," he said. "The demon can't get at you inside there."

The girl looked back at, what was now nothing more than a pile of ash.

"She protected me," she said in a half-whisper.

"Yes, she did. And she would want you to get safely inside the church."

Betsy nodded and moved quickly across the lot, to the door and told Esther she was there to help her back to bed. As the two of them disappeared into the church, the padre turned back to the court.

The cold winter wind was beginning to blow the pile of ash away and within a minute, the only thing left was a black mark on the ground where the brave nun had fallen.

He walked to the spot and knelt down. Reaching down, he picked up the only thing left.

The sister's rosary. It appeared to be nearly untouched by the flames. Raising the wooden cross to his lips, he kissed it and said a prayer for the safe passage to Heaven for the nun.

Then he cried.

"Fredrick Bishop!"

The large black man stopped what he was doing and turned to the sound of the voice and a smile crossed his lips.

"Oh, I'm in trouble now," he said with a slur.

He wasn't just drunk. He was very drunk. To the point of almost falling over.

The detective had been tussling with a

couple of security guards, who appeared to be nothing more than a couple of average sized students in uniform. They were trying to get handcuffs on him, but weren't having much luck.

He had been going on about demons from Hell and how they were going to kill us all.

Sister Clarice marched right up to him and stared him right in the eyes. The look in her eyes made him take a step back and suddenly look a lot smaller than he was.

"Just exactly what are you doing, detective?" she demanded.

Even though she had taken a bit of the fight out of him, he still wouldn't let the security guards put the cuffs on him.

Finally the sister looked at them and asked, "Gentlemen, can you please let me handle this?"

They both stepped back and raised their hands. One said, "He's all yours, sister. Please get him out of here."

She nodded and they turned around and headed outside. They didn't go far, planning to stick around in case she couldn't handle the situation.

"In answer to your question, sishter," he slurred, "I am here to protect my daughter."

"Like this?"

"How are you going to protect me when

you're falling down drunk, daddy?"

Bishop swung around and almost fell down. Coming face-to-face with his daughter took the last bit of fight out of him and his shoulders sagged. It had been nearly twenty years since she saw him in such a state and it hit him hard, realizing what he was doing.

"You're in danger, Ash, and I just wanted to take care of you," he mumbled.

"Like the sister just asked, like this? You're in no condition to take care of anyone right now."

Sister Clarice stepped next to her and said, "We need to get you out of here, Freddie. And Ashley, I think you should come with us. We'll explain it all to you when we get back to the church."

"Okay, I'll go with you, but only to make sure my daddy is going to be okay."

Bethany spoke up and said, "I think the best way for him to be okay is to sleep this off."

"Bethany!" said the detective with a smile. Then the smile disappeared as he asked, with his finger to his lips, "Shouldn't you be in the church so Azrin can't get you?"

"Oh, now you care about me being safe in the church. Not like the other night when you ditched me at your ex-wife's house and left me miles from the church!"

"Did I?"

Sister Clarice held up her hand when she saw Bethany was going to light into him. The younger woman backed down as the sister grabbed the detective by the arm and his daughter grabbed his other arm. Together, the two of them were able to steer him out the door and down the sidewalk toward the car.

The two security guards followed behind at a safe distance.

After the sister and Ashley stuffed her father into the back seat, Clarice turned and walked back over to the guards.

"I am truly sorry for the trouble he put you through, gentlemen. Rest assured, this will be dealt with."

"Thank you for taking over, sister. We didn't really want to arrest him. Just wanted to get him off campus."

Just as the sister was going to say something else, there was a cry of anguish and Ashley screamed, "Sister!"

Whirling around, she saw Ashley was huddled over Bethany, who was on her hands and knees screaming, "No, no, no!"

Running back to the young woman, she knelt down.

"Bethany? What is it, swe ..."

When she touched her arm the vision hit her like a ton of bricks. As if they were standing right there, they saw the attack on

Sister Nina and her death.

"Oh dear God!" cried out the sister.

Jumping back to her feet, she pulled Bethany to hers and asked Ashley to help get her into the car. When they shoved her into the back seat next to the detective, the sister ran around and sat in the driver's seat.

Starting the car, the sister took a quick second to say a quick prayer for their safe passage back to the church.

Then she raced out of the parking lot and onto the city streets at speeds that would make a Formula One driver proud. Bethany was so far gone, she couldn't even marvel at how the sister's rust bucket of a car could even accomplish such a thing.

They had a clear path to the church without any police officers or red lights in sight.

Chapter 27 – The Cavalry

The mood around the church was as dark as it could have been for the next couple of days. Sister Clarice was holed up in her room and not talking to anyone. Not even Bethany.

The cardinal spent an hour on the phone with his uncle, expressing his feelings that this might be a losing battle. The Pope admonished him to keep the faith. It might be a losing battle, but it was not the entire war. Azrin and Lucifer might win a battle here and there, but they would never win it all in the end.

When Cardinal Wright expressed his concerns that Sister Clarice might be slipping away from them, the Pope was momentarily silent. Knowing that the Spirit of God resided deeply inside her, he couldn't conceive of her losing the faith she had. But it deeply concerned him.

Before ending the call the Pope told his nephew to stay the course and he would see if there was anything he could do to help.

Bethany spent most of her time with Esther, both of them trying to console each other. Esther tried to lighten the mood by telling the younger woman about her time as a demon hunter and how it led her to meet the love of her life.

That didn't have the effect Esther would

have hoped because it just brought back memories of how she lost that same love.

When Bethany would tell her about her aunt Suzanne, it had the same effect. The stories would start off happy, but then come back around to the fact that Azrin had killed her. Words would stop flowing and both would feel a sense of melancholy settle over them.

If Azrin could see the inside of the church at that moment, he would have been proud of his accomplishment. Never had his work destroyed happiness like it did at this time. He relished the sadness he was bringing to these humans.

Ashley spent most of her time in her room, but it wasn't really just her room. Her dad was sleeping on the carpeted floor beside her bed and she was looking after him.

It took him a full two days to get to where he could stand up without feeling dizzy. He wouldn't, or couldn't, eat, even though Ashley made sure to bring him something from the kitchen.

One last person was the one Bethany wondered about the most. Betsy seemed to come and go throughout the day. She knew the young woman had been there when Sister Nina was killed, but she seemed to be the least affected by it.

Whenever Bethany found her wandering

the halls of the church, it seemed like the girl didn't expect to be found. She was walking around the dark halls, humming to herself, but when Bethany would find her, it was like a switch was thrown and her whole demeanor changed. The humming would stop and the watery eyes would begin.

When asked by Bethany what she was doing, Betsy replied that she was attempting to walk around and forget the sister's death.

"No, Betsy, that's not what I mean. It appears you can leave this church at any time and go home. Apparently Azrin has no real interest in you. So why do you keep coming back? You're not Catholic, or even religious as far as I can tell."

"You're not Catholic, either," said the girl.

"It's different with me."

"Is it? Anyway, the cardinal said I could come inside the church and I would be safe. I don't really feel safe at home."

"What makes you feel unsafe at home?" asked Bethany.

Betsy just shrugged and said, "I don't. I just feel more safe inside here."

The girl turned and walked away, leaving Bethany watching her go, thinking something just wasn't right. From the vision she and Sister Clarice had witnessed, Betsy was terrified of the demon and had been devastated at the sight of Sister Nina's death.

Now, it was if she was completely past it, but it had happened just a couple of days before. Something just wasn't right.

Later in the afternoon of the third day, Bethany was in the small gym while Esther napped. She worked on some sword drills and was doing the best she could without an instructor. Sister Nina had taught her a lot, but her training was far from over.

The cardinal stepped in once and talked to her, apologizing that he couldn't help her because he wasn't an instructor in swordsmanship. She said it was okay and she was sure the sister would get back to it when she felt better. When she mentioned the sister, the padre went silent.

"You're worried she might not recover from this, aren't you?"

The padre looked at her and it was as if she had read his mind.

"I've never seen her like this, Bethany. I mean, she's lost before, but this time it seems like she is falling into despair and may not recover. I'm at a loss as to what to do."

"I don't know, padre. As close as I've become with her, I can't figure out how to break through her sadness right now."

The padre was going to say something, but

stopped when there was a sound coming from outside. They had both heard it when it first started, but it sounded like it was a long way off. It was a sound both of them recognized and had heard it many times in their lives.

There was a helicopter flying somewhere nearby and they both figured it would fly by and onto somewhere else in the city. Lots of helicopters flew the skies of Chicago, so hearing one wasn't that unusual.

This one, however, seemed to hover directly above the church. It got so loud, the stained glass windows began to rattle.

"What in the world," yelled the padre over the noise as he and Bethany ran from the gym.

As they came out of the gym, they almost ran into Sister Clarice. She had come out of her room at the sound, thinking the church might be under attack.

The three of them stopped in the back foyer and Bethany slipped an arm around the waist of the sister and hugged her close.

"What is going on?" yelled Bethany over the sound of the rotors.

They could tell the sound of the helicopter was moving slowly and the padre yelled it sounded like it was coming from out back. By this time, Ashley and her father had joined the group.

"That's not a police chopper," yelled

Bishop.

The whole group moved slowly to the back doors and the cardinal tried to peer out, but the marbled glass in the doors made it impossible to see what was happening. The rotor wash was banging the doors, so he finally reached over and pushed one door open. The artificial hurricane ripped the door from his hands and it slammed against the side of the building, shattering the glass.

Stepping out, he looked up.

"Oh my," was all he could say, but no one could hear it.

He stepped even further out allowing the others to follow him. They all craned their necks to see the green military helicopter moving slowly from above the church.

It appeared there were two pilots and they were looking down through the glass windows in front of their feet. There was another man in a military uniform, leaning out the open door on the far side of the chopper. It looked like he was yelling into his headset and the pilots were following his guidance.

It took a bit of jockeying of the chopper, but the pilots set it down right in the center of the small parking lot. Its blades were not in danger of hitting anything, but the wash from the rotors was playing havoc with the bushes around the edges.

Cardinal Wright half-expected to hear the rotors begin winding down, but the pilots kept them at just below take off speed. The man in the doorway jumped down to the ground on the other side of the chopper, while the small crowd watched and wondered.

Next, they saw a black duffel bag land on the ground next to his feet, which was all they could see of him.

Sister Clarice looked to the front of the chopper and noticed the young pilot was looking at her. He waved and smiled and she gave a tentative wave back.

The black duffel bag was followed by another set of feet landing on the ground. Two more bags landed on the ground and two more sets of feet. All of this was happening on the other side of the helicopter so no one could see who was getting off.

Then the first set of feet jumped back up in the chopper and the three people being dropped off grabbed their bags and moved away. When they were a safe distance away, the chopper's rotors began to speed up and it was apparent it was leaving.

Three people shielded themselves from the rotor blast on the far side of the parking lot as the helicopter took off. When the helicopter had lifted off and flown away, the group of three black clad people picked up their bags and turned toward the church.

"Father Draper?" said Sister Clarice.

Bethany looked at her, wondering who this Father Draper was.

The three finally started walking toward the stunned audience. The man was most definitely a priest and both ladies wore the same style black, leather habits that Sister Clarice wore.

Sister Clarice started crying and Bethany could feel her body shuddering with each sob.

The new padre and two nuns walked across the parking lot and Cardinal Wright moved to meet them.

Everyone else followed along behind him. Except for Sister Clarice and Bethany. Bethany didn't move because she still had her arm around the sister and the sister appeared to be in no condition to walk that short distance.

Father Draper dropped his bag when he reached the cardinal and they threw their arms around each other. The two sisters walked right past Ashley and Bishop without saying anything.

They walk straight to the other two women and stopped in front of them.

The older one looked at the tears streaming down Sister Clarice's face and said, "Tears of joy, I assume, Clarice?"

The sister finally moved when she stepped

into the waiting arms of the other nun and began crying even harder.

The younger sister, stepped up to Bethany and smiled.

"You must be this Bethany we've heard so much about."

Bethany held out her hand and this new sister used it to pull her into a hug.

"My name is Sister Marisol and I am pleased to meet you."

Bethany pulled back a little and said, "Really?"

Marisol smiled and said, "Sweetheart, any warrior that carries the sword of the cherubim that guarded the Garden of Eden is worth knowing."

They stepped apart and Marisol looked at the other two women, who were still in a hug.

"Alright, Helena. My turn."

Sister Helena laughed and stepped back so Marisol could hug their sister-in-arms. The most Sister Clarice could do was squeak out, "Thank you for coming."

Sister Helena gave Bethany a once over. She looked to be in her mid-fifties and also looked like she would take no guff from anyone.

Not feeling as much like hugging this younger woman, she reached up with both hands, held Bethany's head in her bony hands.

"Like Sister Marisol said, it is good to meet

you, young lady. We hear great things about you."

"You'd think these ladies hadn't seen each other in years."

The four ladies turned to see Father Draper and the cardinal standing there smiling.

"Does she still drop to her knees all the time?"

The cardinal laughed softly and said, "Almost constantly."

"I would have thought she would have grown out of that by now."

"Oh, hush!" said Sister Clarice as she threw her arms around the neck of the priest. "Thank you for coming."

The cardinal spoke up and said, "Might I suggest we move this reunion inside?"

As they were turning to the doors, a friar stepped out with a sheet of plywood and some tools. He set them down against the wall and then looked at the new arrivals.

"You just couldn't make an entrance that didn't involve destroying part of the property?"

"Brother Michael," said the cardinal.

Father Draper stepped in front of the irate friar and said, "You have something to say, brother?"

"Now I gotta clean it up."

The two men stood facing each other and Bethany thought a fight was about to break out. Not a smile on either man's face.

Then Father Draper started laughing and Brother Michael laughed and said, "I knew you couldn't do it."

They hugged each other and then Father Draper looked at the others.

"When I say, brother, I mean it literally."

"He's your brother?" asked Bethany.

"Hey, she's sharp," he said, elbowing his brother in the side.

"Sharper than you know," said Brother Michael.

The padre stepped forward and held out his hand and she took it. He leaned forward and kissed it and said, "I look forward to finding out."

As they moved into the church, Betsy was standing off to the side, in a dark corner. Sister Helena saw her standing there.

"And who are you, child?" she asked.

Sister Clarice offered, "This is Betsy. She was outside when Azrin killed Sister Nina."

"Oh, I'm so sorry," she said to Betsy. "May the grace of God be upon you."

All Betsy could do was nod and then walk away.

Sister Marisol leaned over and whispered in Bethany's ear, "Strange child."

"Yes, my thoughts exactly."

Within the next ten minutes, they assigned

the new arrivals rooms. They put father Draper across the hall from Ashley and her father and the two sisters asked to have small beds brought into Sister Clarice's room. Bethany offered to give up her room for them, but they insisted they wanted to be close the Clarice.

With that, there was no more room at the inn.

Chapter 28 – Sanctuary Breached

"Young lady. Your skill with the blade is rough and lacking."

Bethany took a step back and fought the tears welling up in her eyes. They didn't come because she was being upbraided by Sister Helena. They came because the sister had landed a stinging blow to Bethany's left shoulder. If they had been using real swords, Bethany would now be minus one arm.

"That's because Sister Nina didn't get a chance to finish my training!"

Sister Helena stood back and narrowed her eyes at the young woman.

"Is it going to be your intention to blame our dear departed sister for your lack of skill? This is the third time you've brought that up this hour."

Sister Marisol stood up and asked for a moment. Walking onto the mat, she put an arm around Bethany's shoulders and turned her away from her taskmaster. She was just a couple of years older than Sister Clarice, so much closer to Bethany's age.

The sister walked her off the mats and to a corner of the gym to have a little privacy. Bethany glanced over at the empty seat and wished that Sister Clarice was sitting in it.

As they reached the corner, Bethany

looked back at Sister Helena, who looked like she was thinking, "We don't have time for this!"

"Why does she hate me so much?" asked Bethany softly.

Marisol smiled, which caused the freckles across the bridge of her nose to wrinkle up. Her green eyes shined as her lips turned upward.

"She doesn't hate you, sweetheart. She loves you more than you know. She is tough on you because she is scared to death you may come up against this Azrin demon and won't be prepared for it. That terrifies her."

Bethany looked back across the gym, at the older sister and for a split second saw a softened image of Helena. It was brief, but Bethany realized she had just seen past the façade the older nun was putting up.

Sister Marisol reached up and placed a hand on the side of her face and turned her gaze back to her.

"Sister Clarice has said that you got the measure of Sister Nina after she told you something. What was it?"

The thought of Nina ready to do battle on the mats brought warmth to Bethany's heart.

"She told me to ask for help from Heaven and it would never fail me."

Marisol smiled and said, "I'm guessing you

haven't bothered to ask yet today. I can assure you, Sister Helena asked before she stepped onto the mats with you."

"I keep forgetting," whispered Bethany.

The sister took her head between her hands, leaned forward and whispered in her ear, "Stop forgetting. Make it part of who you are. The power of Heaven will lead you in all aspects of your life, not just when going into battle."

Bethany looked into Marisol's green eyes and nodded.

The sister leaned in and whispered one last thing. "The sooner you get the better of her, the sooner today's training session will end."

"You should have told me that sooner."

"Didn't want the torture to end too soon," said the nun with a giggle.

They both turned and walked back to the mats, hand-in-hand. As Bethany stepped onto the mats, Sister Marisol sat back down on her chair.

Next to the still empty chair.

Bethany closed her eyes for a few seconds and connected with the power of Heaven and felt it wash over her.

When she opened her eyes, she felt something tickling at the back of her mind. Looking to the side and past Sister Marisol, she saw Betsy standing just inside the doors, just staring at them.

Bethany turned and faced her, which caused the two nuns to also look at the girl. Being the center of attention wasn't something Betsy wanted, so she quickly exited through the doors.

"There is something seriously wrong with that young lady," said Sister Helena.

"You think she might be suffering under the sight of seeing Sister Nina killed?" asked Marisol.

"No, sister. She doesn't appear to be weighed down by that event at all. This is something completely different."

Sister Marisol said, "Maybe we should ask the cardinal to send her away."

"We can't turn away a child of God just because she makes us uncomfortable," said Sister Helena.

"If she really is a child of God," said Bethany softly.

Helena looked at her with concern and asked, "What makes you say that?"

Bethany said, "I just... I don't know ... it's ..."

"Young lady," said Sister Helena, "if you have concerns, do not be afraid to speak them. Anything you have to say is as important as what anyone else will say."

"I just get the feeling there is something

inside her that doesn't belong. I witnessed the vision of Sister Nina being killed and Betsy was terrified and screaming. But, by the time Sister Clarice and I got back here, she was walking around like nothing had happened."

"Sister Marisol, could you go to the cardinal and see what he knows about that girl. I concur with Bethany. There is something not right about her."

"Yes, sister," said Marisol as she stood up and headed out of the gym.

Sister Helena looked back at Bethany and prepared to continue her training.

"I hope I'm wrong about her," said Bethany. "I have witnessed my own friends being murdered by Azrin, so I know of the terror she was feeling that day."

"Yes, Bethany, but when you think back to that day, do you still feel that terror?"

"Yes, sister, though Sister Clarice did some good work in walling off Azrin from my mind."

"Well, that girl doesn't seem to feel that horror, even though she should."

Then the sister squared off and said, "Enough chitchat. Let us continue with your training."

Bethany couldn't help but smile as she asked for the power of Heaven again. And it flared in her soul.

For the first time that afternoon, she thought, "This is going to be fun."

"Where are you going?"

Sister Marisol whirled around to see Betsy slipping out of a dark corner. She immediately took a step back from the girl. Something about this young girl was scaring her.

"I just have a little business to discuss with the cardinal. How are you doing today, Betsy?"

"You're going to speak to him about me, aren't you?"

"No. Why would you say that?"

Betsy stepped closer, which caused Marisol to step back

"Because I can tell when you're lying. It's not nice for a nun to lie to a little girl," hissed Betsy.

Sister Marisol couldn't help but feel something evil was sharing the hallway with her. Her hand instantly flew behind her right shoulder, under her veil.

Before she could pull her sword, Betsy's right hand snapped out and the sister felt something grip her by the throat, even though the girl was still five feet away. Trying to clutch at the invisible force around her neck, she could feel massive fingers cutting off her ability to breathe.

Betsy took a couple of steps forward and

Sister Marisol began to lift off the ground. Struggling to break the hold of whatever had her, she could feel her vision beginning to darken. She knew within seconds she was going to be unconscious and completely defenseless.

"What are you doing?"

Betsy looked to her right and could see Ashley standing outside her door. Bishop suddenly appeared, pushing his way passed his daughter and charging toward the two.

Betsy hissed and flung Sister Marisol at him. The nun flew through the air and slammed into the detective with full force. He tried to grab her so she wouldn't get injured further, but they both crashed to the ground and skidded about twenty feet and up against a wall.

Ashley screamed and tried to catch her father and the nun, but got knocked out of the way. As she pushed herself back up, she went to her dad, who was trying to untangle himself from the unconscious nun.

Doors began flying open. The gym door crashed open as Bethany and Sister Helena rushed into the hallway. The door across the hall opened and Esther tottered into view using her walker.

Sister Clarice came out of her room, both of her hands filled with her pistols and the cardinal and Father Draper came running from the office.

"What happened?" yelled the cardinal.

"She attacked …"

The place where Ashley was pointing was empty.

"She was just there! That girl. Betsy!"

Just then they heard the back doors slam open and Sister Clarice and Bethany ran toward the back of the church. As they rushed through the doors, they caught sight of Betsy running around the far corner of the church.

Bethany took off after her and the sister screamed at her to stop. Father Draper ran through the doors just in time to see Bethany disappear around the corner.

"Stay here!" he yelled at Clarice as he took off after the young warrior.

Reaching the street, he heard the screeching of tires on asphalt and saw Bethany running across the nearby intersection, oblivious to the traffic bearing down on her.

"Oh, Father, we don't need to be doing this," he muttered as he set off after her.

As he raced through the intersection, setting off another round of screeching tires, he saw Bethany turn into an alley.

Rounding the corner, he came upon Bethany, about twenty feet away and brandishing her sword. It was blazing and spitting fire, ready for battle.

"You shouldn't be out here alone, young warrior," he said as he moved beside her, his own sword ready to fight.

"If I had waited for you old people I would have lost her."

Father Draper chuckled and warned, "You'll never know what it's like to get old if you keep rushing into these situations."

As they circled around, their backs to each other, he said, "It appears you might have lost her anyway."

"She was fast," said Bethany, her eyes still shifting from side-to-side. "But I don't think we've lost her."

"You still feel her?"

"I'm not sure what I feel right now, but it isn't good."

As they continued to circle, neither one of them could shake the feeling they were being watched.

A garbage can flew from the side of the alley and slammed into the padre, knocking him down. His sword clattered to the ground, skittering away from him.

Bethany whirled around and brought her own sword to bear. Betsy stepped out of a dark space, as if appearing from thin air.

The girl smiled and said, "Ah, the young warrior is out of the safety of her church."

For the first time since she chased Betsy, Bethany realized the gravity of her situation. She was indeed outside the church and looking down, she could see the padre was out cold.

Now she was truly terrified.

Holding her sword in front of her, she kept her eyes locked on Betsy's. The girl smiled the most evil grin. Or maybe it was the demon inside her.

Her sword had no problem discerning what they were dealing with and lashed out with a couple of lightning bolts. These caused the demon to screech in pain. But to Bethany's ears, they sounded like cries of pain from a young girl.

"Kill her!"

Bethany looked down to see the padre had regained consciousness. His voice was raspy and rough and he was trying to push himself back up.

"Silence!" screamed Betsy as the garbage can flew again. The padre blocked it with his arms, but it still knocked him back down, bouncing his head on the cement.

"Stop that!" yelled Bethany as she stepped forward, pointing her sword at the girl.

Betsy backed up, clearly wary of the blade and found herself backed up against the brick wall.

Bethany pressed the sword against the

chest of the girl and said, "I don't want to kill you, but I will."

"Will you?" growled the little girl, but not with a little girl's voice. It was definitely the voice of a demon now. "I don't think you have it in you."

Bethany trembled at the thought of ending Betsy and knew she couldn't do it.

"You're a pathetic excuse for a hunter!" spat the demon voice.

The little girl stepped forward, pressing her body against the tip of the sword. Bethany stepped back, but her blade was having none of it. Lightning erupted from the tip and drove the demon back against the wall.

Then the demon screeched as another blade sliced past Bethany's ear and right through the neck of the girl. As her head fell to the ground, Bethany looked over to see Sister Helena wielding the other sword.

"Don't ever hesitate to destroy a demon, Bethany. They will destroy you in the blink of an eye."

Bethany looked down at the body of the girl and watched as it disintegrated into a pile of ash. A cold breeze came through the alley and blew the pile away, swirling it around her feet.

Turning around, she saw the sister helping Father Draper to his feet. He was still a bit

363

groggy and she leaned him back against the wall until he could get his strength back.

"You gotta watch out for those flying trash cans, Charles."

"Yeah, those things are killers."

Bethany turned around and saw the padre's sword laying on the ground and she bent down to pick it up. The sister and priest yelled at her to stop, but she picked it up without a second thought.

Then turned around and looked at them.

"What?"

"She shouldn't be able to do that," gasped the sister.

Bethany walked over and handed the sword to the padre, who held it to his chest and let its power strengthen him.

After a moment, the padre said, "Let's get back to the church."

Together the three of them headed out of the alley and back across the intersection. This time waiting for the WALK light like they were supposed to.

Walking around to the back parking lot, they found two ambulances. Sister Marisol was being loaded into one. The paramedics were trying to get Detective Bishop in the other one, but being the cantankerous police officer he was, it was a losing battle.

"I am not leaving my daughter here

defenseless!"

"Daddy! Go to the damn hospital!"

Bishop snapped back and looked at her.

"You'd use such language in a church?"

"We're not in the church! We're in the parking lot! Now get in the freakin' ambulance!"

"What's going on?" asked Bethany. "Is he hurt?"

"Yes," said Ashley. "Apparently trying to catch the flying nun he might have broken his arm."

Bethany brought her sword up and pointed it right at his chest.

"Get in the ambulance. I won't tell you again."

"You wouldn't dare stab me!"

"I don't have to stab you."

With that, the sword spit out a lightning bolt that hit the detective in the chest.

"Ow! That hurt!"

"I'll do it again!"

He tried to stare her down, but ultimately turned and climbed into the ambulance, muttering, "These damn women are taking over the freakin' world."

As he sat down, he looked back at Ashley.

"And you! You're becoming more and more like your mother every day!"

She just smiled up at him.

"I'll be safe here until you get back, daddy."

One of the paramedics was getting ready to close the doors of the ambulance when Sister Helena said, "We have one more to go."

She ushered Father Draper to the back of the ambulance, but he insisted he was fine. The paramedic looked into his eyes and said something about a possible concussion.

"I'm telling you, I'm fine."

"You want me to get Bethany to get you in this ambulance?"

"That's some dirty pool right there, sister."

He climbed in and took a seat next to the detective. Looking past the ladies, he called out, "Don't let them take over, Your Eminence."

"I'll try, but I'm not making any promises," said the cardinal.

With that, the doors were closed and the two ambulances made their way out to the street and toward the hospital.

The cardinal shepherded all the ladies back into the church and made sure the doors were locked tight.

Chapter 29 – Confronting The Hero

It was much later when a taxi pulled into the parking lot and dropped off the detective and the padre. Bishop was sporting a shiny new cast on his forearm and the padre had a bandage on the back of his head.

They had to knock on the back doors because the cardinal had decided locked doors were necessary since a demon had somehow found its way into the church.

After a minute, someone looked through the window and saw them and opened the door. It was Brother Michael.

"How are you feeling, Charles?"

"Pretty good considering I got my head smashed by a demon."

"Mother wasn't too happy to hear about that."

"Oh. You didn't call her, did you?"

"Nope. She called because she felt something was wrong. Anyway, I assured her you were fine. You should call her."

Bishop looked around and noticed the place was unusually dark.

"Where is everyone?" he asked.

"In the dining room."

"Dinner was a little late this evening?"

"Well, with the invasion of the church by a demon, things got pushed back a little."

Heading into the dining room, they found all the ladies and one cardinal trying to enjoy a simple meal.

Bishop and Draper could tell the mood was a bit dark. One thing he noticed was the absence of Sister Clarice.

"Gentlemen," said the cardinal. "It's good to see you back. Have a seat and have some dinner."

Bishop walked around and leaned over and gave Ashley a kiss on top of the head and then sat down next to her.

"How's Sister Marisol?" asked Bethany.

Father Draper answered, "She's going to be fine, but they are keeping her for a couple of days."

"I'll have to visit her tomorrow," said Sister Helena.

"I'd like to go with you," said Bethany.

Sister Helena was going to say that wasn't a good idea, but then changed her mind.

"That will be fine. We'll go just after morning meal."

"Not to change the subject," said Bishop, "but where is Sister Clarice?"

It was as if he had asked the forbidden question. Everyone went silent around the table.

"She's in her room," said Bethany softly. "She won't come out."

Brother Michael came out of the kitchen with two plates and set one in front of his brother and one in front of Bishop.

"Has she eaten?" asked the detective.

"I don't think so," said Bethany.

Bishop pushed his chair back and picked up his plate. As he was heading for the door, the cardinal said, "I don't think she wants to talk to anyone right now, detective."

"She's going to talk to me."

Leaving the dining room, he walked to Sister Clarice's room and knocked softly on the door. A few seconds later, the door opened slightly and she peered out through the narrow opening.

"What do you want?"

He smiled and said, "I brought you your dinner."

"I'm not really …"

He pushed the door open and walked into the room.

"I don't really give a rat's ass whether or not you're hungry. We need to talk."

She looked at him and then pushed the door closed. He walked over and set the plate down on the small table and then sat down on the other side.

It was about that time he realized she wasn't dressed as a nun. She was just wearing a plain black t-shirt and a pair of sweatpants. He almost didn't recognize her, having never seen her like this.

He gestured to the chair near the plate and she sat down. When she was seated, she pushed the plate across the table to him.

"I'm fasting, detective. Go ahead and eat."

"You sure?"

"Yes, detective."

As he picked up the fork and stabbed a piece of roast beef, he looked at her.

"What happened to Freddie? Or Fredrick?"

She bowed her head as he stuck the meat in his mouth and began chewing.

"You know, I have all evening," he said with his mouth full.

She looked up at him and said, "Freddie, you just would not understand."

"Then help me understand. Help me understand how the woman who can march straight into Hell and confront the Devil himself, can be brought so low?"

Sister Clarice bowed her head and started crying again. He just continued eating, realizing he hadn't eaten since breakfast that morning.

"I can't talk about this," she said.

"Oh, you will talk about this or I'll start saying things you definitely don't want to hear."

"Like what?" she said, starting to sound a

little more defiant.

"Like, how incredibly beautiful you are when you're not wearing your nun clothes."

Her mouth dropped open as he took a bite of potato.

"I'm just a couple of years older than Ashley, Freddie."

"Yes, you are. And still quite beautiful. I never really noticed it before because you were always wrapped up tighter than a Christmas present. But now, seeing you like this, I can hardly take my eyes off you."

"Please stop," she whispered.

"Then start … talking."

She took a deep breath and shook her head.

"Freddie, we're fighting a losing battle!" she said, raising her voice. At first, it took him by surprise because he'd never heard her like this.

"Are we? Because from where I sit, we're still fighting. Sure, we've taken a couple on the chin, but we're still standing."

"We're still standing? Marvin isn't. Suzanne Kelly isn't! All of Bethany's friends aren't! Your ex-wife is NOT still standing!"

He sat back in his chair, wondering if this is what he had in mind when he said she was going to talk to him. His mouth hung open with some half-chewed roast beef in it.

"And when do we admit defeat?" she continued. "When do we realize we might not win this fight?"

Her eyes were blazing as she vented her anger at him.

"Never, sister! We never admit defeat as long as we can still fight. We don't give up."

"But who are we fighting for?" she pleaded.

"Who are we … Sister, we're fighting for people like Ashley. We're fighting for Bethany and Esther," he said as he set his fork down. "We're fighting for people like Shondra, who got dragged into Hell and didn't deserve to be there. And for someone you might remember from a few years ago, we fight for Isabella."

The image of Isabella stuffing a ketchup-covered Brussels sprout in the mouth made her cry even more. Then she smiled as she pictured Isabella with ketchup running down her chin.

"Now, there's that smile," said the detective.

"You're not playing fair, you know."

Bishop picked up his fork and stuffed another piece of meat in his mouth.

"Just taking a page from my daughter's playbook."

"How so?"

"She tore into me yesterday when I was sober enough to hear her."

"You were pretty drunk that day."

"Yes, I was and for that, I apologize to you. Nearly twenty years on the wagon and I fell off with one massive bender because of that jackass demon from Hell."

She nodded and thought for a moment.

"How are we supposed to win against Azrin?" she asked. "Like I said the other day, we always seem to be one step behind him."

"I don't know, sister. This is your world. I'm just a visitor here."

As he finished the last of the food on his plate and pushed it aside, he leaned forward on the table and stared at her.

"But just like the day when you jumped into Hell, I will follow you anywhere and help in any way I can."

"We need a plan, Freddie and I'm at a loss."

"Well, there is a table full of people in the dining room that would love to have you join them. Maybe they can give us some ideas."

She bit her lip and then nodded. Standing up, she walked over to her wardrobe and pulled out a habit. Pulling it over her head, she shimmied it down until it came to her feet. Then the sweatpants fell to the floor and she kicked them away.

Bishop was a bit disappointed. She was putting on a regular nun's habit, not one of the

373

black leather ones she usually wore.

Pulling a simple veil from the wardrobe, she draped it over her head, leaving it to show her dark hair underneath. Then she pulled a pair of plain, black sneakers out and slipped her feet into them.

"Shall we?" she asked when she was finished.

He sat and looked at her for a moment and she could tell something was wrong.

"What?"

"I don't know," he said as he stood up and picked up his plate. "I just like you better when you're dressed as a badass warrior."

She smiled and said, "Those are my battle clothes. These are my casual clothes."

"So what are the t-shirts and sweatpants?"

"Those are my sleeping clothes."

He smirked and let out, "Oooo."

"Stop it. I'm still about the same age as your daughter."

He reached over and pulled the door open and leaned over as she walked past him.

"And you're still very beautiful."

She just shook her head and sighed.

"Men."

He laughed as he pulled her door closed and they headed for the dining room. Everyone still sat around the table, talking. All went silent when she walked into the room.

Bishop walked over and sat down next to his daughter and Clarice moved toward an empty seat next to Bethany.

Before she sat down, she looked around the table.

"First, let me apologize for the way I've been acting for the past few days. I guess Sister Nina's passing hit me …"

Bethany mumbled, "Murder."

"What?" asked the sister.

Bethany looked up at her and said, "Sister Nina's murder."

Sister Clarice took a deep breath and closed her eyes. Letting the breath out, she nodded.

"Yes, Sister Nina's murder. Thank you, Bethany. Again, I apologize for my recent mood. I ask for your forgiveness."

There were nods and words of forgiveness from around the table. Bethany jumped up and threw her arms around the nun's neck and hugged her close.

After they parted and sat back down, the cardinal tapped his spoon against a glass. Everyone gave him their undivided attention.

"We need to talk about the events of today."

"Yes," said Ashley. "Like how did a demon get inside this church? I thought that was supposed to be impossible."

"I'm afraid I may have had something to do with that," said the cardinal.

Everyone looked at him.

"Upon the attack of the blessed Sister Nina, I directed Betsy to seek refuge in the church. Somewhere along the way, Azrin must have possessed her and, as I had just invited her into the church, he just walked right in."

"But she helped me back to bed," said Esther. "I didn't sense any evil in her at all. Just a scared little girl."

"Yes, Esther. But she came and went later after Sister Clarice and Bethany returned from their mission to retrieve the detective."

Bishop looked down at the table and kept his eyes down. He didn't look up until Ashley placed a hand on top of his.

"When we returned," said Bethany, "I could feel something was off about her."

"Yes," said the cardinal, "but I failed to watch her in that short time during your travels. She possibly could have slipped outside for even just a minute. It would have only taken a second for Azrin to grab her."

"We need to find her family," said Ashley. "They need to know what happened."

"And what shall we tell them?"

Everyone looked at Sister Helena.

"We can't very well go to them and say, oh yes, a demon from Hell possessed your daughter so we had to behead her."

Bethany hung her head and tried to fight back the tears, remembering how she had the point of her sword pressed against the young girl's chest.

She felt a hand settle on hers and give her a squeeze. She looked over into Sister Clarice's eyes. The nun leaned over and whispered in her ear.

"It gets no easier. Ask God to help you through this."

"We still need to let her family know something," said Ashley. "Even if we have to keep the whole truth from them."

"Do we even know where her family is?" asked Bethany.

"No," said the cardinal. "She wasn't a member of this flock and was only out back because she was with some friends watching some boys play basketball."

"Any of the boys or other girls members of this church?" she asked.

"I didn't recognize any of them, but it's not unusual for kids from the neighborhood to use the basketball court. That's why we put it back there. To give them a safe place to play."

Detective Bishop pulled out his phone and said he'd try to get the department to locate the family. He tapped out a message and sent it.

Within a few seconds, his phone pinged

with a new text.

He read the message and said, "Uh oh."

"What?" asked Sister Clarice.

He held up the phone so she could read it from across the table.

"Uh oh," she said.

He looked at the message again and Ashley read it over his shoulder.

GET YOUR GODDAMN ASS
DOWN HERE RIGHT NOW!

Standing up, he said, "Ladies and gentlemen, I bid you farewell. If I don't see you again, it's because I was put in front of a firing squad. It's been a pleasure."

He quickly tapped out a message on the phone as Sister Clarice stood up.

"I'm going with you."

"Oh no, you're not," said Bishop.

"In case you've forgotten, Freddie, your car is miles away from here."

"Which is why I just called an Uber," he said, holding up the phone. "Besides, sweet sister, I don't want you walking into the line of fire I so well deserve."

"Is there anything I can do to help?" she asked.

"Yes," he said with a smile. "Pray for me."

When she smiled again, he said, "You

know, you really are beautiful."

"Oh, stop that!"

He looked at Bethany and asked, "Isn't she just the cutest thing when she gets all flustered?"

Bethany just smiled and nodded.

"I shall return," said the detective as he turned and headed for the door. "Maybe … probably … maybe not."

He disappeared out the door and the cardinal pulled his own phone out and dialed.

"Who are you calling?" asked the sister.

"Oh, just the chief of police."

"You know, Captain Tyrell is going to hate you."

"A chance I will take for a man that would follow a knucklehead nun straight into Hell to rescue a woman he didn't even know."

He got up and walked out of the dining room as he began talking to the chief. Bethany leaned over and poked the sister in the ribs.

"He called you a knucklehead," she said with a giggle.

"A term of endearment."

"Not to dampen the mood," said Father Draper as he stood up, "we still need to figure out what to do about this Azrin."

Bethany raised her hand. Sister Helena slapped her hand down on the table, causing everyone to jump.

"Young lady, if you have something to say, you do NOT need to raise your hand!"

"Yes, sister. I was just wondering why you refer to him as this Azrin? Sister Marisol did the same thing. It's like you don't know who he is."

"We've never been confronted with him, Sister Bethany," said Father Draper, causing Bethany to tense up. "I don't want to scare you, but there are more demons that walk the face of this planet than just Azrin."

She looked at Sister Helena, who just nodded.

"Yes, we have our share of demons in California, but they're a weak bunch. Sister Marisol and I can usually just slap them around a little and send them back to Hell with their tails between their legs."

Bethany smiled. She liked this older nun.

"Was there something I said, Sister Bethany?" asked Father Draper.

Sister Clarice squeezed her hand and said, "She doesn't like to be called Sister Bethany. Says she feels unworthy."

"Unworthy?" barked Sister Helena. She looked up at Father Draper and said, "What in the world?"

"Young lady," he said, "after what we witnessed in the alley today, don't you ever consider yourself unworthy!"

"What happened?" asked Clarice.

"Oh yes, you weren't there," said Sister Helena. "Seems the young lady here may have the Angel's Touch."

Sister Clarice's head whipped around and stared at Bethany.

"I honestly have no idea what they are talking about," mumbled Bethany.

"Did you or did you not pick up Father Draper's sword and hand it back to him?" asked the older sister.

"Well, yes, but I was just trying to be helpful. He was still hurt."

She felt a soft hand settle on her arm and she looked to see Esther looking at her with wonder in her eyes.

"Only a select handful of warriors have what we call the Angel's Touch," said the older woman. "I didn't have it. I don't believe Sister Clarice has it or anyone else in this room, for that matter."

"I don't understand."

Sister Clarice said, "When you pick up another warrior's sword, it should have knocked you into next week."

"But he was hurt."

"It doesn't matter," she said. "It's a safeguard placed on the warrior's weapons so they can't be picked up and used against them if they fall."

Then she leaned over and hugged the young woman close and whispered in her ear. "You might as well give in. Heaven has chosen you."

Bethany dropped her head and then blurted, "I haven't even been to my senior prom yet!"

Sister Clarice hugged her even tighter and said, "There's still time for that. Besides, you haven't even been to school in almost a month. It's safe to say they may have written you off by now."

When they parted, Sister Clarice had a grin on her face.

"You're enjoying this!" said Bethany.

"Immensely."

About that time, the cardinal came back to the table and sat down.

"So, in our midst, we have one of the favored warriors of God," said Father Draper.

"What did I miss?" asked the cardinal.

Sister Clarice wrapped her arms around Bethany's shoulders again and told the cardinal what she had just learned.

"I knew there was something special about you," he said as he picked up his glass and drank.

"I feel like I'm going to be sick," said Bethany, leaning over the table.

"I guess you haven't told her what she will

need to do after we take care of this Azrin situation," said the cardinal.

"Oh no," said Sister Clarice. "We're trying to ease her into it."

"What?" asked Bethany as she sat back up, trying to keep dinner down.

Esther reached over and cupped her face with one of her bony hands.

"You'll need to fly to Rome and meet the Pope."

Bethany's face went white and she jumped up from the table and ran from the dining room.

Sister Clarice looked at the cardinal and said, "You know, I seem to remember having a similar reaction to that news."

The rest of the gathering went on without Bethany, as she sat hunched over the toilet in her bathroom for the next hour.

Chapter 30 – Upping The Ante

A drizzle was falling, making the roads just a little more slippery. Nothing too dangerous, but something that would cause the more cautious drivers to slow down.

A more cautious driver did not exist than Sister Beth. With the water on the roadways, she slowed down by half the speed limit. If the truth were known, part of that was because her eyesight wasn't the best and she was pretty sure she'd lose her driver's license the next time it came up for renewal.

Sitting in the passenger seat, Sister Marissa dozed a little. It had been a long day that started at the children's hospital. With Sister Nina gone, she and Sister Beth picked up her responsibilities until someone else could be found to take them. The recently murdered sister had been one of those that would spend all her time at the hospital, making the children laugh. It was almost as if she needed to be dragged away from there with wild horses.

The children loved her and neither nun had the heart to tell them she would not be returning.

As Sister Beth picked her way slowly along the right hand lane of the freeway, other cars raced past her, but she paid them no mind.

Other than to whisper a silent prayer they would reach their destinations safely.

A little ways ahead was the off-ramp that would take them to the surface streets and then a few blocks back to the orphanage. She was looking forward to crawling into bed and getting some sleep. Unlike the Mother Superior, she obviously couldn't close her eyes and rest.

As she reached the bottom of the off-ramp, she signaled a right turn and began to turn the wheel. There was a set of train tracks that ran alongside the freeway and making the turn, she would drive over them.

There was no red signal, so she knew they wouldn't have to stop, which she thanked Heaven for speeding them on their way.

As she turned, she noticed the tires drifting in the water and let off the gas, but the car slid forward faster than expected.

"Oh no!" she gasped as she turned the wheel to keep the car on the road.

Sister Marissa opened her eyes just in time to feel the car slide off the side of the road and become high-centered on the railroad tracks. She immediately crossed herself when she looked out the windshield.

The last thing both sisters saw was a dark train coming right at them. The front of the engine took on the shape of Azrin's face. His mouth was open in a grin and his eyes were blazing red.

In a split second, a train that had no headlights smashed into the car. The train hurtled forward and didn't even activate the crossing signals. The car exploded in a ball of fire and the force of the crash threw it about a hundred yards down the tracks. The train hit it again and again, completely destroying it.

With one last hit, the remains of the car arced into the air, over the tops of the trees lining the tracks, coming to rest a hundred yards away.

The only bit of mercy for the two sisters was they were killed instantly and didn't suffer burning to death.

"Do you have any idea just how close I am to snapping your badge and gun away from you?" thundered Captain Tyrell.

The detective stood at parade rest, a habit he had from his days in the Marines. His eyes were fixed straight ahead, his hands crossed behind his back.

"Yes, sir!"

The captain looked up from his seated position behind his desk at the wayward detective and scowled.

"What the fuck are you doing?" he yelled loud enough to be heard by everyone in the squad room.

"Sir?"

"Sit your damn ass down!"

"Yes, sir."

Bishop moved around the chair in front of him and sat down and looked at the captain.

"You call me sir one more time and I will fire you! Understood?"

"Sorry, Mike."

The captain stared at him for a moment and then said, "We go way back, Fred. All the way to the academy. You've been there for me way more times than I've been there for you."

"I appreciate that, Mike, and I know we've both seen our share of shit in this job. And if you were to fire me right now, I'd understand it. I deserve it."

"Yes, you do. But I also know you still had feelings for your ex and it was my mistake to send you out there last week. For that, I apologize. And you're not going to be fired. Seems that damned cardinal called the chief again and the chief called me and told me to go easy on you."

Bishop just nodded and took a deep breath. "I'm going to have to ask him to stop that."

"Be straight with me, Fred. What is it we're dealing with here?"

"Captain, if I told you, you would not just

fire me, but would have me committed to Bellvue within an hour."

"So, you're going to stick with your story of this being something Biblical. I don't believe in the Bible, Fred."

Bishop just looked at him and said, "It might be time for you to start believing. I've seen it with my own eyes and I'm ready to commit myself to the loony bin."

"Just tell me, what are we dealing with here?"

Bishop took a deep breath and then said, "A demon."

"A demon. That's what you think is causing all this mayhem?"

"Yes, sir. I've see …"

A knock on the door interrupted him and the captain called out for them to come in. Shirley, his receptionist, opened the door.

"Detective, that little girl you asked us to find? We've found her."

"You found her? Really?"

Knowing Betsy had been killed in the alley earlier that afternoon, Bishop was unsure of what to think.

"Where?"

"Her home," said Shirley as she handed a piece of paper to him. "You should get over there. They say it's really bad."

"Another attack?"

She just nodded and backed out of the door and closed it.

"I don't believe this," he mumbled as he looked at the paper.

"Should I send someone else out there to handle this?" asked the captain.

The detective took a breath and stood up.

"No, Mike. I got this. I need to go pick up the sister and head out there."

"You could always leave her out of this," said the captain.

"I wish I could, but she's even madder at me than you. If I ghosted her she'd bring down Hellfire on me."

"We've got to stop this son of a bitch."

"You're preachin' to the choir, Mike. Preachin' to the choir."

He turned and headed out of the office and to the garage to check out another car. While he walked, he pulled his phone and dialed a number, halfway hoping she wouldn't pick up.

Rolling onto the street toward the address Shirley had given him, he saw a sight that was becoming all too familiar. Police cars and ambulances completely blocked the street off. A small crowd was gathered on the far side of the street.

The sister sat next to him, not having said a word since they got in the car and made the drive. He wasn't sure if it was because she was mad at him or something else.

One thing she had done after he called her was get dressed like a warrior again. She looked like she was ready to fight. She had even taken her sword back from Bethany.

As he parked the car and prepared to get out, she just sat and looked at the house across the street. He could read it in her face.

Other than her mission to come find him, she hadn't been out of the church. This was her first time back in the field since Azrin had attacked her.

"You going to be okay?"

She turned and looked at him.

"No, Freddie, I'm not going to be okay. This is so far past anything I've ever dealt with and I don't know what to do."

He didn't know what to say to that, so he didn't say anything.

"I guess sitting here isn't going to be the answer, either," she said as she unbuckled her seatbelt and opened the door.

He met her at the front of the car and they made their way across the street and under the Crime Scene tape. As they walked up the sidewalk, he saw something that should have brought a smile to his face, but he couldn't muster one.

"Officer Danton, it's good to see you back

on the job."

Mary turned around and just shook her head.

"I wish I could say it was good to be back, detective. This one is just so evil I can't …"

She couldn't even bring herself to finish the sentence. She looked at the sister.

"Is this ever going to stop, sister? I can't even get that monster out of my head."

The sister reached over and squeezed Bishop's arm.

"You go on inside. I need to talk to Mary for a moment."

He just nodded and headed up the steps and into the house.

The sister stepped in front of Mary and reached up and placed her hands on the sides of her face. She was suddenly assailed with the vision of the attack that sent Mary to the hospital.

The demon was obviously taking great delight in the pain and suffering he was inflicting. She could hear him laughing each time he struck Mary. She could tell it was nothing more than a show he was putting on for her benefit.

Mary's breathing became ragged and hurried as Sister Clarice pulled her forehead to hers and they touched. The sister began praying and after a couple of minutes, the officer's breathing eased and her whole body began to relax.

They both could hear Azrin raging at being shut out of another mind. He didn't like having his toys taken away.

As they parted, Mary wiped the tears away from her face. For the first time in days she was finally at peace.

"In answer to your question," said Sister Clarice, "yes, this is going to end. One way or another, I intend to end it."

Mary gasped when she caught a fleeting glimpse of the sister in a life or death struggle with the demon and losing the battle. That the sister could lose her own life in vanquishing the demon was terrifying to her.

Sister Clarice patted her on the shoulder again and said, "I guess I better get in there and see how bad this is."

"Please don't go in there, sister. It's worse than anything I've ever seen."

"I have to bear witness to the evil we face, Mary. The only way I shall defeat him is to know what he is capable of."

"I'm afraid we will lose you."

Sister Clarice forced a pained smile and said, "God promises none of us immortality in this life. Only in the next one."

With one last pat on the shoulder, she turned and headed in the door to the row house. What she saw was so far beyond the horror she could have imagined.

The entire living room was covered in blood, as if a red paint bomb had gone off in the room. The color of crimson coated every surface.

Like with Esther, there were two people on their knees, their arms outstretched upward. Their eyes were burned out of their sockets and their mouths frozen in cries of anguish.

They were facing a third figure, a young girl, who was spiked to the wall. Again, in the form of Jesus hanging on the cross.

"Where is Detective Bishop?" she asked one of the crime scene investigators.

The man could only point toward the kitchen door. Stepping through, she could see the back door was open, leading to a small backyard.

When she walked to the door, she could see him standing just off the porch, staring straight ahead. She could tell he was trying to control his breathing and it wasn't easy.

"Why does God allow this monster to continue like this?"

He hadn't turned around, but somehow sensed her presence behind. Maybe it was the sound her habit made as she walked. Maybe he could just feel her spirit when she was close.

"Freddie, if I had a dollar for every time I

wondered that myself, I'd be a very rich woman."

He turned around and she could see the tears in his eyes were very close to falling down his dark cheeks. Reaching into her pocket, she pulled out a clean tissue and handed it to him.

"She was just fourteen," he said as he dabbed his eyes dry. "She had her whole life ahead of her."

She could only nod in agreement.

"As did Bethany's friends, or Suzanne Kelly, or your ex-wife."

"How are we supposed to stop him?"

"I'm thinking there may be only one way to stop Azrin," she said, "but I'm not ready to divulge what that is just yet."

"Why not?" he demanded.

"Because the cardinal will not approve and The Holy Father most certainly won't."

"Then don't do it."

"It may come down to not having any other choice," she said softly.

He just stared at her for a moment before speaking.

"Your idea is something that could end with your death, isn't it?"

When she hesitated to answer, he knew he was correct.

"Sister Clarice, I strongly advise you to reconsider that course of action."

She stepped to the edge of the porch, which put her almost eye-to-eye with him.

"Freddie, if you have any better ideas I am certainly willing to listen. You've seen what we're up against. He seems to move in and out of our world with ease, most likely with the full support of Lucifer. He could be across the city at this moment, carrying out another attack and will be done and gone before we even hear about it."

"There has to be another way," he said as he wiped more tears from his eyes. "I can't stand the thought of losing you to this monster."

Reaching up, she cupped his cheek.

"There is no guarantee that you will lose me, sweet man. But also realize, there is no guarantee that I will live forever."

"I won't let it happen."

She just smiled and said, "It may not be your choice. It rests in the hands of God."

"Well, I'd like to talk to Him, then."

She smiled again.

"You know how to do that."

Bishop was about to say something when his phone rang. Looking at the display, he had a confused look on his face. Holding up the phone, she could see the reason for his confusion.

"Why is he calling me?" he asked.

She just shrugged as he answered the call, placing it on speaker.

"Cardinal Wright?"

"Please take the phone off speaker, detective."

A look of terror crossed her face as he tapped the button to turn off the speaker.

"Okay, what's up?"

He listened for a moment and then his eyes closed and his head dropped.

"Yes sir, I understand."

Hanging up the phone, he slipped it back into his pocket. He took a deep breath, hoping what he had heard was just a dream. Opening his eyes, he looked into the sister's and knew if it was a dream, it was a nightmare.

"It's happened again," he said softly. "We need to go."

"What's happened, Freddie?"

He stepped past her, patting her on the shoulder.

"Let's just go."

Chapter 31 – The Aftermath

The rain that started three days ago had not let up at all. It seemed almost poetic as the detective and the sister stood at the edge of the road, looking into the trees. From there they could almost see the wreckage about a hundred yards away.

"It doesn't make any sense, detective."

Bishop looked at the uniform cop standing next to them.

"What's that, officer?"

"There is no way on God's green Earth that car could have ended up there. They could have been going over a hundred miles per hour and they still wouldn't have ended up there."

"Do we know how fast they were going?"

"A couple of traffic cams showed them traveling well under the speed limit. Being as how we're dealing with a couple of senior ladies here, I don't see them driving like race car drivers."

"Any cameras show the actual accident?"

"No, sir and that's another strange thing. There is a traffic cam pointed right at the railroad crossing back there, but at the time we figured the accident happened, that camera just happened to go on the fritz."

"Maybe it didn't happen at the crossing?" mused Bishop.

"We're pretty sure it did," said the officer. "There's debris and pieces of the car at the crossing and scattered all along the tracks until that point over there. That's where it appears the car went into the woods."

"And yet we don't see a train stopped here," said Bishop.

"That's another thing," said the officer. "We've contacted the rail dispatcher. A train came through about an hour before the accident. That was over three hours ago. There is not another train scheduled through that crossing until early tomorrow morning."

Bishop looked over at the sister, whose face was wet. He couldn't tell what was tears and what was rain. He was pretty sure it was equal amounts of both.

"Do you think we need to go over there?" he asked her.

When she looked at him he knew he had overestimated the amount of rain on her face. Most of the wetness was tears.

She looked at the officer and asked, "Have the bodies been removed?"

"Yes, sister. About an hour ago."

"Thank you," she said with a very shaky voice.

"We don't really need to go over there," said Bishop. "We can always just wait for the report in the morning."

"No, we do need to go over there. Given what we're fighting, we can't pass up any opportunity to find a clue on how to catch this bastard."

"Sister?"

When she realized what she had said, she covered her mouth and said, "Sorry."

Bishop looked at the officer and said, "Thank you, officer. Oh, which way is the easiest way to get over there?"

"There's a small path just over there," he said, pointing to an opening in the trees.

Bishop held out his arm and the sister put hers through and they set off for the path. The officer just watched them go, wondering at the strange sight of the large, black detective and the petite nun walking arm-in-arm. But he figured with all the strange things he had seen on this job, this was the least strange of all.

It took them ten minutes to reach the wreck site and Sister Clarice felt an increasing sense of evil. So much that she almost felt the need to sit down.

A team of CSIs diligently worked around the remnants of the car. It surprised Sister Clarice to see Shondra was one of them.

When the woman saw the two of them, she almost ran over and threw her arms around the sister and hugged her. She held on for what seemed like an unnecessary amount of time, but the sister didn't push her away.

When she finally pulled back, Shondra said, "I've thought about you every single moment since last week."

Then she looked at Bishop and said, "You, too."

Bishop just forced a smile and nodded.

"Give us your best guess what happened here," he said.

"Well, I can tell you right off, anything I tell you is going to be just that, a guess."

"Let's hear it."

She led them to the car and said, "As best we can figure, an old-fashioned steam train hit this car."

"Steam train? There can't be more than a couple dozen of those still running around this country."

"You're right," she said. We contacted a historical society specializing in those trains. They informed us that only eleven are operational, with a few others being restored."

"And I'm sure you're going to tell us where the nearest running one is."

"Yes, sir. It's in Kansas City and has been for the last three weeks. It hasn't moved from there since last month."

"So, what makes you think that's the kind of train that hit this car?" he asked.

She motioned for them to follow her

around to the front of the car.

"When we saw this, it was like nothing we'd ever seen before."

The front end of the car was smashed in and looked like it had been sent through a cheese slicer.

"What in the world?" said the detective.

"I don't know why," said Shondra, "but when I saw this, I immediately thought of the old trains. When I sent a picture to the man I talked to at the historical society, he said it looked like the car had been hit by a train with a cow catcher on the front."

"Cow catcher?" asked the sister.

"It's a piece that used to be on the front of the old trains," said the detective, "that would knock cows and deer off the tracks so they wouldn't go under the wheels of the trains. It would leave marks like this on a car."

Looking at Shondra, he said, "This means the car would have been facing down the tracks, straight at the train."

"Right, but we found no skid marks at the crossing. Not surprising though, with all the rain. I doubt their tires left any marks."

Sister Clarice walked around to the driver's door, which was laying on the ground a few feet away. The fire department had cut it away to get into the car.

Crouching down, she looked into the car

and noticed a rosary laying on the center console. Brushing away some of the broken glass, she sat down in the seat and picked up the beads.

As she held the rosary between her fingers, a vision assaulted her mind that almost drove the breath from her lungs. The rosary belonged to the Mother Superior and it contained a vision of the last thing she saw.

The car slipped sideways onto the tracks and became stuck there. Then a train's headlight could be seen coming around the curve and at great speed. It only took a few seconds for the train to reach the car.

Sister Clarice cried out as she saw the face of Azrin in the front of the train, grinning as he was about to end the lives of those two wonderful women.

"Hello ladies," she could hear the demon growl. "Oh, and goodbye."

The sister almost wanted to laugh when she heard the last words of the Mother Superior.

"Sister Clarice is going to destroy you!"

Then she relived the sickening crunch of the train hitting the car. She immediately realized what a cow catcher was and it sent the car tumbling down the tracks. After a couple more hits, the train launched the car into the air, over the tops of the trees and into the woods where it now sat.

Sister Clarice could only feel relief in that the sisters didn't endure any of it. They were both killed instantly when the train hit them.

As she sat in the car, she wept for those two ladies and held the rosary up to her lips and kissed it.

I don't know what to do, Sister Marissa.

She bowed her head and wept again. After a moment, she felt a hand settle on her shoulder and she looked up to see Bishop looking down at her.

She got out of the car and placed a hand against his chest to steady herself.

"It was him," was all she could say.

"Well, we kind of knew it had to be."

She nodded as she took his hand and placed the rosary in it.

"This belonged to Sister Marissa. She looked after you and guarded you as you were growing up. I think she would have wanted you to have it."

He took the rosary from her and held it up. Though he couldn't see the vision the sister had, he could feel the spirit of the departed Mother Superior warming his hand.

He brought the beads to his own lips and kissed them and then stuck the rosary in his pocket. He made a mental note that he would never go anywhere without them.

403

"I don't think there is anything else we can learn here," he said. "Let's head back to the church."

She just nodded as she took his offered arm again and he helped her back down the soggy path and back to the car.

The drive back to the church was a very quiet one. Not a single word was spoken during the drive back to the church.

For the detective's part, he was trying to figure out how to enlist the cardinal's help to keep the sister from doing something so monumentally stupid and getting herself killed.

Sister Clarice was trying to figure out how to put her plan into motion when she knew everyone around her would do whatever they could to stop her. She was pretty sure the detective was trying to come up with just such a plan to do that as he drove.

Chapter 32 – Arming A Warrior

The next day, Sister Marisol returned to the church and appeared to be in good health. Any sign of concussion or injury was gone.

The three sisters took up the training of Bethany with a gusto that wore the young woman out. When she would complain and beg for a moment to rest, Sister Helena would bark that Azrin would give her no rest during a battle.

Sisters Clarice and Marisol had to act as a buffer between Bethany and the gruff, older nun.

As the afternoon of training drew to a close, Sister Helena asked Bethany to walk with her. They walked through the dark corridors on the far side of the church, away from the guest rooms. And away from prying eyes and listening ears.

They came to a small chapel tucked in the back of the church. The three monks that worked in various duties around the church were the only ones to use it. At this time it was empty and dimly lit.

Sister Helena walked to the small altar and had her back to Bethany. She was looking up at the small crucifix that hung on the wall behind the altar.

Looking at the crucifix, she said, "You

bring more fear to my heart than I have ever felt before, child."

Bethany didn't know what to say to that, as she looked at the older nun's back.

"I don't mean to," she finally mumbled.

Sister Helena turned around and looked at her.

"Young lady, speak up as a proud warrior of God. Your mumbling and hesitancy to say anything are unbecoming of your station in life."

"I didn't ask for any of this," said Bethany with a little more force and confidence.

Sister Helena stepped up to her. They were both the same height, so they looked each other in the eyes.

"I know you didn't, child, and that's what makes me so fearful. I am not fearful *of* you. I am fearful *for* you."

"What do you mean?"

The sister reached up and placed her hands on each side of Bethany's face and for a moment just stared into her eyes.

"You're so young. Much younger than I was when I received this calling. Even Sister Clarice wasn't as young when she picked up the sword and battled Azrin for the first time."

The nun looked deeply into Bethany's eyes and the younger woman could see some sadness in the older eyes.

"Your youth is what scares me. I don't think you fully understand what is being asked of you."

Bethany pulled back a little. Not enough to break contact with the nun, but just enough to stare back at her.

"A demon from Hell killed five of my friends while I watched. That same demon killed my aunt and Esther's husband. He killed Sister Nina and Detective Bishop's ex-wife. He has killed countless others, but for some reason left me alive. He seems bent on destroying Sister Clarice, a woman I dearly love, and wants to destroy this entire city. What do I not understand?"

A single tear began running down the nun's cheek as she shook her head.

"What you don't understand is Azrin isn't after Sister Clarice. She's just in the way."

"Who is he after?"

"He's after you, sweetheart."

Bethany took a step back and looked at the sister.

"After me? Why on Earth would he be interested in me?"

"We've already discussed that. At dinner the other night?"

"You mean this so-called Angel's Touch?"

"Yes, Bethany, and it is a very real thing. The fact that you could pick up Father Draper's sword without any ill effects is just one sign that you have it."

Bethany walked over and sat down in one of the small pews. Sister Helena just stood in front of the altar, her hands clasped in front of her.

"I'm nothing special, Sister Helena. The fact that Sister Clarice's sword seems to like me just means it's a bad judge of character."

"I think the only reason you say that is because you wish it were true."

The sister sat down sideways in the pew in front of her and reached over, taking one of Bethany's hands in hers.

"I know this is a lot for you to take in. You are young and this kind of thing should not have been dropped on your shoulders like this. Haven't you wondered why Azrin let you live while your friends died?"

"He said it was because he wanted me to tell the demon hunter what I had seen. He wanted me to tell the story."

"Any one of your friends could have done that."

Bethany looked into the eyes of the elderly nun.

"Why didn't he kill me? Why not let Kyle live? He was the only one that stood up to Azrin, trying to protect me and Lydia."

"Trying to protect you was most likely

what got Kyle killed. Now, ask yourself, would Kyle have traded places with you? Would he have wanted to live if he knew it meant you would die?"

Bethany dropped her head and whispered, "No."

"You said that when Azrin finally came for you, he went to grab you, but then pulled back."

"Yes, it was almost as if he couldn't touch me and I think it gave him second thoughts about killing me. But he did push past whatever was stopping him and grabbed me by the throat."

"Yes, he did, but stopped short of killing you, not because he wanted you to relate the story of his deeds that afternoon. He knew that if he killed you, angels from Heaven might come down to avenge your death. Having the Angel's Touch doesn't just mean you can pick up a fallen hunter's weapons. It also means the very hosts of Heaven are watching over you and ready to lend you any help you might need."

"You mean like a guardian angel?"

Sister Helena smiled and said, "Yes, but in your case you have an entire Heaven of guardian angels."

Just then Sister Marisol stepped into the chapel and signaled to her companion.

"Yes, Sister Marisol?"

"It's arrived."

"Excellent," said Sister Helena as she pushed herself up from the pew. Then patting Bethany on the shoulder, she said, "Come along, child. We have something for you."

Sister Helena walked out of the chapel, followed by the other two.

"What do you have for me?" whispered Bethany.

Sister Marisol smiled and said, "You'll see." Then she slipped her arm through Bethany's and they walked together behind the older nun.

As they came around the corner by the small foyer at the back doors, Bethany came to a stop.

"Come on," said Sister Marisol as she tugged Bethany forward.

Standing in the foyer was the cardinal and Father Draper.

And three very large men, all dressed in what looked like black military fatigues. They all stood at least six feet tall and looked to be as tough as any soldiers Bethany could imagine. The only thing that gave them away were the white squares at the base of their throats.

"Sister Helena," said the one that appeared to be the leader. He stepped forward and took her hand and bent at the waist and kissed it.

"Always a delight to see my favorite demon hunter."

"Ha!" said Sister Helena. "I always thought Sister Clarice was your favorite, Father Damien."

"She is, but she isn't here right now," he said with a smile.

"Are you talking about me behind my back?"

They turned to see Sister Clarice walking slowly around the corner, her hand resting lightly on Esther's shoulders. Ashley was walking on the other side of the elderly demon hunter.

One of the other soldiers, probably the youngest of the three, stepped forward and bowed low to Esther.

"A great honor to see you again, Esther."

"Oh, stop that, Father Samuels," she said. "You're younger than my own son."

He smiled as he leaned over and kissed her on the cheek and she could not hide the blush or the twinkle in her eyes.

The two soldiers stepped back and stood tall. Father Damien looked at Bethany and raised his eyebrows.

"And this must be Bethany. The young lady that is setting the entire Vatican on fire."

"Fire!" said a bewildered Bethany. "I ..."

"He means figuratively, sweetheart," said

Sister Marisol in her ear.

"Oh."

"Father Karras, if you please," he said as he stepped aside.

The third soldier stepped forward, carrying a case. He had a look of awe on his face as he looked at the young woman. He lifted the case up, holding it horizontally and the other two priests stepped to each side and placed their hands under the ends of the case.

Father Karras reached across the case and released three clasps, each one springing open and the clicks could be heard echoing through the church.

"Sister Bethany," he said as he motioned for her to open the case.

Sister Marisol urged her forward and it took a few seconds for her to step up to the case. The two holding the case looked like they would stand there forever, if needs be, until she opened the case.

Reaching out, she lifted the lid, halfway expecting to see a guitar in it, because that's what the case looked like. She was hoping for a nice Gold Top Les Paul.

What she saw was anything but a classic guitar.

She saw a very plain looking sword. Though the blade looked shiny, she could tell it was old. The hilt was covered in a rather mundane brown leather and the pommel was just an ordinary metal knob.

"I don't understand," she said, looking at Father Karras.

"Take the sword from the case and you will."

"Oh no! I'm not falling for that again."

Sister Clarice stepped up behind her and put her hands on her shoulders.

"Sweetie, you can't keep using my sword."

"Do I have to?" she whined.

The sister wrapped her arms around her shoulders from behind and whispered in her ear.

"Like I've said before, you don't have to do anything. But you will always wonder *what if* if you don't pick up the sword."

Bethany swallowed hard and then reached forward. She could feel the power of the sword as her fingers got closer. Her fingers were tingling from the energy. A couple of small lightning bolts shot from the hilt, arcing into her fingertips. Having felt it before with the sister's sword, she didn't pull back.

Wrapping her fingers around the hilt, she felt the sword lock her grip around the leather and she placed her other hand just below the first.

As she lifted the sword from the case, it began to glow and then it burst into flames.

413

White flames.

As she held the sword up, her hair whipped around her face and shoulders. She could feel the sister lift her hands off her shoulders and step back.

A power unlike anything she had felt before surged up her arms and into her chest. She still had enough awareness to feel her heart beating so hard in her chest she thought it would burst out.

Raising the blade up, she pointed it at the ceiling and a pillar of fire shot from the tip and hit the stone ceiling twenty feet above their heads. The cardinal looked up, glad the ceiling was stone and not something that would burn readily.

A roar came from the blade and everyone began backing away slowly. They were quite sure the blade would never hurt them, but it is never unwise to be cautious.

Bethany's eyes lit up with a golden fire and her face became almost translucent. She closed her eyes and let the power flow through her body.

After a full two minutes, the blade began to fade until it was an ordinary gray metal again. When she finally opened her eyes, Bethany looked at those that stood in front of her. Everyone was speechless because of what they had just seen.

Sister Helena, one of the toughest, crankiest demon hunters in the sisterhood, had tears streaming down her face. As if she had just witnessed the face of God, Himself.

Father Karras reached into a pocket in the case and pulled out a set of straps with a scabbard attached. Stepping up to her, he motioned her to turn around which she did.

As he helped her put the straps over her shoulders, positioning the scabbard just behind her head, Sister Clarice stepped forward to help buckle the straps in front.

Bethany could see tears in the sister's eyes, just fighting to begin falling.

"Still thinking of declining your calling?" the sister asked softly.

Bethany smiled and cried, "I think I've pretty much given up on that idea."

After finishing the buckles, the sister reached up and cupped her cheek.

"Put the sword away, sweetie."

After Bethany slid the sword into the scabbard, she felt a tap on her shoulder. Turning around she looked up into the eyes of Father Damien. He held out his hand and she took it.

"It is a great pleasure to meet you, Sister Bethany."

As she shook his hand, she looked around and could see the others were nodding their agreement.

"Looking back at Father Damien, she asked, "Do I still have to go meet the Pope?"

"Umm, yes. That's kind of a requirement."

She could feel her stomach starting to churn again and ran to a wastebasket in the corner and emptied the contents.

Father Damien watched her and then looked at Sister Clarice.

"Didn't you do the same thing when told about meeting His Holiness?"

"Oh hush," she said with a smile.

Just then the back door of the church opened and Bishop walked in. He looked at the assembled group.

"What did I miss?"

Before anyone could answer, the silence was broken by a young woman over in the corner, retching into the wastebasket.

"You told her about meeting the Pope again, didn't you?" he asked.

When Sister Clarice giggled, Bishop said, "You people need to stop tormenting her like that."

When she walked over, he pulled a handkerchief from his pocket and handed it to her. After she wiped her mouth, she put her arms around him and he hugged her.

"They're being mean to me, detective. You should arrest them."

He laughed softly as he hugged her close.

"Detective," said Father Damien. "I need to warn you, you are dangerously close to touching that sword she now carries. Please do not do that."

As he looked down, he saw his hand was close to touching the pommel and he drew his hand slowly away from it.

Father Damien nodded to Cardinal Wright and he stepped forward and took Bethany by the hand and led her into the circle of the others.

"Sister Bethany," said Father Damien, "It is with great pleasure I welcome you into the Sisters of the Templar. As you progress, you will find this church, and this world would not still be standing if it were not for this sisterhood. We are honored to have you."

Then he did something she could never have expected. He dropped to one knee in front of her and bowed his head.

"Oh, please don't do that!" she blurted.

When he rose, he reached forward and lifted her chin.

"Bethany, there has not been a warrior with the Angel's Touch in over a hundred years."

"Really?"

"Now, please don't get sick again, but believe me when I tell you, His Holiness is more nervous about meeting you than you are of meeting him. I could see it in his eyes yesterday as the three of us stood in his office and he gave us that blade."

Father Karras spoke up and said, "And please guard that blade. It will protect you to the fullest of its abilities, but it is actually quite valuable."

"Valuable? How so?"

"It is the sword of a king, Sister Bethany," said Father Samuels. "It was the sword King David would carry into battle."

She could feel the entire weight of history fall upon her shoulders. The sword on her back was thousands of years old and had been carried by one of the most famous kings of the Bible.

Then one of the monks stepped into the foyer and signaled the cardinal.

"Ladies and gentlemen, it seems lunch is now ready. I'm guessing even Bethany is a little hungry now."

Bethany felt her empty stomach growl, letting her know it was time to eat. Apparently, even warriors of God needed to eat from time to time.

Chapter 33 – Confronting Our Hero

It didn't take Bethany long to realize this new blade was something special. When she held it, she felt like it was talking to her. Not in words, but in the feelings that she could understand completely.

Talking to the blade became natural to her in just a couple of days' time. She now understood how Sister Clarice could speak to her sword as if it were alive.

She spent a lot of time in the gym, training with Sisters Helena and Marisol. Esther would come by and watch the training, sometime lamenting how she missed being able to do those things.

Sister Clarice and Father Draper worked together, rebuilding her strength. He even took to making sure she spent at least half an hour in the small garden behind the church, sitting on a bench, with her sword in her hands. The power of the sword flowed into her body, strengthening her and building her confidence.

One thing the padre noticed was how quiet she had become. The cardinal said he had noticed the same thing and it was beginning to worry him.

It all became clear to him when Bishop stopped by to check on Ashley and asked the cardinal if he could talk to him privately.

After sitting down in his office, the cardinal asked what was on his mind.

"I'm worried about Sister Clarice."

"I think we all are, detective," said the cardinal. "We just have to be patient with her as she heals."

"That's not what I'm talking about, sir."

"Then enlighten me."

"I believe she's thinking of doing something really stupid to end this fight with Azrin and I think it may bring her to great harm."

"She said that?"

"No, sir. Not in so many words. It was more of a feeling I got when we were leaving the scene of Sister Beth and Sister Marissa's crash."

Neither spoke for a moment.

Then the cardinal said, "I shall have to have a little chat with our warrior nun."

Standing up, he held out his hand.

"Thank you for alerting me to this. Rest assured, I will do everything in my power to keep her from harm. You were right a few days ago when you said I loved her. I do love her, but not in the way you think. To lose her would be a crushing blow to the church."

"Thank you, padre. I just felt I needed to say something."

"And I'm glad you did."

The two of them left the office, Bishop going to find his daughter and the cardinal to look for a certain nun.

His heart was a mass of confusion. On the one hand he would never dream of telling Sister Clarice how to do her job. He was determined to protect her by discovering and thwarting her plans.

When he walked into the garden, she was sitting with her back to him, her sword held up in front of her face. He could hear the crackling of the lightning being emitted from the blade.

"Did you need me, padre?"

It shook him slightly that she asked that question without turning around. He was quite sure his approach had been too quiet for her to hear him, especially over the sounds the sword was making.

"Um, yes. Can you stop by my office when you are finished?"

"Yes, cardinal."

About twenty minutes later she knocked on his door and opened it. He was sitting behind his desk, his hands folded in front of his chin. It was obvious he was waiting for her.

"Close the door, please."

She closed the door and walked to one of the chairs across his desk and sat down. Smoothing her black leather habit, she sat back and could feel the sword in its scabbard at her

421

back. It emitted a low power that told her to prepare herself.

Prepare myself? From the cardinal?

Cardinal Wright took a deep breath and then let it out.

"It has come to my attention that you may do something foolish in your attempt to stop Azrin. Please tell me I have it all wrong."

Her blue eyes stared at him, the little golden flecks growing brighter by the second.

"The detective needs to mind his own business when it comes to my business," she said, working hard to remain calm.

"His business? His business and my business are to see that we can help you in any way AND ... to do what we can to keep you safe. Tell me if I have that wrong."

Sister Clarice bowed her head and closed her eyes. After a moment she looked up.

"We know that my calling is one of danger and that my life may be given at any moment. It is not a calling I take lightly, nor will I shirk from it."

"Sister Clarice, the detective has accused me of being in love with you and on that matter he would be correct."

He could see her sit up a little straighter, not knowing what to make of his words.

"However, my love for you is the same love I feel for all my brothers and sisters that toil in the fields of our Lord. Only with you, it is stronger than I have ever felt before. When I am near you I feel the presence of God, the Holy Father."

After composing herself, she said, "I'm sorry. I don't know what to say to this."

"Sister, let's ignore the fact that I am more than forty years your senior. Losing you would be a tragedy I don't think this church could survive it."

A tear began to trail down her cheek and she wiped it away.

"It survived the loss of Sister Agatha. Sister Marissa and Sister Beth gave their lives and the church still stands. You personally witnessed Sister Nina giving her life to protect a child from Azrin. How would my death mean anymore than theirs?"

The cardinal just looked at her from across the desk. He was at a loss for words when thinking he could lose this warrior sitting across from him.

"I promise I will not go looking for Azrin in a way that will result in my death. You may think I'm suicidal, but I am not."

"That's all I ask, sister."

The sister stood up and said, "Now, if you have nothing else, I need to go find the detective and have a little chat with him."

"Go easy on him. I think he is more

terrified of losing you than I am. If that's possible."

As she pulled the door closed, he couldn't shake the feeling that her time was fast approaching and there was nothing he could do to slow it down.

Reaching for a tissue, he dried his eyes and begged God not to take her. The only feeling that settled down over his soul was to be strong, no matter what happens.

Chapter 34 – He Walked Right In

The day dawned gray and windy. Though there was the look of a storm coming in, Sister Clarice felt as if this was something different. A feeling in her soul told her today would be one that would test her to her spiritual limits.

Sitting in the garden, she could smell the scent of rain, but none had fallen. There were many things about the atmosphere of the day that didn't feel right. Though this was an early winter day, there was no chill in the air. As a matter of fact, each time the wind blew around her, she could feel a bit of warmth, something she shouldn't have been feeling.

Sitting on a park bench in the middle of the garden, she stared at a faded rosebush in front of her. The changing season had long since robbed the bush of its green leaves and red flowers.

A wave of sadness washed over her soul as she stared at the bush, fighting the feeling she might never see that bush bloom again. Sitting in this garden had become one of her favorite things ever since she came to Chicago. Even though she could hear the street noise just over the wall, there seemed to be a quiet tranquility in the green space around her.

However, there wasn't much greenery around her. Though the gardener did what he could do to keep the space clean and inviting, there was no holding back the seasons.

Just like in the garden, a life also has its seasons and she couldn't shake the feeling she was locked deep inside her own winter.

As she tried to center her thoughts, she reached out with her mind to find what was bothering her. Her eyes were closed and her breathing was slowing.

Something bad was coming and it was a feeling she had never felt before. As if the evil was coming right to her doorstep and was about to barge right in.

She just about jumped out of her skin when she felt someone sit down beside her in the bench.

"I'm sorry, sister," said Bethany. "I didn't mean to startle you."

Sister Clarice leaned over and rested her head on Bethany's shoulder.

"That's okay, sweetie. I was just lost in my thoughts."

"I understand. I should go and leave you to your meditation."

As she went to stand up, the sister reached out and held her arm.

"No, no, please sit. I could use your company."

Bethany sat back down, this time a little closer to the nun and rested a hand on her shoulder.

"Anything I can help with?"

"I don't know," said the sister. "I'm just feeling a bit out of sorts today. Like something just isn't quite right with the world."

"What do you mean?"

"That's the thing, Bethany, I'm not quite sure. It's like something I know I should be familiar with, but it's like it's staying just outside the circle of my sight."

Bethany looked around, not quite sure if she was supposed to be able to see whatever was bothering the sister. She wasn't quite sure if she should admit to the sister that she was feeling uncomfortable, too. It was a feeling she had had since she woke up that morning.

As they sat together, they heard the door open and turned to see the padre come through the door, followed by a young man and woman. The padre began leading the couple around the garden, showing them the various plants and statues contained within.

When they reached the bench where the sister and Bethany were sitting, they stopped and the padre introduced the couple. "Sister Clarice, Bethany, I'd like to introduce to you two new members of our flock. This is Scott and Natalie Hearst."

The two ladies stood up and the sister held out her hand. Scott took her hand and she felt a

427

warmth of peace and goodness come from him.

"Welcome," said Sister Clarice. "It is so wonderful to have you with us. I'm sure you will both be quite happy with this congregation."

"Thank you, sister," he said. "We look forward to becoming part of this church family."

"Oh my, that is a wonderful accent. Reminds me of Sean Connery."

Scott smiled and said, "As a matter of fact, his hometown is just down the road from my hometown."

"Oh really? And where is that?"

"A little place called Harburn."

"I spent a few months in Scotland, but I don't think I know that one."

"I'd be surprised if you did, sister. There are less than fifty people living there."

The sister smiled and nodded, then turned her attention to Natalie.

Holding out her hand, she asked, "Natalie, are you from there, too?"

Natalie just stared down at her hand for a moment, but made no effort to take it. When she looked back up, the sister could see a blank look in her eyes.

"Natalie, is something wrong?" she asked.

Scott looked at his young wife and

furrowed his brow.

"Sweetie? What's wrong?"

This was when Bethany realized something was wrong. Even the padre sensed something was amiss and stepped around to look at Natalie.

Scott reached out and put a hand on his wife's shoulder in an attempt to get her attention. She looked to her left, at the hand resting on her shoulder and a deep growl came from her throat.

In an instant Bethany's sword was drawn and it began glowing and spitting fire. A look of terror filled Scott's eyes when he saw the sword. Natalie's savage backhand sent him tumbling down the garden path, colliding with a garden vase.

"How did he get in here?" yelled Bethany.

Before anyone could answer, the padre grabbed Natalie in a bear hug from behind, hoping he could keep anything bad from happening. How the padre intended to hold a demon from Hell was anyone's guess.

Natalie threw her arms wide, throwing the padre backwards and into the dormant rosebushes. A roar came from Natalie's throat. A roar that obviously did not belong to the sweet blonde-haired, blue-eyed woman standing in the middle of the garden.

As Bethany was trying to figure out what

to do, she realized that Sister Clarice hadn't drawn her own sword.

"Sister!" she yelled.

That seemed to snap the sister out of whatever trance she was in and she immediately armed herself. Now there were two swords brandished, spitting sparks and fire and ready to do battle.

Just then the door of the church burst open and Father Draper and the two sisters came running out. At first they didn't see Scott or the padre, and they were confused about the two women holding swords to the pretty young lady.

Then Sister Marisol saw the padre struggling in the rosebush and she ran to him. When she did that, the other two realized what was going on. Father Draper produced a broadsword from under his smock and Sister Helena took a roundabout path to get to Scott and see if he was okay.

Sister Clarice stepped forward, pointing her sword directly at Natalie's chest. She felt a grave hesitation in her heart, because she knew that Natalie had nothing to do with this.

"Azrin, you will come out of her and leave her unharmed!" exhorted the sister.

Natalie's eyes came up and they were burning red.

"Now why would I do that?" the demon

growled.

The sister took another step forward and pressed the point of her sword to the chest of the young woman.

"Because I command you, by the power of God, ruler of Heaven and Earth to leave this woman and face us directly."

"I take no orders from you or your god. I serve only Lucifer, the one true God."

"Please don't hurt her!"

Bethany looked over her shoulder and could see Scott was sitting up with the help of Sister Helena. She could see the horror in the young man's eyes, seeing his young bride about to be run through with a sword.

Even though Sister Helena tried to hold him back, he staggered forward until he was standing directly behind Sister, Clarice.

"What's wrong with her?" he pleaded.

Without taking her eyes off the woman, Bethany said, "Demon."

"She's no demon!"

"Not her," said Bethany. "The demon inside her."

Natalie looked at him and her lips curled up in the most evil grin.

"Hi, honey. Don't you recognize me?"

At the sound of the demon's voice, Scott's hand flew to his mouth and he bit his finger. Sister Helena pulled him back and held him.

"Stand back, young man," she whispered in his ear. "She may still be saved."

The point of a sword settled down on Natalie's shoulder and Father Draper reached forward and grabbed her by the back of the neck.

"I believe you were commanded to leave her. Do it now and leave not one scratch on her."

At that moment, three more came out the back door and into the garden. First came Bishop, who immediately turned around and tried to stop his daughter and Esther from coming out the door. Neither one of them were having any of it and pushed past him, which was an incredible feat when Esther banged her walker against his shin.

"Son of a bitch!" yelled the detective as he felt her almost break his leg. "You two get back in the church!"

Esther looked at him with fire in her eyes.

"Don't tell me what to do, detective! I can see that bastard with my own eyes."

Shuffling down the path as fast as her wobbly legs and walker could carry her, she came to a stop directly behind Father Draper.

"It's him," she said.

Father Draper nodded over his shoulder, "I know, sweet lady. I can see him just as clearly as you can."

A groan came from Natalie as her shoulders began to roll back and forth. It became plain she was struggling to push Azrin out and the demon was struggling to keep his hold.

"Fight him, honey!" cried Scott. "You're the strongest woman I know!"

For a few seconds the struggle continued and for a brief moment it looked like Natalie would win the battle. But just as quickly as the fight started it ended with Azrin taking complete control over her again.

"I actually quite like this body," growled Azrin. "I think I'll keep it and use it to do many great and terrible things in this world."

"No!" screamed Scott as he tore free from Sister Helena and charged forward.

He wasn't quite as fast as he thought because Sister Helena showed a bit of speed for an older woman and she grabbed him by the back of the collar. Yanking him backwards, she pulled him away from the confrontation like only an old-school nun could do.

"I told you to stay out of this young man."

"She's my wife!"

"Aww, you must be the father," growled Azrin.

"What?" stammered Scott.

"Oh," said Azrin from Natalie's grinning mouth, "she hasn't told you yet. Leave it to a woman to keep secrets."

"I don't …"

"She's pregnant, Scott," whispered Sister Helena.

"Oh my god!"

Father Draper tightened his grip on the back of her neck and did a bit of growling himself.

"I command you by the power of God, The Father, to leave her and the child unharmed. Come out of her, demon!"

Another struggle ensued and this time it was epic. Natalie's voice could be heard, coming from deep inside, screaming for the demon to let her go. She could be forgiven for the few choice, four-letter words that were peppering her demands.

There was a moment when it appeared there were two entities occupying the same body. One a young woman and the other, a larger demon with a charred black body with fire under its skin.

Father Draper's sword still sat on Azrin's shoulder, but his hand wasn't large enough to maintain his grip on the demon's neck.

Bethany jumped forward and grabbed Natalie's hand and pulled. Azrin still had a death grip on Natalie's soul and he didn't appear willing to give it up.

"Please help me!"

Bethany looked and could see she was looking directly into Natalie's eyes. The real Natalie.

"Come to me, Natalie," she said directly to the woman.

Pulling even harder, the two became even more separated and Azrin was roaring over losing his grip.

"Hey, remember me?"

Azrin looked to the side and saw nothing, but a 9mm pistol aimed directly at his head.

BAM!

The gun spit fire and lead and the bullet tore through Azrin's head, right between the eyes. This was enough for him to lose his hold on Natalie and Bethany pulled her into her arms.

"You're safe, you're safe," said the newest demon hunter to the sobbing woman. "Go to Scott."

After she ushered Natalie away, she turned back to see Bishop empty his entire magazine into the head of the demon. One thing that amazed her, was the growing silence from outside the walls. It was as if the sounds of the gunfire was bringing the world to a halt on the city street.

With one great effort, Azrin swiped at Bishop and knocked him back towards the door of the church.

"Daddy!" yelled Ashley as she ran to him.

It was quite clear Azrin was not ready to give up and he climbed to his feet and roared. As he did this, the wounds to his head sealed up, closing any injury he was suffering;

Sister Clarice charged in, her sword aiming directly at the gut of the demon. He turned to avoid the blade, but not fast enough. The point drove through the side of the demon bringing a screech of pain.

Bethany lunged forward and skewered Azrin's shoulder and Father Draper drove his blade into the back of one of the demon's knees.

Azrin dropped to one knee, trying to swing his massive fist at his attackers, but came up empty each time.

Sister Clarice pulled her sword out, wanting to go for the head. She knew the only way to kill Azrin was to remove everything from the shoulders up. This would finally put an end to the reign of terror by this demon.

As she swung the sword, the demon reached up and grabbed it, yanking it out of her hands. The sound of the sword sizzling in the demon's hand could be heard all over the garden. He tossed the sword away, it coming to rest near the feet of the fallen detective and his daughter.

Shrugging off the other two blades, Azrin

rose to his feet and looked around. Bethany was looking for an opening to sink her blade again. But Azrin's next move caught her and Father Draper by surprise.

With lightning speed, Azrin lunged forward and grabbed Sister Clarice by the throat and lifted her off the ground. As she struggled to break free of his grip, he pulled her face to his.

"Hello, little bug. I've been waiting for this day."

Then he roared in pain.

Looking down, he saw Father Draper had rammed his sword through his side. He took a swing at the padre's head with his free hand, but missed, which gave the priest the opportunity to twist the blade.

Azrin roared again in pain.

Bethany moved forward, ready to sink her own blade into the gut of the demon, but Azrin saw it coming and used Sister Clarice as a shield. Bethany had no clear path to strike past the struggling nun. As she tried to move to the side to open up the target, Azrin kept the sister in between them.

The demon smashed a fist into the side of Father Draper's head. The padre dropped like a rock and Azrin pulled his sword out and flung it over the wall. The sound of it clattering into the street could be heard by all.

Then he turned Sister Clarice around in his hand, so he could hold her facing Bethany.

"What are you going to do, little one?" growled Azrin looked at Bethany and shook the sister like a rag doll in front of her. "You can try to kill me, but you have to go through your precious sister to do it."

"Do it," croaked a raspy voice.

Bethany's eyes went from the demon's to the eyes of the nun. She was beginning to turn blue as she continued to struggle to breathe.

"I can't, sister," cried Bethany.

"Aww," said Azrin, looking at the young woman. "You'll let the world burn simply because you can't do what it takes to kill me."

As Bethany struggled to come to terms with what she might have to do, the sister raised her right leg and then let it fall back down. The sister nodded at her and a small smile crossed her lips.

"No," cried Bethany.

Azrin turned Sister Clarice's head back to him and said, "I'll let you go. All you have to do is denounce your feeble god. I mean, where is he? Why does he not protect you?"

"My God is waiting," she croaked.

"Waiting? What is he waiting for?"

"To welcome me into His arms."

In a flash, her right hand came up and the dagger it held slammed into the eye of the demon, driving deep into its head. As he roared in pain, he crushed the nun's neck and flung her away like a used tissue.

Bethany watched in horror as the sister's body crashed to the pavement. When she came to rest, the nun's eyes were glassy and unfocused. She was not moving and looked like she would never move again.

As he flailed at the dagger, trying to remove it, a blade sliced through the air and removed his arm at the elbow. As it fell to the ground, it disintegrated into dust.

The blade swung again, this time from the other direction and removed his other arm from just below the shoulder. It joined his other arm as a pile of dust.

Screeching in pain, he looked up into the eyes of the newest demon hunter, who had more rage and hatred on her face than he thought possible.

Staggering to his feet, he saw the blade coming straight at him and driving through his gut. The sword emitted a storm of lightning bolts, even after Bethany pulled it out to prepare for another attack.

Taking a step backwards in an attempt to get away from her, he felt another stabbing pain, this one coming from behind. This blade slammed through the demon's body from the back, coming out of his chest, almost skewering

Bethany in the process, causing her to recoil from it, pulling her blade out of the demon.

"Sorry about that, Bethany."

Bethany looked around to the back of the demon and saw Ashley standing there, her hands firmly gripping the hilt of Sister Clarice's sword.

"That's okay. Just give a girl a little warning next time. Hey, how are you … nevermind."

Looking back at Azrin, she continued.

"I'd tell you to ask your boss about Sister Clarice's blade, but sadly, you're not going to be seeing him anymore. But you see, this blade is the one that expelled your boss from the Garden of Eden and then was carried by the cherubim guarding the Eastern Gate."

Ashley pulled the blade, wanting to stab the demon again and Azrin used that moment to try to make his escape. He began to fade from view, but Bethany was having none of it. She stabbed him again, her blade locking him into this world.

"Not so fast!"

Azrin looked down with his one good eye and saw Bethany's blade had been run through him all the way to the hilt.

"Remember this blade?" roared Bethany, again with a voice straight from Heaven. "Of course, you don't."

She moved right up in his face. Even

though the heat would fry most people's faces, Bethany felt nothing.

Azrin found he couldn't move. He couldn't blink out of sight, going back to his own realm. The sword was never going to let him go.

"Let me enlighten you, demon," growled Bethany. "This is the sword carried into battle by King David when he led the armies of Israel. I don't think it likes you."

She got even closer to his face and she could sense the fear coming from him.

"If you think you are going to slither off to your world, only to come back later and cause more trouble, you are sadly mistaken."

Reaching down, she pulled a dagger from a sheath on her boot. Holding it up, in front of Azrin, she turned it around a couple of times, letting him see the emblem.

"See this blade? Sister Clarice gave it to me. It's a matched set with the one in your eye."

Twirling the dagger in her hand, she slammed it into the demon's other eye, causing him to scream in pain and fall to his knees. She made sure to embed the blade solidly in his molten eye and even wiggled it back and forth for good measure.

Looking over the top of the demon's head, she stared at Ashley, who still had hold of the sister's sword. She scrunched up her face as she looked at the sight.

"Interesting," she said.

The detective hobbled up behind his daughter and reached to the sword to spare his daughter of having to wield it. Or maybe he wanted to get his own pound of flesh from the demon.

Before Bethany could stop him, his hand came in contact with the hilt and it almost dislocated his shoulder as it threw his hand off.

"Son of a bitch!" yelled Bishop as he danced around, holding his arm.

"Master! Help me!"

Bethany looked back at the blinded Azrin, who was still immobilized on two blades.

"Oh, do call him. I'd like to have a little talk with him."

"Oh no you don't!" yelled Bishop, as his arm flopped uselessly at his side. "I've met that jackass and I don't ever want to see him again."

"Master!"

"Shut him up," moaned the detective.

"Yes, I really wish you would."

Everyone turned to see a tall, dark, winged man standing there. Bishop almost fell over backwards as he tried to back away from the King of Hell.

"Hello, Freddie. We meet again."

"Not because I wanted to."

Bishop reached over and put his good arm around a terrified Ashley and gently urged her away, leaving Sister Clarice's sword embedded in the sniveling demon. When they got a few feet away, he put her behind him, which she didn't struggle against.

Bethany showed no inclination of backing away from Satan, even though she could feel the evil pouring off him.

"You're the one that set this demon loose on the world?" she sneered.

"Yes, I am," he said with a slight bow.

"He killed a bunch of innocent people," she said as she let go of the dagger in Azrin's head and turned to face the devil.

"Thousands of innocent people die every day. Where is your outrage for them?"

She stared at him, but realized she had no good answer for that question.

Turning he looked down the path and saw Sister Clarice cradled in the arms of the cardinal.

"Aw, that's such a shame. I told him to leave her alone. I'll be taking her now," he said as he took a couple of steps toward her.

Instantly, two nuns stepped in between him and their fallen sister.

"You will not lay one finger on her," growled Sister Helena as her own sword began glowing. Sister Marisol's blade was no less bright as it prepared for the fight of all fights.

"Master, please!" screeched Azrin.

"Oh shut up! You have failed me for the last time!" yelled Satan and he snapped his finger. The demon began to dissolve into a pile of ash on the ground. Within seconds he was gone.

"Hey!" yelled Bethany. "I wasn't finished with him yet."

Lucifer turned and faced the defiant demon hunter.

"I was. Or would you like me to bring him back?" growled the dark one.

She was ready to go toe-to-toe with Satan, but she looked around. She could see the face of the cardinal between the two nuns standing guard and he shook his head. She looked back at Bishop and he shook his head adamantly.

Even Esther was showing reluctance to bringing the demon back.

Looking back at Satan, she said, "Just promise me he is gone for good."

"I make no promises," said the devil as he took a couple of steps toward her and leaned down, staring her in the face. "And I don't take orders from you."

A blinding flash washed out the garden for a second, accompanied by a loud crack of thunder.

"How about from me, brother?"

As everyone was able to open their eyes, a figure appeared, standing in the middle of the

444

garden. A tall man, as tall as Lucifer, only dressed in white, with shocking white hair. A gold plated sword hung from his hip and his hand rested on the pommel.

"This is not your fight, Michael," growled Satan.

"You lay one hand on her and I'll make it my fight. Now, go back to where you belong and don't ever raise Azrin again. You do, my brothers and I will pay you a visit."

Satan just stood there, trying to stare down the archangel, but it ended when Michael waved his right hand and the devil disappeared.

Bethany walked over to him with tears streaming down her face. She kept her face down, not feeling worthy to be in his presence.

"Why didn't you come earlier? Before Sister Clarice was killed?"

Michael reached out and cupped her chin and lifted her face. Staring down into her eyes, he just smiled and she could feel his power radiate into her.

"Sister Bethany, it was her time. She has much work to do in the Kingdom of Heaven."

Then he caressed her cheek and said, "Her work here was finished. It's up to you to continue where she left off."

He cupped her cheek and she gasped as more power flowed into her.

"Now, I need you to go to your room. There is something there for you."

"What?"

He smiled and said, "Just go."

She looked over and saw Father Draper and Cardinal Wright performing the last rites on Sister Clarice. The other two nuns were just watching her and the archangel. Her heart felt like it was going to break in two when she looked at the body of Sister Clarice.

She felt like she should go to the sister, but when an archangel from Heaven tells you to go to your room, you best do as you're told.

As she turned to walk away, Michael called after her.

Looking back at him, he said, "Just remember, Father is watching you with great interest. He expects great things from you."

Suddenly she felt it again. Throwing her hand over her mouth, she ran for the church, hoping she would make it to the bathroom before she threw up.

"There she goes again," said Bishop.

Ashley timidly walked over and looked up at Michael.

"Are you really Michael, the archangel?"

"Yes, Ashley, I am. Who else would send Lucifer back to Hell with his tail between his legs?"

Ashley raised an eyebrow and said,

"Jesus."

Michael laughed and said, "Touché. Of course, Big Brother wouldn't even need to wave His hand. He'd just say go and Lucifer would be gone."

She motioned to the swords and daggers laying on the ground and said, "So, I guess I'm supposed to take up Sister Clarice's sword?"

She could hear her father suck in a breath.

"No, Ashley," said Michael, "that was a one-time thing so you could help Bethany. Do not touch that sword again. Besides, you have a different calling. Something your father can probably give you some insight into."

"Oh no," stammered Bishop. "I don't want her going into law enforcement."

"Fredrick, you would deny your own daughter her calling in life?"

"Yeah, daddy. You know I've always wanted to be a cop like you."

He just looked back and forth between the two of them and knew he had lost this battle. He walked over to the nearest bench and plopped down. His spirits rose a little when Ashley came over and sat next to him and wrapped her arms around him.

Nothing could assuage the pain in his heart, though, when he looked down the path and saw Sister Clarice lying motionless on the ground. Even though he had been warned this could happen, he felt his heart being ripped out of his chest.

"Love you, daddy."

Those three words brought him back to the present and the arms of his daughter wrapped around him.

"Love you, too, princess."

They watched as Michael walked over and reached down and helped Scott and Natalie up from their knees. They had been huddled in a corner and Scott had his arms wrapped around his wife and soon-to-be mother of his child. He was never going to let her out of his sight again.

"You two have been given a great gift today. Don't waste it."

"We won't," said Scott, choking to get the words out.

Natalie reached out and touched Michael's hand.

"Will our child be healthy and happy?"

Michael smiled and said, "Yes, Natalie. Well, for the first twelve years at least."

The color drained from the faces of the two nearly parents.

"Wh … what happens after twelve years?" whined Natalie.

Michael leaned forward, a serious look on his face and whispered into both their ears.

"Then she becomes a teenager."

He straightened back up and laughed softly.

"That's not funny," said Natalie.

"It's a little funny," said Michael.

"I thought so, too," said Scott with a grin. "You two will be just fine."

He patted them on the shoulders and then turned his attention to the small knot of priests and nuns gathered around Sister Clarice. He stepped in between the two sisters, with the two priests standing on the other side of the body.

Looking down at the fallen nun, he just heaved a heavy sigh. He crouched down and set a hand on her forehead.

"Fly away home when you're finished, sweet sister."

"Is she not finished?" asked Cardinal Wright.

"Not quite yet. She just has one more thing left to do."

He stood back up and looked around the circle.

"Father Draper, your prayers are being heard and you can expect some help in your field of labor."

"Oh, thank you," said the New York City padre.

"And ladies," Michael said, looking at the two nuns, "keep up the good work. Those hippie demons out there don't know who they're messing with."

Both of them just bowed their heads to him.

Then he looked at Cardinal Wright and asked, "Are you going to be okay?"

He looked up at the archangel and for the first time that afternoon, a tear rolled down his face.

"I don't know."

"I know you worked with her the longest and I know this will be one of the darkest times of your life. Stay strong and keep God close and you'll be fine."

"I don't know what to do now," said the cardinal, gesturing to the body on the ground.

"Well, first I would say call your uncle. He'll know what to do. Also, ask Bethany to come out here in a little while and gather up those blades. She's the only one that can handle all of them. The brethren will be here not long after you make the call to collect Sister Clarice's body and her blades."

"Excuse me, sir."

Michael turned and smiled at Scott and said, "Just call me Michael. Sir makes me feel old."

Scott smiled and asked, "Michael, where will she be laid to rest? She gave her life to save me and Natalie. We'd like to know where we can visit her grave?"

The archangel smiled and said, "Are your passports up to date? The cardinal will be able to tell you where you can visit her."

Then he clapped his big hands together and said, "Well, I think I need to get back to where I belong. Have a blessed life, all of you."

As he began walking to the center of the garden, he was stopped by someone. Pushing a walker in front of her.

"Can you take me with you?"

He looked down and smiled. Leaning over, he kissed her on the cheek.

"No, sweet Esther. It is not your time."

"But I miss Marvin."

"Oh Marvin, good gosh. What a royal pain in the butt."

"What?"

"He is still his same old cantankerous self. Do you know, he is, at this moment, sitting on a bench just inside the gates and says he isn't moving until you get there. There are angels trying to coax him to move along, but he won't budge."

"Oh, Marvin."

"Anyway, you still have work to do here. When that's finished, I will personally come down here and take you home."

"But what can I do? I'm just a broken down old woman."

Michael smiled and reached out, putting his large hand on top of her head. Esther squeaked in pain and her body started contorting. When he was finished, Esther stood up straight and looked up at him.

"You're going to need a good, strong, healthy body to keep up with the kids."

"What kids?"

Michael straightened up, looked around, winked at the detective and then began fading from view.

"Go check your phone, Esther," was the last thing she heard from him.

She reached out and set her hands on the walker and then stopped and looked at it. Picking it up, she carried it over to the back door of the church and set it next to the wall.

When she got to her room and picked up her phone, she cried when she read the message:

MOM, WOULD YOU LIKE TO COME
LIVE WITH US HERE IN TEXAS? WE'D
LOVE TO HAVE YOU AND I KNOW
SHERRY WOULD LOVE TO HAVE
SOME HELP WITH THE KIDS.
LOVE, DEREK.

Chapter 35 – Coming To Terms

When Bethany walked into her room, there was nothing out of the ordinary. Walking across the room, she looked into the bathroom, but saw nothing to indicate why Michael had sent her there.

"Bethany."

Her heart stopped. There was only one person that had that voice. Spinning around, she saw her, standing on the other side of the room.

Sister Clarice.

As she rushed toward her, the sister held up her hand and stopped her. It was then she realized she could see right through the sister to the brick wall behind her.

Skidding to a stop, the only thing Bethany could do was moan, "No."

"Yes, sweetie, I'm afraid so," said the spirit of the sister. "But please don't mourn for me."

"How can I not mourn for you?" cried the younger woman. "You are the best friend I've ever had."

Sister Clarice just smiled.

"I'm happy that you think of me that way. And I finally found out why Azrin was coming after me and the detective."

"Why?"

"He wasn't. He was coming after you,

Bethany. Lucifer knew if he could get me to fall, you would have no protection in this life."

"I still don't understand why it comes back to me."

"Because, sweetheart, Lucifer is terrified of you. You are destined to be the strongest warrior for God this world has ever seen."

The spirit stepped closer to Bethany and she could feel the electricity in the air become more static. The hairs all over her body began to stand up in reaction to the closeness of the ghost.

"I will always be your friend," said the sister, "in this life and the next. There is so much I would have liked to have told you to help prepare you for what's to come in your life."

"I still haven't decided I want to become what you think I am."

The sister smiled and said, "You can continue to lie to yourself, but you can't lie to me. You never could."

"So, I really do have to go to Rome and meet the Pope?"

"It's not nearly as bad as you think. As a matter of fact, he is more nervous about meeting you than you are him."

The sister reached up and cupped a ghostly hand to the side of Bethany's face and the younger woman drew in a deep gasp. The feeling of the spirit actually touching her sent a shock of warmth and peace through her entire body.

Her eyes closed spontaneously as the spirit of Heaven flooded every fiber of her body. She felt as if her soul was being sent on a journey through the entire universe in an instant. Entire worlds were opened up to her eyes.

Billions of civilizations became known to her and she came to the realization that all those beings across the vastness of the universe wanted the same thing.

To live with peace and happiness, free from turmoil and the influences of evil. She saw families of the universe just trying to do the best they could.

One of the last things she saw was a multitude of men and women fighting evil across time and space. They had answered the call and fought bravely to keep the darkness at bay.

As the vision faded, she could feel a tear rolling down her cheek and she felt it only right to let it continue until it fell to the floor.

When she opened her eyes, she almost cried out in desperation.

The sister no longer stood in front of her.

"Sister?" she wailed. "Sister, please come back."

Then she felt the touch of the sister's lips

on her cheek.

"I'll always be watching over you."

Reaching up, Bethany touched the spot where the feeling of the kiss still lingered.

"I love you, sister."

As the feeling faded, she didn't notice the sound of the door to her room opening.

"Who are you talking to, Bethany?"

Turning around, she saw Esther looking at her. Another thing she noticed was Esther was standing up straighter and stronger looking than she had ever seen.

"Sister Clarice. She was just here."

Esther smiled and walked over. Reaching out, she pulled Bethany's head to hers and kissed her on the forehead.

"Get used to that. I used to get visits from my predecessor all the time. Back when I was new to the order and had no idea what I was doing."

"So she will come to me?"

"When you need her most, but don't go bothering her just because you need someone to talk to. She's going to be quite busy where she is now. If you need someone to talk to, just give me a call."

"Sounds to me like you're leaving here, too, Esther."

"I've had an offer I can't refuse," she said with a laugh. "Besides, I think I'm getting a bit tired of these cold Chicago winters."

For some unknown reason, Bethany threw her arms around the grandmother and hugged her close. Esther patted her on the back and then looked up at her.

"Now, you have a bit of work to do, that only you can do. There are a couple of swords and daggers laying on the ground in the garden and you are the only one that can pick all of them up."

"Omigosh! I can't believe I left my sword on the ground!"

"You had other things on your mind. Now go pick them up and apologize to them for leaving them in such a state."

"I hope they will forgive me."

"Let me tell you one little secret about the blades, Bethany. You are their boss, though they will try to tell you otherwise."

Bethany smiled as the two of them turned to the door and walked back to the garden.

In just a short amount of time she found she loved Esther just as she would her own grandmother. She still couldn't picture this old woman as a badass demon hunter, but then again, she still couldn't picture herself doing it either.

For the next few hours, Bethany wandered the dark halls of the church. Hoping each time she turned a corner, she would see Sister Clarice and find out it was all a bad dream.

No such luck. Walking past the sister's room, she fought the urge to go inside, knowing the sister's body was laying covered on her bed.

The police had never been contacted. Though Detective Bishop had been there when she died, how do you tell the department she was murdered by a demon from Hell?

The two padres made sure to give her all assurances that the sister's body was going to be handled properly, but they never gave any specifics.

At eight sharp, the back doors of the church burst open and four somber looking priests entered. The same four Bethany had met just a few weeks earlier.

Bethany was sitting in the chapel meditating when she heard the doors open. The urge to get up and see who had come in was overwhelming, but she sat still in the chapel.

It wasn't until she heard the cardinal and some other men talking and walking did she look toward the door. What she saw made her gasp.

Six priests and two nuns formed a procession in the hallway, but what surprised her was what they were pushing down the corridor.

A silver casket on a rolling cart.

As they went by, the two nuns stopped and motioned for her to follow them. As she exited the chapel, they each took a side and held her hands as they walked to the sister's room. She felt a great warmth from each of their hands as they tried to give her strength.

As they walked into the room, the two sisters moved to prepare Sister Clarice's body to be moved to the casket. Bethany felt her knees get weak, but she willed herself to be strong. As she closed her eyes to ask for strength, she felt a heavy hand settle on her shoulder.

Looking back, she saw the detective give her a forced smile. Ashley was standing next to him and she was biting her lips to keep from breaking down.

"How you doing, sweetheart?" asked the detective.

"Not too good, I'm afraid," she said barely above a whisper.

"You hang in there. Everyone in this room is here to help you through this."

As the sisters uncovered the body, Bethany could see the burn marks the demon had left on her neck when he grabbed her. It wasn't the only sign of fire in the room. Bethany's heart was beginning to burn with rage as she saw her deceased friend.

A few weeks earlier she had seen five of her friends killed by the same demon, but this one hurt more than all the others combined.

When the largest of the priests stepped forward, they made room for him and he lifted Sister Clarice's body from the bed and placed her gently in the coffin.

It was at that moment Bethany felt the full weight of what had happened wash over her soul. With tears streaming down her cheeks, she stepped forward and stood at the head of the casket.

Looking down, she could see a bit of pain on the face of the nun. The pain she had felt as she was dying. For some reason, unknown to her, she leaned over and kissed the sister on the forehead and placed a hand over her eyes.

A warmth passed from her hand to the sister and when she removed her hand, the look of pain had been replaced with a look of quiet serenity.

"Goodbye, sister," she whispered. "I look forward to speaking with you many times in the future."

Father Draper stepped forward and said a prayer over the body and the casket was closed. After the latches were secured everyone turned and looked at Bethany.

Feeling a bit self-conscious, she asked,

"What?"

The padre stepped forward and said, "These gentlemen are not here to only take Sister Clarice's body to Rome. They are also here to escort you there."

"Now?"

Father Samuels stepped forward and bowed, making Bethany feel even more uncomfortable. Looking at the Father, she could see he wasn't much older than Sister Clarice, maybe even younger.

"Sister Bethany, we realize you might not be ready to leave this very minute. I will be staying here until you are ready and I will escort you to Rome."

"Thank you, Father Samuels."

With that, the rolling cart was wheeled out of the room and down the corridor. The small group of people followed along behind the casket, many with tears rolling down their faces. Even the big, bad detective's cheeks were covered with tears. His tears were a mix of sadness and regret. Regret for the way he had treated the sister before he really got to know her.

Bethany walked behind the four priests pushing the cart, the two sisters on each side of her, holding her hands.

When they reached the back doors and they were opened, there was a black hearse waiting with it's back door open.

Bethany finally broke down as the casket was loaded into the hearse and the back doors were closed. In a bit of a surprise, when she turned to someone for comfort, she turned into the waiting arms of Sister Helena. The elder nun did not hesitate to wrap her arms around the young woman and hold her tight.

Fathers Damien and Karras shook hands all around and then got in the hearse. As it was pulling out of the back parking lot, Bethany could only stare at it as it disappeared into traffic.

"Goodbye, sister," she whispered. "I love you."

Just then two things happened simultaneously. A couple monks came out, carrying some baggage. And a black SUV pulled into the parking lot, containing Agents Tyler and Perry.

When she exited the SUV, Agent Perry walked straight to Bethany and asked, "How are you doing?"

"Not very well."

"I can understand that. I wish we could have been here and tried to help."

Agent Tyler came around the vehicle and looked at the gathering.

"I guess we have three for the airport?"

Bethany swung around and looked. Sister

Marisol smiled and said, "It's time for the three of us to head back to our fields of labor."

"So soon?"

Sister Helena leaned over and kissed her on the cheek.

"I'm afraid so, sweetheart. We're getting word our demons out in California are getting a little rowdy. We need to get back there."

Bethany looked at Father Draper.

He shrugged and said, "Yes, the demons in New York City never take a break. I think I'll go back there and whoop on a few of them to take out my anger over losing Sister Clarice."

She smiled and said, "Well, when I get back from Rome, give me a call if you need any help."

"Will do," said the padre with a laugh.

The three of them got in the SUV and within seconds they were gone.

One of the monks came out carrying another set of luggage.

Bethany whined, "Who's leaving now?"

Esther took her hand and squeezed it.

"It's time for me to go, too," she said just as a taxi pulled into the parking lot.

"I feel like I'm losing everyone I care about," cried Bethany.

Esther cupped her cheek with her hand and smiled up at her.

"Sweetheart, you aren't losing anyone. You

have a whole world of people that care about you."

"Not to mention the entirety of Heaven," said the cardinal.

Esther pulled her face down and kissed her on the cheek.

"You're going to be fine, Bethany."

The taxi driver took her bags and put them in the cab and waited with the door open.

The last thing Esther said to her was, "You're going to make Sister Clarice proud. I just know it."

Then she sat in the cab and in no time it was gone, leaving just four more people standing there with Bethany.

She looked at the detective and Ashley and said, "I suppose you're going to leave me, too."

Bishop smiled and said, "I'm just going back to work. Here in Chicago. When you get back, you can call me anytime. We can do lunch."

Bishop put his arms around her and hugged her. When they parted, Bethany looked at Ashley, who was busy tapping away on her phone.

Just then Bethany's phone rang in her pocket.

Ashley smiled and said, "There. Now you have my number, too. Call me anytime."

After a quick hug, the detective and his

daughter walked to his car and repeated the same disappearing act the others had.

Turning around, she looked at the only two people left.

Cardinal Wright held up his hands and said, "I'm not going anywhere."

Father Samuels laughed and said, "And I'm not going anywhere until you're ready to go."

"I'm going to need just a couple of days," said Bethany. "I need to call my dad and see if he will come back and see me before I leave."

"That will be a lot easier than you think," said the cardinal. "He never left town. He's staying in a hotel just a couple of blocks from here."

"Really?"

Father Samuels stepped to her side and held out his arm.

"Fancy a short walk, Sister Bethany?"

She smiled and put her arm through his and as they headed out to the street, Cardinal Wright called after them. "Don't you two stay out too late."

The following day, Bethany told Father Samuels she would be ready to go the next day. He just nodded and went to the office to call for the Vatican jet to come pick them up.

The hardest part of the whole ordeal was when the padre took her into the sister's room

465

and instructed her to remove anything she felt she'd like to keep. Anything that she didn't take would most likely be sent to the thrift store, except for a few items that would be placed in memory of the sister in the foyer.

Because they were the same size, Bethany took the sister's habits and other clothing to her own room and placed them quietly in her own wardrobe. Other than the jacket which she continued to wear, Bethany chose to wear only the black rock band t-shirts. She vowed to do some research and figure out why the sister would wear each one.

Sure she would never wear the habits, even without the wimple or veil, she still couldn't stand the idea of them being disposed of. Taking one habit, she hung it from a hook just under the crucifix on her wall. She wanted it to be one of the first things she saw every time she entered the room.

The next day her father showed up to drive her and Father Samuels to the airport. As they were standing on the tarmac, the Vatican jet idling in the background, she finally saw her father cry.

"Your mother would be so proud of you."

"I don't know about that, daddy. You're the only one who came running when you heard about the trouble I was in."

"Go easy on her, punkin. One day she will open her eyes and see what an amazing woman you're turning out to be."

After a quick hug and kiss, she turned and headed for the jet. Father Samuels was waiting patiently at the bottom of the stairs and offered his hand as she started up. After she disappeared into the jet, the padre walked back across the tarmac and held out his hand to her father.

"Sir, I just want to say, I hope you know how important Sister Bethany will be in the fight against evil. God is watching over her."

"But, can you watch over her, too?"

Father Samuels smiled and said, "With my very life, sir."

After a quick handshake, the padre jogged to the plane, but it still took twenty minutes to get airborne.

Even the Pope's personal jet needs to wait in line at O'Hare airport.

The End

I hope you've enjoyed this story about Sister Clarice, Detective Bishop and Bethany. And others. These *Campfire Stories* are stand alone novels, but that doesn't mean we won't see any other stories. Who know what kind of trouble Bethany might find herself in?

I would appreciate it if you could visit your favorite bookseller's website and leave a rating. Obviously I would love to get 4 and 5 star ratings, but more than that, I'd like to get honest ratings so I can see how these stories are being received. Thank you for taking the time to read my stories.

Check the next page for a quick preview of the book that preceded this one. Darius James is in for the fight of his life and his horse just knows he's going to get killed this time.

Preview of:
Daruius James: Monster Hunter

1 – A Hunter Rides Into Town

Time is a funny thing. Some say that it flies, while others say it crawls. Well, it certainly can't do both. Can it?

Time also marches on, like an army across the face of history, leaving in its wake the detritus of humanity scattered across the landscape.

It has been many centuries since any person witnessed more than a few decades of time slipping by. If you read the Bible and believe in that sort of thing, people used to live hundreds of years; some even reaching more than a thousand years old.

But now, a person was lucky to see their sixtieth birthday, most succumbing to the harsh life of this world in less than forty years. The real old-timers might see their fiftieth, but not much more than that.

This was the world of steam-driven locomotives and ocean-crossing ships. The age of gas lamps and wind-up pocket watches. In the old west, it was the day of traveling for days on horseback to reach a destination that wasn't served by the railroads.

It was the world that passed before the eyes of the man in the dirty brown duster, leather boots and two Colt six-shooters on his hips. His silvery gray eyes looked out across the barren landscape of Northern New Mexico and saw little to his liking.

His horse, black as the bottom of a coal mine, plodded along and snorted a few times to chase the flies away from its nose. But, the flies of New Mexico are an insistent bunch and would cause the horse to waggle its head now and then to shoo them away.

"I know, Midnight," said the man. "We've been on the trail for far too long."

One of us a lot longer than the other.

"Are you saying I'm old?"

Your eyes have seen many centuries that mine have never seen or hope to see.

"There are days when I wonder if that's a curse or a blessing," the man mumbled.

You can always say you're done with this life.

The man laughed and patted the horse on the neck.

"If I did that, I would get sent straight to Hell and you wouldn't have anyone to keep you company."

That's true. And I wouldn't be able to watch you get into and out of trouble like you do.

"See there, I am here for your amusement."

Midnight snorted and waggled his head again. The sun was falling behind the mountains to the west and these two travelers knew they were walking toward their next adventure.

–

Holding his Colt six-shooters waist high, the man looked back and forth across the scene. It took a few seconds for his eyes to adjust to the darkness before he set foot inside.

The gloom in the abandoned farmhouse was almost complete, but not quite. The full moon outside shone through a few holes in the roof, giving him just enough light to see his targets.

At the moment, he did not know where those targets were. He could feel them with his senses; could almost smell them, but see them? Nope, couldn't do that.

His eyes swept across the rafters of the old house, having learned at a young age that his enemies liked to hang out there and drop on top of him. It only took about a half a dozen times of that happening for him to learn. That and having his mentor laugh at him every time it occurred.

What the hell does that old coot know? He's dead and I'm not.

Stepping as quietly as possible, he crossed the open room of the farmhouse and could hear the old floorboards creaking under his boots. His spurs jingled each time his heels hit the ground. The cavalry sword hanging from his waist knocked gently against his leg.

His heart would race, but he'd been doing this for so long, it was hard for him to get it pumping any faster than normal. There was only one thing that could get his heart rate up and this wasn't it.

Moving to the center of the open room, he turned in a circle, his eyes looking for any movement that shouldn't be there, but he had no doubt they were close.

Come on out and play, you mangy sonsabitches. I ain't got all night.

Then he laughed to himself. He had all the time in the world and then some. He just didn't appreciate being kept waiting. Not that he had anywhere else to be. He had seen the lights of a small town in the distance and he realized he was hungry and was going to have a nice, hot dinner this evening.

If he could get this task taken care of before it got too late.

"Inconsiderate bastards! Come out and meet your doom," he mumbled to himself.

Oh yes, that should bring them right out.

"You hush out there."

Incoming!

Before he had time to register what Midnight had said, something crashed through the roof of the farmhouse, landing in front of him. Make that *two* somethings.

The gunslinger backed away from the two late arrivals and found himself in a corner. Not the most ideal spot to be in, but it kept his attackers from flanking him.

With two targets on different sides of the room, he wondered how he always got himself into situations like this. The answer was quite obvious.

You're an idiot! No doubt about it!

"If you don't shut up, I'm making you

gallop to town when I'm finished."

If you get hurt, I'm not picking you up.

"You can't pick me up, anyway," mumbled the man.

The situation he found himself in wasn't new. This was something that he had been doing since he was a young man. Never mind the fact that it had been over four hundred years since he could call himself a young man. That thought alone caused him to laugh to himself. Obviously, age brought no more wisdom than experience.

Backed into the corner, he could keep both of his attackers in sight without having to turn his head. Just a shift of his eyes kept both of them at bay.

The two assailants, one male and one female, shifted back and forth on their feet, their dark cloaks swinging in the slight breeze coming in through the broken door. Both were bald and their bare heads glinted in the moonlight. Their fingertips came to sharp points as they curled into claws.

"You two really don't want any of this," said the man as he raised his pistols and trained them on each one.

Both of them hissed at him like feral cats, baring their fangs. They each took a step toward the stranger, trying to come at him from different directions.

Deciding it was time to put an end to this, the man pulled both triggers. The Colts erupted with the fire and thunder of Hell itself. He didn't need to aim. He knew exactly where his pistols were pointing, having done this for so many years.

Continued in:
Darius James: Monster Hunter

Other books by D Glenn Casey

Beware The Boogerman
A Cold Shivers Nightmare #1

Where it all began.

How do you fight the thing monsters are afraid of?

After Deputy Debbie did her tour in the Army as an MP, she returned to her hometown, marched into the sheriff's office and demanded a job. Her daddy is the sheriff. Now, you can call her Deputy Debbie -- or if you're really brave, Dinkie.

Her hometown of Prattville isn't like other towns. It's where monsters go when they retire. The sheriff's job is to keep the peace between the human folk and the vampires, goblins, werewolves and other scary residents that call Prattville home.

But when a tragic past re-emerges, Debbie's best friend disappears -- again -- in the midst of a spate of attacks on monsters, Debbie fears the worst.

What's killing monsters? Where is it hiding Debbie's friend? And how is one little human woman supposed to fight something that can shred a goblin, decimate a vampire and put two large trolls in the hospital?

All she knows is she has to try. Her best friend's life depends on it.

477

More demons. Lots more demons.

Shattered Prisons
A Cold Shivers Nightmare #2

When things go bump in the night, maybe you should just sell the house and move.

For the last few months before her death, artist Julie's beloved Nana started to talk about strange things - evil demons, dark angels and bad humans. Julie let her prattle - it was just harmless talk, wasn't it? Wasn't it?

Now on her own with her grief in a big empty house, Julie's beginning to think that maybe there was something to Nana's wild talk. Most normal families have skeletons in the closet. Julie's family is a little more unusual ... her closet has demons.

Demons are on the loose, a friend is in peril, and a family legacy has been thrust upon her surprised shoulders. Can Julie transform into a badass demon fighting machine or will she cower behind her easel?

With the forces of evil on the prowl - released from their prisons by a clumsy friend - Julie must scramble to train and take her place beside Templar Knights, demon-fighting monks and a feisty Dominican nun who has an obsession with cherry pie.

Want another story about demons? And angels?

Into The Wishing Well

Welcome to the afterlife.
Please take a number.

Melanie, a kind-hearted soul, faced an unexpected turn of events after her untimely demise. Heaven, closed for new arrivals, left her wandering her town as a spirit, unaware of the celestial bureaucracy. However, her predicament took a sinister turn when a diabolical demon set his sights on capturing her soul, igniting a celestial war between Heaven and Hell. Caught in the crossfire, Melanie found herself protected by Angels and Archangels, while Lucifer's minions eagerly sought her capture. In this supernatural conflict, the fate of both realms unexpectedly rested upon Melanie's ghostly shoulders, making death merely the beginning of her extraordinary journey.

Crossing The Veil
A Cold Shivers Nightmare #3

They heard voices from the other side. Perhaps they should have ignored them.

Carol Hamilton, a brilliant quantum physicist, embarks on a quest to find her missing parents after opening a doorway to another universe, drawing unwanted attention. Tasked by the military to rescue her parents, Carol teams up with mysterious strangers, raising suspicions. As she grapples with her father's haunting voice and the potential consequences of her actions, Carol must confront the possibility of her quest leading to the universe's demise.

Wicked Rising
The Chronicles of Wyndweir - Book One

by D Glenn Casey

Garlan has finished his trials in the Land of the Dragons and he is heading home. The only thing he can think of is being reunited with the woman that has stolen his heart.

But, there is evil rising in the Eastern Desert and war is on the horizon. Everyone he knows is expecting him to rise up and be a leader and vanquish this evil. He'd rather they find someone else.

The Tales of Garlan
Prequel to the Chronicles of Wyndweir

by D Glenn Casey

Garlan went to live with the old wizard, Sigarick when he was eight years old. Now, in his twenty-third year it's time to prove he's actually learned something.

These four short stories tell of wizard duel, clearing thugs from villages and facing a final set of trials that could very well kill him. All in a days work for Garlan.

Printed in Great Britain
by Amazon